The Post Office Girl

D0784222

STEFAN ZWEIG

Sort Of
BOOKS

The Post Office Girl

STEFAN ZWEIG

Translated from the German by
JOEL ROTENBERG

with an afterword by
WILLIAM DERESIEWICZ

The Post Office Girl (Rausch der Verwandlung) by Stefan Zweig © 1982 by Williams
Verlag AG, Zurich and Atrium Press Ltd, London
Translation copyright © 2008 by Joel Rotenberg: all rights reserved.
Afterword © William Deresiewicz (reprinted with permission from the June 9, 2008,
issue of The Nation; www.thenation.com).
Author photo published by kind permission of Atrium Press Ltd, London.

Thanks to Sara Kramer and Edwin Frank of New York Review Books, Lindi Preuss of
Williams Verlag AG, Zurich, and Sonya Dobbins of Atrium Press.

This English translation first published in the UK 2009 by
Sort Of Books, PO Box 18678, London NW3 2FL.

Printed and bound by CPI Group (UK) Ltd, Croydon, CR0 4YY
on Forest Stewardship Council (Mixed Sources) certified paper.

Reprinted 2009 (twice), 2010 (twice), 2011, 2012

272 pp
A catalogue record for this book is available from the British Library
ISBN 978-0-9542217-2-0

Mixed Sources
Product group from well-managed
forests and other controlled sources
www.fsc.org   Cert no. TT-COC-002227
© 1996 Forest Stewardship Council
FSC

CONTENTS

PART ONE

ONE VILLAGE post office in Austria is much like another: seen one and you've seen them all. Each with identical meager furnishings provided (or rather issued, like uniforms) during Franz Josef's rule, all drawn from the same stock, their sad look of administrative stinginess is the same everywhere. Even in the most remote mountain villages of the Tyrol, in the shadow of the glaciers, they stubbornly retain that unmistakable odor of old Austrian officialdom, a smell of stale cheap tobacco and dusty files. The layout never varies: a wooden partition perforated by glass wickets divides the room, according to a precisely prescribed ratio, into This Side and That Side—the public sphere and the official one. The state's failure to give much thought to the significant amount of time spent by its citizens in the public area is clear from the absence of seating or any other amenities. In most cases the only piece of furniture in the public area is a rickety stand-up desk propped against the wall, its cracked oilcloth covered with innumerable inkblots, though no one can remember finding anything but congealed, moldy, unusable goo in the recessed inkwell, and if there happens to be a pen lying in the grooved gutter, the nib is always bent and useless. The thrifty Treasury attaches as little significance to beauty as to comfort: since the Republic took Franz Josef's picture down, what might be called interior decoration is limited to the garish posters on the dirty whitewashed walls inviting one to attend exhibitions which have long since closed, to buy lottery tickets, and even, in certain neglectful offices, to take out war loans.

With these cheap wall coverings and possibly an admonition not to smoke, heeded by no one, the state's generosity to the public ends.

But the area beyond the official barrier evidently demands more respect. Here the state arrays the unmistakable symbols of its power and reach. The iron safe in the corner may actually contain considerable sums from time to time, or so the bars on the windows seem to suggest. The centerpiece gleaming on the wheeled worktable is a well-polished brass telegraph; next to it the more unassuming telephone receiver sleeps on a black nickel cradle. These two items are accorded a certain amount of space betokening honor and respect, for, via copper wires, they link the tiny, remote village with the width and breadth of the Reich. The other postal implements are forced to crowd together: the package scales and weights, the letter bags, books, folders, brochures, and index files, the petty cash, the black, blue, red, and indigo pencils, the clips and clasps, the twine, sealing wax, moistening sponge, and blotter, the gum arabic, the knives and scissors, the bookbinder's bone folder, all the varied equipment of the postal service lies in a jumble on a desk hardly broader than a forearm is long, while the many drawers and boxes hold an inconceivable profusion of papers and forms, each different from the last. But the seeming extravagance with which these objects are scattered about is deceptive, for every last piece of this cheap equipment is stealthily and inexorably enumerated by the state. From this pencil stub to that torn stamp, from the frayed blotter sheet to the used bar of soap in the metal sink, from the lightbulb illuminating the office to the iron key for locking it up, the Treasury is unyielding in demanding that its employees account for each and every piece of public property either in use or consumed. Next to the iron stove hangs a detailed inventory, typewritten, officially stamped, and bearing an illegible signature, which catalogues with relentless precision even the humblest and most worthless items in the post office in question. No object not on this list has any place in the official area, and, conversely, every item entered on it must be present and to hand at all times. Orderly and by the book—that's the official way of doing things.

It stands to reason that this typed inventory would also specify the individual whose job it is to raise the wicket every day at eight o'clock, the one who sets in motion the inert implements, who opens the mailbags, stamps the letters, pays the postal orders, and writes the receipts, who weighs the packages and deploys the blue, the red, the indigo pencils to scrawl strange hieroglyphics on them, who lifts the telephone receiver and switches on the telegraph machine. But for some reason the name of this individual, known to the public as a postal official or the postmaster, is not listed there. The name is on another official record, in another drawer, in another section of the postal administration, but is similarly kept on file, updated, and subject to review.

Within this official area sanctified by the bureaucratic aristocracy, no visible change is allowed. The eternal law of growth and decline is suspended at the barrier of officialdom; while outside, around the building, trees come into bloom and become bare again, children grow up and die old and gray, buildings fall into ruin and rise again in another form, the bureaucracy demonstrates its more than earthly power by staying the same forever. For any object within this sphere which is used up or worn out or lost is replaced by another identical object, requisitioned and delivered by the appropriate agency, thus providing the inconstant world with an example of the superiority of the powers that be. The substance passes, the form remains. On the wall hangs a calendar. Each day a page is torn off, seven times a week, thirty times a month. By December 31 the calendar has been used up, but a new one has been ordered, in the same format, the same size, the same style; the year changes, but the calendar remains the same. On the table is a columned ledger book. When the left side is filled, the amount is carried to the right, and so on from one page to the next. When the last page is full and the end of the book has been reached, a new one is begun, of the same type, in the same format, indistinguishable from the old one. Whatever disappears is back the next day, as unchanging as the work of the office, and thus the same objects lie immutably on the same tabletop, always the identical pages and pencils and clips and forms, always different and always the same. Nothing leaves this realm of the Treasury, nothing is added to it, life goes on here without fading or flowering, or rather death never ends. The many kinds of objects differ only in their rhythm of attrition and renewal, not in their fate. A pencil lasts a week; then it has run its course and is replaced by an identical new one. A postal service manual lasts a month, a lightbulb three months, a calendar a year. The rush-seat chair is allotted three years until it's due to be replaced, the individual who sits out his life on it some thirty or thirty-five years of service; then a new individual is seated on the chair, just the same as the old one.

In 1926, in the post office in Klein-Reifling, an inconse-quential village not far from Krems, some two hours by train from Vienna, this interchangeable fixture "civil servant" is a member of the female sex and, as this facility belongs to a lower census class, has the bureaucratic designation of postal official. Not much more of her is visible through the wicket than the pleasant profile of an ordinary young woman, somewhat thin-lipped and pale and with a hint of circles under the eyes; late in the day, when she turns on the harsh electric lights, a close observer might notice a few slight lines on her forehead and wrinkles around her eyes. Still, this young woman, along with the hollyhocks in the window and the sprig of elder that she has put in the metal washbasin today for her own pleasure, is easily the freshest thing in the Klein-Reifling post office; she seems good for at least another twenty-five years of service. Her hand with its pale fingers will raise and lower the same rattly wicket thousands upon thousands of times more, will toss hundreds of thousands, perhaps millions of letters onto the canceling desk with the same swiveling motion, will slam the blackened brass canceler onto hundreds of thousands or millions of stamps with the same brief thump. Probably the wrist will even learn to function better and better, ever more mechanically and unconsciously, detached more and more completely from the conscious self. The hundreds of thousands of letters will always be different letters, but always letters. The stamps different stamps, but always stamps. The days different, but each one lasting from eight o'clock until noon, from two o'clock until six o'clock, and the work of the office, as the years come and go, always the same, the same, the same.

Perhaps, behind her wicket on this soundless summer morning, the ash-blond postal official herself is musing about these events to come, or perhaps she's just lost in a languid daydream. In any case her hands, unoccupied, have slipped off the worktable and into her lap, where they rest, folded, slender, tired, pale. On this blue, stiflingly hot July morning, there's little to do in the Klein-Reifling post office. The morning's work is done, the hunchbacked, tobacco-chewing postman Hinterfellner has long since delivered the letters, there will be no packages or trade samples from the factory arriving for shipment before evening, and the country people have neither the time nor the inclination to write to anyone just now. The peasants are far off in the vineyards, hoeing under the shelter of their yard-wide straw hats, while the children on summer vacation romp bare-legged in the brook, and the irregular pavement outside the door lies empty in the seething, brassy noontime blaze. It's good to be inside now, good to dream. The papers and official forms doze in their drawers and on their shelves in the shadows cast by the lowered blinds, the metal office equipment glints feebly and lazily through the golden half-light. Silence covers everything like thick golden dust, except for a miniature summer concert: the thin violins of the gnats and the dusky cello of a bumblebee caught between the windowpanes. The only thing in constant motion in the room (somewhat cooler now) is the wood-framed clock on the wall between the windows, which gulps down a drop of time every second. But it's a weak, monotonous sound, lulling rather than stimulating. Thus the postal official sits in a kind of pleasant waking paralysis at the center of her little sleeping world. She'd meant to do some needlework—this is clear from the needles and scissors there at hand—but she has neither the will nor the strength to pick up the embroidery lying rumpled on the floor. She leans back comfortably in her chair, hardly breathing, eyes closed, and basks in the strange and wonderful feeling of permissible idleness.

Clack! She starts. And again, harder, more metallic, more insistent: clack, clack, clack. The telegraph hammers wildly, the mechanism whirs: that rare visitor to Klein-Reifling, a telegram, is requesting a respectful reception. The postal official pulls herself out of her lazy half sleep, moves quickly to the wheeled table, and starts the tape. But no sooner has she deciphered the first words of unwinding type than she feels herself flushing to the roots of her hair: she's never seen her own name on a telegram here. Now the entire dispatch has been banged out. She reads it once, twice, three times and still doesn't understand. What can this be? Who could be sending her a telegram from Pontresina? "Christine Hoflehner, Klein-Reifling, Austria, Welcome, come any time, choose your day, wire arrival time in advance. Best, Claire—Anthony." She ponders: Who is this Anthony who's expecting her? Is somebody in the office playing a silly prank? But then she remembers something her mother said weeks ago, that her aunt would be coming over to Europe this summer, and, that's right, her name is Klara. And Anthony, that must be Klara's husband, Anton is the name her mother has always used. Yes, now it's coming back, a few days ago there was a letter for her mother from Cherbourg—Christine herself took it to her. She was tight-lipped about it, didn't say what it was. But this telegram is addressed to her, Christine. Does it mean she's supposed to go up to Pontresina to see her aunt? There's been no mention of it. Her eyes return to the still-unglued tape, the only telegram she's ever received in her own name here. She reads and rereads the strange document, at a loss, curious, disbelieving, confused. No, it can't possibly wait until her lunch hour. She has to ask her mother what it all means right now. She snatches up the key, locks the office, and runs home. In her excitement she neglects to disconnect the arm of the telegraph; the brass hammer, forgotten in the empty room, goes on clacking and clattering furiously over the blank and unmarked tape.

Electricity moves at a speed greater than thought, a speed too great for thought to grasp. These twelve words, which have landed like a white, soundless thunderbolt in the airless humidity of the Austrian post office, were written only minutes before and three countries away, in the cool blue shadow of glaciers, under the clear violet Engadine sky, and the ink was not even dry on the telegraph form when the message, the summons, burst upon a bewildered consciousness.

Here's what happened. Anthony van Boolen, born in Holland but for many years an established cotton broker in the American South; Anthony van Boolen, a good-natured, phlegmatic, and when you come down to it utterly insignificant man, had just finished his breakfast on the terrace (all glass and light) of the Palace Hotel. Then came the nicotine-laden culmination of the meal, the tuberous brownish-black Havana that he'd had specially imported in an airtight tin. This rather stout gentleman rested his legs on a wicker chair as he took the first and most invigorating puff with the schooled pleasure of the experienced smoker, then unfurled the paper spinnaker of the *New York Herald* and sailed off into the vast typeset sea of the stock market and brokerage listings. Meanwhile, across from him at the table, his bored wife, Claire (formerly Klara), divided her grapefruit into sections. She knew from many years of experience that any conversational sally against the usual early-morning wall of paper would have no hope of success. Thus the comical bellhop, brown-capped and apple-cheeked, was not unwelcome when he suddenly pivoted sharply in front of her with the morning mail. The tray held a single letter. But it was evidently something of great interest, for, ignoring long experience, she tried to interrupt her husband's morning reading: "Anthony, excuse me a moment," she said. The newspaper did not move. "I don't want to disturb you, Anthony, but listen for just a second, it's urgent. Mary" (she automatically gave the name its English form) "Mary has just sent her regrets. She can't come, she says, she'd like to but she's in a bad way with her heart, it's serious, and her doctor thinks she couldn't stand the two thousand meters. He says it's out of the question. But if it's all right with us she'd be glad to send Christine here for two weeks in her place, you know who that is, the youngest one, the blond. You saw a photo of her once before the war. She works in a post office, but she's never taken a proper vacation, and if she puts in for it she'll get it immediately, and of course after so many years she'd be glad to 'pay her respects to you, dear Klara, and Anthony,' etc., etc."

The newspaper did not move. Claire became impatient. "So what do you think, should we ask her to come? . . . It wouldn't hurt the poor thing to get a breath or two of fresh air, and anyway it's only right. As long as I'm over here I really ought to meet my sister's child, we're hardly family anymore. Do you have any objections to my inviting her?"

The newspaper rustled a little. A smoke ring rose over the top edge of the paper, round, a pretty blue; then, in a ponderous and indifferent tone: "Not at all. Why should I?"

With this laconic decision the conversation ended and a fate began to take shape. After an interval of decades a family tie was being renewed, for, despite the almost aristocratic-sounding name with its impressive but actually quite ordinary Dutch "van," and even though the couple's conversation was in English, this Claire van Boolen was none other than the sister of Marie Hoflehner and hence incontestably the aunt of the Klein-Reifling postal official. Her departure from Austria more than a quarter of a century earlier had come in the train of a somewhat shady business which she recalled only vaguely (memory is always happy to oblige) and of which her sister too had never given her daughters a clear account. At the time, however, the affair had caused quite a sensation and would have had still greater consequences had not prudent and clever men soon deprived public curiosity of the spark that would have inflamed it. At that time Mrs. Claire van Boolen had been plain Fräulein Klara, a simple dress model in an exclusive boutique on the Kohlmarkt. But, flashing-eyed and graceful as she was then, she'd had a devastating effect on an elderly lumber baron who had gone along with his wife to a fitting. Full of last-ditch impetuosity, the rich and still fairly well-preserved businessman fell for the lively, shapely blond within a matter of days and began courting her with a generosity that was rare even in his circles. Before long the nineteen-year-old model, much to the indignation of her respectable family, was riding in a hackney coach wearing the finest clothes and furs, items which until then she'd only modeled in front of mirrors for finicky and usually hard-to-please customers, but which were now her very own. The more elegant she became, the more she pleased her elderly benefactor, and the more she pleased the old businessman, who'd been thrown into a complete tizzy by his unexpected success in love, the more lavishly he decked her out. After a few weeks she'd softened him up so thoroughly that divorce papers were already being secretly drafted and she was well on her way to becoming one of the wealthiest women in Vienna—but then the wife, alerted by an anonymous letter, intervened aggressively and foolishly. Understandably infuriated at being abruptly put out to pasture like a hobbled horse after thirty tranquil years of marriage, she bought a revolver and set upon the mismatched couple in their love nest, a recently established cheap hotel. She fired two shots at the home wrecker on the spot. One went wide; the other hit Klara in the upper arm. The wound would prove trivial, but everything else was awkward indeed: neighbors scurrying past, loud cries for help through smashed windows, doors flying open, swoons and scenes, doctors, police, investigations, and, looming at the end of it all, apparently unavoidable, the court hearing, feared by all parties because of the scandal. Fortunately, there are clever lawyers—not just in Vienna but everywhere—who are practiced in hushing up such troubling episodes for the well-to-do. Counselor Karplus, the proven master of them all, immediately dispelled the imminent dangers of the affair. He respectfully summoned Klara to his office. Looking extremely elegant, with a fetching bandage, she read with curiosity through the contract, which stipulated that she depart for America immediately, before anyone could serve her with a summons; once there she would receive a one-time payment for damages and a certain sum of money on the first of every month for five years, provided she kept her mouth shut. Klara, who in any case had little wish to go back to being a dress model in Vienna after this scandal, and whose own family had thrown her out, glanced through the four foolscap pages of the contract without protest, rapidly calculated the amount, found it surprisingly high, and thought she'd see what would happen if she demanded an additional thousand gulden. This too was granted. She signed the contract with a quick smile, traveled across the sea, and never regretted her decision. Even during the crossing all sorts of marriage opportunities presented themselves, and a decisive one soon came along: in a New York boarding-house she met Anthony van Boolen. At the time he was only a minor commission agent for a Dutch exporter, but he quickly resolved that he would set up on his own in the South using the small capital which she contributed and whose romantic origin he never suspected. After three years she had two children, after five years a house, and after ten years a considerable fortune (the same war that was wrathfully crushing the wealthy in Europe was causing wealth to grow by leaps and bounds everywhere else). By now their two sons, grown up and business-minded, were already taking the reins at their father's brokerage, and af-ter so many years the two older people could permit themselves a relatively lengthy and leisurely trip to Europe. And strangely: when the low shores of Cherbourg emerged from the fog, in that fraction of a second Claire suddenly felt her sense of home change completely. She'd long since become deeply American, yet she felt an unexpected pang of nostalgia for her youth just because this bit of land was Europe. That night she dreamt of the little cribs in which she and her sister had slept side by side, a thousand tiny details came back to her; suddenly realizing she hadn't written a word for years to her impoverished, widowed sister, she felt ashamed. The feeling gave her no rest. She went straight from the landing to send her the letter inviting her to come, enclosing with it a hundred-dollar bill.

But now the invitation was to be passed on to the daughter. Mrs. van Boolen had only to beckon: the liveried bellhop was there like a brown ramrod. He heard and obeyed the brief request for a telegraph form and sprinted finally with the completed sheet to the post office, his cap tight over his ears. A few minutes later the symbols sprang from the clattering telegraph up to the roof and into the vibrating strand of copper, and, more quickly than the rattling trains, inexpressibly more quickly than the automobiles with their trails of swirling dust, the message flashed through a thousand kilometers of wire. In no time it had crossed the border, had passed through Vorarlberg with its thousand peaks, through cute little Liechtenstein, the many valleyed Tyrol, and already the magically transformed communication was whizzing down from the glaciers into the middle of the valley of the Danube and into a transformer in Linz. There it paused a moment; then, quicker than quick, the message shot through the rooftop circuitry in Klein-Reifling and into the startled telegraph receiver, and from there straight into a heart that was stunned, confused, and brimming with feverish curiosity.

Around the corner, up a dark creaky staircase, and Christine is home in the small-windowed attic room she shares with her mother in a narrow farmhouse. A broad projecting gable, though it helps to keep the snow away during the winter, also deprives the upper story of any ray of sun; not until evening does a weak sunbeam sometimes creep as far as the geraniums on the sill. It's always musty and damp in this gloomy garret, it smells of decayed roofing and mildewy varnish; ancient odors permeate the wood like fungus. In ordinary times the room would probably have been used only for storage, but the severe housing shortage of the postwar period has made people accept modest living conditions. It's a good thing only two beds, a table, and an old chest have to squeeze in. The inherited leather armchair took up too much room, so it went to a junk dealer at a low price. Later this turned out to be a serious mistake, for now whenever old Frau Hoflehner's bloated, dropsical feet fail her, the bed is the only place left for her to rest them.

Tired and worn out before her time, she blames her sick legs, thick and swollen lumps with ominous blue veins under flannel bandages, on two years spent working as a caretaker in a basement room, with nothing between her and the cold earth, in an infirmary to which she was assigned during the war (everyone had to make a living). Since then the heavy woman has moved with a labored wheezing; any exertion or excitement makes her clutch her heart. She knows she won't last long. It's a good thing that, amid all the confusion after the breakup of the monarchy, her brother-in-law the privy councillor had no trouble finding the Post Office job for Christine, miserably paid though it is and in such an out-of-the-way hole. But still: a little bit of security, a roof over your head, room to breathe, just barely; might as well get used to it—after all, the casket's an even tighter fit.

It always smells of vinegar and damp in the cramped box, of sickness and confinement to bed. The door to the tiny adjoining kitchen doesn't close properly, so the insipid fumes of reheated food creep in like a stewing fog. Coming in now, Christine automatically flings open the window. The sudden noise awakens the old woman on the bed, and she can't help moaning, the way a broken-down trunk might creak when anyone even approaches it: her rheumatic body knows pain is coming and dreads it, the pain that any movement causes. So first the unavoidable moan; then she lurches to her feet. "What is it?" she asks. Even asleep, she knew it couldn't be noon yet, couldn't be lunchtime. Something must have happened. Her daughter hands her the telegram.

The weathered hand gropes among the drugstore articles on the night table and with effort (every movement hurts) finds the steel-rimmed glasses. But once she's made out what's on the sheet of paper, it's as though an electric shock goes through her heavy body. She gasps, struggles for breath, sways, and finally collapses with all her weight onto Christine. She clings fiercely to her startled daughter, quakes, laughs, wheezes, tries to speak but can't. Finally, hands pressed to her heart, she sinks exhaustedly into the chair. She takes a deep breath and pants for a moment. But then a confused torrent of broken, half-intelligible sentences bursts from her toothless, working mouth, interspersed with floods of wild triumphant laughter. Tears roll down her cheeks and into her sagging mouth as she stammers and waves her hands, hurling the jumble of excited words at her bewildered daughter. Thank God, it's all turned out well, now she can die in peace, a useless, sick old woman like her. That's the only reason she made the pilgrimage last month, in June, that's all she asked for, the only thing, that her sister Klara would come back before she died and look after Christl, poor child. So now she's happy. See, she didn't just send a letter, no, she spent good money on a telegram, saying that Christl should come up to her hotel, and she sent a hundred dollars two weeks ago, yes, Klara always had a heart of gold, she was always good and kind. And Christine can use that hundred dollars for more than just travel, yes, she can dress up like a princess before she goes to visit her aunt at that posh resort. Oh, she'll get an eyeful there, she'll see how those high-class people live it up, the people with money. For the first time she'll have it as good as the rest, thank heavens, and by the saints she's earned it. Because what has she ever gotten out of her life—nothing, just the job and responsibility and slaving away on top of having to take care of a useless, sick, unhappy old woman who should have been dead and buried long ago and who if she had any sense would finally just give up once and for all. It was on her account and because of the damned war that Christl's entire girlhood was ruined, it always tore her old mother's heart out to see her missing the best years of her life. But now she can make her fortune. She should just make sure to be polite to her aunt and uncle, always polite, always humble, and not be frightened of her aunt Klara, she always did have a heart of gold, she's good, and she'll certainly help her get out of this stifling hole, this one-horse town, once she herself is dead and buried. No, Christine shouldn't think twice if her aunt ends by offering to take her along, she should just get out of this rotten country, away from these no-goods, don't worry about her. She can always find a spot in a nursing home and when you get down to it how much time does she have left...Ah, now she can die in peace, everything will be fine now.

The bloated old woman, swathed in mufflers and petticoats, keeps getting up to labor on her massive legs over the creaking floorboards. She dabs her eyes with the big red handkerchief, overcome by happiness; she waves her arms more and more wildly, pausing amid her excited rambling to sit down, moan, blow her nose, and catch her breath for a new flood of words. She keeps thinking of something else to say, keeps talking and talking and clamoring and rejoicing and moaning and weeping all at once over the wonderful surprise. Suddenly, in a moment of exhaustion, she notices that Christine, upon whom she's bestowing all this joy, is standing there in a daze, pale and awkward, with wondering eyes and in some perplexity, not knowing what to say. Frau Hoflehner finds this exasperating. Once more she struggles out of the chair and goes to the bewildered young woman, cheerily takes hold of her, gives her a heavy, wet kiss, pulls her close, and shakes her as if to wake her up: "Well, say something! It's for you, silly, what's the matter with you? You stand there like a stone with nothing to say for yourself, and what an opportunity! So be happy! Why aren't you happy?"

Regulations strictly prohibit postal workers from leaving the premises for any length of time while the post office is open to the public, and even the most urgent private matter is subject to the Treasury's priorities: official before personal, the letter of the law before the spirit. Thus a few minutes later the Klein-Reifling postal official is back behind her wicket, ready for work again. No one missed her. The loose forms still slumber on the table where she left them, the telegraph which not so long ago set her heart beating is turned off and silent, glinting yellow in the gloomy room. Thank goodness no one came, no one needed anything. Now the postal official can with a clear conscience think over the confusing message that sprang off the wires—with all the excitement she still doesn't know if it's welcome or disturbing. Gradually her thoughts come into focus. She's being asked to go away, away from her mother for the first time ever, for two weeks, perhaps longer, to visit strangers, no, to visit her aunt Klara, her mother's sister, at a fancy hotel. She's going to take a vacation, an actual, honest vacation, after so many years she's finally going to have a break, see the world, see something new, something different. She turns it over in her mind. Actually it is good news, Mother's right, she's right to be so happy about it. Christine has to admit it's the best news she's had in years and years. To be allowed to get out of harness for the first time, to be free, to see new faces, a bit of the world, it's a gift from heaven, isn't it? But she hears her mother's astonished, alarmed, almost angry question: "Why aren't you happy?"

Mother's right: Why is it I'm not happy? Where's the flutter, the excitement? She keeps listening for a response inside, some reaction to this fine surprise out of the blue, but no: all she feels is confusion, fear, and mistrust. Strange, she thinks, why is it I'm not happy? A hundred times I've taken postcards out of the mailbag, picture-postcards showing gray Norwegian fjords, the boulevards of Paris, the bay of Sorrento, the stone monoliths of New York, and haven't I always put them down with a sigh? When will it be me? When will it be my turn? What have I been dreaming about during these long empty mornings if not about being free someday from this meaningless grind, this deadly race against time? Relaxing for once, having some unbroken time to myself, not always in shreds, in shards so tiny you could cut your finger on them. For once getting away from this daily grind, the alarm clock, destroyer of sleep, driving you to get up, get dressed, get the furnace going, get milk, get bread, light the fire, go to work and clock in, write, make phone calls, then go straight home again to the ironing board, the stove, wash, cook, do the mending and the nursing, and at last fall asleep dead tired. A thousand times I've dreamed of it, tens of thousands of times, here at this very table, here in this ramshackle coop, and now it's finally sinking in, I'm going to travel, get away from here, be free, and yet—Mother's right—why is it I'm not happy? How come I'm not ready?

She sits with shoulders slumped, staring at the wall, waiting for an answer, waiting to feel some joy. She's holding her breath without knowing it, listening to her body like a pregnant woman, listening, bending down deep into herself. But nothing stirs, everything is silent and empty like a forest where no birds are singing. She tries harder, this twenty-eight-year-old woman, to remember what it is to be happy, and with alarm she realizes that she no longer knows, that it's like a foreign language she learned in childhood but has now forgotten, remembering only that she knew it once. When was the last time I was happy? She thinks hard, and two little lines are etched in her bowed forehead. Gradually it comes to her: an image as though from a dim mirror, a thin-legged blond girl, her schoolbag swinging above her short cotton skirt. A dozen other girls are swirling around her: it's a game of rounders in a park in suburban Vienna. A surge of laughter, a bright trill of high spirits following the ball into the air, now she remembers how light, how free that laughter felt, it was never far away, it tickled under her skin, it swirled through her blood; one shake and it would spill out over her lips, it was so free, almost too free: on the school bench you had to hug yourself and bite your lip to keep from laughing at some funny remark or silliness in French class. Any little thing would set off waves of that effervescent girlish laughter. A teacher who stammered, a funny face in the mirror, a cat chasing its tail, a look from an officer on the street, any little thing, any tiny, senseless bit of nonsense, you were so full of laughter that any-thing could bring it out. It was always there and ready to erupt, that free, tomboyish laughter, and even when she was asleep, its high-spirited arabesque was traced on her young mouth.

And then it all went black, snuffed out like a candle. It was the first of August, 1914. That afternoon she was at the pool. In the cabin she'd seen her smooth, naked sixteen-year-old body emerge like a flash of light from her blouse, almost fully formed, sleek, white, flushed, full of health. It was marvelous to cool off, splashing and swimming, to race with her friends across the rattling boards—she can still hear the laughing and panting of the half-dozen teenage girls. Then she trotted home, quickly, quickly, her feet light, for of course she was late again. She was supposed to be helping her mother pack: in two days she'd be going over to the Kamp Valley for summer vacation. So she takes the steps three at a time and goes straight through the door, out of breath. But, strangely, her mother and father fall silent when she comes in, and they don't look at her. She'd heard her father speaking in an unusually loud voice, but now he seems oddly interested in the newspaper; her mother must have been crying, because now she crushes her handkerchief nervously and rushes to the window. What's happened? Did they have a fight? No, never, that can't be it, for now her father wheels about and puts his hand on her mother's trembling shoulder, she's never seen him so tender. But her mother doesn't turn, the silent caress only makes her tremble more. What's happened? They pay no attention to her, neither of them so much as looks at her. Even now, twelve years later, she remembers how afraid she felt. Are they angry with her? Did she do something bad, perhaps? Fearfully—a child is always full of fear and guilt—she slinks into the kitchen, where she gets the news from Božena, the cook, and Geza, the officer's servant from next door (and he'd know). He says now it's starting, the damn Serbs are going to be goulash. Otto will have to go as a reserve lieutenant and also her sister's husband, both of them, that's why her parents are upset. And in fact the next morning her brother, Otto, is suddenly standing in the room in his pike-blue infantryman's uniform, his brocade sash fastened at an angle, a gold sword knot on his saber. As a grammar-school substitute teacher he usually wears an ill-brushed black Prince Albert—a pale, thin, towering boy with stubbly hair and yolk-yellow down on his cheeks who looks almost ridiculous in solemn black. But now, pulled up straight in the close-fitting uniform, with a rigid set to his mouth, he seems entirely new and different to his sister. She looks up at him with a silly teen-ager's pride and claps her hands: "My, don't you look smart." Then her mother, usually so gentle, gives her a shove, making her elbow hit the armoire: "Aren't you ashamed of yourself, you heartless creature?"—an angry outburst relieving a hurt she can't express. Now, nearly shrieking, she weeps openly, her mouth working and trembling, and in desperation she clings with all her strength to the young man, who resolutely looks the other way, tries to assume a manly bearing, and says something about duty and country. Her father has turned his back—he can't look. The young man, face pale and jaw set, frees himself almost roughly from his mother's impulsive embrace. He covers his mother's cheeks with quick, harried kisses, hastily holds out his hand to his father (whose posture is unnaturally stiff), and darts past Christine with a quick goodbye. The saber rattles down the stairs. Her sister's husband, a municipal official who's been conscripted as a train sergeant, comes by that afternoon to say goodbye. This is easier; he knows he won't be in danger. He makes himself comfortable and pretends it'll be fun, jokes en-couragingly, and leaves. But two shadows remain behind—her brother's wife, four months pregnant, and her sister with her small child. The two of them come for dinner every evening, and each time the lamp seems to burn lower. All eyes regard Christine severely if she says anything cheerful, and in her bed at night she's ashamed at how bad she is, how unserious, how much she's still a child. Without meaning to she grows silent. There's no laughter left in the rooms, no one sleeps well. If she wakes up during the night she sometimes hears a faint steady sound like a ghostly faucet drip in the next room: it's her mother, unable to sleep, on her knees before the illuminated Virgin, praying for her brother for hours on end.

And then 1915: seventeen years old. Her parents seem a decade older. Her father is dwindling as though eaten away from inside; he struggles from room to room, sallow and stooped, and everyone knows he's worried about business. For sixty years, since her grandfather's time, there's been no one in the entire monarchy who could dress chamois horn or do game taxidermy like Bonifazius Hoflehner and Son. Her father prepared hunting trophies for the castles of the Esterházys, the Schwarzenbergs, even the archdukes, working with four or five assistants, painstakingly, exactingly, and honorably, from morning till late at night. But in times as deadly as these, when the only thing people shoot is people, no one comes in for weeks on end. Yet the daughter-in-law's pregnancy, the grandson's illness, it all costs money. The shoulders of the now taciturn man slump more and more, and they give way completely one day when the letter arrives from the Isonzo, for the first time not in Otto's handwriting but his commander's. Even without opening it they know what it is: a hero's death at the head of the company, eternal remembrance, and so forth. The house becomes quieter and quieter; her mother has stopped praying, the light over the Virgin has gone out; she's forgotten to fill it with oil.

1916: She's eighteen. There's a new catchphrase in the household, used constantly: too expensive. Her mother, her father, her sister, her sister-in-law escape from their troubles into the smaller-scale misery of the bills, from morning until night they reckon up their poor daily life aloud. Meat, too expensive, butter, too expensive, a pair of shoes, too expensive: Christine hardly dares to breathe for fear it might be too expensive. The things most necessary to a bare existence flee as though terrified, burrowing like animals into lairs of extortionate prices—you have to hunt them down. Bread has to be begged for, a handful of vegetables inveigled from the grocer, eggs brought in from the country, coal carted by hand from the train station: thousands of freezing, hungry women vie with one another in pursuit of quarry that's scarcer every day. Her father has something wrong with his stomach, he needs special, easily digestible food. Ever since he had to take down the BONIFAZIUS HOFLEHNER sign and sell the business, he hasn't been talking to anyone, he just presses his hands to his belly sometimes and moans when he thinks he's alone. The doctor really ought to be called. But: too expensive, her father says, preferring to double up furtively in his distress.

And 1917—nineteen. They buried her father two days after New Year's; the money in the bankbook was just enough for them to dye their clothes black. It's getting more and more expensive to live, they've already rented out two rooms to a pair of refugees from Brody, but it's not enough, not enough, even if you slave until late at night. Finally her uncle the privy councillor finds a job for her mother as a caretaker in the Korneuburg Hospital and one for her as a clerk. If only it wasn't so far— leaving at daybreak in an ice-cold train car and not back until evening. Then cleaning, mending, scrubbing, darning, and sewing, until, without thinking, without wanting anything, you fall like an overturned bag into a grudging sleep from which you'd prefer not to wake.

And 1918—twenty. The war still on, still not a day to yourself without worries, still no time to glance in the mirror, to poke your head out into the street. Christine's mother is beginning to complain, her legs are swelling up in the damp, uncellared ward, but Christine has no strength left for sympathy. She's been living too long with infirmity; something in her has gone numb since she started having to type admission records for seventy or eighty atrocious mutilations every day. Sometimes a little lieutenant from the Banat toils into the office on his crutch to see her (his left leg is shattered), his hair golden-blond like the wheat of his homeland but terror etched into the still-unformed child's face. In his quaint Swabian dialect he tells homesick stories (poor blond lost child) about his village, his dog, his horses. One evening they kiss on a bench in the park, two, three feeble kisses, more pity than passion, then he says he wants to marry her as soon as the war is over. A tired smile is her only response; she doesn't dare think that the war might ever end.

And 1919—twenty-one. The war has in fact ended, but poverty has not. It only ducked beneath the barrage of ordinances, crawled foxily behind the paper ramparts of war loans and banknotes with their ink still wet. Now it's creeping back out, hollow-eyed, broad-muzzled, hungry, and bold, and eating what's left in the gutters of the war. An entire winter of denominations and zeroes snows down from the sky, hundreds of thousands, millions, but every flake, every thousand melts in your hand. Money dissolves while you're sleeping, it flies away while you're changing your shoes (coming apart, with wooden heels) to run to the market for a second time; you never stop moving, but you're always too late. Life becomes mathematics, addition, multiplication, a mad whirl of figures and numbers, a vortex that snatches the last of your possessions into its black insatiable vacuum: your mother's gold hair clasp off your neck, her wedding ring off her finger, the damask cloth off the table. But no matter how much you toss in, it's no use, you can't plug that black hellish hole, it does no good to stay up late knitting wool sweaters and rent all your rooms out and use the kitchen as a bedroom, doubling up with someone else. Sleep, though, that's still the one thing you can't begrudge yourself, the only thing that doesn't cost money: the hours when you throw your spent, wan, now gaunt, still-untouched body on the mattress, unconscious of this ongoing apocalypse for six or seven hours.

And then 1920–1921. Twenty-two, twenty-three years old, the flower of youth, it's called. But she doesn't hear that from anyone, and she herself has no idea. From morning till night, just one thought: how to get by, with money tighter and tighter all the time. Things have gotten just a touch better. Once more her uncle the privy councillor has helped out by going personally to his poker buddy in the postal administration to cadge a temporary postal worker's position, in Klein-Reifling—a wretched hole in the wine country, but it's permanent employment, it's a foothold. The bare wage is only enough for one, but she's had to take her mother in (her brother-in-law didn't have room) and make everything stretch twice as far; each day still begins with making do and ends with counting up. Every matchstick is itemized, every coffee bean, every speck of flour in the dough. But you're breathing, you're alive.

And 1922, 1923, 1924—twenty-four, twenty-five, twenty-six. Are you still young? Are you already old? Her temples show a scribble of a few fine lines, her legs are sometimes tired, in the spring her head aches strangely. But there's progress, things are getting better. There's money in her hand, hard and round, she has a permanent position as "postal official," her brother-in-law is even sending her mother two or three banknotes at the beginning of every month. Now would be the time to try, in some small way, to be young again; even her mother is urging her to go out and enjoy herself. Her mother finally gets her to sign up for a dancing class in the next town. These thumping dance lessons aren't easy, her fatigue is too much a part of her. Sometimes she feels her joints are frozen—even the music can't thaw them out. Laboriously she practices the assigned steps, but she can't really get interested, she's not carried away, and for the first time she has a feeling: too late, toil has exhausted her youth, the war has taken it away. Something must have snapped inside her, and men seem to sense it, for she isn't really being pursued by any of them, even though her delicate blond profile has an aristocratic look among the coarse faces, round and red like apples, of the village girls. But these postwar seventeen- and eighteen-year-olds aren't waiting quietly and patiently, waiting for someone to want them and take them. They're demanding pleasure as their right, demanding it as impetuously as though it's not just their own young lives that they're living but the lives of the hundred thousand dead and buried too. With a kind of horror Christine, now twenty-six, watches how they act, these newcomers, these young ones, sees their self-assurance and covetousness, their knowing and impudent eyes, the provocation in their hips, how unmistakably they laugh no matter how boldly the boys embrace them, and how shamelessly they take the men off into the woods—she sees them on her way home. It disgusts her. Surrounded by this coarse and lustful postwar generation she feels ancient, tired, useless, and overwhelmed, unwilling and unable to compete. No more struggling, no more striving, that's the main thing! Breathe calmly, daydream quietly, do your work, water the flowers in the window, ask not, want not. No more asking for anything, nothing new, nothing exciting. The war stole her decade of youth. She has no courage, no strength left even for happiness.

Christine sighs as she pushes her thoughts aside. Just thinking about the horrors of her early life makes her feel tired. All the trouble Mother has caused! Why leave now and go visit an aunt she doesn't know, be among people she isn't comfortable with? But my God, what can she do? That's what Mother wants and it would make her happy if she went, so Christine really shouldn't fight it. And why fight it anyway? She's so tired, so tired. Slowly, resignedly, the postal official takes a sheet of foolscap from the top shelf of her desk, folds it carefully in the middle, puts a sheet of ruled paper underneath as a guide, and writes, in a clear, clean hand with lovely shading, to the postal administration in Vienna, asking that, for family reasons, she immediately be permitted to begin the vacation to which she is legally entitled and requesting that a substitute be sent next week. Then she writes to her sister in Vienna, asking that she obtain a Swiss visa for her, lend her a small suitcase, and come out so they can discuss a few things having to do with their mother. And during the next few days she slowly, carefully gets everything ready for the trip, without joy, without expectation, without interest, as though this were not her life but just more work and responsibility.

Preparations have been going on all week. The evenings are spent in energetic sewing, mending, cleaning, and fixing up of old clothes; and her sister, instead of buying anything new with the dollars Christine sent her (better to save the money, was her anxious thought), has lent her some things from her own wardrobe—a canary-yellow travel coat, a green blouse, a mosaic brooch that their mother bought in Venice when she was on her honeymoon, and a small straw suitcase. This will do, Christine thinks, in the mountains you don't dress up, and whatever she's missing, if it comes to that, would be better bought once she's there. At last the day comes. The schoolteacher from the next village, Franz Fuchsthaler, carries the flat straw suitcase to the station himself; he doesn't want to miss this chance to do a favor for a friend. A scrawny little man, anxious blue eyes hidden behind spectacles, he showed up at the Hoflehners' to offer his help as soon as he heard the news; they're the only people he's friendly with in the remote vineyard village. His wife has been in the state hospital for tuberculosis at Alland for more than a year—all the doctors have given up on her case—and both his children are staying with relatives elsewhere; so almost every evening he sits in silence in his two lonely rooms, making modest little objects with the care of a craftsman. He puts plants into herbaria, inking the names in calligraphy (red for the Latin, black for the German) underneath the pressed flower petals; he binds his beloved brick-red Reclam booklets in brightly colored pasteboard with his own hands and uses a drawing pen with an ultrafine point to simulate printed letters on the spines with microscopic accuracy and remarkable detail. Late at night, when he knows the neighbors are all asleep, he plays a somewhat labored but enthusiastic violin from scores he wrote out himself, mostly Schubert and Mendelssohn, or copies the finest verses and thoughts out of borrowed books onto white textured quarto sheets, which, when he has a hundred of them, he binds into an album with a glossy cover and a brightly colored label. He's like a Koranic calligrapher who loves the handwriting with its delicate curves and shading for the mute joy of it, its silent expressive flair. For this quiet, unprepossessing, passive man who has no garden in front of his subsidized flat, books are like flowers. He loves to line them up on the shelf in multicolored rows; he watches over each of them with an old-fashioned gardener's delight, holds them like fragile objects in his thin, bloodless hands. He never goes to the village inn: he abhors beer and smoke as the holy do evil. If he's outside and hears the boorish voices of brawlers or drunks behind a window, he hurries past with quick, outraged steps. The Hoflehners are the only people he's been seeing since his wife fell ill. Often he drops in after dinner, to chat with them or (they're fond of this) to read aloud from books, especially the *Wildflowers* of Austria's own Adalbert Stifter. His voice is actually somewhat dry, but it soars musically when he's in the grip of emotion. His timid and somewhat cramped soul always feels subtly more expansive when he looks up from the book and sees the young woman listening, her blond head bowed. She seems so sensitive, so attentive, and that makes him feel she understands him. Christine's mother has noticed his growing feeling and knows that, once his wife has met her inevitable fate, he'll look more boldly at her daughter. But Christine is stoic and says nothing: it's been a long time since she gave any thought to herself.

The schoolteacher carries the suitcase on one shoulder, the slightly lower one (he ignores the laughing schoolboys). It's not much of a load, but Christine hurries ahead so nervously and impatiently that he pants to keep up with her; her departure has unexpectedly put her in a dreadful state. Three times, despite the doctor's express orders, her mother stumbled down the stairs and followed her into the entry, inexplicably anxious to hold on to her; three times the stout old woman had to be led back up sobbing, though time was short. And then it happened, as so often in recent weeks: in the midst of her weeping and carrying on, the old woman suddenly became winded and had to be put to bed, gasping for breath. Christine left her in that condition, and now her worry is becoming a guilty feeling: "My God, I've never seen her so upset, what if something happens to her and I'm not there? Or if she needs something at night—my sister isn't coming from Vienna till Sunday. The bakery girl, she gave me her solemn word she'd stay with her in the evening, but you can't depend on her; she'll abandon her own mother if there's a chance to go dancing. No, I shouldn't have done it, I shouldn't have let myself be talked into it. Traveling, that's something for people who don't have someone sick at home, not for people like us, especially if it's so far away you can't go home whenever you want. And what will I get out of all this gadding about anyway? How am I supposed to enjoy myself if I can't relax, if I've got to be thinking every minute about whether she might need something, and nobody's there at night, and they don't hear the bell downstairs, or they don't want to hear it? They don't like us in the house, the landlord and the landlady; if they had their way they'd have rented our rooms to someone else long ago. And the secretary from Linz, I asked her to look in for a minute in the evening and at midday, but all she said was, 'All right,' that cold prune-face, the kind of thing that didn't tell you whether she really would or not. Maybe I ought to wire them to call it off? What does my aunt care whether I come or not? Mother's kidding herself that we matter to them. If we did, they'd have written once in a while during all that time in America, or sent a care package during the bad years the way thousands of people did. All those packages I handled myself, and never one for Mother from her very own sister. No, I shouldn't have given in, and I'd call it off now if it was up to me. I don't know why, but I've got such a bad feeling. I shouldn't go, I shouldn't go."

The shy little blond man gasps out reassuring things as he hastens to keep up. No, don't worry, he'll look in on her mother that day himself, that's a promise. She has the right if anyone does to give herself a vacation at long last, she hasn't had a day of rest in years. He'd be the first to tell her if it was irresponsible. But not to worry, he'll send news every day, every day. He blurts out whatever comes into his head to set her mind at ease, and in fact his urgent talk does her some good. She's not really listening to what he's saying, but she feels she has someone she can depend on.

At the station, the train already has the signal. Christine's timid escort clears his throat in discomfort and embarrassment. She notices that he's been shifting from one foot to the other—he has something to say but lacks the courage to say it. At last, during a pause, he bashfully takes a white folded object out of his breast pocket. She must forgive him, of course it's not a gift, just a little something, maybe it'll come in handy. Surprised, she opens the long handmade paper construction. It's a map of her route from Linz to Pontresina, to be unfolded accordion-style. All the rivers, mountains, and cities along the train route

are microscopically labeled in black ink, the mountains shaded
in with finer or coarser hatching corresponding to their altitude and with meter figures shown in tiny numerals, the rivers
drawn in blue pencil, the cities marked in red; distances are
indicated in a separate table at bottom right, exactly as on the
Geographical Institute's large maps for schools, but here neatly,
painstakingly, lovingly copied by a little assistant schoolmaster. Christine blushes with surprise. Her pleasure encourages
the timid little man and he produces another small map, this
one square and trimmed in gold braid: a map of the Engadine,
copied from the large-scale Swiss ordnance map, with every
hill and dale artfully reproduced down to the tiniest detail. In
the center is a building given special distinction by a tiny circle
around it in red ink: that's the hotel where she'll be staying,
he explains, he located it in an old Baedeker. This is so she'll
always be able to find her bearings on outings and never have
to worry about getting lost. She's truly moved and thanks him.
This sweet man must have secretly spent days in libraries in
Linz or Vienna finding models to copy, must have sharpened
his pencils a hundred times and bought special drafting pens
to draw and ink these maps, tenderly, patiently, for nights on
end, just to produce from his meager means something that was
suitable and practical and would delight her. Her journey hasn't
even begun, but he's anticipated it as though experiencing it
himself, at her side for every kilometer of the trip; her route
and what will happen to her must have been in his thoughts
day and night. She's touched, and as she now extends her hand
to him in thanks (he's still in shock over his own daring) she
sees his eyes behind his glasses as though for the first time.
They're the fine mild blue of a child's, a blue suddenly deeper
and tinged with emotion. Abruptly she feels a new warmth,
an affection and trust unlike anything she's felt for a man. At
that moment what was only a vague feeling becomes a decision.
She's never held his hand so long, with such earnestness and

gratitude. He too senses the changed mood, feels hot at the temples, gets flustered, breathes deeply, and struggles to find the right thing to say. But the locomotive is already snorting like an angry black beast, with air eddying off both sides and almost blowing the paper out of her hand. There's only a moment left. Christine boards hurriedly. Through the window she sees only a fluttering white handkerchief, quickly vanishing in the steam and distance. Then she's alone, for the first time in many years.

For the entire overcast evening she huddles exhausted in the corner of the wood-paneled car. The countryside is dimly visible through the window, now wet with rain. At first small villages flit past indistinctly in the twilight, like startled animals running away; then everything fades into opaque and feature-less fog. There's no one else in her third-class compartment, so she stretches out on the wooden bench, feeling for the first time how tired she is. She tries to think, but the monotonous stuttering of the wheels breaks the flow of her thoughts, and the narcotic cowl of sleep tightens over her throbbing forehead— that muffled and yet overpowering railroad-sleep in which one lies rapt and benumbed as though in a shuddering black coal sack made of metal. Beneath her body the rackety wheels speed on like driven slaves; above her thrown-back head time goes by silently, without form or dimension. So completely does she sink into this surging black tide that she's startled awake the next morning when the door bangs open and a man, broad-shouldered and mustachioed, severely confronts her. It takes a moment for her to collect herself and realize that this uniformed man means her no harm, isn't going to arrest her and take her away, but only wants to inspect her passport, which she brings out of her handbag with cold-stiffened fingers. The official scrutinizes the photo for a moment and compares it with her nervous face. She's trembling violently (with an unreasonable and yet immutable fear, dinned into her by the war, of somehow violating one of the thousand-and-one regulations: back then everyone was always breaking some law). But the gendarme amiably returns her passport, gives his cap a casual tug, and closes the door more gently than he opened it. Christine could lie down again if she wanted to, but the shock has banished sleep. She goes to the window, curious to look out, and her senses awaken. It was only a moment ago (for sleep knows no time) that the flat horizon was a loamy gray swell merging into the fog behind the icy glass. But now rocky, powerful mountains are massing out of the ground (where have they come from?), a vast, strange, overwhelming sight. This is her first glimpse of the unimaginable majesty of the Alps, and she sways with surprise. Just now a first ray of sun through the pass to the east is shattering into a million reflections on the ice field covering the highest peak. The white purity of this unfiltered light is so dazzling and sharp that she has to close her eyes for a moment, but now she's wide awake. One push and the window bangs down, to bring this marvel closer, and fresh air—ice-cold, glass-sharp, and with a bracing dash of snow—streams through her lips, parted in astonishment, and into her lungs, the deepest, purest breath of her life. She spreads her arms to take in this first reckless gulp, and immediately, her chest expanding, feels a luxurious warmth rise through her veins—marvelous, marvelous. Inflamed with cold, she takes in the scene to the left and the right; her eyes (thawed out now) follow each of the granite slopes up to the icy epaulet at the top, discovering, with growing excitement, new magnificence everywhere—here a white waterfall tumbling headlong into a valley, there neat little stone houses tucked into crevices like birds' nests, farther off an eagle circling proudly over the very highest heights, and above it all a wonderfully pure, sumptuous blue whose lush, exhilarating power she would never have thought possible. Again and again she returns to these Alps sprung overnight from her sleep, an incredible sight to someone leaving her narrow world for the first time. These immense granite mountains must have been here for thousands of years; they'll probably still be here millions and millions of years from now, every one of them immovably where it's always been, and if not for the accident of this journey, she herself would have died, rotted away, and turned to dust with no inkling of their glory. She's been living as though all this didn't exist, never saw it, hardly cared to; like a fool she dozed off in this tiny little room, hardly longer than her arm, hardly wide enough for her feet, just a night away, a day away from this infinitude, these manifold immensities! Indifferent and without desires before, now she's beginning to realize what she's been missing. This contact with the overpowering is her first encounter with travel's disconcerting ability to strip the hard shell of habit from the heart, leaving only the bare, fertile kernel.

Forgetting herself completely in this first explosive moment, full of passionate curiosity, she continues to stand in front of the landscape, her flushed cheek pressed to the window frame. She no longer thinks about what she's left behind. Her mother, the office, the village, all are forgotten; forgotten too is the tenderly drawn map in her handbag from which she could have learned the names of all the peaks, all the streams tumbling into the valleys; forgotten is her own self of the day before. All that's left is soaking up this ever-changing magnificence, these shifting panoramas, and inhaling the freezing air, sharp and pungent like juniper, this mountain air that makes the heart beat faster and harder. Christine doesn't move from the window during the four hours of the trip. She's so absorbed that she loses track of time, and her heart gives a lurch when the engine stops and the local conductor, his words strangely accented but unmistakable, announces her destination.

"Good Lord!" Abruptly she comes to herself. There already

and she hasn't given a thought to anything, how to greet her aunt, what to say. Hurriedly she fumbles for her suitcase and umbrella—mustn't leave anything behind!—and rushes after the other passengers who are getting off. With military discipline, two ranks of colorfully capped porters fan out and set upon the arrivees, while the station buzzes with shouted names of hotels and loud welcomes. She is the only one with no one to meet her. Increasingly uneasy, her heart in her throat, she looks in all directions, searching anxiously. No one. Nothing. Everyone's expected, everyone knows where to go, everyone but her. The travelers are already crowding around the cars from the hotels waiting in a shiny, colorful row like a regiment at the ready, the platform is already starting to empty. Still no one: they've forgotten her. Her aunt didn't come; maybe she left, or she's ill; they wrote calling it off but the telegram didn't arrive in time. My God, is there at least enough money for the trip back! But first she gathers her remaining strength and goes up to a porter with "Palace Hotel" on his cap in gold letters, and asks in a small voice if a van Boolen family is staying there. "Sure, sure," replies the stout, red-faced man in a guttural Swiss accent. Oh, and he was told there would be a young lady at the station. If she'd just step into the car and give him the baggage-compartment receipt for her large bags. Christine flushes with mortification, noticing for the first time that her seedy little straw suitcase is swinging with telltale lightness in her hand, while in front of all the other cars stand spanking-new and metallically gleaming tank turrets of wardrobe trunks, seemingly straight from the store window, splendid towers among the colorful cubes and prisms of luxurious Russian calf, alligator, snakeskin, and smooth glacé kid. The distance between those people and herself must be glaringly obvious. Shame grips her. Quick, some lie! The rest of her luggage will be along later, she says. So then we can be off, announces the majestically liveried porter (thank goodness without surprise or disdain), opening the car door.

Once shame touches your being at any point, even the most distant nerve is implicated, whether you know it or not; any fleeting encounter or random thought will rake up the anguish and add to it. This first blow marks the end of Christine's unselfconsciousness. She climbs uncertainly into the dull black hotel limousine and involuntarily recoils when she sees she's not alone. But it's too late to go back. She has to move through a cloud of sweet perfume and pungent Russian leather, past knees reluctantly swung out of the way—she does this timidly, shoulders hunched as though with cold, eyes downcast—to get to a seat in the back. She murmurs a quick embarrassed hello as she passes each pair of knees, as if this courtesy might excuse her presence. But no one answers. She must have failed the sixteen inspections, or else the passengers, Romanian aristocrats speaking a harsh, vehement French, are having such a good time that they haven't noticed the slender specter of poverty shyly and silently perched in the farthest corner. With the straw suitcase across her knees (she doesn't dare to set it down in an empty spot), she slumps over for fear that these no doubt snooty people might take notice of her, doesn't dare lift her eyes even once during the entire trip; she looks down, seeing only what's under the bench. But the ladies' luxurious footwear only makes her conscious of the plainness of her own. She looks with chagrin at the women's legs with their arrogant poise, pertly crossed beneath summer ermines, and the boldly styled ski socks of the men. This netherworld of opulence is enough to drive waves of shame into her cheeks. How can she hold her own next to this undreamed-of elegance? Each timid glance brings a new pang. A seventeen-year-old girl across from her holds a whining Pekinese lazily sprawled in her lap; its felt-trimmed coat bears a monogram, and the small hand scratching it is rosily manicured and sparkles with a precocious diamond. Even the golf clubs leaning in the corner have elegant new grips of smooth cream-colored leather; each of the umbrellas casually tossed there has a different exquisite and extravagant handle. Without thinking she quickly moves her hand to cover up her own umbrella's handle, made of cheap fake horn. If only no one looks, no one notices what's only now become clear to her! She cringes further in alarm, and with each eruption of laughter anxiety runs up and down her hunched spine. But she doesn't dare look up to see if she is the joke.

Release from this torment finally comes when the car crunches into the graveled forecourt of the hotel. A clang like a railway-crossing bell summons a colorful squadron of porters and bellhops out to the car. Behind them stands the reception manager, dressed in a black frock coat to make a distinguished impression, his hair parted with geometric precision. First out the open car door is the Pekinese: it leaps out, jingling and shaking itself. Next come the women, who hike up their summer furs over athletically muscled legs and descend easily, chattering loudly all the while; the perfume billowing after them is almost stupefying. It would undoubtedly be good manners for the gentlemen to allow the young woman now timidly getting up to go first, but either they've come to the correct conclusion about her station or they fail to notice her at all; in any case they stride past her and up to the reception clerk without a glance back. Christine remains behind uncertainly, holding the straw suitcase, which she suddenly detests. She thinks she might give the others a few more paces' head start to keep them from looking too closely at her. But she waits too long. As she steps onto the running board of the car, nobody from the hotel springs forward to meet her: the obsequious gentleman in the frock coat has gone in with the Romanians, the bellhops are busy towing the luggage, and the porters are thunderously moving heavy chests about on the roof of the car. No one pays any attention to her. Evidently, she thinks, mortified—evidently, undoubtedly, they take her for the help, at best those gentlemen's serving girl, because the porters are maneuvering baggage past her with complete indifference, ignoring her as though she were one of their own. Finally she can't bear it any longer and with the last of her strength manages to get through the door of the hotel and go up to the desk clerk.

But who dares to approach a desk clerk in the high season, this luxury-liner captain standing at the command behind his desk, steadfastly holding his course amid a storm of problems. A dozen guests wait shoulder to shoulder before him as he writes notes with his right hand and fires off bellhops like arrows with every look and nod while at the same time giving out information left and right, his ear to the telephone receiver, a universal man-machine with nerve fibers forever taut. Even those authorized to come near him have to wait, so what can an inhibited and uninitiated newcomer expect? This lord of chaos seems so unapproachable that Christine retreats timidly into an alcove to wait until the whirlwind has died down. But the straw suitcase is getting heavier in her hand. She looks in vain for a bench to set it down on. But as she glances around, she thinks she notices (imagination, probably, or nerves) two people in lobby club chairs looking at her ironically, whispering and laughing. Her fingers are getting so weak that in another moment she'll have to let go. But at this critical point an artificially blond, artificially youthful, very elegant lady steps up smartly and sharply scrutinizes her profile before venturing, "Is it you, Christine?" And hearing Christine's automatic "Yes" (more whispered than spoken), her aunt envelops her with airy kisses on both cheeks and the mild scent of face powder. But Christine, grateful that at last something warm and kindred has appeared, throws herself into this purely ceremonial embrace with such passion that her aunt, interpreting this clutching as family feeling, is quite moved. Gently she pats Christine's heaving shoulders. "Oh, I'm awfully glad you came too, both Anthony and I, we're so glad." And then, taking her by the hand: "Come on, you'll certainly want to freshen up a little, your Austrian trains are supposed to be so dreadfully uncomfortable. Why don't you go fix yourself up. Don't be too long, though—the bell rang for lunch just now, and Anthony doesn't like to wait, that's a weakness of his. Everything's ready for you, the desk clerk will give you your room right away. But be quick, won't you? Nothing fancy—it's come as you are for lunch."

Her aunt motions, a liveried lad swiftly takes the suitcase and umbrella and runs for the key. The elevator shoots soundlessly two stories up. The boy opens a door in the middle of the corridor, flourishes his cap, and steps aside. This must be her room. Christine goes in. But on the threshold she stops short, as though she were in the wrong place. Because with all the will in the world, the postal official from Klein-Reifling, accustomed to shabby surroundings, can't just flick a switch and really believe that this room is for her, this extravagantly scaled, exquisitely bright, colorfully wallpapered room, with open French doors like crystalline floodgates, the light cascading through. The unchecked golden torrent covers every corner of the room, every object in it is bathed in a deluge of fire. The polished surfaces of the furniture sparkle like crystal, friendly reflections glint on brass and glass, even the carpet with its embroidered flowers breathes with the lushness and naturalness of living moss. The room glows like a morning in paradise. The onslaught of blazing light everywhere is dazzling, and for a moment Christine's heart seems to stand still; then she closes the door behind her, quickly and with a slightly guilty conscience. Her first reaction is to marvel that anything like this can exist at all, so much gleaming magnificence. Her next thought is one that for years has been indissolubly linked to anything desirable: what this must cost, how much money, what an incredible amount of money! Certainly more for a single day than she earns at home in a week—no, in a month! She looks around in embarrassment (how could anyone dare to feel at home here) and steps carefully onto the luxurious carpet; then she begins to go up to the treasures one at a time, awestruck and yet burning with curiosity. First she cautiously tries out the bed: will it really be all right to sleep there, on that effulgence of cool white? And the flowered silk duvet, spread out like down, light and pillowy to the touch. A push of a button turns on the lamp, filling every corner with its rosy glow. Discovery upon discovery: the washbasin, white and shiny as a seashell with nickel-plated fixtures, the armchairs, soft and deep and so enveloping that it takes an effort to get up again, the polished hardwood of the furniture, harmonizing with the spring-green wallpaper, and here on the table to welcome her a vibrant variegated carnation in a long-stem vase, like a colorful salute from a crystal trumpet. How unbelievably, wonderfully grand! She has a heady feeling as she imagines having all this to look at and to use, imagines making it her own for a day, eight days, fourteen days, and with timid infatuation she sidles up to the unfamiliar things, curiously tries out each feature one after another, absorbed in these delights, until suddenly she rears back as though she's stepped on a snake, almost losing her footing. For unthinkingly she's opened the massive armoire against the wall—and what she sees through the partly open inner door, in an unexpected full-length mirror, is a life-sized image like a red-tongued jack-in-the-box, and (she gives a start) it's her, horribly real, the only thing out of place in this entire elegantly coordinated room. The abrupt sight of the bulky, garish yellow travel coat, the straw hat bent out of shape above the stricken face, is like a blow, and she feels her knees sag. "Interloper, begone! Don't pollute this place. Go back where you belong," the mirror seems to bark. Really, she thinks in consternation, how can I have the nerve to stay in a room like this, in this world! What an embarrassment for my aunt! I shouldn't wear anything fancy, she said! As though I could do anything else! No, I'm not going down, I'd rather stay here. I'd rather go back. But how can I hide, how can I disappear quickly before anyone sees me and takes offense? She's backed as far as possible away from the mirror, onto the balcony. She stares down, her hand on the railing. One heave and it would be over.

Again the martial clang of the bell from downstairs. Goodness! It comes to her—her aunt and uncle are waiting in the lounge, and here she is dawdling. She hasn't washed up, hasn't even taken off her disgusting bargain-basement coat. Feverishly she unstraps the straw suitcase to get out her toilet articles. But when she unrolls the rubber bundle and puts everything on the smooth glass plate—the coarse soap, the small prickly wooden brush, the obviously dirt-cheap washing things—she feels again that she's exposing her entire lower-middle-class life to a haughty, sneering curiosity. What will the maid think when she comes in to straighten up, certainly she'll go right back down and make fun of the beggarly guest for the rest of the staff to hear. One person will tell another, everyone in the hotel will know it in no time, and I'll have to walk past them, every day, have to look down quickly and know they're saying things behind my back. No, her aunt can't help, there's no hiding it, it'll leak out. With every step she takes she'll split a seam, her clothes and her shoes will reveal the naked truth of her shabbiness to everyone. But now it's time to get going, her aunt is waiting, and her uncle gets impatient easily, she says. What to wear? God, what to do? First she thinks of the green rayon blouse her sister lent her, but what was the showpiece of her wardrobe yesterday in Klein-Reifling seems miserably flashy and common to her now. Better the plain white one, because it doesn't stand out so much, and the flower from the vase: perhaps the blazing headlight of it on her blouse will distract attention. Then she scurries down the stairs with downcast eyes, rushing past all the hotel guests for fear they'll look at her, pale and breathless, her temples throbbing, and with the queasy feeling that she's walking over a cliff.

From the lobby her aunt sees her coming. Something funny about that girl. How gracelessly she dashes down the stairs, the lopsided, embarrassed way she passes people! A nervous thing, probably; they should have told us! And my God, how awkwardly she's standing in the entry now, she's probably near-sighted, or something else isn't right. "Is something the matter, child? You're so pale. Are you ill?"

"No, no," she stammers, distracted—there are still so many people in the lobby, and that old lady in black with the lorgnette, the way she's staring! Probably at her absurdly unpresentable shoes.

"Come on, child," her aunt urges, and puts her arm around her, not imagining what a favor, what a great thing she's do-ing for her intimidated niece. Because Christine finally has a little bit of cover—a cloak and half a hiding place: her aunt is shielding her, at least from one side, with her body, her clothes, her imposing appearance. With this escort Christine, nervous as she is, succeeds in crossing the dining room with reasonable composure, to a table where fat, phlegmatic Uncle Anthony is waiting. He gets up now, a good-natured smile on his broad jowly face. He regards his newly arrived niece with his red-rimmed but bright Dutch eyes and gives her a heavy, worn paw. The main reason he's so cheerful is that now he doesn't have to wait any longer for lunch. Like a true Dutchman, he likes to eat, a lot and at leisure. He hates disruptions, and since yesterday he's been secretly dreading some impossible chic flibbertigibbet who'd disturb his meal with chattering and too many questions. But now that he sees his niece, self-conscious, charming, pale, and meek, he begins to feel better. She'll be easy to get along with. He gives her a friendly look and says jovially, to buck her up, "First you have to eat. Then we'll talk." She pleases him, this shy slip of a girl who doesn't dare to look up, who's so unlike those flappers over there, whom he detests in a grouchy sort of way because a gramophone always rattles to life when they show up and because they sashay through the room as no woman in Holland ever would have in his day. He pours Christine some wine himself, although bending over makes him grunt a little, and he motions to the waiter for service.

But if only the waiter, with his starched and ironed cuffs and equally starchy face, hadn't put such strange delicacies on her plate, all these unfamiliar hors d'oeuvres, chilled olives, colorful salads, silvery fish, heaps of artichokes, mysterious creams, a delicate goose-liver mousse, these pink salmon steaks—all of it exquisite without a doubt, subtle and light. And to get hold of these strange objects, which of the dozen utensils at her place is she supposed to use? The little spoon or the round one, the miniature knife or the broader one? How to cut it all up without revealing to the waiter's professional eye and to her proficient neighbors that this is her first time ever in such a posh dining room? How to avoid committing some gross gaucherie? She unfolds her napkin slowly to gain a little time, lowering her eyes and stealing glances at her aunt's hands in order to copy what they do. But at the same time she has to respond to her uncle's friendly questions. He speaks a thick Dutch-inflected German that needs to be followed closely, and the chunks of English that he's always slipping in make it even harder. She needs all her nerve in this battle on two fronts, but her feeling of inferiority has her constantly imagining whispers behind her back and derisive or sympathetic looks from people nearby. Fear of betraying her poverty and lack of worldliness to her uncle, her aunt, the waiter, to everyone there, and the simultaneous effort of making carefree, even cheery conversation under the most terrifying strain make the half h   ͻm an eternity. She contends bravely until the fruit cͬ her aunt finally notices her confusion, without ur it: "Child, you're tired, I can tell. No wonder, been traveling all night in one of those miser trains. No, don't be embarrassed, feel free to nap for an hour in your room, then we'll be off. No, there's nothing we wanted to do, Anthony always has a rest after lunch too." She gets up and helps Christine to her feet. "Just go on upstairs and lie down. Then you'll be refreshed and we can go for a brisk walk." Christine takes a deep breath of thanks. An hour hidden behind a closed door is an hour gained.

"So how do you like her?" she asks as she comes in. Anthony is already unbuttoning his jacket and vest for his siesta.

"Very nice," he yawns, "a nice Viennese face...Oh, hand me the pillow...Really very nice and modest. A little poorly dressed, that's all, I think so anyway...I mean...I don't know how to say it...We don't see such things anymore... And I think if you're going to introduce her as our niece to the Kinsleys and everyone else, she'll have to be dressed more presentably...Couldn't you help her out with something from your wardrobe?"

"I've already taken out the key." Mrs. van Boolen smiles. "I was stunned myself when I saw her trailing into the hotel in that outfit...It was something a person wouldn't be caught dead in. And you didn't see her coat, yellow as an egg yolk, really a specimen—you could display it in a shop with Indian curios ...Poor thing, if she only knew how barbarically she's decked herself out, but my God, where would she find out...The damned war laid everybody low in Austria, you heard her say herself that she's never been three miles beyond Vienna, never met people...Poor dear, you can tell she feels out of place here, she goes around in terror...But put it out of your mind, you can depend on me, I'll set her up properly. I've got plenty here, and what I don't have I'll pick up at the English shop; no one will know, and why shouldn't she have something special for a few days, the poor thing."

While her husband dozes on the ottoman, she musters the two almost wall-high garment bags standing like caryatids in the entry. During her two weeks in Paris Mrs. van Boolen went to a good many dress shops, not just museums. The hangers rustle with crêpe de chine, silk, batiste. She pulls out a dozen blouses and outfits, one after another, then puts them back, studying, deliberating, figuring, trying to decide what to give her young niece. Sorting through the iridescent gowns and the black ones, the delicate fabrics and the heavy ones is a slow process, but enjoyable. At last a shimmering froth of sheer garments is piled on the chair along with all sorts of stockings and underthings, all so light they can be picked up with one hand; she takes them to Christine's room. To her surprise the door swings open when she pushes on it. At first she thinks the room is empty. The window is wide open, looking straight out onto the countryside; there's no one in the chairs, no one at the desk. She goes to put the clothes down on one of the chairs and finds Christine asleep on the sofa. The unaccustomed glasses of wine have gone to her head; her uncle had poured her one after another—all in good fun—as she drained them quickly, not knowing what else to do. She'd intended just to sit down and think things over, get everything straight in her mind, but then drowsiness had gently laid her head on the cushions.

The helplessness of a sleeper is always either moving or slightly ridiculous to other people. As Christine's aunt tiptoes closer, she is moved. In her sleep the frightened girl has drawn her arms over her chest, as though to protect herself. This simple gesture is touching, childish, as is the half-open, almost frightened mouth; the eyebrows too are somewhat raised, as though she's in the grip of a dream. Even in her sleep, her aunt thinks with sudden clear-sightedness, even in her sleep she's afraid. And how pale her lips are, how colorless her gums, how pasty her complexion, although the sleeping face is still young and childish. Probably poorly nourished, overtaxed from having to go to work at an early age, tired out, worn down, and not even twenty-eight. Poor girl! Christine's unconscious self-revelation in her sleep suddenly makes Mrs. van Boolen feel almost ashamed. Disgraceful of us, really. So tired, so poor, so worried to death—they needed help and we should have given it to them a long time ago. Back there you're wrapped up in a dozen charitable causes, you're giving charity teas, making Christmas donations, you don't even know who they go to, and your own sister, your closest relative, for all these years you've forgotten her, yet you could have worked wonders with a few hundred dollars. Yes, she might have written, reminded me—always that foolish pride of the poor, that unwillingness to ask! Fortunately now at least we can help out and give this pale quiet girl a little happiness. Moved once more, she doesn't know why, she goes back to the strangely dreamy profile. Is it her own image as seen in a mirror long ago? Is she remembering an early photo of her mother in a narrow gold frame that hung over her bed as a child, or her own loneliness in the boardinghouse? In any event she's unexpectedly overcome with tenderness. And tenderly, gently, she strokes the sleeper's blond hair.

Christine is instantly awake. Taking care of her mother has accustomed her to being alert at the slightest touch. "Am I late already?" she stammers guiltily. All office workers are afraid of being late for work. For years she's gone to sleep afraid and awakened afraid at the first blast from the alarm clock. The first thing she does is check the time: "I'm not too late, am I?" The day always begins with fear of having neglected some responsibility.

"But child, why panic?" her aunt says soothingly. "We have time coming out our ears here, we don't know what to do with it all. Take it easy if you're still tired. Of course I don't want to disturb you, I was just bringing some clothes for you to look at, maybe it would be fun for you to wear some of these things while you're here. I brought so much from Paris, it's just filling up my trunk, so I thought it would be better if you wore a few things for me."

Christine feels herself flushing, down to her chest. So she'd been disgracing them from the moment they saw her—no doubt her aunt and uncle were both ashamed on her account. But how sweetly her aunt tries to help, veils her handouts, goes out of her way not to hurt her.

"But how could I wear your dresses, Aunt?" she stammers. "They're certainly much too fancy for me."

"Nonsense, they suit you better than they do me. Anthony complains that I'm dressing too young anyway. He'd like to see me looking like his great-aunts in Zaandam, heavy black silk up to the neck, buttoned up like a Protestant, and a starched white housewife's bonnet on my head. On you he'd like these things a thousand times better. So tell us now which one you want for this evening."

In a flash she's taken one of the filmy garments and held it skillfully against her own (suddenly with the casual, graceful movements of the long-forgotten dress model). It's ivory-colored, with floral edging in a Japanese style; it seems to glow in contrast to the next one, a midnight-black silk dress with flickering red flames. The third is pond-green with veins of silver, and all three seem so fantastic to Christine that she doesn't dare to think they could be hers. How could she ever wear such splendid and fragile treasures without constantly worrying? How do you walk, how do you move in such a mist of color and light? Don't you have to learn how to wear clothes like these? She gazes humbly at the exquisite garments.

But she's too much a woman not to yearn too. Her nostrils flare, and her hands have begun trembling strangely because they'd like to finger the material. Christine struggles to master herself. Her aunt, from her experience as a model long ago, knows this hungry expression, this almost sensual excitement which grips women when they see luxury. She can't help smiling at the sudden light in this quiet blond girl's eyes as they flicker restlessly and indecisively from one garment to another. She knows which garment Christine is going to choose, knows too she'll regret not taking the others. Her aunt finds it amusing to overwhelm her still more. "There's no rush, I'll leave all three here for you. You can choose the one you like best for today and tomorrow you can try on something else. I've also brought stockings and underthings—all you need now is something fresh-looking and attractive to put a little color in your cheeks. If you don't mind we'll go right over to the shops and buy everything you need for the Engadine."

"But Aunt," Christine whispers, startled and shaken. "What did I do to deserve this...You shouldn't be spending so much on me. And this room is much too expensive for me, really, a plain one would have been fine." But her aunt just smiles and looks at her appraisingly. "And then, child," she declares dictatorially, "I'll take you to our beautician, she'll make you more or less presentable. Nobody but one of our Indians back home would have a hank of hair like that. You'll see how much freer your head will be without that mop hanging down your neck. No, no argument, I know what's best, leave it to me and don't worry. And now get yourself together. We have lots of time, Anthony is at his afternoon poker game. We want to have you all fixed up to present to him this evening. Come, child."

Soon boxes are flying off the shelves in the big sports shop. They choose a sweater in a checkerboard plaid, a chamois belt that cinches the waist, a pair of fawn walking shoes with a pungent new smell, a cap, snug colorful sport stockings, and all sorts of odds and ends. In the fitting room Christine peels off the hated blouse like a dirty rind: the poverty she brought with her is packed out of sight in a cardboard box. She feels oddly relieved as the horrid things disappear, as though her fears were being hidden away forever. In another shop a pair of dress shoes, a flowing silk scarf, and yet more wonders. Christine has no experience of this kind of shopping and is agog at this new marvel, this buying with no concern for cost, without the eternal fear of the "too expensive." You choose things, you say yes, you don't think about it, you don't worry, and the packages are tied up and on their way home, borne by mysterious messengers. Your wish is granted before you've even dared to make it. It's strange, but intoxicatingly easy and pleasant. Christine surrenders without further resistance and lets her aunt do as she pleases. But when her aunt takes banknotes out of her bag she averts her eyes nervously. She tries not to listen, not to hear the price, because what's being spent on her has got to be such a fortune, such an unimaginable amount of money: she's made do for years on less than what her aunt's gone through in half an hour. She contains herself until they're leaving, then seizes the arm of her gracious benefactress and gratefully kisses her hand. Her aunt smiles at her touching confusion. "But now your hair! I'll take you to the hairdresser's and drop in on some friends while you're there. In an hour you'll be freshly done up and I'll come get you. You'll see what she does for you, already you're looking completely different. Then we'll go for a walk and tonight we'll try to have a really good time." Christine's heart is thumping wildly. She lets herself be led (her aunt means her nothing but good) into a tiled and mirrored room full of warmth and sweetly scented with mild floral soap and sprayed perfumes; an electrical apparatus roars like a mountain storm in the adjoining room. The hairdresser, a brisk, snub-nosed Frenchwoman, is given all sorts of instructions, little of which Christine understands or cares to. A new desire has come over her to give herself up, to submit and let herself be surprised. She allows herself to be seated in the comfortable barber's chair and her aunt disappears. She leans back gently, and, eyes closed in a luxurious stupor, senses a mechanical clattering, cold steel on her neck, and the easy incomprehensible chatter of the cheerful hairdresser; she breathes in clouds of fragrance and lets aromatic balms and clever fingers run over her hair and neck. Just don't open your eyes, she thinks. If you do, it might go away. Don't question anything, just savor this Sundayish feeling of sitting back for once, of being waited on instead of waiting on other people. Just let your hands fall into your lap, let good things happen to you, let it come, savor it, this rare swoon of lying back and being ministered to, this strange voluptuous feeling you haven't experienced in years, in decades. Eyes closed, feeling the fragrant warmth enveloping her, she remembers the last time: she's a child, in bed, she had a fever for days, but now it's over and her mother brings some sweet white almond milk, her father and her brother are sitting by her bed, everyone's taking care of her, everyone's doing things for her, they're all gentle and nice. In the next room the canary is singing mischievously, the bed is soft and warm, there's no need to go to school, everything's being done for her, there are toys on the bed, though she's too pleasantly lulled to play with them; no, it's better to close her eyes and really feel, deep down, the idleness, the being waited on. It's been decades since she thought of this lovely languor from her childhood, but suddenly it's back: her skin, her temples bathed in warmth are doing the remembering. A few times the brisk salonist asks some question like, "Would you like it shorter?" But she answers only, "Whatever you think," and deliberately avoids the mirror held up to her. Best not to disturb the wonderful irresponsibility of letting things happen to you, this detachment from doing or wanting anything. Though it would be tempting to give someone an order just once, for the first time in your life, to make some imperious demand, to call for such and such. Now fragrance from a shiny bottle streams over her hair, a razor blade tickles her gently and delicately, her head feels suddenly strangely light and the skin of her neck cool and bare. She wants to look in the mirror, but keeping her eyes closed is prolonging the numb dreamy feeling so pleasantly. Meanwhile a second young woman has slipped beside her like a sylph to do her nails while the other is waving her hair. She submits to it all without resistance, almost without surprise, and makes no protest when, after an introductory "*Vous êtes un peu pâle, Mademoiselle*," the busy salonist, employing all manner of pencils and crayons, reddens her lips, reinforces the arches of her eyebrows, and touches up the color of her cheeks. She's aware of it all and, in her pleasant detached stupor, unaware of it too: drugged by the humid, fragrance-laden air, she hardly knows if all this is happening to her or to some other, brand-new self. It's all dreamily disjointed, not quite real, and she's a little afraid of suddenly falling out of the dream.

Her aunt finally appears. "Excellent," she pronounces to the salonist with the air of a connoisseur. Before they leave for their walk she requests that they pack up some additional packets, pencils, and bottles. Christine avoids the mirror as she gets up, only touching the nape of her neck lightly. From time to time as they walk along she looks down surreptitiously at the taut skirt, the brightly patterned stockings, the shiny elegant shoes, and senses that her step is surer. Pressed close to her aunt, she allows everything to announce itself: the landscape with its vivid green and the panoramic sweep of the peaks, the hotels like castles of luxury at challenging vantages high on the slopes, the expensive stores with their provocative, extravagant window displays, furs, jewelry, watches, antiques, all of it strange and foreign next to the vast desolate majesty of the glacier. The horses in their fine harnesses, the dogs, the people are marvelous too, their own clothes as bright as Alpine flowers; the entire atmosphere of sunshiny insouciance, a world without work or poverty whose existence she never dreamed of. Her aunt tells her the names of the mountains, the hotels, points out prominent hotel guests as they pass by; she listens and looks up at them in awe. It seems more and more marvelous that she can be walking here, that it's permitted, and she feels more and more uncertain that she is the one experiencing this. At last her aunt looks at her watch.

"We have to go back. It's time to get dressed. We only have an hour till dinner. And lateness is the only thing that can make Anthony angry."

Christine finds her room already tinged by dusk. The early infiltration of dusk is making everything in it seem vague and silent. The sharp oblong of sky behind the open balcony door is still a deep, saturated blue, but the colors inside are beginning to dim at the edges, fading into the velvety shadows. Christine goes out onto the balcony, facing the immense landscape with its swiftly unfurling play of colors. First the clouds lose their radiant white, gradually reddening, subtly at the beginning, then more and more deeply, as if provoked despite themselves by the quickening sunset. Then shadows well up from the mountainsides, shadows that were weak and isolated during the day, lurking behind the trees, but now they're massing together, becoming dense and bold, as though a black pool from the valley were rushing up to the peaks, and for a moment it seems possible that darkness might inundate the mountaintops too and the whole vast sweep turn suddenly black and void—in fact there's already a slight breath of frost, an invisible wave of it rising out of the valleys. But now the peaks are glowing in a colder, paler light: the moon has appeared in the blue that's far from gone. It floats like a streetlight, high and round, over the space between two of the mightiest peaks, and what was just now a real scene with colors and details is becoming a silhouette, a solid black-and-white cutout, sprinkled with small, uncertainly flickering stars.

Unaccustomed to this dramatic transition, this vast unfolding palette, Christine gazes at it numbly. She's like someone used to nothing more than fiddle and pipes hearing the roar of a full orchestra for the first time: the sudden revelation of natural majesty is too much for her senses. She clutches the rail in awe, gazing with such concentration and losing herself so much in the view that she forgets herself, forgets the time. But luckily the ever-considerate hotel has a timekeeper, the relentless gong that reminds the guests of their responsibility to ready themselves for their extravagant meals. The first metallic swell gives Christine a start. Her aunt was quite clear that she was to be on time for dinner.

But which of these splendid new dresses should she choose? She lays them out again side by side on the bed, glistening like dragonflies. The dark one glints seductively from the shadows. Finally she decides on the ivory-colored one for today, on the grounds that it's the most modest of the three. She picks it up carefully, amazed at how light it is in her hand, no heavier than a handkerchief or a glove. She quickly strips off the sweater, the heavy Russia leather shoes, the thick socks, everything stiff and heavy, impatient for the new lightness. It's all so delicate, so soft and weightless. Just handling these sumptuous new underthings makes her fingers tremble, the feel of them is wonderful. Quickly she takes off the stiff old linen underthings; the yielding new fabric is a warm, delicate froth on her skin. She has an impulse to turn on the light to look at herself, but then takes her hand from the switch; better to put off the pleasure. Perhaps this luxuriously sheer fabric only feels so filmy, so delicate in the dark, under the light its spell will evaporate. After the underthings, the stockings, then the dress. Carefully (it's her aunt's, after all) she puts on the smooth silk, and it's marvelous, streaming freely down from her shoulders like a glittering cascade of warm water and clinging to her obediently, you can't feel it on you, it's like being dressed in the breeze. But go on, go on, don't get lost in delectation too soon, finish quickly so you can see! The shoes now, a few quick movements, a couple of steps: done, thank goodness! And now—her heart thumps—the first look in the mirror.

Her hand flips the switch and the bulb lights up. The room that had faded away is again dazzlingly bright; the flowered wallpaper, the carefully polished furniture is there again, the elegant new world is back. She's too nervous to bring herself within range of the mirror right away. A sidelong peek from a sharp angle shows only a strip of landscape beyond the balcony and a little of the room. She lacks the final bit of courage for the real test. Won't she look even more ridiculous in the borrowed dress, won't everyone, won't she herself see the fraud for what it is? She edges toward the mirror as though humility might make the judge more lenient. She's close now, eyes still downcast, still afraid to look. Again the sound of the gong comes from downstairs: no more time to waste! She holds her breath with sudden courage like someone about to take a leap, then determinedly lifts her eyes. Lifts her eyes and is startled, even falls back a step. Who is that? Who is that slender, elegant woman, her upper body bent backward, her mouth open, her eyes searching, looking at her with an unmistakable expression of frank surprise? Is that her? Impossible! She doesn't say it, doesn't pronounce the word consciously, but it has made her lips move. And, amazingly, the lips of the reflected figure move too.

She catches her breath in surprise. Not even in a dream has she ever dared to imagine herself as so lovely, so young, so smart. The red, sharply defined mouth, the finely drawn eyebrows, the bare and gleaming neck beneath the golden, curving helmet of hair are new, her own bare skin as framed by the glittering dress is completely new. She moves closer to the mirror, trying to recognize the woman that she knows is herself, but her temples throb with fear that the exhilarating image might not last, might vanish if she came any closer or made some sudden movement. It can't be real, she thinks. A person can't suddenly change like that. Because if it's real, then I'm...She pauses, not daring to think the word. But the woman in the mirror, guessing the thought, begins to smile to herself, at first slightly, then more and more broadly. Now the eyes are quite openly and proudly laughing at her, and the parted red lips seem to acknowledge with amusement: "Yes, I am beautiful."

It's a strange and wonderful feeling to admire her own body, the breasts unconstrained beneath the close-fitting silk, the slender yet rounded forms under the colors of the dress, the relaxed bare shoulders. Curious to see this slim new body in motion, she slowly turns to one side as she watches the effect: again her eyes meet those of her reflection, proud and pleased. Bolder now, she takes three steps back: again the quick movement is lovely. She ventures a rapid pirouette, making her skirts twirl, and again the mirror smiles: "Excellent! How slender, how graceful you are!" She has a restless, experimental feeling in her limbs, she feels like dancing. She races to the middle of the room, then comes back toward the mirror; the image smiles, and it's her own smile. She tests and inspects the image from all sides, caressing it with her eyes, smitten with herself, unable to have enough of this alluring new self that smiles as it approaches from the mirror, beautifully dressed, young, and remade. She feels like throwing her arms around this new person that is herself. She moves so close that the eyes almost touch, the real ones and those of the reflection, and her lips are so near their counterparts that for a moment her breath makes them disappear. She strikes more poses to get different views of her new self. Then the sound of the gong downstairs comes for a third time. She gives a start. My God, I can't keep my aunt waiting, she must be angry already. Quickly, on with the jacket, the evening jacket, light, colorful, trimmed with exquisite fur. Then, before her hand touches the switch to turn out the light, an eager parting glance at the beneficent mirror, one last look. Again the shining eyes, again the happy smile that's her own, yet not her own. "Excellent, excellent," the mirror smiles at her. She hurries down the hallway to her aunt's room; the cool silky fluttering of the dress makes the quick movement a pleasure. She feels borne along, carried by the wind. She was a child the last time she flew like this. This is the beginning of the delirium of transformation.

"It fits you very well! Like a glove," says her aunt. "It doesn't take a lot of tricks when you're young. The dressmaker doesn't have problems unless the dress has to hide rather than reveal. But, seriously, it's a perfect fit, you're hardly the same person. It's clear now what a good figure you have. But you've got to hold your head up too, don't be mad at me for saying it but you're always so unsure of yourself, so hunched over when you walk, you cringe like a cat in the rain. You've still got to learn how to walk the way Americans do, free and easy, chest out like a ship in the wind. Lord, I wish I were as young as you are." Christine blushes. So she's really not betraying anything, she's not ridiculous, not provincial. Meanwhile her aunt has continued the inspection, looking her over appreciatively from head to toe. "Perfect! But your neck needs something." She rummages in her chest. "Here, put these pearls on! No, silly, don't worry, get hold of yourself, they're not real. The real ones are in a safe back home, honestly we wouldn't bring them to Europe for your pickpockets to take." The pearls feel cool and strange as they roll on her bare skin, making her shiver a little. Then her aunt is back for a last once-over: "Perfect! It all looks fine. It would make a man happy to buy you clothes. But let's go! We can't let Anthony wait any longer. Will he be surprised!"

They go together. Negotiating the stairs in the revealing new dress is strange. Christine feels as light as if she were naked. She's floating, not walking, and the steps seem to glide up toward her. On the second landing they pass a gentleman in a smoking jacket, an older man with a razor-sharp part in his smooth white hair. He greets Christine's aunt respectfully, pauses to let the two of them go by, and in that moment Christine senses a special attention, a masculine look of admiration and something close to awe. She feels herself blushing: never in her life has a man of means, a real gentleman, acknowledged her presence with such respectful distance and yet such knowing appreciation. "General Elkins (I'm sure you know the name from the war), president of the London Geographical Society," her aunt announces. "He made great discoveries in Tibet in between his years of service. A famous man. I'll have to introduce you. The cream of the cream. He mixes with royalty." Her blood roars happily in her ears. A genteel, traveled man like that, and he didn't spot her right away as a gate-crasher or a pretender and turn up his nose: no, he bowed as though she were an aristocrat too, an equal.

And then reinforcement from her uncle, who gives a start as she approaches the table. "Oh, this is a surprise. Look what's happened to you! You look damn good—sorry, you look splendid." Again Christine feels herself blushing with pleasure, and a delicious shiver runs down her spine. "I guess you're trying to make a compliment," she tries to joke. "Am I ever," he says with a laugh, puffing himself up unconsciously. The creased dickey suddenly tautens, the avuncular stolidity is gone, and there's an interested, almost greedy light in the small red-rimmed eyes nestled in flesh. The unexpected pleasure of this lovely girl's presence puts him in an unusually merry and eloquent mood. He delivers himself of so many thoughtful, expert opinions on her appearance, getting perhaps a little too analytical and personal, that Christine's aunt good-naturedly reins in his enthusiasm, telling him not to let her turn his head, younger men know how to do it better and more tactfully too. Meanwhile the waiters have approached and are standing respectfully by the table like ministrants beside the altar, awaiting a nod. Strange, Christine thinks, how could I have been so afraid of them at lunch, these polite, discreet, wonderfully noiseless men who seem to want nothing but to be inconspicuous? She boldly helps herself. Her fear is gone now, and she's starting to be ravenous after her long journey. The light truffled pâtés, the roast meats artfully arranged on beds of vegetables, the delicate, frothy desserts brought to her plate by silver serving knives as if anticipating her wishes all seem fantastically delicious. Nothing requires any effort, any thought, and in fact she's no longer even surprised. It's all wonderful, and the most wonderful thing of all is that she's allowed to be here, here in this bright, crowded, yet hushed room full of exquisitely adorned and probably very important people who ... but no, don't think about that, stop thinking about that, as long as you're allowed to be here. But the best thing is the wine. It must be made of golden grapes ripened in the southern sun, it must come from some happy, faraway land; it gives off a transparent, amber glow and goes down unctuously like sweet chilled cream. At first Christine takes shy, reverent sips; but then, tempted by the constant kindnesses of her uncle, who's enjoying her obvious pleasure, she allows him to refill her glass repeatedly. Unconsciously she's becoming talkative. Effervescent laughter is suddenly pouring from her throat like uncorked champagne; she herself is amazed at the carefree bubbly swirl of it between her words. It's as though a bulwark of anxiety has burst. And why would anyone be anxious here? They're all so nice, her aunt, her uncle, these refined, grand people around her everywhere are so fancy and good-looking, the world is beautiful, life itself is beautiful.

Sitting across from her, broad, comfortable, and complacent, her uncle is thoroughly enjoying her sudden high spirits. Ah, he's thinking, to be young again and have a vivacious, glowing girl like that. He feels exhilarated, stimulated, lively, almost reckless. Normally he's phlegmatic and on the grumpy side, but now he's dredging up drolleries, even suggestive ones, unconsciously trying to stoke the fire that's doing his old bones so much good. He's purring like a tomcat, feeling hot in his dinner jacket, and there's a suspiciously high color on his cheeks: he looks like Jordaens's *Bean King*, flushed with drink and good cheer. He toasts her repeatedly and is about to order champagne when his amused warden, Christine's aunt, lays a warning hand on his arm and reminds him of the doctor's orders.

Meanwhile a rhythmic rumble of dance music has started up in the adjoining lounge. Christine's uncle sets down the butt of his Brazilian cigar in the ashtray and twinkles at her: "So? I can see it in your eyes, you'd like to dance, wouldn't you?"

"Only with you, Uncle," she says, gaily laying it on thick (my God, I've gotten a little tipsy, haven't I). She's close to laughing, there's such a funny tickling in her throat, she can't keep the happy trill out of her voice. "Don't kid me," growls her uncle. "These goddamn strapping boys here, three of them put together wouldn't be as old as I am, and they all dance seven times better than a gouty gray rhinoceros like me. But it's on your head. If you're brave enough, by all means."

He offers his arm in the Biedermeier manner, she takes it and chatters and laughs and doubles over and laughs, her aunt looks on with amusement, the music roars, the room glitters, full of bright colors, other guests watch with friendly curiosity, waiters move a table back, everything's friendly, happy, and welcoming, it doesn't take much courage to push off into the colorful swirl. Uncle Anthony is not in fact a brilliant dancer. The paunch that he's put on heaves with every step; he leads clumsily and uncertainly. But the diabolical music drives everything along, strongly syncopated, lurid, lively and spirited and yet rhythmically precise, with a pleasantly slashing ride cymbal, a soothing fiddle, and a jarring, kneading, pummeling beat, hard and propulsive. The musicians are tawny Argentineans in brown jackets with gold buttons, and they play like fiends, in fact they look like fiends, like liveried and festooned demons, and every one of them seemingly out of his head. The thin saxophonist with glittering spectacles gurgles and squeals drunkenly on his instrument. The fat curly-haired pianist next to him, even more frantic, seems to be hitting keys at random with a practiced zeal, while his neighbor the drummer pounds furiously, mouth open. All of them are jumping up and down as though electrified, or bitten by something, ferally, fiercely laying about them with their instruments like maniacs. But this demonic noise factory is actually as precise as a sewing machine (Christine realizes this); all the extravagant behavior, the grinning, the fluffed notes, the gesticulations, the showy fingering, the shouts and jokes as the musicians urge one another on, it's all been practiced down to the last detail in front of the mirror and the music stand, the entire frenzy is totally put on. The leggy, narrow-waisted, pale, powdered women seem to know it too, for they're not visibly distracted or excited by this simulated fervor (which is repeated every evening). With their fixed, lipsticked smiles, their rouged fluttering hands, they lean slackly on their partners' arms, their cool far-off gazes seeming to indicate that they're thinking of something else, or (most likely) of nothing. She's the only one who has to hide her excitement and lower her eyes, her blood stirred by this wickedly thrilling, brashly gripping music with its pose of passion. And when it abruptly stops she takes a deep breath, as though out of danger.

Her uncle is breathing hard too, wheezing heavily and with dignity. At last he can mop his forehead and catch his breath. He leads Christine back to the table in triumph, and, a nice surprise, her aunt has ordered sorbets for both of them. Just now Christine was feeling in the mood for something cool, even if she hadn't quite realized it, and here's a frosty silver dish without her having to ask. What a fantastic world, where unspoken wishes are granted. How could anyone be anything but happy here?

All the world's sweetness might be in this one thin straw of scalding ice. Heart thumping, fingers trembling avidly, she looks about for someone or something to receive her overflowing gratitude. There's her uncle, that fine old fellow, in the deep chair next to her, looking a little done in, still puffing and gasping and wiping the sweat from his forehead with his handkerchief. He tried hard to please her, maybe too hard. Of course she appreciates it, and she gently strokes the heavy, lined hand resting on the back of his chair. This gesture of a shy young creature so recently come to life makes the old man brighten; he takes a fatherly pleasure in the look of gratitude in her eyes. But isn't it unfair to thank him alone and not her aunt too? It was her aunt who brought her here, took her under her wing, dressed her in style, and gave her a measure of blessed protection in this rich, intoxicating atmosphere. So she reaches for her aunt's hand too and sits between the two of them, her eyes shining in the light-filled room, like a child under the Christmas tree.

The music starts up again, on a darker note, more romantic and quieter, black and silky: a tango. Her uncle makes a helpless face and excuses himself—his sixty-seven-year-old legs are not up to this slinky dance. "No, Uncle, I'm a thousand times happier to sit here with the two of you," she says and really means it, continuing to hold their hands on both sides. She feels good with these people, her blood relations, completely protected by them. But now a shadow looms: a tall, broad-shouldered man is bowing before her, his clean-shaven hawk-like face tanned like a climber's above the snowy expanse of his smoking jacket. He clicks his heels in the Prussian manner and in a pure Northern German scrupulously asks her aunt's permission. "Of course," smiles her aunt, proud of her protégée's rapid success. Christine gets to her feet awkwardly, a little weak in the knees. To be chosen by some unknown elegant man from among all these beautiful, smart women—it's a bit of a shock. She takes a deep breath, then puts a trembling hand on the man's shoulder. From the first step she feels herself being gently but authoritatively led by this impeccable dancer. All she has to do is yield to the barely perceptible pressure and her body fits itself to his movements; once she submits to the insistent, coaxing rhythm, her feet magically know where to go. Dancing was never so easy. It's no effort to follow her partner's will; it's as if she has a new body under the new dress, or has learned and practiced the caressing movements in a forgotten dream. A dreamy confidence has descended upon her; her head leans back as though pillowed, her eyes are half closed, she's entirely detached, no longer part of herself, and to her own amazement she feels she's floating weightless through the room. As she's being borne along she occasionally glances up at the hard-eyed face close to hers and thinks she sees a glimmer of a pleased and approving smile; then it seems to her she's grasping the leading hand with a more intimate pressure. A small, tingly, almost voluptuous worry flickers within her: How would she protect herself if hard masculine hands like these grasped her more firmly, if this strange man with the hard, arrogant face suddenly grabbed her and pulled her close? Wouldn't she give in completely, submit the way she's doing now? The sensuality of these half-conscious thoughts begins to spread throughout her increasingly relaxed and yielding limbs. People in the crowd have begun to notice this perfect couple. Again she has the strong, intoxicating feeling of being watched and admired. Responding to the will of her partner, she's increasingly sure of herself, moving and breathing with him; and this new physical pleasure, entering through her skin, mounts within her—she's never felt like this before.

When the dance is over, the tall blond man (he's introduced himself as an engineer from Gladbach) politely escorts her back to her uncle's table. The faint warmth of his touch vanishes and now she feels weaker and diminished, as though the loss of contact has caused some of her new strength to ebb away. As she sits down, still a little flustered, she smiles weakly and happily at her amiable uncle, not noticing someone else at their table: General Elkins. He stands politely and bows. He's come to ask her aunt to introduce him to this "charming girl": he's standing before her as though she were a fine lady, his back straight, his serious face bent forward respectfully. Christine tries to collect herself. My God, what can I say to such a terribly distinguished and famous man, whose picture (as she's learned from her aunt) has been in all the papers and who's even been in films? But there's no getting around it, General Elkins is asking her to forgive his poor German. He did study at Heidelberg, he says, but that was more than forty years ago, sad as it is to have to own up to a number like that, and a magnificent dancer like her will have to show some forbearance if he ventures to ask her for the next dance: he still has a piece of shrapnel in his left leg from Ypres. But in the end one needs forbearance to get by in this world. Christine is too embarrassed to reply, but when she dances with him, slowly and carefully, she's surprised to find that conversation comes easily. Who am I, anyway, she thinks with a chill, what's come over me? How can I be doing this? I was always so stiff and clumsy, the dance teacher said so, yet now I'm leading him instead of the reverse. And how easily I'm talking, perhaps even with some intelligence, because he's listening so graciously, this eminent man. Has this new dress, this new world made me so different? Or was this inside me all along, and I was just too fainthearted, too timid? That's what Mother always said. Maybe everything's not so hard, maybe life is so much easier than I thought, you just need courage, you just need to have a sense of yourself, then you'll discover your hidden resources.

When the dance is over, General Elkins guides her back through the room at a leisurely pace. She walks proudly on his arm, feeling her neck straighten as she looks ahead confidently, sensing that this makes her look younger and more beautiful. She told General Elkins straight out that this was her first time here and that she didn't know the real Engadine (Maloja, Sils-Maria), but this revelation hasn't made him any less respectful. Instead he seems pleased: Won't she permit him to drive her to Maloja tomorrow morning? "Of course," she says, awed and happy, and presses the distinguished old man's hand with a kind of comradely gratitude (where is she getting the nerve?). In this room, so unfriendly even that morning, she feels increasingly at home and sure of herself now that all these people are practically fighting each other off to please her, now that she sees how a little contact can create an easy sociability, while down in her own narrow little world people envy each other the butter on their bread and the rings on their fingers. She gives her uncle and aunt an enraptured report of the general's gracious invitation. But she's not allowed much time for conversation: the German engineer crosses the room for the next dance. Through him she meets a French doctor, also an American friend of her uncle's, and a parade of other people whose names she's too excited and happy to catch. In the last ten years she hasn't met as many gracious, polite, elegant people as she has in these two hours. She's being asked to dance, offered cigarettes and liqueurs, invited on drives and a climbing expedition: everyone seems curious to meet her and everyone treats her with a respect that apparently comes naturally to all of them. "You're a sensation, child," her aunt whispers, pleased by the stir her charge is creating. Her uncle stifles a tired yawn. He denies the obvious out of vanity but gives in finally. "Yes, perhaps that's the best thing, we'll all have a good rest. Not too much at once. Tomorrow's another day and we'll make a good job of it." Christine takes a last look at the enchanting room, luminous with candelabras and electric lights, pulsating with music and dancing. She feels she's stepped out of a bath, renewed and refreshed, every nerve quivering. She takes the old man's arm and impulsively bends to kiss his hand in gratitude.

Then she's alone in her room, stunned, confused, overwhelmed by her own self, by the sudden silence all around. Her skin burns under the loose dress, she's tense with excitement. Now the room seems confining. She pushes the balcony door open. Snow showers onto her bare shoulders. She goes out onto the balcony, where, shivering happily and breathing easily now, she looks out, full to bursting, over the empty landscape, her small heart beating under the great dome of night. There's silence here too, but a bigger, more elemental silence than the one inside, a soothing silence instead of an oppressive one. The mountains that were glittering earlier are now in their own shadow, crouched like massive black cats, with glinting snowy eyes. The air is thin under the almost full moon like an irregular yellow pearl amid a spray of brilliant stars, its wan, cool light faintly illuminating the misty contours of the valley. An inhuman landscape, divinely silent, gently overwhelming, unlike anything she knows, but her excitement seems to flow out into the bottomless calm as she gradually loses herself in the silence. Suddenly a bronze mass of sound rolls through the frozen air: it's the church bell down in the valley, echoing off rock faces to the left and right. Christine gives a start, as though she were the bell being struck. She listens to the bronze notes rumbling into the sea of mist. With bated breath she counts: nine, ten, eleven, twelve. Midnight! Is it possible? Only midnight? Only twelve hours since she arrived, shy, inhibited, and panicky, with a dried-up, paltry little soul, really just one day, half a day? In this instant, shaken to her very depths, this ecstatic human being has a first inkling that the soul is made of stuff so mysteriously elastic that a single event can make it big enough to contain the infinite.

In this new world even sleep is different: blacker, denser, more drugged, you're completely submerged in yourself. As she awakens Christine hauls her drowned senses out of these new depths, slowly, laboriously, bit by bit, as though from a bottomless well. First she has an uncertain sense of the time. Through her eyelids she sees brightness; the room must be light, it must be day. It's a vague, muffled feeling, followed by an anxious thought (even while she's still sleep): Don't forget about work! Don't be late! The train of thought she's known for the last ten years begins automatically: The alarm clock will ring now... Don't go back to sleep... Responsibility, responsibility, responsibility... Get up now, work starts at eight, and before that I'll have to get the heat started, make coffee, get the milk, the rolls, tidy up, change mother's bandages, prepare for lunch, and what else? There's something else I have to do today... Right, pay the grocer lady, she reminded me yesterday... No, don't doze off, stay alert, get up when the alarm goes off... But what's the problem today... What's keeping it... Is the alarm clock broken, did I forget to wind it... Where's the alarm, it's light in the room... Goodness, maybe I've overslept and it's already seven or eight or nine and people are cursing at the wicket they way they did that time when I wasn't feeling well, right away they wanted to complain to the head office... And so many employees are being let go these days... Dear God, I can't be late, I can't oversleep... The long-buried fear of being late is like a mole tunneling under the black soil of sleep. Abruptly the last of it falls away.

Where am I? Her eyes grope upward. What has happened to me? Instead of the slanting, smoke-stained, cobweb-gray attic ceiling with the brown wooden beams, a blue-white ceiling, clean and rectilinear with gilt molding, floats above her. And where's all this light coming from? A new window must have appeared overnight. Where am I? She looks at her hands, which are lying not on the brown, patched old camelhair blanket but on a light, fluffy, blue one embroidered with reddish flowers. The first shock: this isn't my bed. And not my room—that's the second. And the third and greatest: now fully awake, she looks around and remembers everything—vacation, holiday, freedom, Switzerland, her aunt, her uncle, the magnificent hotel! No worries, no responsibilities, no work, no time, no alarm clock! No stove, no one waiting, no pressure from anyone: the terrible mill of hardship that's been crushing her life for ten years has ground to a halt for the first time. You can lie in your soft warm bed, aware of the blood flowing in your veins, the light waiting behind the delicately gathered curtains, the soft warmth on your skin. You don't have to worry about letting your eyes close again, you deserve to be lazy, you can dream and stretch and spread out, you belong to yourself. You can even (she remembers now, her aunt told her) press this button at the head of the bed, on which a bellboy is represented at postage-stamp scale: all you have to do is reach over, and, by magic, two minutes later the door opens, the bellboy knocks and enters politely, pushing a cute little cart on little rubber wheels (she marveled at one of them in her aunt's room), with coffee, tea, or cocoa the way you like them in fine dishes and with white damask napkins. Breakfast is there all by itself, you don't have to grind the coffee, light the fire, toil at the stove with your feet in slippers in the cold, no, no, it's all been done, white rolls and golden honey and delicacies like the ones yesterday come riding in, a magic sleigh floating up to the soft white bed without your having to lift a finger. Or you can press the other button, marked with a picture of a girl in a little white bonnet, and in she scurries after a gentle knock, wearing a bright apron and a black dress, asking what madam wishes, whether she should open the shutters or pull the curtains open or closed or draw a bath. You can make a hundred thousand wishes in this enchanting world and they'll all be granted just like that. You can want or do anything here, but you don't have to. You can ring or not, you can get up or not, you can go back to sleep or lie in bed, whatever you want, your eyes open or closed, and bask in a flood of fine carefree notions. Or you can think about nothing at all and just laze mindlessly, time belongs to you, not the reverse. You're not driven onward by that frantic mill wheel of hours and seconds, you glide through time, eyes closed, as though in a rowboat with oars pulled in. Christine lies there, enjoying this new feeling, her blood pulsing pleasantly in her ears like faraway Sunday church bells.

But no (she sits up energetically)—this is no time for daydreaming. Don't waste any of this time, this time that brings more wonders every second. At home you can dream for months, years on end, in the creaky, broken-down wooden bed with the hard mattress at night, and at the ink-spotted worktable while the peasants are off in the fields, the clock on the wall like a sentinel, ticking inexorably and punctiliously. There, dreaming is better than being awake; here in this celestial world, sleep is a waste of time. She's out of bed with a final decisive movement and splashes some cold water on her face and neck; now, refreshed, into the new clothes. Overnight her skin has forgotten their soft rustle and shimmer. The clinging caress of the luxurious fabric is a new pleasure. But don't linger on these small delights, don't waste time. Time to leave now, get out of this room, go somewhere, anywhere; sharpen this feeling of happiness and freedom, stretch your limbs, fill your eyes, be awake, wider awake, vividly awake in every sense and every pore. She pulls on her sweater, jams on her hat, and dashes downstairs.

The corridors are still gray and empty in the cold morning light, but in the lounge downstairs shirtsleeved hotel workers are cleaning the runners with electric carpet sweepers. The puffy-eyed night clerk shows ill-humored surprise at the sight of this excessively early guest, but sleepily doffs his cap. Poor fellow, so here too there's hard work, unseen labor, ill-paid drudgery, there's such a thing as having to get up and be on time. But let's not think about that. What's it to me? I don't want to be aware of anyone but me, me, me. Go on, go on by. Outside the cold air pounces, scrubs eyelids, lips, and cheeks like an icy cloth. This mountain air does chill you, down to the bone. The only thing for that is to run, that'll get the blood circulating.

This path must go somewhere. It doesn't matter where. Up here anywhere is as magical and new as anywhere else.

Christine sets off at a vigorous pace, surprised that no one is out yet. At six in the morning the swirl of people that thronged the paths at midday yesterday must still be packed away in the great stone crates of the hotels, and the very landscape lies in a kind of gray trance. The air is soundless, the moon, so golden yesterday, is gone, the stars have vanished, the colors have faded, the misty cliffs are as drab and colorless as cold metal. Only high up, among the highest peaks, are there thick clouds moving restlessly, as if some invisible force were stretching them, pulling them. Now and then a cloud separates from the dense mass, floating up like a fat white cotton ball; it changes form as it climbs, suffused with a light from nowhere, bordered with gold. The sun must be nearby, already at work somewhere behind the peaks—not yet in sight, but warming the turbulent atmosphere. So move toward it, then, upward, higher! This trail here, perhaps, graveled, as gently winding as a garden path, it can't be hard; and in fact it's plain sailing. She's not used to this sort of thing and is surprised by the joyous spring in her step. The path's gradual turns and the buoyancy of the air draw her upward. A sprint like this warms the blood in no time. She tears off her gloves, sweater, hat: the skin should have a chance to breathe in this rousing chill, not just the lips and lungs. As she quickens her pace she becomes more confident, lighter on her feet. She should really stop (her heart is hammering in her chest, her pulse pounding in her ears, her temples throbbing), and she pauses for a moment to look down from this first bend and shake the moisture out of her hair: forest, white streets ruled straight amid the dense green, the river, curved and gleaming like a scimitar, and above it all the sun suddenly pouring through the notch. Wonderful, but her momentum won't let her stop. The insistent drumming of her heart and the rhythm of the muscles and tendons keep urging her forward, and she presses on, spurred and intoxicated by her own excitement, with no idea how far or how high or where she's going. After an hour, perhaps, she comes to a vantage point where the slope of the mountain is cambered like a ramp, and throws herself down on the grass: enough. Enough for today. Her head is swimming, but she's strangely happy. Her blood is pulsing under her eyelids, her skin feels raw where it was exposed to the wind, but the almost painful sensations are a new kind of pleasure. She never knew the blood could flow so strongly, the pulse could pound so eagerly, was never as aware of her own physicality, her light-footedness and energy, as in this extravagant, narcotic exhaustion. Clouds float overhead in an undreamed-of blue and the panorama down below opens up as she lets her hands dig pleasantly into cold fragrant Alpine moss. Washed by the sun and scoured by gusty mountain winds, she lies in a pleasant daze, awake and dreaming at once, savoring the tumult within her and the driving, tempestuous movement of nature for an hour or two, until the sun begins to burn her lips. She jumps to her feet and quickly gathers a few flowers—juniper, gentian, sage—still so cold that there are ice crystals among the petals. Then she hurries down, at first maintaining the measured stride of a tourist, straight and tall, before she yields to the pull of gravity, leaping from one stone to the next with increasing speed and daring. She feels self-confident and happy as never before, could almost sing as she whirls down the hairpin turns into the valley as though carried by the wind, skirt and hair fluttering behind her.

At nine, the appointed hour, the young German engineer is in front of the hotel in his tennis whites, waiting for his trainer to arrive for the morning match. It's still too cold to sit on the damp bench and the wind keeps probing with deft icy fingers under his thin, open-collared linen shirt, so he paces vigorously up and down on frozen feet, spinning his racket to warm his hands. Hang it, has the trainer overslept? The engineer looks about impatiently and happens to glance up at the mountain path. There's something strange off in the distance, something bright and colorful and in turbulent motion, bounding curiously down the path. Wait, what's that? Wish I had my field glasses. But the hurtling brightly colored object is coming on fast: it will be clearer in a moment. The engineer shades his eyes with his hand and can make out someone speeding down the mountain path. It must be a woman or a young girl with hair blowing and arms swinging, seemingly carried by the wind. Good grief, not a good idea to take the curves at full tilt. She's crazy, but great to look at, coming down at a speed like that. Automatically he takes a step forward for a better view. The girl looks like a goddess of dawn, a maenad, all energy and fearlessness. He can't make out her face yet, her speed and the glare of the rising sun are making her features indistinct. But to get to the hotel she'll have to pass the tennis court—this is where the path ends. She's getting closer, bits of gravel are rolling into view, he can hear her steps on the curve above, and suddenly she charges up. He's stepped in her way on purpose and she stops short to keep from running into him; her hair flies back and the damp hem of her dress is pushed against her legs. She's an arm's length away from him, breathing hard. She laughs with surprise, suddenly recognizing her dance partner. "Oh, it's you," she exclaims in relief. "Sorry—I almost ran into you!" He doesn't reply right away, but good-humoredly, even raptly, gazes at her glowing in front of him with wind-frozen cheeks, her chest rising and falling, still full of energy. All he does is smile broadly, captivated by this vision of youth and vigor. At last he speaks. "Well done! That's what I call a good clip. I'd like to see any professional mountain guide do that. But..." (he looks at her again, considering and smiling again with approval) "...if my neck were so young and fresh-looking, I'd look out

71

I didn't break it. You're damn well not taking care of yourself! Good thing it was just me who saw you and not your aunt. And mainly, you shouldn't be taking this kind of morning excursion by yourself. If you ever need somebody along who's in fair-to-middling shape, yours truly is warmly recommended." He looks at her once more and she feels herself becoming embarrassed by the surge of unexpected interest in his eyes. Never in her life has a man looked at her so admiringly; she tingles with new pleasure. She shows him the bouquet to shake off the embarrassment. "Look what I got! Fresh-picked, aren't they wonderful?" "Yes, wonderful," he replies in a tense voice, ignoring the flowers and looking into her eyes. These insistent, almost intrusive attentions are even more embarrassing. "Forgive me, I have to go to breakfast now," she offers, "I'm probably late already," and tries to move past. He bows and steps aside, but she feels instinctively that he's following her with his eyes and tenses up unconsciously as she moves away. Her surprise that a man might feel so strongly about her, might find her beautiful and perhaps even desire her, enters her blood like the fragrance of the wildflowers and the invigorating bite in the air.

Intoxication surges in her again as she enters the lobby. It seems stuffy here now; everything is too close, too heavy. She tosses hat, sweater, belt, whatever is confining and oppressive, into the wardrobe, and wishes she could tear the clothes off her tingling skin. The two older people at the breakfast table look up in surprise as she approaches, her step light, cheeks glow-ing, nostrils quivering, somehow taller, healthier, sleeker than yesterday. She lays the bunch of wildflowers, still moist with dew and glinting with melting ice crystals, in front of her aunt: "I picked them up on...I don't know the name of the mountain, but I went up there, oh" (she takes a deep breath) "it was wonderful." Her aunt looks at her with admiration. "What a glutton for punishment you are! Out of bed and straight up into the mountains without breakfast. The likes of us ought to follow your example. Better than any massage, I'm sure. Anthony, just look at her though, she's transformed. Look what the fresh air has done to her cheeks. You're glowing, child! But tell us where you got this." Christine tells them, unaware how quickly and hungrily she's eating and how much. Butter, jam, and honey vanish at a tremendous rate; the amused old gentleman beckons to the waiter, who smiles slightly as he refills the basket with croissants. She's too carried away to notice her aunt and uncle smiling more and more broadly at her unseemly appetite, only feels the pleasant burning in her cheeks as they begin to thaw. She's relaxed now and leans back in the wicker chair, eating, talking, and laughing gaily; further encouraged by the kind faces of her aunt and uncle and ignoring the astonishment of people around them, she spreads her arms wide in the middle of her story and her elation bursts out of her: "Oh, Aunt, I never knew what it was to really breathe."

The floodgates have been opened. At ten she's still at the breakfast table. The breadbasket is empty. Her appetite, stimulated by the high altitude, has cleaned it out. General Elkins appears in his stylish sportswear to remind her of the planned drive. Walking respectfully behind her, he takes her to his car, of the best British make, lacquered and gleaming with nickel plate. The bright-eyed, clean-shaven chauffeur is himself an English gentleman. General Elkins makes sure she's comfortable, spreads blankets over her knees, then, again lifting his hat carefully, takes a seat next to her. All this respect is a little confusing; the emphatic, almost humble politeness of this man makes Christine feel like an impostor. Who am I that he treats me this way? My God, she thinks, if he ever knew what stupid, menial donkey work I do, glued to my chair at the Post Office desk! But the chauffeur spins the steering wheel and the rapid acceleration soon brings her back to the here and now. The machine can't really stretch out in the resort's narrow streets. She's childishly proud to see these strangers admiring the car—luxurious even here—and many of them eyeing her, undoubtedly the owner, with slightly envious awe. General Elkins provides a running commentary on the landscape like a geography professor, getting caught up in the details like anyone with a special interest, but he seems stimulated by Christine's evident attentiveness as she leans forward. His rather cold, dour face gradually loses its English austerity; a kind smile makes his somewhat thin and severe lips more friendly when he hears her youthful "Oh" or "Terrific" or sees her turn with interest to take in passing views. His smile is almost wistful as he glances at her lively profile; her unbridled enthusiasm is weakening his reserve. The chauffeur continues to accelerate. The road is like a carpet. The luxury car climbs smoothly and silently. There's no hint of strain from its metallic heart, it takes the sharpest curves with ease. The rising roar of the wind is the only indication of how fast they're moving, the feeling of safety adding to the thrill of speed. The valley darkens as the cliffs converge sharply. Finally the chauffeur stops the car at an overlook. "Maloja," General Elkins explains and helps Christine out with the same deferential courtesy. The grand view shows the road down below, winding elaborately like a stream. The mountain, dropping off suddenly into a vast, broad valley, seems to have given out here, unable to continue on up toward the summits and glaciers. "The lowlands start down there—that's the beginning of Italy," Elkins tells her. "Italy," says Christine wonderingly, "is it really so close?" Her astonishment expresses such longing that Elkins asks immediately, "You've never been there?" "No, never." And her "never" is so ardent, so full of yearning, that all her secret anxiety resonates in it: I'll never see it, never. Ashamed to hear the change in her voice, afraid he might guess her deepest thoughts, her private worry about her poverty, she tries to turn the conversation away from her, asking foolishly, "You know Italy, of course, General?" His smile is serious, almost melancholy. "Where haven't I knocked about? I've been around the world three times, don't forget I'm an old man." "No, no," she protests, bewildered. "How could you say such a thing!" And her bewilderment is so honest, this young girl's protest is so real and full of feeling, that the sixty-eight-year-old man's cheeks are suddenly warm. He may never have another chance to hear her so impassioned. His voice becomes soft. "You have young eyes, Miss van Boolen, that's why you see everything as younger than it is. I hope you're right. It may be that in fact I'm not yet as old and gray as my hair. But what wouldn't I give to be able to see Italy again for the first time." He looks at her again, now with the vague abject shyness that older men often have with young women, as though asking their indulgence for no longer being young. Christine is curiously touched and thinks suddenly of her father, the way she loved to stroke the bent old man's white hair gently, almost reverently: he had the same look of kindhearted gratitude. Lord Elkins doesn't say much on the way back; he seems reflective, withdrawn. When they drive up to the hotel, he jumps out with an almost pointed liveliness in order to help her out of the car before the chauffeur does. "Such a wonderful drive—thank you very much," he says, before she can thank him, "it was the best outing I've been on in a long time."

At the table with her aunt and uncle she gives an enthusiastic account of how gracious and friendly General Elkins was. Her aunt nods sympathetically: "Good that you brightened him up a little. He's had a lot of bad luck. His wife died young, while he was on his expedition in Tibet. He kept writing to her every day for four months because he hadn't gotten word. When he came back he found the pile of unopened letters. And his only son was shot down by the Germans at Soissons, the same day he himself was wounded. He lives alone now in his huge castle in Nottingham. I understand why he travels so much—what he's really doing is running away from those memories. But keep him off that, don't talk about it, or he'll tear up right away." Christine is moved as she listens. It hadn't occurred to her that there might be unhappiness up in this halcyon realm. She'd thought everyone had to be as happy as she is. She feels like going over to squeeze the hand of this old man who's been hiding his secret sadness with such poise. On impulse she looks over toward the other end of the dining hall, where he sits alone with military erectness. He happens to look up and bows slightly as he meets her eyes. She's touched to see him alone in the big room filled with light and luxury. You really ought be nice to someone so nice.

But there's so little opportunity here to think about anyone in particular, time is going by too fast, bringing too many surprises: each fleeting moment sparkles with new delights. After lunch, when her aunt and uncle have gone upstairs for a short nap, Christine thinks she'll sit quietly in one of the soft adjustable armchairs on the terrace in order to at last bask in this metamorphosis she's gone through, run over it in her mind. But no sooner has she leaned back, allowing the images of the crowded day to slowly, dreamily pass by, than her dance partner from yesterday, the bright-eyed German engineer, appears before her and offers his strong hand— "Get up, get up!": would she come over to their table, his friends are asking to be introduced. Uncertainly (she's still afraid of anything new, but conquers her anxiety for fear of seeming rude) she lets herself be led to the lively table, where there are a dozen young people sitting and chatting. To her dismay, the engineer introduces her around the table as Fräulein von Boolen. Her uncle's Dutch name, altered to a German aristocratic one, seems to elicit special respect from everyone (she notices it in the way the men stand politely). Evidently they're thinking of the wealthiest family in Germany, the Krupp-Bohlens. Christine feels herself blushing: Goodness, what is he saying? But she lacks the presence of mind to set them straight, you can hardly contradict these polite strangers to their faces and say: No, no, my name is not von

Boolen but Hoflehner. So with an uneasy conscience she lets the unintentional deception go unchallenged, her fingers trembling nervously. All these young people, a fresh-faced, high-strung girl from Mannheim, a Viennese doctor, a French bank director's son, a somewhat noisy American, and a few more whose names she doesn't catch, are plainly making a fuss over her: they're all asking questions, in fact she's the only one they're speaking to or trying to speak to. Christine is awkward for the first few minutes. She flinches slightly each time someone addresses her as "Fräulein von Boolen"—it gives her a twinge—but gradually she gets caught up in the friendly high spirits of the young people, is delighted over the swiftly developing camaraderie, and in the end is taking part without inhibition. Everyone's so kind, what is there to be afraid of? Her aunt comes by, happy to see her protégée so well accepted, gives her a good-natured smile when she hears the others address her as Fräulein von Boolen, and finally reminds her that they had planned to take a walk while her uncle was at his inevitable afternoon gambling. Is it really the same path as yesterday, or does a broadened soul have a more joyful view of things than a cramped one? In any event the path she walked before, so to speak with clouded eyes, now seems new, more colorful, the view more magnificent, as though the mountains had become taller, the meadows a deeper or richer green, the air purer and more crystalline, and the people more beautiful, more animated, more friendly and outgoing. Everything has lost its strangeness since yesterday; she regards the massive forms of the hotel with a kind of pride now that she knows there's none finer (and is beginning to realize how much it costs to stay there). The slim-legged, perfumed women no longer seem so unearthly, no longer seem to belong to some higher caste as they drive by in their cars, now that she's ridden in such a luxurious one herself. She no longer feels out of place among them and unconsciously imitates the easy, bold, carefree walk of the athletic young women. They pause at a café; Christine's aunt is again amazed by her appetite. Whether because the mountain air is tiring or because strong emotions are actually chemically consuming energy that must be replaced, no matter, she easily devours three or four brötchen with honey, along with cocoa, then chocolates and fluffy pastries: she feels she can never have enough food and talk and looking and pleasure—surrendering to brute self-indulgence is the only way to make up for years and years of terrible hunger. She occasionally feels the touch of men's friendly and interested gazes from adjoining tables and unconsciously throws out her chest, lifts her head, returns the interest with an interested smile of her own: So you like me—who are you? And who am I?

At six, after another shopping trip, they're back at the hotel. Christine's friendly benefactress has discovered all sorts of new fripperies that she needs. Now her aunt, who has been continually delighted to see Christine's amazing passage from down in the dumps to high spirits, pats her hand gently: "So now you can do something for me, something hard! Are you brave?" Christine laughs. What could be hard here? Everything's fun up here in this blissful world. "No, don't think it'll be that easy! You're going to go into the lion's den and carefully pry Anthony loose from his game. I repeat, carefully, because he can really snarl if anyone bothers him there. But I can't let him be, doctor's orders are that he has to take his pills at least an hour before meals, and gambling from four to six in a stifling room is more than enough anyway. Number 112 on the first floor, the suite of Mr. Vornemann of the great Petroleum Trust. Knock on the door and just tell Anthony I sent you—he'll understand. He might growl—no, he wouldn't growl at you! Toward you he's still respectful."

Christine accepts the assignment without much enthusiasm. If her uncle likes to gamble, why should she be the one to nag him! But she doesn't dare to argue. She knocks lightly. The gentlemen all look up from their table, a long rectangle with strange diamonds and numerals on its green cloth. It seems young women don't intrude here very often. Her uncle, taken aback at first, laughs out loud. "Ah, Claire put you up to it! She's taking advantage of you! Gentlemen, this is my niece! My wife sent her to break it up. I propose" (he pulls out his watch) "exactly ten more minutes. You'll permit that?" Christine smiles uncertainly. "Well, I'll take full responsibility," Anthony says, proud to show off his authority in front of the gentlemen. "Hush now! Sit here next to me and bring me luck, I need it today." Christine sits down timidly behind him. She understands nothing of what's going on. Someone's holding a long thing like a shovel, or a toboggan, and deals out cards with it; someone says something and then celluloid disks, white, red, green, slide here and there; a rake gathers them up. It's actually boring, Christine thinks, it's funny that such rich, distinguished men would be playing for these round things. But in some way she's still proud to be sitting here in her uncle's broad shadow, close to men who undoubtedly have influence in the world, you can tell from their big diamond rings, their gold pencils, their hard, emphatic features, even their fists, which could probably pound the table like hammers during meetings. Christine glances respectfully from one to another, paying no attention to the game she doesn't understand, and looks rather foolishly taken aback when suddenly her uncle turns to her and asks, "Should I take it?" Christine has grasped at least that one of them is the banker and is fending everyone off, so he's playing a difficult game. Should she say yes? She'd prefer to whisper "For God's sake, no!" so as not to have any responsibility. But she doesn't want to seem fainthearted, so she stammers an uncertain "Yes." "Good," her uncle teases, "it's on your shoulders. We'll go fifty-fifty." The incomprehensible cartomancy starts up again. She understands none of it, but thinks she can tell that her uncle is winning. His movements are becoming quicker, he's making strange gurgling sounds in his throat, he seems to be enjoying himself thoroughly. Finally, passing the toboggan on to someone else, he turns to her: "You did great work. And since we're sharing equally, here's your half." He pulls some chips out of his pile—two yellow ones, three red ones, a white one. Christine takes them with a laugh, not thinking anything. "Another five minutes," he reminds her (he has his watch in front of him). "Come on, come on, tiredness is no excuse." The five minutes pass quickly. They all get to their feet, gather up their chips, and cash them in. Christine is waiting diffidently at the door; her chips are on the table. Her uncle calls out: "Well, what about your chips?" Christine steps closer, not understanding. "Cash them in." Christine still doesn't understand; he takes her to one of the men, who looks briefly, says, "Two hundred fifty-five," and puts down two hundred-franc bills, a fifty-franc bill, and one of those heavy silver coins. Christine gazes with surprise at the foreign money on the green table, then looks at her uncle uncertainly. "Just take it," he says, almost annoyed, "that's your share! And now let's go, we have to be on time."

Christine clutches the three bills and the silver coin in bewilderment, still incredulous. Back in her room, she examines over and over the three rectangular rainbow-hued slips of paper that have come her way. Two hundred fifty-five francs. She does the conversion quickly—about three hundred fifty schillings. To make this much money at home, she'd have to work for four months, a third of a year, sitting at the office from eight until noon, from two until six precisely, and here it just flies into your hand in ten minutes. Can it be true, was there some mistake? Incredible! But the bills rustle in her fingers just like real money, and they're hers, her uncle said, they belong to her, to her new self, this new, unfathomable other person. These crackling banknotes—she's never had so much money at one time. As she anxiously and reverentially hides the bills like loot in her suitcase, shivers of dread and pleasure run down her spine. Her conscience can't grasp this contradiction: at home money has to be saved so patiently, coin by dark heavy coin, while here it casually flutters into your hand. A violent, fearful shudder runs through her entire being—as though she'd been witness to a crime. Something in her would like to understand this, but there's no time, she has to get dressed, choose a dress, one of the three exquisite dresses, has to go back downstairs to feel things, experience things, to enter the trance, to dive down into the wonderful fiery current of extravagance.

Names have a mysterious transforming power. Like a ring on a finger, a name may at first seem merely accidental, committing you to nothing; but before you realize its magical power, it's gotten under your skin, become part of you and your destiny. During the first few days Christine heard the new name von Boolen with secret glee. (Oh, they don't know who I am! If they only did!) She wore it thoughtlessly, like a mask at a costume ball. But soon she forgets the unintentional deception and begins to deceive herself, becoming what she feigns to be. If at first it was embarrassing to be addressed as a rich aristocratic stranger, a day later it's a thrill, and after two or three days it seems the most natural thing in the world. When she was asked her first name by one of the gentlemen, "Christine" (she goes by "Christl" at home) didn't seem impressive enough for the borrowed title; "Christiane," she answered daringly, and thus she's now known at every table as Christiane von Boolen. She's introduced and addressed as Christiane von Boolen and has had no trouble getting used to the name, just as she's gotten used to the room with the soft colors and polished furniture, the luxury and comfort of the hotel, the unquestioning matter-of-fact attitude toward money, and all the intoxication of desire, felt in so many ways. If someone who was in on it all suddenly addressed her as Fräulein Hoflehner, she'd wake up like a sleepwalker and tumble off the roof of her dream, so completely has the new name become a part of her, so passionately is she convinced that she's another person, that other person.

But haven't these few days in fact already turned her into another person? Hasn't the Alpine air actually pumped new blood into her veins, hasn't the more plentiful and more luxurious food stirred it, fortified it? Undeniably Christiane von Boolen looks different now, younger, fresher than Postal Official Hoflehner, as different as Cinderella from her ugly stepsisters. The mountain sun has tanned her once-pale, slightly sallow skin as brown as an Indian's; the muscles of her neck are tauter; her new clothes have given her a new walk, more casual, an easy stride with a sensual swing to the hips and a surge of self-confidence in every step. Frolicking about outside has done wonders to revitalize her, dancing has toned her, and her newly discovered vigor, the youth she'd forgotten was there, pushes her again and again to test her powers: her heart beats harder, she's constantly aware of an effervescence, a ferment expanding and contracting inside her, an electric thrill she senses to the tips of her fingers—a strange, strong, new pleasure. Suddenly it's hard to sit still; she always has to be outside frisking about. She's like a gusting wind, always busy, always driven by curiosity, now here, now there, indoors, outdoors, upstairs and downstairs. She never takes the stairs one step at a time, but always three at once, as though she might be missing something, always impelled by inner excitement. Her urge to play, her need to express affection and gratitude is so strong that her hands are always grabbing someone or something. Sometimes she has to spread her arms and look off into the distance to keep from laughing or crying out. Her youthful energy is a force field around her: anyone near her is immediately caught in the whirlpool of high spirits in which she moves. Conversations brighten when she takes part, always sunny and lighthearted, and not only her aunt and uncle but total strangers observe her uninhibited enthusiasm with pleasure. She hurtles into the hotel lobby like a stone through the window, the revolving door whirling behind her; she gives the little bellhop tugging at her sleeve a cheerful slap on the shoulder with her glove. Off with the hat and the sweater, it's all oppressive and constraining. She carelessly fixes herself up at the mirror: the dress smoothed down, the tousled hair shaken back, and that's it: still disheveled, her cheeks pink from the wind, she heads straight for one of the tables (she knows everyone now) to report on what she's been doing. She always has something to report, she's always just experienced something, it was always terrific, wonderful, indescribable, everything fills her with ardent enthusiasm; even a perfect stranger feels that here is a person full to bursting who can endure her excess of gratitude only by passing it along to someone else. She can't see a dog without patting it, she lifts every child onto her lap to kiss its cheeks, she has a friendly word for every maid and waiter. If someone is grumpy or apathetic, she soon lifts his spirits with good-natured kidding; she admires every dress, every ring, every camera, every cigarette case, she picks up everything and gazes at it enthusiastically. She laughs at every joke, is enchanted by everything she eats, likes everyone she meets, finds every conversation amusing; everything, everything is wonderful in this singular, lofty realm. Her passionate goodwill is irresistible, everyone around her feels her ardor; the grouchy privy councillor in her armchair looks cheerful behind her lorgnette when she sees her, the desk clerk greets her with special friendliness, the starchy waiters adjust her chair attentively, and even the sterner older people are gladdened by so much joy and responsiveness. There's some shaking of heads when she's naïve or gushy, as she can be at times, but she encounters warm and welcoming faces on every side, and after three or four days everyone from Lord Elkins down to the last bellhop and elevator boy has decided that this Fräulein von Boolen is an enchanting creature, "a charming girl." And she feels their looks of approbation and takes pleasure in being looked at, feels it as an intensification of her own existence and her daring to exist, and the affection that surrounds her makes her happier still.

The man in the hotel who most clearly demonstrates a personal interest, a romantic inclination, is, unexpectedly, General Elkins. With the diffidence of age, the delicate and touching uncertainty of a man long past the perilous fifty-year mark, he's been trying to find inconspicuous opportunities to get near her. Even Christine's aunt notices that he's dressing more brightly, more youthfully, is choosing more colorful ties. She may be wrong, but she even thinks his temples have become less white, evidently by artificial means. He's been coming to Christine's aunt's table with noticeable frequency, finding all sorts of pretexts; every day he sends flowers to both women's rooms (so as not to be too obvious); he's been bringing Christine books, German ones bought specially for her, mostly about climbing the Matterhorn (just because she once happened to ask who was the first to brave it) and about Sven Hedin's Tibetan expedition. One morning when a sudden cloudburst has kept everyone indoors, he sits with Christine in a corner of the lounge, showing her photographs—his house, his garden, his dogs. He lives in an odd tall castle, dating perhaps to Norman times, the round ivied towers making it look like a fort. The pictures of the inside show great halls with old-fashioned fireplaces, framed family portraits, model ships, and heavy atlases. It must be dreary living there alone during the winter, she thinks, and as if he's guessed her thoughts, he says, pointing to a pair of hunting dogs in the photos, "If not for them I'd be completely alone." This is his first allusion to the death of his wife and son. She shivers slightly as his eyes avoid hers self-consciously (he goes back to the photos immediately): Why is he telling me all this, showing me all this, why does he ask with such strange solicitude if I could be comfortable in an English house like that, is he trying to tell me, a rich, distinguished man like him...She doesn't dare to finish the thought. She's too inexperienced to realize that this lord, this general, who seems remote, far above her world, is waiting, with the fainthearted- ness of an older man who isn't sure he's still in the running and is terrified that he's about to make a fool of himself in courtship, for any tiny sign, for some encouraging word. She's afraid to believe in herself, so how could she understand? His hints both please and disturb her; she feels them as tokens of special sympathy but doesn't dare to put too much stock in them, while he for his part struggles to find the right interpre- tation of her noncommittal embarrassment. She comes away quite moved from any time spent with him. Sometimes she thinks she sees romantic intentions in his shy sidelong glances, but then his brusque formality muddles things again (the old man has retreated abruptly, though she doesn't realize that). This needs to be pondered. What does he want from me, can it be what it seems? This needs attention—calm consideration and clear thinking.

But how could she think, when would she think? She has no time to herself. No sooner does she appear in the lounge than someone from the merry band is there to drag her along somewhere—on a drive or a photo excursion, to play games, chat, dance; there's always a shout of welcome, and then it's bedlam. The pageant of idle busyness goes on all day. There's no end of games played, things to smoke, nibble on, laugh at, and she falls into the whirl without resistance when any of the young fellows shouts for Fräulein von Boolen, for how can she say no, and why would she, they're all so warm, these fresh-faced guys and gals, young people of a sort she's never known, always boisterous and carefree, always nicely dressed in new ways, always joking, always with money to spend, always thinking of new things to do; as soon as you sit down with them the gramophone starts up with music for dancing, or the car is there and five or six of them squeeze in and streak sixty, eighty, a hundred kilometers, so fast it pulls your hair. Or you loll in the bar with your legs crossed, nurse a cold drink, a cigarette in your mouth, casually, indolently lounging about without lifting a finger while listening to all sorts of delightful, funny stories, it's all so easy to get used to and so wonderfully relaxing, and she drinks in this tonic air as if with new lungs. Sometimes it seems like sheet lightning in her blood, especially in the evening when she's dancing or when one of the lithe young men presses close in the dark. Behind the companionship they have romance on their minds too, but it's different, more open, bolder, more physical, a pursuit that sometimes frightens the inexperienced Christine when she feels a firm hand on her knee in a dark car or when strolls arm in arm take a more affectionate turn. But the other young women, the American and the Mannheim girl, good-humoredly put up with all of it, not bothering themselves beyond discouraging excessively daring fingers with a friendly slap. Why be prissy—yet it's always well to keep in mind how the engineer starts up a little more relentlessly every time or the little American fellow tries to lure you gently toward the woods on hikes. She doesn't go, but she feels a small new pride, aware of being desired, knowing now that her body, bare, warm, and untouched beneath her dress, is something men would like to breathe in, feel, stroke, enjoy. She senses some subtle narcotic within her, compounded of unknown alluring substances. Constantly courted by so many charming and elegant strange men, dizzy from being the center of such an intense circle of admirers, she shakes herself awake for a moment and wonders in bewilderment, "Who am I? Who am I really?"

"Who am I? And what do they all see in me?" Day after day she asks herself this question, continually astonished. New and different attentions make themselves felt every day. The moment she wakes up, the maid comes into her room with flowers from Lord Elkins. Yesterday her aunt gave her a leather handbag and a charming little gold wristwatch. The newcomers, the Trenkwitzes from Silesia, have invited her to their estate; the little American quietly slipped a small gold pocket lighter that she'd admired into her leather handbag. The little Mannheim girl is warmer than her own sister, bringing chocolates up to her room in the evening and chatting with her until midnight. Christine is almost the only one the engineer dances with, and every day there's a swirl of new people, all of them pleasant and respectful and warm. The minute she comes down or comes in, someone's there to ask her on a drive, to the bar, to go dancing, on some escapade, she's never alone for a moment, never has a boring empty hour. And continually she asks herself in bewilderment, "Who am I? For years people on the street walked past without a glance, for years I've been sitting there in the village and no one gave me anything or bothered about me. Is it because the people there are all so poor, their poverty makes them tired and mistrustful, or is there suddenly something in me that was always there and yet not there, something that just couldn't get out? Can it be that I was actually prettier than I dared to be, and smarter and more attractive, but didn't have the courage to believe it? Who am I, who am I really?" She asks herself this question in the brief moments when they leave her alone, and something strange happens that she herself is unable to understand: confidence turns into insecurity again. In the first few days she was just bewildered and surprised that all these distinguished, elegant, charming strangers had accepted her as one of their own. But now that she feels she's been particularly well received, now that, more than the others, more than the strawberry blond American who's so fabulously dressed, more than the amusing, high-spirited, sparklingly clever Mannheim girl, she is exciting the interest, the curiosity, the eagerness of all these men, she's troubled again. "What do they want from me?" she asks herself, and in their presence becomes even more troubled. It's so strange with these young men. At home she never paid any attention to men and never felt troubled in their presence; among those provincials, with a stolidity that only beer could take the edge off, with their gross clumsy hands, their crude jokes rapidly turning vulgar, and their blatant forwardness, sensual thoughts never crossed her mind. When one of them, lurching out of the tavern, made a suggestive noise, or someone at work would try to sweet-talk her, she felt nothing but disgust: they were animals. But these young men here, their hands manicured, always meticulously shaven, so suave that the most risqué remarks seem casual and amusing, who can put a caress into even the most fleeting touch, they sometimes arouse her interest, yet trouble her in a way that's quite new. Her own laughter sounds strange to her—she realizes she's backing off anxiously. She feels somehow uneasy in this company; it seems so friendly, yet she has a feeling of danger. Particularly with someone like the engineer, who is unabashedly putting himself forward and making a play for her, sometimes the atmosphere of sensuality makes her feel slightly dizzy.

Fortunately she's rarely alone with him. Usually there are two or three other women present, and she feels more secure. At difficult moments she glances at them out of the corner of her eye to see if they are coping better, and can't help picking up all sorts of little tricks from them: how to feign indignation or brightly look away when somebody goes a bit too far, and especially how to call a halt when things are really getting too close for comfort. But she's soaking up the atmosphere now even when she's not with the men, especially in her conversations with the little Mannheim girl, who talks about the most ticklish subjects with a frankness that's new to Christine. A chemistry student, intelligent and shrewd, high-spirited, sensual but able to exercise self-control at the last moment, her sharp black eyes take in everything. From her Christine learns about all the affairs going on in the hotel. That the little thing with the garish makeup and the peroxided hair is not at all the daughter of the French banker as she makes out but his paramour, that they may have separate rooms, but at night... She's heard it herself from next door... And that the American had something going with the German movie star on the boat, three American women were in competition for him, and that the German major is a homosexual, the elevator boy told the upstairs maid all about it. Just nineteen years old to Christine's twenty-eight, she runs down the entire scandal sheet in a casual, conversational tone of voice, with no hint of outrage, as though these were quite natural things, just a matter of course. And Christine, afraid that any overt astonishment might betray her inexperience, listens with curiosity, occasionally glancing at the spirited girl with a strange kind of admiration. That slender little body, she thinks, must already have done all sorts of things I know nothing about, or she wouldn't be talking that way, so naturally and sure of herself. Just thinking about all those things makes Christine uncomfortable. Her skin burns sometimes as though she were soaking up warmth through a thousand tiny new pores, and on the dance floor her head spins. "What's wrong with me?" she asks herself. She has begun to find out who she is, and, having discovered this new world, to discover herself.

Another three days, four days, an entire mad week has flashed by. Sitting at dinner in his smoking jacket, Anthony says peevishly to his wife, "I've had it now with all this being late. The first time, well, it can happen to anyone. But to gallivant around all day, making you sit and wait, that's just bad manners. What on earth is she thinking?" Claire tries to mollify him: "My God, what do you expect. They're all that way nowadays, forget it, it's the postwar generation, all they know is being young and having fun."

But Anthony throws down his fork irascibly. "Confound this eternal fun. I was young once too and I cut loose, but I never permitted myself bad manners, not that it was even a possibility. The two hours in the day when that Little Miss Niece of yours deigns to grant us the honor of her presence, she's got to be on time. And another thing I insist on—will you just tell her, give her a good talking to!—is that she stop bringing that crowd of kids to our table every evening. What do I care about the thick-necked German with his prison buzz cut and his Kaiser Wilhelm whiskers or the Jewish civil service candidate with his ironic quips or the flapper from Mannheim who looks like she just stepped out of some nightclub. It's such a merry-go-round that I can't even read my paper. How did I end up associating with these brats? Tonight, though, I insist on peace and quiet, and if anybody from that noisy bunch sits at my table I'm going to start smashing things." Claire doesn't argue— that can't help when blue veins are pulsing on his brow—but what's really annoying is that she has to admit he's right. She herself was the one who pushed Christine into the social whirl to start with, and it was fun to see how smartly and gracefully the girl modeled the outfits. From her own youth she still has a confused memory of how delightful it was that first time when she dressed in style and lunched at the Sacher with her patron. But these last two days Christine has simply gone too far. She's like a drunkard, aware of nothing but herself and her own state of exaltation, never noticing how the old man's head nods in the evening, not even paying attention when her aunt admonishes her, "Come on, it's getting late." She's startled out of her frenzy for no more than a second. "Yes, of course, Aunt, I've promised just this last dance, just this one." But a moment later she's forgotten everything, she doesn't even notice that her uncle, tired of waiting, has gotten up from the table without saying good night, doesn't consider that he might be angry; how could anyone ever be angry and aggrieved in this wonderful world. In her giddiness, unable to imagine that everyone isn't burning with enthusiasm, isn't in a fever of high spirits, of passionate delight, she's lost her sense of balance. She's discovered herself for the first time in twenty-eight years, and the discovery is so intoxicating that she's forgetting everyone else.

Now she bursts feverishly into the dining room, unceremoniously tearing off her gloves as she goes (who could find fault here?), merrily greets the two young Americans in English as she goes by (she's picked up all sorts of things), and spins like a top across the room to her aunt, whom she hugs from behind, kissing her cheeks. Then a small surprise: "Oh, you're so far along? I'm sorry!...I was just saying to those two, Percy and Edwin, that they wouldn't make it to the hotel in forty minutes in their shabby Ford no matter how hard they tried! But they didn't believe me...Yes, waiter, go ahead and serve, both courses, so I can catch up...So, yes, the engineer drove, he's a great driver, but I noticed right away that the old jalopy wouldn't go over eighty, with Lord Elkins's Rolls-Royce it's something else again, and what a ride...To tell the truth it might also have been because I tried taking the wheel, with Edwin next to me of course...It's easy, all that black magic... And I'll take you for a drive, Uncle, you'll be the first, won't you, you've got the guts... But Uncle, what's the matter? You're not mad at me because I'm a little late, are you?...Honestly, it wasn't my fault, I told them they wouldn't make it in forty minutes...But you can't trust anybody but yourself...This vol-au-vent is excellent, and am I thirsty!... Oh, it's easy to forget how nice it is here with you. Tomorrow morning they're off again to Landeck, but I said I wouldn't be going, I have to go out walking with you again, but you know the action just never stops..."

All this is like the crackling of flames in dry wood. Not until Christine begins to flag does she notice that her spirited monologue is being met with a cold, hard silence. Her uncle is staring at the fruit basket as though the oranges interested him more than Christine's chatter; her aunt is toying nervously with her silverware. Neither says a word. "You're not annoyed with me, Uncle, not seriously?" Christine asks uneasily. "No," he says gruffly, "but finish up." It sounds so angry that Claire is embarrassed to see Christine instantly crestfallen, like a slapped child. She doesn't dare to look up. She meekly puts the partly cut apple on her plate; her mouth quivers. Her aunt steps in quickly to distract her. She turns to Christine and asks, "So what do you hear from Mary? Do you have good news from home? I've been wanting to ask you." But Christine grows paler yet, she trembles, her teeth even chatter. It hadn't crossed her mind! She hasn't received a single piece of mail in the entire week she's been here, and she didn't even notice. Or actually she'd sometimes wonder about it for a moment and think she ought to write, but then some flurry of activity would always intervene. Now everything she's been neglecting comes home to her, like a blow to the heart. "I can't explain it, but there's nothing from home. Maybe something got lost?" Her aunt's expression too has become sharp and severe. "Peculiar," she says, "very peculiar! But maybe it's because you're Miss van Boolen here and the mail for Hoflehner is still with the desk clerk. Have you checked with him?" "No," says Christine in a small, stricken voice. She remembers clearly, she'd been going to ask three or four times, every day actually, but there was always something going on and she always forgot. "Excuse me, Aunt, just a moment!" she says, jumping up. "I'll go see."

Anthony lets the newspaper fall. He was listening to all of it. He looks after her angrily. "What did I tell you! Her mother desperately ill, she told us herself, and she doesn't even care, just goes about playing the flapper all day long. Now you see I was right." "Really unbelievable," Christine's aunt says with a sigh, "she knows how it is with Mary and she hasn't troubled her head about it once in eight days. And at the beginning she was so touchingly worried about her mother, told me with tears in her eyes how terrible it was to leave her there by herself. Incredible how she's changed."

Christine is back, her steps halting now, confused and ashamed. She looks fragile in the wide armchair. She feels like cringing, as though to avoid a well-deserved blow. In fact the desk clerk had three unclaimed letters and two cards. Fuchsthaler has been sending complete news every day with touching care, and she—it falls like a stone on her conscience—she scrawled just a single quick card in pencil from Celerina. Not once has she looked at her honest and dependable friend's beautifully crosshatched, tenderly drawn map, or even taken his little gift out of the suitcase. Wanting to forget her former, other, Hoflehner self, she's wound up forgetting everything she left behind, her mother, her sister, her friend. "Well," her aunt says, seeing the unopened letters trembling in Christine's hand, "aren't you going to read them?" "Yes," Christine murmurs. Obediently she tears open the envelopes and skims through Fuchsthaler's clear, clean lines without looking at the dates. "Today things are somewhat better, thank God," says one. The other reads, "Since I gave you my word of honor, *verehrte Fräulein*, that I would frankly inform you as to the condition of your *sehr verehrte Frau* mother, I must unfortunately report that yesterday we were not unconcerned. The commotion over your departure gave rise to a state of excitement that is not without risk..." She turns the pages quickly. "The injection has had a certain calming effect, and we are again hoping for the best, though the danger of a recurrence has not been entirely eliminated." "Well," Christine's aunt asks, noticing her agitation, "how's your mother?" "Fine, fine," says Christine out of sheer embarrassment, "I mean, Mother has been having troubles again, but they've passed, and she sends her best, and best regards too from my sister." She doesn't believe what she's saying. Why hasn't Mother written, even a line, she thinks nervously. I wonder if I shouldn't send a wire or try to phone the post office, my substitute must certainly know what's going on. But I've got to write immediately, it's really disgraceful that I haven't. She doesn't dare look up for fear of finding her aunt's eyes watching her. "Yes, it'll be good if you write them a regular letter," says her aunt, as if she'd guessed her thoughts. "And send the warmest regards from the two of us. By the way, we're going straight up to our room, not to the lounge this time. All the late nights are taxing Anthony too much. Yesterday he couldn't get to sleep, and after all he's here for a rest too." Christine senses the underlying reproach and feels cold shock tightening about her heart. She approaches the old man shamefacedly. "Please, Uncle, don't be angry with me. I had no idea I was tiring you out." Still irked but touched by her humility, he gives a growl of concession. "Oh, well, we old folks always sleep badly. I enjoy being in the thick of things once in a while, but not every day. And anyway you don't need us now, you've got plenty of company."

"No, absolutely not, I'm going with you." Carefully she helps the old man into the elevator and is so warm and solicitous that her aunt's displeasure gradually softens. "You've got to understand, Christl, nobody wants to stop you from having fun," she says as they glide up the two stories, "but it can only do you good to get a decent night's sleep. Otherwise you'll get overtired and that's not why you're on vacation. It can't hurt to take a break. Just stay quietly in your room this time and write some letters. Frankly, it doesn't look right for you to be running around by yourself with those people all the time, and I'm not too wild about most of them anyway. I'd rather see you with General Elkins than with that young whatever he is. Believe me, you'll be better off staying in your room tonight."

"I will, I promise, Aunt," says Christine humbly. "I know you're right. It was just that . . . I don't know . . . these days have been making my head spin, it might also be the air and all. But I'm happy to have a chance to think things over calmly for once and write some letters. I'm going to my room now, you can count on it. Good night!"

As she unlocks the door to her room, Christine thinks: She's right, and she only has my best interests at heart. I really shouldn't have let myself get carried away like that, what's the point of rushing about, there's still time, eight days, nine days, and what could happen to me if I wire for extra sick days, I've never taken a vacation and never missed a day in all my years of work. They'll believe me at the head office, and the substitute will be only too pleased. It's so quiet in this beautiful room, you can't hear a sound from downstairs, you can collect your thoughts for once, mull it all over. And I have to read the books Lord Elkins lent me. No, first the letters, that's why I'm up here, to write my letters. It's disgraceful, eight days without a word to my mother or my sister or that nice Fuchsthaler. I ought to send a card to the secretary too, it's only right, and I promised my sister's children I'd send them one. And I made another promise, what was it—God, I'm completely confused, what promises have I been making to whom—right, I told the engineer I'd go with him on that outing tomorrow morning. No, I can't be alone with him, not with him, and also—tomorrow I have to be with my aunt and uncle, no, I'm not going to be alone with him again...But in that case I should really call it off, I should take a quick run down so he won't be kept waiting for nothing tomorrow...No, I promised my aunt I'd stay here...Anyway I can call down to the desk clerk and he'll tell him...The telephone, that's the best way. No, forget that...How would it look if they wind up thinking I'm sick or confined to quarters here and then they all make fun of me. Better to send a note, ha, I'd rather do that, I'll include the other letters so the desk clerk can mail them tomorrow morning...Where on earth is the letter paper?...Can you believe it, the folder is empty, how can that happen in a posh hotel like this...Just cleaned out...Well, I can ring, the maid will bring some right up...But can you still ring after nine? Who knows, they might all be asleep already, and maybe it would even look funny to ring at night just for a few sheets of paper...Better to run down myself and get some from the library...If only I don't run into Edwin on the way...My aunt's right, I shouldn't let him get so close...I wonder if he goes as far with other women as he did in the car this afternoon...All down my knee, I don't know how I could have permitted it...I should have moved away and refused to put up with it...I've only known him for a few days. But I couldn't move a muscle... Terrible how you suddenly go all weak, lose all your willpower, when a man touches you like that...I never could have imagined how your strength just gives out...Are other women like that, I wonder... They never say so, they talk so brazenly, tell you such wild stories...I should have done something, otherwise he'll wind up thinking I'll let anyone touch me that way...Or think I want them to...Ghastly what that was like—I shivered down to my toes...If he did that to a really young girl, I bet she'd lose her head completely—and when he suddenly squeezed my arm as we rounded the curves, terrible the way he...He has such slender fingers, I've never seen nails like that on a man, as immaculate as a woman's, yet it's like a vise when he grabs you...I wonder if he really does that with everyone... Probably so...I'll have to watch for that the next time I see him dancing...It's awful that I'm so ignorant, everybody else my age knows the ropes—they'd be able to get some respect... Wait, what was Carla saying, that the doors here open and close all night long...I'd better bolt mine right now...If only they were honest with you, didn't beat around the bush like that, if only I knew what the others do, whether they get so upset and mixed up too...Nothing like this ever happened to me! No, there was that time two years ago, when that elegant gentleman spoke to me on the Währinger Strasse, he looked much the same, standing so straight and tall... There would have been no harm in it in the end, I could have had dinner with him as he proposed...That's how people get to know each other...But I was worried I'd be late getting home...I've had that silly worry all my life and I've shown consideration for everyone, everyone...And time goes by and you start to get crow's feet...The rest of them were smarter, they understood things better...Really, would any other girl be sitting here alone in this room, with the lights blazing downstairs and all the fun going on...Just because my uncle is tired...Nobody else would be on the sidelines this early... What time is it in fact...Just nine o'clock, only nine...I certainly won't be able to sleep, forget it...I feel so horribly hot suddenly...Yes, open the window...That's nice, the cold on my bare shoulders...I should take care I don't get a chill... Bah, always this stupid worrying, always so cautious and careful...Where has it gotten me...The air feels wonderful through this thin dress, it's like having nothing on...Why did I put it on, anyway, who am I wearing it for, this beautiful dress...Nobody can see me in it if I'm sitting around in this room...Maybe I should take a quick run downstairs?...I do have to get some letter paper, or I could even write the letters down there in the library...It couldn't do any harm...Brr, it's gotten cold, I'd better close the window, it's freezing in here now...And I'm going to be sitting in that empty armchair?...Nonsense, I'll run downstairs and warm up fast down there...But what if Elkins sees me or somebody else does and tomorrow my aunt finds out? Bah...I'll just say I went down to give the letters to the desk clerk...There's nothing she can say to that...I won't stay down there, I'll just write the letters, both of them, then come straight back up...Where's my coat? No, no coat, I'm coming right back, just the flowers...

But they came from Elkins...Oh, never mind, they look nice... Maybe I should look in on my aunt just to be on the safe side, to be sure she's asleep...Nonsense, no need for that...I'm not a schoolgirl anymore...Always this stupid worrying! I don't need permission to run down for three minutes. So...

She hurries downstairs uneasily, as though trying to outrace her own hesitation.

She succeeds in slipping unnoticed into the library, though the lounge is seething with dancers. She finishes the first letter and the second is nearly done. Then she feels a hand on her shoulder. "Got you! What a trick to hide in here. For the last hour I've been looking in every nook and cranny for Fräulein von Boolen, everyone I ask just laughs, and here she is hunkered down like a rabbit in the crosshairs. But now let's get moving!" The tall thin man is standing behind her. Again she feels his ominous grip as a fluttering in her nerves. She smiles weakly, frightened by the ambush and yet pleased that just half an hour was enough for him to miss her so much. But she still has the strength to defend herself. "I can't go dancing tonight, I mustn't. I still have letters to write. They have to be on the early train. And then I promised my aunt I'd stay upstairs this evening. No, it's out of the question, I can't. She'd be angry if she knew I came down again."

Confidences are always risky: a secret entrusted to a stranger makes him less of one. You've given away something of yourself, given him the advantage. And now in fact those hard covetous eyes become intimate. "Aha, you're on the lam. Absent without leave. No, don't worry, I'm not going to tell, not me...But since I've been cooling my heels for an hour, I won't let you go so easily now, no, not a chance. In for a penny, in for a pound! Since you've come down without permission, you won't need permission to stay with us."

"What are you thinking! Impossible. My aunt might come down. No, it's out of the question!"

"Well, now, we'll want to make a factual determination right away, make sure Auntie is asleep. Do you know which windows are hers?" "But why?" "Very simple. If the windows are dark, then your aunt's asleep. And once you've undressed and gone to bed you don't get dressed again just to see if the little one's being good. My God, the times we used to sneak out at technical school. We'd oil up the keys to keep them from rattling, take our shoes off, and slip out through the entrance hall. An evening like that was seven times as much fun as an official holiday. So! Synchronize watches!" Christine has to smile; the way everything is settled here so easily and casually, the way all difficulties are straightened out! A girlish sense of fun gives her an itch to make a monkey out of her excessively strict guardian. But she can't give in too quickly. "Nothing doing, I can't go out in the cold like this! I haven't got my coat."

"We'll find you something. Just a second," and he's dashing off for his ulster, hanging soft and woolly in the wardrobe. "It'll do, put it on!"

"But I ought to ..." she thinks, then thinks no more about what she ought to do, because one arm is already in the soft coat. Resistance would be childish now. She laughs with a comfortable mischievous feeling as she wraps herself in the strange masculine garment. "Not through the main door," he says with a smile at her mantled back, "through the side door here, and we'll go for a stroll underneath your aunt's window." "Really, just for a second," she says, and the minute they're in the dark she feels his arm in hers as though it were the most natural thing in the world. "So where are the windows?" "Second floor left, the corner room there with the balcony." "Dark, pitch-black, hurrah! Not a glimmer. They're having a good long snooze. Right, and now I'm in charge. For starters, back to the lounge!" "No, not on your life! If Lord Elkins or somebody else sees me there, he'll tell them first thing tomorrow, and they're very angry with me as it is ... No, I'm going up now."

"Then we'll go somewhere else, to the bar on the way to St. Moritz. We can drive there in ten minutes. Nobody knows you there, so there'll be nobody to tattle."

"What are you thinking! The things you come up with. If someone here sees me get into the car with you, the entire hotel will be buzzing with nothing else for two weeks." "That'll be taken care of, leave it to me. Of course you're not going to be making a formal departure from the main entrance where the excellent management keeps seventeen lamps burning. What you do is you follow the forest path there for forty paces until you're hidden in the shadows. I'll be along with the car in a minute, and in fifteen minutes we'll be there. So that's settled, case closed."

Again Christine is amazed at how easy it is. Her resistance wavers. "You make it sound so simple." "Simple or not, that's how it is and that's how it's done. I'll run right over and get the car cranked. In the meantime you can go on ahead." "But when will we be back?" she interposes again, hesitantly and more weakly now.

"Midnight at the latest."

"Do I have your word?"

"You have my word."

A railing to clutch at. "Fine, then, I'm depending on you."

"Keep left until you get to the road. Don't walk under the lights. I'll be along in a minute."

She takes the suggested path. Why am I doing what he says, she wonders. I really ought to...I should...But she can't think anymore, can't remember what she really ought to do, because already she's seduced by this new game, already slinking through the dark like an Indian, muffled in a strange man's coat, once more leaving her life as it is, once more transforming herself into something different from what she has known. She waits for a second in the shadows; then two broad fingers of light come feeling their way along the road, the high beams silvery among the pines, and already the driver has spotted her, extinguishing the piercing glare of the lights as the car, huge and black, crunches up. Now the interior lights are discreetly extinguished too; the speedometer's tiny glowing blue disk is the only color in the darkness, so black after the blast of light that Christine can't make anything out. But the car door opens, a hand reaches out to help her in, and the latch clicks behind her, the whole thing eerily quick, dizzying, fantastic, like something in a film. Before she can speak or breathe the car pulls away, and as the initial acceleration thrusts her back she feels herself being seized and embraced. She wants to help herself and gestures fearfully toward the back of the chauffeur at the wheel in front of them, as rigid and motionless as a small mountain; the witness so near at hand makes her ashamed, though she knows his very presence will protect her from the worst. But the man next to her says not a word. She only feels her body clasped warmly and urgently, his hands on hers, on her arms, on her breasts, his mouth, imperiously strange and violent, seeking hers, hotly and wetly forcing open her gradually relenting lips. She wanted and expected all this without knowing it, wanted this assault, this terrible hunt for kisses over throat and shoulders and cheeks; his mouth is like a burning brand, now here, now there on her quivering skin, and the need for restraint under the chauffeur's watchful eyes is part of the game too, growing until it becomes an intoxication in its own right. She closes her eyes without a word or thought of defense. She allows any breath of protest to be sucked away, lifts her body so that it too can feel what her lips feel. It all continues on some abstract plane, how long she couldn't say, breaking off abruptly only when, after sounding the horn in warning, the chauffeur brings the car into a lighted drive and stops it in front of the bar of the great hotel.

Confused and ashamed, she gets out, swaying a little and quickly smoothing down her rumpled dress and disordered hair. Won't everybody notice, she wonders, but no, no one pays any attention to her in the semidarkness and crush of the bar. Someone politely leads her to a table. How opaque a life can be, how completely the mask of social propriety can hide the passions; this is something new. She never would have thought it possible that she could be sitting next to a man, coolly, calmly, her head high, thinking clearly, could be making casual conversation with his well-pressed shirtfront two minutes after feeling his lips at her clenched teeth and bending under the weight of him, and none of these people has any idea. How many women have played a part in front of me, she thinks in shock, how many of the ones I knew back home in the village. All of them were leading double lives, in all sorts of ways, in a hundred different ways, private and public, while I took their restraint as an example to follow, innocent fool that I was. She feels his knee announce itself under the table. She sees his face as though for the first time, hard, tanned, vigorous, his decisive mouth beneath the trimmed beard, his eyes accosting her, boring into her. A kind of pride stirs in her: this man, so solid, so masculine, wants me, just me, and I'm the only one who knows. "Are we going to dance?" he asks. "Yes," she answers, meaning much more. Dancing isn't enough, it seems to her now. This much contact is only making her impatient for something more passionate, more unrestrained, and she struggles not to let it show.

She downs a quick cocktail, then another. The kisses she's had, the kisses she wants are burning her lips. It's unbearable to sit among these people. "We have to go back," she says. "Whatever you like." The intimacy of this first *du* comes as a soft blow, and in the car she falls into his arms without a thought. Urgent words now come between the kisses. Just an hour with him, her room is on the same floor, none of the hotel people will still be awake. She drinks the impassioned entreaties in like liquid fire. There's still time, I can still put up a fight, she thinks confusedly, already beaten. She says nothing, doesn't reply, simply accepts the onrush of words she's hearing from a man for the first time.

The car stops where she got in. The chauffeur's back is still motionless as she gets out. The lights in front of the hotel are dark. She goes in alone, walking quickly through the lobby. She knows he'll follow, already hears him not far behind, taking three steps at a time with athletic ease. In a moment he'll catch me, she thinks. A mad, mixed-up fear grips her suddenly, and she breaks into a run, staying ahead of him. She leaps through the door and bolts it, collapses into a chair, and draws a deep breath of relief. Saved!

Saved, saved! She's still shaking. Another minute and it would have been too late. I felt so uncertain and frail and weak. Horrible! Anyone could have taken me at a moment like that— I had no idea. Yet I was so sure. It gets you so fired up, so tense. Awful. A good thing I still had the strength to run in here ahead of him and lock the door, or God knows what would have happened.

She undresses quickly in the dark, heart pounding. She lies with eyes closed in the downy embrace of her warm bed, still shaking as her excitement slowly subsides. Silly, she thinks, why was I so scared. Twenty-eight years old and I'm still saving myself, still denying myself, still waiting and shilly-shallying and scared. Why am I saving myself? For whom? Father scrimped and saved, Mother and I, everyone, the bunch of us scrimped and saved all through those terrible years, while the others were living, I never had the guts, for anything, and what did we get? And suddenly you're old and faded and you die and you don't know anything and you never lived and you never knew anything. That horrible narrow little life back there is going to start up again, and here, here is where everything is, and you have to seize it, but I'm afraid, I lock myself in and save myself like a teenage girl, cowardly, cowardly, and stupid. Silly. Silly? Maybe I shouldn't have bolted the door, maybe... No, no, not today. But I'm still going to be here, eight days, fourteen days, wonderful, endless time. No, I'll stop being so stupid, so cowardly, accept everything, enjoy everything, everything...

Christine falls asleep with a smile on her lips and her arms flung wide, unaware that this is her last day, her last night in this exalted realm.

Someone who's on top of the world isn't much of an observer: happy people are poor psychologists. But someone who's troubled about something is on the alert. The perceived threat sharpens his senses—he takes in more than he usually does. And there's someone who's been troubled about Christine for some time now, who sees her as a threat, though Christine is unaware of it. The girl from Mannheim, enraged by Christine's social success, has devoted herself to doing something about it; Christine has been foolish enough to mistake her confidential chitchat for friendship. Before Christine's arrival the engineer had been flirting hard with Carla and hinting at more serious, possibly matrimonial intentions. The critical point had not come; the right moment for the crucial tête-à-tête was still perhaps a few days away. Then Christine showed up, an extremely unwelcome distraction, because the engineer's interest has been moving more and more unmistakably in Christine's direction ever since. The engineer has a logical mind and it may be that he's interested in the aura of wealth around Christine, her aristocratic name; or maybe it's her infectious glow, her brimming happiness. In any event the little Mannheim girl saw herself being put on the shelf, and responded with the jealousy of a schoolgirl and the focused anger of an adult. The engineer has been dancing almost exclusively with Christine, has been sitting at the van Boolen table every evening. Christine's rival realized it was high time to tighten the reins if she didn't want to lose him. And with the instinct of the hyperalert she has long sensed that there was something wrong about Christine and her exuberance, something out of place, and while the others succumbed and responded to the magic of that abandon, Carla set about unraveling the mystery.

A methodically cultivated intimacy was the first step. On walks she'd affectionately take Christine's arm and whisper confidences (half of them made up), hoping to tease out something compromising in return. In the evening she visited the unsuspecting Christine in her room, sat on her bed next to her, and stroked her arm; Christine, eager to please everybody in the world, responded gratefully and warmly. She took the bait and answered every question, instinctively dodging only those inquiries that touched on her deepest secret. When Carla asked how many maids she had, for example, or how many rooms there were in her house, Christine answered evasively, saying she was living in seclusion in the country because of her mother's illness, though things had of course been different before. But Carla, full of malicious curiosity, noticed small inconsistencies and seized upon them with ever greater tenacity; slowly but surely she located the chink in Christine's armor, discovering that this stranger, who with her sparkling clothes, pearls, and air of wealth has been threatening to eclipse her in Edwin's eyes, actually comes from modest, even straitened circumstances. Unwittingly Christine revealed the gaps in her worldliness. She didn't know that polo was played on horseback, wasn't familiar with common perfumes like Coty and Houbigant, didn't have a grasp of the price range of cars; she'd never been to the races. Ten or twenty gaucheries like that and it was clear she was poorly versed in the lore of the chic. And compared to a chemistry student's her schooling was nothing. No secondary school, no languages (she freely admitted she'd long since forgotten the scraps of English she'd learned in school). No, something was just not right about elegant Fräulein von Boolen, it was only a question of digging a little deeper; and the shrewd little schemer set about it, with all the force of her childish jealousy.

After two busy days of whispering, eavesdropping, and snooping, she hit pay dirt. Hairdressers are professional gossips; when only the hands are busy, the tongue is seldom still. The brisk Madame Duvernois, whose hair salon also traded in news of all kinds, laughed a silvery high C when Carla, as her hair was being washed, asked about Christine. "*Ah, la nièce de Madame van Boolen*" (the laughter was like a jet of water) "*ah, elle était bien drôle à voir quand elle arrivait ici*"; she'd had a hairdo like a peasant girl's, thick rolled braids and heavy iron hairpins, Madame had had no idea that such frightful things were made in Europe, she must still have two of them in a drawer somewhere, preserved as a historical curiosity. That was a generous clue, and the little fox pursued it aggressively. Next she cleverly got the chambermaid on Christine's floor to talk, and soon she knew it all: how Christine had arrived with a tiny little straw suitcase, how all her clothes and underthings had promptly been bought for her or lent to her by Mrs. van Boolen. Lively questioning and some palm-greasing brought out every detail, down to the umbrella with the horn handle. And since malice is always lucky, Carla happened to be there when Christine asked for her mail under the name Hoflehner; an artfully nonchalant question yielded the surprising intelligence that Christine's name was not von Boolen at all.

This was enough, more than enough. The powder was spread; all Carla had to do now was light the fuse. Privy Councillor Frau Strodtmann, widow of the great surgeon, sat in the lobby day and night like a sentry, armed with her lorgnette. Her wheelchair (the old woman was paralyzed) was the hotel's

undisputed social news desk and, most important, the final
court of appeal as to what was proper and what wasn't—an
aggressive, fanatical intelligence agency laboring around the
clock in the secret war of all against all. Clara sat with Frau
Strodtmann and unloaded the precious cargo smoothly and
quickly, giving no hint that she was anything but a friend. That
Fräulein von Boolen (at least that's what everyone calls her
here) is such a charming girl, you'd never guess where she came
from. But isn't it simply splendid of Mrs. van Boolen to take
this shopgirl or whatever she is and pretend so sweetly that she's
her niece, dress her up in style in her own clothes and give her
a new identity. Yes, Americans do have a more democratic and
generous way of thinking about these matters of social standing
than backward Europeans like us who are still playing at high
society (here the privy councillor's head bobbed like an angry
hen)—eventually they'll be giving her an education and even
a proper ancestry, not just clothes and money. Needless to
say, the protective wing offered to the girl from the provinces
was characterized in the liveliest terms. Every last deliciously
damaging detail was handed over to the news desk. That very
morning the story began circulating throughout the hotel,
picking up dirt and debris on its way as gossip will. Some said
Americans got up stenographers as millionaires all the time, did
it on purpose to annoy the aristocrats (there was even a play
about it over there). Others argued that Christine was probably the old man's lover, or even his wife's. In short, the thing
worked like a charm, and on the evening of Christine's escapade
with the engineer she had no suspicion that she was the main
topic of conversation throughout the hotel. No one wanted to
be the one who'd been taken in, so they all claimed to have
noticed a hundred fishy things before. And since memory is
subject to the will, everything they'd found so charming the
day before was now something to snicker at. They all knew
about Christine's innocent and reluctant deceit while she, her

warm young body wrapped up in happiness, her lips parted in a sleeper's smile, was still deceiving herself.

The subject of a rumor is always the last to hear it. That morning, pursued by prying, mocking eyes, Christine has no suspicion that she's walking through the licking flames of a ring of fire. She graciously sits down next to the privy councillor, the most dangerous spot of all. The old lady prods her with questions, but Christine doesn't notice how nasty they are (people all around are leaning in to listen). She charmingly kisses her white-haired antagonist's hand before she goes off to take the planned walk with her aunt and uncle. She doesn't notice the slight smirk on the faces of some of the guests as they return her greeting. Why would anyone be anything but pleasant? Bright and serene, she looks upon the malicious crowd with trusting eyes. She flutters through the room like a flame, beatifically confident of the goodness of the world.

At first her aunt also notices nothing. There does seem to be something disagreeable in the air this morning, but she can't put her finger on it. Herr and Frau von Trenkwitz, a Silesian landowner couple staying at the hotel, are very particular about the company they keep, setting great store by high birth and class and ruthlessly ignoring all commoners. They've made an exception of the van Boolens, mostly because they're Americans (already nobility of a kind) without being Jews, but perhaps also because their second-oldest son, Harro, whose property is heavily encumbered by high-interest mortgages, is going to arrive tomorrow and it might not be a bad thing for him to make the acquaintance of an American heiress. A stroll with Mrs. van Boolen was planned for ten this morning, but at nine thirty (on receipt of the information from the privy councillor's desk) they send the desk clerk to deliver the inexplicable message that, unfortunately, it won't be possible. And strangely, instead of stopping to apologize and give some explanation for this late cancellation, they pass by the van Boolens' table at lunchtime with no more than a stiff nod. Mrs. van Boolen, morbidly sensitive in all social matters, immediately suspects something. "Odd," she thinks, "did we offend them? What's happened?" Strange too that no one comes to sit with her in the lounge after lunch (Anthony is taking his afternoon nap; Christine is writing in the library). The Kinsleys or other new friends they've made here usually come by to chat, but now, as though by mutual agreement, everyone's staying at their tables, and she waits alone in her deep armchair, oddly hurt that all her friends aren't coming over and that that self-important Trenkwitz hasn't even apologized.

Finally someone does approach, and he's different too, stiff-legged, awkward, solemn: Lord Elkins. He averts his eyes strangely beneath his reddish, tired-looking lids. Usually he meets your eyes so directly. What's the matter with him? He bows almost ceremonially. "May I sit with you?"

"Of course, Lord Elkins. Need you ask?"

Once more she's surprised. He seems so uncomfortable, he examines his shoes, unbuttons his coat, adjusts the creases in his trousers; strange, strange. What on earth is wrong, she thinks, he looks as though he's about to give a speech.

At last the old man finds the resolve to lift his bright clear eyes under the heavy lids. It's like a blast of light, like a sword flashing.

"I say, my dear Mrs. van Boolen, I should like to discuss something of a private nature with you. No one can hear us here. But you must allow me the liberty of being quite forthright. All this time I've been considering how the business might be hinted at, but hints are to no purpose in serious matters. Anything personal or awkward must be approached with that much more clarity and directness. So ... I feel I shall be doing my duty as a friend if I speak quite without reservation. Will you permit me that?"

"But of course."

The old man doesn't look very relieved. For a moment he delays again as he takes his shag pipe out of his pocket and fills it laboriously, his fingers trembling strangely (is it age or agitation?). Finally he looks up and says clearly, "What I have to say to you concerns Miss Christiana."

He hesitates some more.

Mrs. van Boolen is slightly shocked. Can the almost seventy-year-old man really be thinking seriously about...She's already realized that Christine is very much on his mind. Can that really have gone so far that he...But then Lord Elkins looks up with a sharp, inquisitive expression and asks, "Is she really your niece?"

Mrs. van Boolen looks almost offended. "Of course."

"And is her name really van Boolen?"

Now Mrs. van Boolen is becoming seriously bewildered.

"No, no . . . But she's *my* niece, not my husband's, she's the daughter of my sister in Vienna . . . But I beg you, Lord Elkins, I know your intentions are friendly. What is the meaning of this question?"

Elkins looks deeply and intently into his pipe. It seems to be of immense interest to him whether the tobacco is burning evenly, and he spends some time poking it about with his finger. He remains hunched over. At last he says, almost without opening his thin lips, as if speaking to his pipe, "Because . . . well, because a very peculiar bit of gossip has suddenly cropped up here, to the effect that . . . I thought it my duty as a friend to get to the bottom of the matter. Since you tell me she really is your niece, the whole tale has been put to rest as far as I'm concerned. I was immediately persuaded that Miss Christiana was incapable of being untruthful, it was just that . . . well, people here are saying such strange things."

Mrs. van Boolen feels herself turn pale, and her knees shake.

"What . . . Please be candid . . . What are people saying?"

The pipe begins to glow, a red disk.

"Well, you know that this kind of hotel society, which isn't a real society, is always more unforgiving than society itself. That cold-blooded popinjay Trenkwitz, for example, is personally offended to be sitting at the same table with someone who is not a member of the nobility and has no money. It seems he and his wife have been wagging their tongues all over the place with a story that you played a joke on them by dressing up a lower-middle-class girl and presenting her to them as a lady under a false name—as though that blockhead knew what a real lady was anyway. I'm sure I don't have to impress upon you that the great respect and the great...the very great... the genuine liking that I have for Miss Christiana would not be diminished in the slightest if she really came from...from straitened circumstances...Perhaps she wouldn't have any of that marvelous responsiveness and joy if she were as accustomed to luxury as this stuck-up lot. So I personally have nothing against your good-heartedly giving her your clothes, quite the contrary; and if I inquired about the truth of the matter it was only so as to be able to deal a crushing blow to this vile talk."

Shock has mounted from Mrs. van Boolen's knees into her throat. She has to take three deep breaths before she can summon the strength to respond calmly.

"My dear Lord Elkins, I have no reason at all to keep the slightest thing about Christine's background secret from you. My brother-in-law was a prominent businessman, one of the wealthiest and most respected in Vienna" (here she was exaggerating greatly) "but lost his fortune in the war as the most decent people did. His family didn't have an easy time of it. They considered it more honorable to work than to let us support them, and so Christine now works as a civil servant, in the post office, which, I hope, is not shameful."

Lord Elkins looks up with a smile. His slump has vanished and he's plainly feeling more at ease.

"You're talking to someone who was himself a civil servant for forty years. If that's something to be ashamed of, then I share the shame. But now that we've spoken clearly, we need to be thinking clearly too. I knew right away that all this cattiness was low gossip—it's one of the few advantages of age that one is rarely wrong about people. Let us accept things as they are: Miss Christiana's situation will, I fear, not be an easy one from here on in. There's nothing more vindictive, nothing more underhanded, than a little world that would like to be a big one. A conceited oaf like that Trenkwitz will be kicking himself for the next ten years for having been polite to a Post Office employee. That sort of thing bothers an old nitwit like him more than toothache. And it's not impossible that others too will be less than tactful toward your niece. At the very least she'll find that people are chilly and impolite. Now I should like to prevent that, for (as I'm sure you've noticed) I have an extraordinarily high regard for your niece...extraordinarily high, and I should be happy if I might be of help in sparing her any disappointment, as she's so wonderfully guileless."

Lord Elkins breaks off, his face once again old and gray in thought.

"Whether I shall be able to protect her in the long run, that...that I cannot say. That depends...that depends on the circumstances. But in any case I wish to make it clear to these fine ladies and gents that I respect her more than the entire moneyed mob of them and that whoever goes so far as to treat her rudely will have me to deal with. There are certain jokes I shan't tolerate, and as long as I'm here they'll have to watch themselves."

He stands up abruptly, more resolute and firm than Mrs. van Boolen has ever known him to be.

"Will you permit me to ask your niece on a drive?" he asks formally.

"But of course."

He bows and walks off toward the library (Mrs. van Boolen looks after him in shock), his cheeks reddened as though by a biting wind and his fists clenched. What does he want, Mrs. van Boolen thinks, still stunned. Christine is writing and doesn't hear him come up. From behind he sees only her lovely fair hair on her neck as she bends over the paper, sees the form that has reawakened desire in him after so many years. Poor child, he thinks, she's so carefree, she knows nothing, but they'll get you somehow and there's no way to protect you. He touches her shoulder. Christine gives a start and gets to her feet respectfully. From the beginning she's always felt the need to demonstrate her respect to this exceptional man. He forces a smile: "My dear Fräulein Christiana, I'm coming with a request. I'm not feeling well today, I've had a headache since early this morning, can't read, can't sleep. I thought some fresh air might do me good, a jaunt in the car, and I should certainly get the most out of it if you would accompany me. Your aunt has already given me permission to ask. So if you'd like...?"

"But of course... I'd be... delighted, I'd be honored..."

"Then let's be off." He courteously offers his arm. It surprises her and embarrasses her a little, but how can she refuse this honor! Lord Elkins walks with her the length of the lounge, slowly, steadily, and firmly. He gives each person a quick sharp look, not something he normally does. There's unmistakable threat expressed in his bearing: hands off! Ordinarily he's friendly and polite, barely noticed as he moves among them like a quiet gray shadow; but now he fixes each of them with a challenging gaze. It's immediately clear to everyone what this display of respect means, his taking Christine's arm. The privy councillor watches guiltily, the Kinsleys nod almost apprehensively as the fearless old paladin with his snow-white hair and icy gaze strides through the broad room with the young woman, she proud and happy, suspecting nothing, he with a hard, soldierly set to his mouth as though standing at the head of a regiment about to attack an entrenched enemy.

Trenkwitz happens to be outside the hotel door when they emerge; he greets them automatically. Lord Elkins looks past him, lifts his hand halfway to his hat and lets it fall carelessly as if acknowledging a waiter. It's a gesture of indescribable contempt, like a rebuff. He releases Christine's arm, opens the car door, and doffs his hat as he helps the lady in, with the same courtesy he once showed the daughter-in-law of the King of England during an automobile trip to the Transvaal.

Mrs. van Boolen was a good deal more frightened by Lord Elkins's discreet disclosure than she let on; without realizing it, he had reopened an old wound. Down in that dim stratum of things half known and things better left forgotten, that treacherous zone consciously entered only under duress and with trepidation, the long-since respectable and quite ordinary Claire van Boolen harbors an ancient and ineradicable fear, one that surfaces sometimes in dreams and disturbs her sleep: the fear that her own past might be discovered. When, as Klara, thirty years ago, she had found herself adroitly eased out of Europe and had met and was going to marry Anthony van Boolen, she had lacked the courage to confess to that honest but somewhat philistine burgher the troubled origins of the small capital she was contributing to their union. Lying resolutely, she'd said that the two thousand dollars was an inheritance from her grandfather, and never once during their entire married life had her guileless and adoring husband doubted the truth of this statement. There was nothing to fear from his stolid good nature, but the more proper Claire became, the more she was possessed by the mad idea that some silly happenstance, a chance meeting or anonymous letter, might suddenly bring her long-ago affair to light. For that reason she'd doggedly and purposefully avoided encounters with her compatriots for years. She wouldn't let her husband introduce her to a Viennese business friend, and as soon as she was fluent in English she refused to hear a word of German. She aggressively terminated all correspondence with her own family, sending no more than a brief telegram even in the most important matters. But the fear did not subside; quite the contrary, it grew as she moved up the social ladder, and the better adapted she became to puritanical American ways the more nervous she was that some casual bit of talk might bring that nasty spark smoldering under the ashes to a blaze. When a dinner guest happened to remark that he'd lived for a long time in Vienna, that was enough to keep her awake all night, feeling that burning in her heart. Then came the war, and at a stroke everything that had come before was pushed back into an inaccessible and almost mythical era. The newspapers and magazines from that time were turning to dust, people in Europe had other things to worry about now, talked about different things; it was over, forgotten. Like a foreign body encapsulated in scar tissue, which may cause some aching when the weather changes but is otherwise hardly felt and thus not so foreign anymore, that awkward bit of her past was forgotten amid the comfort, contentment, and wholesome activity of her new life. She was the mother of two strapping sons, she lent a hand in the business occasionally, belonged to the Philanthropic League, was vice president of the Association for Former Internees, was highly respected and honored in the city; and, after having to repress her ambitions for so long, at last she had an outlet—a new house where all the best families came to call. Little by little she forgot the episode —this was the most critical thing for her peace of mind. Memory is so corrupt that you remember only what you want to; if you want to forget about something, slowly but surely you do. Klara the dress model finally died, to be reborn as the impeccable wife of the cotton merchant van Boolen. The episode was so little in her thoughts anymore that she wrote her sister to arrange a reunion the moment she arrived in Europe. But now she's learned that, inexplicably, evil-minded people are looking into her niece's background: didn't it stand to reason that they'd include her too, that she herself would become the focus of attention? Fear is a distorting mirror in which anything can appear as a caricature of itself, stretched to terrible proportions; once inflamed, the imagination pursues the craziest and most unlikely possibilities. What is most absurd suddenly seems the most probable: she realizes with horror that at the next table is an old Viennese, director of the commercial bank, seventy or eighty years old, by the name of Löwy, and suddenly she thinks she remembers that the maiden name of her late patron's wife had also been Löwy. What if she were his sister, or his cousin! And doesn't he seem to find it easy to chime in with some suggestive remark or other (old men do like to go on about scandals recalled from their youth!). Cold sweat breaks out on Claire's brow. Fear has done its work well, and now she thinks old Herr Löwy looks remarkably like her patron's wife: the same thick lips, the same hooked nose. In a hallucinatory fever of anxiety she has no doubt that he's her brother, and of course he'll recognize her and dredge up the old story in all its detail, and that'll be nectar and ambrosia to the Kinsleys and Guggenheims, and the next day Anthony will get an anonymous letter which will at a stroke demolish thirty years of trusting marriage.

Claire feels faint and steadies herself on her armrest for a moment before hurling herself from her seat with the energy of despair. She makes an effort to nod pleasantly to the Kinsleys as she passes their table. They're perfectly friendly, smiling back with that stereotypical American smile of greeting which she herself has long since unconsciously learned. But Claire is so irrationally frightened that she imagines it's a different kind of smile—ironic, malicious, knowing, treacherous. There even seems to be something wrong with the way the elevator boy looks at her, the way the chambermaid passes by without a word. She enters her room exhausted, as though she's been trudging through deep snow.

Anthony has just risen from his siesta. He's combing his sparse hair before the mirror, his suspenders flopping and his collar open, his cheeks still creased from sleep.

"Anthony, we have to talk," she says, breathing heavily.

"What's the problem?" He puts some pomade on his comb and parts his hair precisely.

"Please stop that." She can bear it no longer. "We have to think everything over calmly. It's something very unpleasant."

The phlegmatic Anthony has long since become accustomed to his wife's excitability and is rarely inclined to believe that such announcements require urgent attention. He doesn't turn from the mirror. "I hope it's not as bad as all that. Not a wire from Dickie or Alvin?"

"No, but stop that! You can get dressed later."

"Well?" Anthony puts down his comb at last and sits resignedly in the armchair. "So what's the matter?"

"Something terrible has happened. Christine must have been careless or done something stupid. It's all come out, the entire hotel is talking about it."

"Oh? What's come out?"

"Well, the business with the clothes . . . The fact that she's wearing my clothes, that she came here looking like a shopgirl and we dressed her from head to toe and presented her as a stylish lady—people are saying all sorts of things . . . And now you know why the Trenkwitzes cut us dead . . . Of course they're furious because they had something in mind with their son and think we were conning them. We've been compromised now in front of the whole hotel. That little blunderer must have done something stupid! My God, what a disgrace!"

"Why is it a disgrace? All Americans have poor relatives. I wouldn't want to look too closely at the nephews of the Guggenheims, or the Roskys for that matter, or those Rosenstocks from Kovno. I'll bet you'd see quite a contrast there too. I don't see why it's a disgrace that we dressed her up respectably."

"Because...because..." (Claire is raising her voice nervously) "because they're right—that kind of person doesn't belong here, not in this world...I mean, somebody who...who just doesn't know how to behave so you can't tell where she came from...It's her fault...If she hadn't made such a spectacle of herself, no one would have noticed, if she'd just kept a low profile, the way she did at the beginning...But always running about, always bright and cheery and so forward with everyone, she's got to talk to everyone and mingle with everyone, be in on everything, always at the head of the parade. Everyone's friend...So it's no wonder people started to ask who she is and where she came from, and now...now it's a total scandal. Everybody's talking about it and making fun of us...They're saying terrible things."

Anthony gives an easy guffaw. "Let them talk...I don't care. She's a nice girl, I like her no matter what they say. And whether she's poor or not is nobody's goddamn business. I didn't borrow a penny from anybody here and I couldn't care less if they think we're classy or not. If anybody thinks there's something wrong with us, they'll just have to live with it."

"But I care. I care."

Claire's voice is becoming shriller. "I won't listen to talk that I bamboozled people and put forward some poor girl as a duchess. I can't stand it if we invite someone like Trenkwitz and that boor sends the desk clerk to make his excuses for him. No, I'm not going to let people turn their backs on us, I don't need that. God knows I came here to enjoy myself, not to feel angry and upset. I won't have it."

"So" (he covers a small yawn with his hand) "what do you want to do?"

"Leave!"

"What?" Anthony, usually so indolent, pulls himself up as though someone stepped on his toes.

"Yes, leave, tomorrow morning. These people are mistaken if they think they can put me on trial, make me testify to the hows and whys and say I'm sorry too. Not for the likes of those Trenkwitzes and the rest of them. I don't like this crowd here anyway. Except for Lord Elkins they're a boring, noisy bunch of mediocrities. They won't get a word out of me. Besides, it's not good for me here, the altitude is bad for my nerves, I can't sleep at night—you don't notice, of course, you just lie down and you're asleep. For the last week I've been wishing I had your temperament. We've been here three weeks now—that's more than enough! And as far as the girl is concerned, we've done our duty toward Mary and then some. We invited her, she amused herself and had a rest, even went a little too far, but now that's it. My conscience is clear."

"Yes, but where ... where is it you want to go so suddenly?"

"To Interlaken! It's at a lower altitude, and we can meet up with the Linseys who were so pleasant to talk to on the boat. They really are nice, not like this motley crew here, and just the day before yesterday they wrote to say we ought to come. If we leave tomorrow morning, we can be there for dinner."

Anthony is still a little reluctant. "It's all so sudden! Do we have to leave tomorrow? There's plenty of time left!"

But he soon gives in. He always gives in, knowing from long experience that if Claire wants something intensely she'll get it in the end and it's a waste of energy to protest. And it's all the same to him anyway. People who are comfortable with themselves don't react strongly to what goes on around them, and Anthony is too confirmed in his apathy to care whether it's Linseys or Guggenheims he has for gambling partners, whether the mountain outside the window is the Schwarzhorn or the Wetterhorn, or whether the hotel is the Palace or the Astoria. He just wants to avoid conflict. So he doesn't put up much resistance, listens patiently as Claire calls down to the desk clerk and gives him instructions, looks on with amusement as she hurriedly pulls out the suitcases and madly piles the clothes in, lights his pipe, strolls over to his card game, and, as he shuffles and cuts, gives no further thought to his departure or his wife or least of all Christine.

While everyone, friends and strangers alike, is gossiping excitedly about how Christine arrived and how she'll be leaving, Lord Elkins's gleaming gray car is cutting a smooth, bold swath through the windy blue of the high valley, following the white road twisting down to the Lower Engadine. Already they're near Schuls-Tarasp. Lord Elkins's intention in asking Christine along had been more or less to bring her under his protection in a way that would be clear to everyone and then return her to the hotel after a short drive. But, as he climbed in next to her and saw her leaning back, talking cheerfully, with the sky reflected in her untroubled eyes, he felt it was senseless to cut short such a sweet moment for her and for him too, and he told the chauffeur to drive on. No need to hurry back, she'll hear the news soon enough, the old man thinks (he can't help stroking her hand). Actually she ought to be given some warning, be gently prepared in some unobtrusive way for what to expect from that bunch—that way the sudden chill won't be so painful. So he drops occasional hints about the privy councillor's malice and discreetly warns about Christine's little friend. But Christine, full of the ardor and optimism of youth, innocently defends her worst enemies: the old privy councillor is so sweet, she cares so much about everyone, and Lord Elkins has no idea how clever and amusing and fun the little Mannheim girl can be—probably she's just shy when he's around. Anyhow, all the people here are so wonderful, so cheerful, so kind to her, really, sometimes she feels ashamed, she doesn't deserve all this.

The old man stares at the tip of his cane. Ever since the war he's had a low opinion of people and of nations, they're selfish, all of them, without the imagination to see the injustices they're perpetrating. The idealism of his youth, a belief in the moral mission of mankind and the enlightened spirit of the white race that he took from the lectures of John Stuart Mill and his followers, was buried once and for all in the bloody mire of Ypres and the chalk quarry at Soissons where his son met his death. Politics disgusts him, the cool conviviality of the club and the showy self-congratulation of the public banquet repel him; since the death of his son he's avoided making new acquaintances. His own generation's sour unwillingness to recognize the truth and its inability to adapt to the postwar era anger him, as does the younger generation's smart-alecky thoughtlessness. But with this girl he's regained belief, a vague devout gratitude for the mere existence of youth; in her presence he sees that one generation's painfully acquired mistrust of life is fortunately neither understood nor credited by the next, and that each new wave of youth is a new beginning. How wonderfully grateful she is for the tiniest thing—it delights him, while at the same time he feels a passionate desire, stronger than ever, almost painful, to bring something of this marvelous warmth into his own life, perhaps even bind it to him. I could protect her for a couple of years, he thinks. Perhaps she'd never find out, or not for a while, about the vileness of a world that prostrates itself before God but tramples on the poor. Ah—he looks at her from the side: her eyes are closed, her mouth open like a child's as she drinks in the onrushing air—just a few years of youth would be enough for me. She cheerfully chatters away, turned toward him gratefully, but the old man is only half listening. A sudden boldness has come over him. He's considering how he might subtly court her in what might be the last hour.

They have tea at Schuls-Tarasp. Then, on a bench on the promenade, he begins, carefully and indirectly. He has two nieces, he says—about Christine's age—in Oxford. If she wanted to come to England, she could stay there; he'd be delighted to have her, and if his set, an old man's society of course, didn't seem too tiresome, he'd be happy to show her around London. Of course he doesn't know if it's even possible for her to leave Austria and go to England, if there might not be something to keep her at home, emotional ties, he means. What he's asking is clear, but Christine, bubbling with enthusiasm, fails to understand. Oh, no, how she'd love to see the world, it's supposed to be fantastic in England, she's heard so much about Oxford and the regattas, there can't be another country where it's so much fun to be outside doing things, where it's so great to be young.

The old man's face darkens. About him she has said nothing. She's only thinking of herself, about her own youthful life. Again he loses his nerve. No, he thinks, it would be criminal to take a young person, so happy and so full of energy, and shut her up with an old man in an old castle. No, don't let yourself be rejected, don't make a fool of yourself. Take your leave, old man! On your way! Too late!

"Hadn't we better be getting back," he asks in a suddenly changed voice. "I don't want your aunt to start worrying."

"Of course," she replies, adding enthusiastically, "Oh, it's been so nice, it's all so fantastically beautiful here."

The old man is sad for her and for himself and says little in the car next to her. She has no suspicion of what is happening in him and will happen to her. She looks brightly out onto the landscape, her cheeks flushed in the wind.

The gong is sounding as they pull up in front of the hotel. She presses the old man's hand in thanks and dashes upstairs to change. For the first few days, getting dressed was a worry, an effort, a trial, yet also an exciting game. She'd wonder at herself in the mirror, at the spangled creature she'd unexpectedly become. Now she knows she's beautiful, elegant, and smart every evening, it's something she takes for granted. The sheer, bright dress slips on with a few quick movements. She gives her lips a confident touch-up, tosses her hair into place, throws on a scarf, and she's ready, as comfortable in her borrowed finery as in her own skin. A last glance over her shoulder at the mirror, and, satisfied, she goes to get her aunt for dinner.

But at the door she stops short in surprise. The room has been taken apart, it's been totally ransacked, with half-filled suitcases, and hats, shoes, and articles of clothing spread on chairs and strewn over the bed and the table. The room that was once so orderly is now a hopeless mess. Her aunt, in her dressing gown, is just now kneeling on top of a recalcitrant suitcase. "What... what's happening?" says Christine in amazement. Her aunt deliberately doesn't look up. She pushes angrily at the suitcase, her face red, groaning, "We're going... Oh, damn thing! Will you close... We're going away."

"Really, when?... Why?" Christine's mouth falls open. She's paralyzed.

Her aunt hammers again at the catch, which finally snaps shut. She straightens, panting.

"Yes, it's really a shame, I'm sorry too, Christl! But I said from the start that the thin air up here wouldn't agree with Anthony. It's not the right thing for old people. This afternoon he had another asthma attack."

"Oh!" The old man emerges unsuspectingly from the next room. Christine approaches and puts her arm around him gently, quivering with alarm. "How are you, Uncle? Feeling better, I hope! My God, I had no idea, or I wouldn't have gone out! But really, I mean it, you look fine. You're feeling better?"

She gazes at him in bewilderment, genuinely alarmed. She has no thought of herself. She hasn't yet understood that she'll be leaving, has grasped only that her good-natured old uncle is ill; she's frightened for him, not for herself.

Anthony, as stolid and healthy as ever, is embarrassed by so much sympathy and concern. It takes him a moment to understand the repugnant farce he's embroiled in.

"No, dear child," he growls (damn it all, why is Claire using me as an excuse!). "I'm sure you've realized by now that Claire always exaggerates. I feel fine, and if it were up to me we'd stay." Baffled and irritated by his wife's lie, he adds almost roughly, "Claire, stop with the damn packing, there's plenty of time for that. On our last evening we want to relax with the dear girl." Claire goes on busying herself with the packing, saying nothing. Probably she fears the inevitable explanations; Anthony meanwhile looks pensively out the window (let her get herself out of this one, I'm not going to lift a finger). Christine stands mute and confused between the two of them, feeling she's in the way. Something's happened, something she doesn't understand. Lightning has struck; now she waits with beating heart for the thunder which doesn't come and doesn't come and yet must come. She doesn't dare to ask any questions, doesn't dare to think, but knows with every nerve in her body that something bad has happened. Did they have a fight? Is there bad news from New York? Perhaps something in the stock market, something to do with business, a bank failure, there's something like that in the papers every day. Or maybe her uncle really did have an asthma attack and he's hiding it on her account. Why are they leaving me to stand here like this, what am I doing here? But nothing, silence, silence, just her aunt's unnecessary bustling around and her uncle's restless pacing and the loud thumping of her own heart.

A knock at the door comes as a relief. A waiter enters, followed by a second waiter carrying a white tablecloth. To Christine's astonishment they clear the smoking things off the table and begin setting it carefully.

"You see," her aunt explains finally, "Anthony thought it was better to have dinner up here in our room tonight. I hate those

awkward goodbyes, all those questions about where we're going and for how long. Besides, almost all my things are packed
now, Anthony's smoking jacket too. And it's quieter and more
comfortable here, isn't it."

The waiters roll the cart in and serve from the nickel-
plated chafing dishes. Once they're gone I'll get an explanation,
Christine thinks, worriedly watching the faces of her aunt and
uncle. Her uncle is bent low over his plate, angrily spooning his
soup; her aunt looks pale and embarrassed. Finally she begins:
"Christine, I know our sudden decision comes as a surprise! But
in America everything's done fast, that's one of the good things
you learn over there. Don't stick around where you don't want
to be. If a business isn't doing well, give up and start another. If
you don't feel right somewhere, you pack your bags and leave.
I didn't want to tell you, because you've been having such a
splendid vacation, but we've been feeling out of sorts here for
some time. I've been sleeping poorly all along and Anthony just
can't take it either, the thin air at this altitude. Today a telegram
happened to arrive from our friends in Interlaken and we just
decided to go, probably only for a few days, and then on to Aix-
les-Bains. Yes, we do everything fast (I know it's a surprise)."

Christine bows her head over her plate in order not to look
at her aunt. Something in her tone bothers her, the brightness of her talk, every word artificially brisk and full of false
enthusiasm. There has to be something behind it. Something
else must be coming, and it comes: "Of course it would have
been best for you to come along," her aunt goes on, pulling off
a chicken wing. "But I don't think you'd like Interlaken, it's
no place for young people, and one has to consider whether
all that toing and froing in the last few days of your vacation
would really be worth the trouble. You've picked up fabulously
here, this powerful fresh air has done wonders for you. Yes, I
always say there's nothing better than the high mountains
for young people, Dickie and Alvin ought to come here

sometime. Obviously for worn-out old hearts like ours the Engadine is all wrong. So as I say, of course we'd love it, Anthony's so used to having you around, but on the other hand it's seven hours each way, that would be too much, and anyway we'll be back next year. But of course if you want to come along to Interlaken..."

"No, no," Christine says, or rather her lips say it, the way a patient going under anesthesia might continue counting after losing consciousness.

"Myself, I think you'd be better off going straight home. There's a wonderfully comfortable train that leaves around seven in the morning—I asked the desk clerk. That would put you in Salzburg by late tomorrow night and back home the next morning. I can picture how happy your mother will be, you look so tanned and fresh and young, really magnificent, and the best thing would be for you to go right home and show them."

"All right," Christine hears herself say quietly. Why is she still sitting here? They just want her gone, and fast. But why? Something must have happened, something. She eats mechanically, tasting bitterness in every bite. I have to say something, something casual, she thinks—she doesn't want them to see that her eyes are stinging, that her throat is quivering with anger. Something matter-of-fact, something cool and indifferent.

Finally she has a thought. "I'll go get your clothes so we can pack them," she says, standing up. But her aunt pushes her back gently.

"No, child, there's still time for that. I'll pack the third suitcase tomorrow. Just leave everything in your room, the maid will bring it." And then, suddenly embarrassed: "By the way, you know that dress, the red one, why don't you keep it, I really don't need it anymore, it fits you so well, and of course the odds and ends too, the sweater, the underthings, that goes without saying. The other two gowns are all I'll be needing for Aix-les-Bains, it's wonderful there, you know, a fantastic hotel too, I'm told, and I hope Anthony will feel well there, the warm baths, and the air is much milder and..." Now that the hard part is over, her aunt rattles on. Having gently broken it to Christine that she'll be leaving tomorrow, she knows it's smooth sailing from here, and she perks up as she talks about hotels and traveling and America—the most wounding stories— and Christine, downcast, sits through them meekly though her nerves are strained by the shrill, desperately blasé stream of talk. If only it were over. Finally a brief pause. "I don't want to keep you up. Uncle should rest and you too, Aunt, you must be tired from your packing. Is there anything else I can help with?"

"No, no." Her aunt stands up too. "I can easily pack the last few things myself. But it would be better for you too if you got to bed early. You'll have to be up by six, I think. You won't be mad if we don't take you to the train, will you?"

"No, no, there's no need for that, Aunt," Christine says tonelessly, looking at the floor.

"And you'll write to tell me how Mary is doing, won't you, write as soon as you get there. And as I say, we'll see each other next year."

"All right," Christine says. Thank God I can go now. A kiss for her uncle, who is strangely embarrassed, a kiss for her aunt, and then she moves toward the door (go now, quickly!). But at the last moment—her hand is on the doorknob—her aunt rushes up with fear in her heart (though for the last time). "You'll be going to your room now, won't you, Christl," she says urgently, "go to bed and get a good night's sleep. Best not to go down again, you know, or...or...or tomorrow morning everyone will come to say goodbye to us...And we don't like that...It's better just to go without a big song and dance and then send a few postcards later...I can't bear it when people give you flowers and...come to see you off. So you won't go down, will you, just go right to bed...You'll promise me?"

"Yes, of course," says Christine with the last of her voice and pulls the door shut. Not until weeks later does she realize she hadn't spoken even a word of thanks.

Outside the door the strength that Christine summoned with so much effort deserts her. Holding on to the wall, she makes it back to her room in a daze, the way an animal that's been killed by a shot lurches on for a few steps before falling. In her room she drops into a chair and doesn't move. She doesn't understand what has happened. Behind her forehead she feels the pain of an unexpected blow, but who dealt it? Somebody did something, did something to hurt her. She's being chased off, but doesn't know why.

She tries to think, but she's numb inside, filled with something dim, hard, unresponding. Around her there's more hardness, a glass coffin more ghastly than a dank black one, its lights brilliant and taunting, its comfort mocking, and silent, horribly silent, while within her the question "What did I do? Why are they driving me away?" cries out for an answer. The dull pressure is intolerable, as though the entire hotel with its four hundred guests, its bricks and beams and huge roof lay on her chest, along with the poisonously cold white light and the beckoning chairs and mirror, the enticing bed with its flowered coverlet; if she goes on sitting in this chair she might freeze, smash the windows in fury, or scream, howl, weep so loudly that everybody wakes up. Just get away from here, leave! Just . . . she doesn't know what, but get out, get out, to keep from suffocating in this dreadful airless silence.

She jumps up and runs out with no idea what she's doing, leaving the door swinging and the brass and glass glittering meaninglessly at each other under the light.

She moves downstairs like a sleepwalker. Rugs and paintings, hotel equipment, steps and light fixtures, guests, waiters and chambermaids, objects and faces glide spectrally by. A few people look up, surprised she doesn't acknowledge their greetings. Her gaze is closed off; she doesn't know what she's looking at or where she's going or why but negotiates the stairs with inexplicable assurance.

Some mechanism that regulates her actions is broken. She's running blindly now, pursued by a nameless fear, with no goal in mind. She stops short at the entrance to the lounge; something stirs, some memory of dancing and laughing and cheerful socializing. "Why am I here? Why did I come?" she wonders, and the power of the room is gone. She can't go on; the walls are swaying, the carpet is slipping, the chandeliers are swinging in wild ellipses. I'm falling, she thinks, the floor is moving out from under me. She instinctively grasps a curtain with her right hand and regains her balance. But her limbs have lost their strength. She can't go forward, can't go back. She stands with all her weight against the wall, face convulsed and rigid, eyes closed, breathing hard, unable to go on.

Just then the German engineer runs into her. He's hurrying to his room for some photos he wants to show a certain lady, but now he spots the figure oddly pressed against the wall, motionless, breathing heavily, with unseeing eyes; for a moment he doesn't recognize her. But then his voice takes on its breezy boyish tone: "There you are! Why aren't you coming to the lounge? Or are you on some secret mission? And why... What is it... Are you all right?" He stares with surprise. Christine has flinched at his first word. Now she's trembling all over like a sleepwalker who hears her name called.

Her eyebrows are arched in alarm; she looks frantic, stricken. She raises her arm as though to ward off a blow.

"What's wrong? Are you ill?" He steadies her, and just in time, for Christine is swaying strangely—her head is suddenly spinning. But she gives a feverish start when she feels the warm touch of his arm.

"I have to talk to you . . . right away . . . but not here . . . not in front of the others . . . I have to talk to you alone." She doesn't know what she wants to say to him, she just wants to talk, with someone, to let out a wail.

Her voice, usually so calm, is shrill, and the engineer is taken aback. He thinks: She's probably ill. They put her to bed, that's why she didn't come down, and she sneaked off—she must have a fever, you can tell by her glassy eyes. Or maybe it's a fit of hysteria—women do have them—anyway easy does it, don't let on she looks sick, just play along.

"Of course, Fräulein" (he's speaking to her like a child) "al- though. . ." (best not to be seen) "although why don't we step outside . . . into the fresh air . . . I know it'll do you good . . . The lounge is always so terribly overheated. . ." Soothe her, calm her down, he thinks, and as he takes her arm he casually checks her wrist for fever. No, her hand is ice-cold. Curious, he thinks with growing unease—very strange.

The lamps in front of the hotel sway brightly overhead; to the left the woods are deep in shadow. That's where she waited yesterday. It seems like a thousand years ago and the memory is gone from every cell in her body. He leads her there gently (quick, into the dark, who knows what's wrong with her), and she allows herself to be led. First distract her, he reflects, keep it light, no serious discussion, just some casual chat, that's the most reassuring thing.

"This is much nicer, isn't it . . . Here, put on my coat . . . Ah, what a marvelous evening . . . Look at the stars . . . Silly of us to spend the whole evening in the hotel the way we always do." But Christine continues to shake and doesn't hear him. What stars, what evening, she's aware only of herself, the self suppressed, repressed for years, now rearing up to shatter her. She grips his arm fiercely, completely unaware of what she's doing.

"We're leaving...We're leaving tomorrow...forever...I'll never come back, never...You hear, never again...Never...No, I can't bear it...never...never." She's feverish, the engineer thinks, look how her whole body is shaking. She's sick, I have to get a doctor right away. But she clutches the flesh of his arm savagely. "But why, I don't know why...Why do I have to go so suddenly...Something must have happened...I don't know what. At lunch they were both so nice and said nothing about it, and this evening...this evening they said I have to leave tomorrow...tomorrow, tomorrow morning...right away, and I don't know why...why I have to go away so suddenly...away...away, like some useless thing you toss out the window...I don't know why, I don't know...I don't understand it...Something must have happened."

Ah, the engineer thinks. It's all clear now. Just a while ago he'd gotten a report of the talk that was going around about the van Boolens and was shocked despite himself; he'd almost asked her to marry him! But now he realizes that her uncle and aunt are sending the poor thing away as fast as they possibly can so she won't cause further embarrassment. The bombshell has dropped.

Keep out of it, he reflects quickly. Change the subject! He ventures a few generalities: Oh, surely that's not the last word, maybe her relatives will reconsider, and next year...But Christine isn't listening or thinking. Her pain has to come out, a child's rage, and she stamps her foot. "But I don't want to! I don't want to...I'm not going home now...What will I do there, I can't stand it now...I can't...That'll be the end of me...I'll lose my mind there...I swear to you, I can't, I can't, and I don't want to...Help me...Help me!"

It's the cry of someone drowning, shrill and half choking, her voice flooded by tears, a fit that shakes her so much that his own body absorbs it. "No, don't cry," he pleads, moved despite himself, automatically drawing her closer to soothe her. She slumps against his chest, out of sheer exhaustion, just to have a living person to lean on, someone to stroke her hair, so she isn't so terribly, helplessly alone and rejected. Bit by bit the convulsive sobbing subsides, becoming more inward, a quiet weeping.

To him this is strange: here he is hidden in the shadows just twenty paces from the hotel (someone might see them, might walk by any time), holding a sobbing young woman in his arms, feeling the warmth of her heedlessly pressed up against him. He's overcome with sympathy, and a man's sympathy for a suffering woman is always tender. Just soothe her, he thinks, calm her down! With his left hand (she's still holding on to his right hand to keep from falling) he strokes her hair, bends to kiss it to still the sobs, then her temples, and finally her mouth. But what she says is wild.

"Take me with you, take me along... Let's go... wherever you want... Let's just go and never come back... Not back home... I can't bear it... Anywhere, just not back here... Anything but back here... Wherever you want, for however long you want... Let's just go!" She shakes his arm like a tree. "Take me along!"

Break it off, thinks the sensible engineer, now alarmed. Break it off, quickly and decisively. Calm her down somehow, take her back inside, or things will get awkward.

"Yes, darling," he says. "Of course... But it's no good rushing into things... We'll talk it over. Why don't you sleep on it... Maybe your relatives will change their minds and regret what they said... Things will be clearer tomorrow." But she quivers urgently: "No, not tomorrow, not tomorrow! Tomorrow I'll have to leave, tomorrow morning... They're pushing me away... Sending me off like a package, express mail, special delivery... I won't be sent away like that... I won't..." And, taking hold of him more fiercely: "Take me with you... right away... Help me... I... I can't bear it any longer."

This has to stop, the engineer thinks. Don't get mixed up in it. She's not in her right mind, she doesn't know what she's saying. "Yes, yes, dear, of course," he says, stroking her hair, "I understand...We'll talk it all over inside, not here, you can't stay here any longer...You might catch cold...in that thin dress without a coat...Come along, we'll go in and sit in the lounge..." He carefully removes his arm. "Come on now, dear."

Christine stops sobbing and stares at him. She hasn't heard or understood a word, but her body knows the warm arm is gone. She knows physically, instinctively, and finally intellectually that this man is withdrawing, that he's cowardly, cautious, and afraid, that everyone here wants her gone, all of them. Now she snaps out of it. "Thank you," she says shortly. "Thank you, I'll go on my own. Forgive me, I was feeling out of sorts for a moment. My aunt was right: the air up here isn't good for me."

He starts to say something but she ignores him and goes on ahead, her shoulders rigid. Just so I never see his face again, no one's, never see any of them again, be gone, never again humiliate myself in front of these arrogant, cowardly, self-satisfied people, get out of here, take nothing more from them, no more gifts, never be taken in again, never betray myself to them, any of them, anyone, go, better to die in some corner. And as she moves through the hotel that dazzled her before, through the lounge she adored, past the people like so many painted and well-dressed stones, she feels only one thing: hate for him, for everyone here, for all of them.

All night Christine sits motionless in the chair by the table, her thoughts revolving dully around the feeling that everything is over; not an actual pain so much as a drugged awareness of something painful going on deep down—the way a patient under anesthesia might be aware of the surgeon's knife cutting into him. She sits there in silence, empty eyes on the table, but something's happening, something beyond her benumbed awareness: that new creature, the manufactured changeling that had taken her place for nine dreamlike days, that unreal yet real Fräulein von Boolen, is dying in her. She's still sitting in that other woman's room, with that other woman's pearls around her frozen neck, a bold slash of red lipstick on her lips; the beloved dragonfly-light gown is still on her shoulders, but now it's like a winding-sheet. It's no longer hers, nothing here, nothing in this other, exalted, more blessed realm belongs to her anymore, it's all as borrowed and alien as on the first day. Nearby is the bed, smoothly made up with its white flowered coverlet, soft and warm, but she doesn't lie down: it's no longer hers. The gleaming furniture, the gently suspiring carpet, the brass, silk, and glass on every side, none of it belongs to her now. The gloves on her hands, the pearls around her neck, everything belongs to that other one, that murdered doppel-gänger Christiane von Boolen who is no more, yet lives on. She tries to push the artificial self aside and find the real one again; she forces herself to think about her mother, keep in mind that she's sick or maybe even dead, but no matter how she prods she can't muster any pang or feeling of concern. One feeling drowns out all the others, a boundless rage, a dull, clenched, impotent rage without outlet or object (her aunt, her mother, fate), the rage of someone who has suffered an injustice. All she knows is that something has been taken from her, that now she must leave that blissfully winged self to become a blind grub crawling on the ground; knows only that something is gone forever.

She sits all through the night, frozen with fury. None of the life of the hotel reaches her through the upholstered doors; she doesn't hear the untroubled breathing of sleepers, the moans of lovers, the groans of the sick, the restless pacing of the sleepless, doesn't hear through the closed glass door the morning breeze that's already blowing outside; she's aware only that she's alone in the room, the building, all of creation, a bit of breathing, twitching flesh like a severed finger still warm yet without feeling or strength. It's a cruel death-in-life, a gradual freezing to death; she sits rigidly as though listening for the moment when that warm von Boolen heart will finally stop beating. Morning comes after a thousand years. The staff can be heard sweeping the hallways, the gardener is raking the gravel in front of the hotel. It's beginning, inescapably: day, the end, the departure. Now she must pack her things, leave, be that other, Postal Official Hoflehner of Klein-Reifling, forget the one whose breath had quickened to see the finery that is now no longer hers.

Christine gets up stiffly. She's exhausted, light-headed; the four steps to the armoire seem like a great journey. She weakly pulls the door open and is shocked to see the Klein-Reifling dress and the hated blouse she came in, dangling there as white and ghastly as a hanged man. Taking them off the rod she shudders as if touching a dead thing. She is going to have to get back into that dead Hoflehner person! But there's no choice. The dress rustles like satiny paper as she takes it off. One after another she sets aside all the other new clothes, the underthings, the sweater, the pearls, the ten or twenty pretty things she's acquired. The shabby straw suitcase is quickly packed. She takes only the genuine gifts, a mere handful that fit easily.

Done. She surveys the room again. Dress, dancing shoes, belt, pink chemise, sweater, gloves—all lie helter-skelter on the bed as though an explosion had ripped that fantastic creature Fräulein von Boolen to shreds. Christine shudders at the remains of the phantom that she was. She looks around to make sure she hasn't forgotten anything that belongs to her. But nothing does. Others will sleep in this bed, others will see the golden landscape through this window, others will see themselves reflected in this mirror, but not her, never again. This isn't goodbye, this is dying.

The hallways are still empty as she steps out with her ancient little suitcase. She goes to the stairs automatically, but in her poor clothes she feels that she, Christine Hoflehner, no longer has the right to use the carpeted, brass-railed steps, the grand staircase. Instead she takes the winding cast-iron servants' stairs near the lavatory. In the lobby downstairs, gray and only half cleaned, the nodding night clerk starts up suspiciously. What was that? A young woman, indifferently or even poorly dressed, a shabby suitcase in hand, is darting shamefacedly to the door like a shadow, without a word to him. He leaps forward and blocks the revolving door with a shoulder.

"Excuse me, where do you wish to go?"

"I'm leaving on the seven o'clock train." The clerk is stunned to realize that a hotel guest (a lady!) wants to carry her own luggage to the station. He asks suspiciously, "May I...may I have your room number?"

Christine understands now. Ah, the man takes her for an intruder. And he's right too! But the thought doesn't anger her. On the contrary, she has an unpleasant desire to be mistreated. Give me trouble, make it hard for me, all the better. She answers calmly, "Room 286, billed to my uncle, Anthony van Boolen. Christine Hoflehner."

"One moment." The night clerk releases the door to check his book, but she feels his eye on her. Then he gives a nervous bow and says politely, his tone different now, "Oh, madam, I beg your pardon, I see the day clerk was informed that you'd be checking out...I thought, because it's so early...and also...madam will surely not be taking her own luggage, the car will bring it twenty minutes before the train leaves. Please proceed to the breakfast room. Madam has plenty of time for breakfast."

"No, nothing more. Goodbye!" She leaves without a glance. He gazes after her in astonishment, shakes his head, and goes back to his desk.

Nothing more. Good. Nothing, from anyone. She keeps her eyes down as she walks to the station, the suitcase in one hand, the umbrella in the other. The mountains are already bright and in a moment the blue will break through the restless clouds, the wonderful gentian blue of the Engadine that, without putting a name to it, Christine loved, but perversely she keeps her eyes down, to see nothing more, receive nothing more, from anyone, even God. She doesn't want to see it, doesn't want to be reminded that from now on and forever these mountains are for other people, the playing fields and the games, the hotels and their glittering rooms, the thundering avalanches and the hushed forests, not for her, ever again! As she passes in her cheap raincoat, with her old umbrella, on her way to the station, she averts her eyes from the tennis courts, where, she knows, proud bronzed people in glowing white, cigarettes in their mouths, will soon be exercising their supple limbs; from the shops, still closed, with their thousands of luxuries (for other people, other people), the hotels and markets and cafés. Away from here, away from here. Don't look, forget it all.

At the station she hides in the third-class waiting room. Here in the eternal third class, the same all over the world, with its hard benches, its shabby neutrality, she feels almost at home. When the train pulls in, she hurries to board: no one must see her or recognize her. But suddenly she hears her name—is it a hallucination? Hoflehner, Hoflehner. Someone's calling her name, her hated name—is it possible?—the length of the train. She trembles. Is someone still jeering at her, even as she's leaving? But it comes again clearly, so she leans out the window. The desk clerk is standing there waving a telegram. She must excuse him, he says, it came yesterday evening, but the night clerk didn't know where to deliver it; he just now learned that madam was leaving. Christine opens the envelope. "Sudden deterioration, come quickly, Fuchsthaler." And then the train leaves... It's over. Everything is over.

There's an inherent limit to the stress that any material can bear. Water has its boiling point, metals their melting points. The elements of the spirit behave the same way. Happiness can reach a pitch so great that any further happiness can't be felt. Pain, despair, humiliation, disgust, and fear are no different. Once the vessel is full, the world can't add to it.

Thus the telegram causes Christine no new distress. Her intelligence grasps clearly that she ought to feel shock, alarm, anxiety, but however alert she is the emotions don't function. They don't acknowledge the message, don't respond, like a numb leg that the doctor sticks with a needle. The patient sees the needle, knows perfectly well that it's sharp, knows it will hurt terribly as it goes in, and he tenses for a pain that must convulse him. But the glowing needle goes in, the paralyzed nerve doesn't respond, and the patient realizes with horror that part of his body has no feeling, that he's carrying a little bit of death in his own warm body. In the same way Christine is horrified by her indifference as she reads and rereads the letter. Mother's ill, she must be in a desperate state or those penny-pinchers back home wouldn't have spent so much on a telegram. Maybe she's already dead, chances are she is. But not a finger trembles, her eyes remain dry, though just yesterday the mere thought had overwhelmed her. Total paralysis—a paralysis that spreads to everything around her. She doesn't notice the rhythmic clangor of the train beneath her, the red-faced men eating wurst and laughing on the wooden seat opposite her, the cliffs outside the window becoming little hills covered with flowers and washing their feet in the white froth of streams—all these prospects, so vivid on Christine's first journey, are numb to her numb eyes. When the passport official barges in at the border she finally feels something: she wants something hot to drink, something to thaw out this terrible frozenness a little, relax her clenched and seemingly swollen throat, so that she can breathe, let it out at last.

She goes to the station buffet and has a glass of tea with rum; it burns in her bloodstream and revives the numb brain cells so she can think again. It occurs to her now that she should wire ahead to tell them when she'll be arriving. Just around the corner to the right, the porter says, you have plenty of time.

At the counter the window is closed, so she raps on it. Reluctant footsteps approach and the window goes up with a clatter. "What is it?" says a woman in glasses with a peevish gray face. Christine is too shocked to respond immediately. This weathered fossil of an old maid with tired eyes behind steel-rimmed spectacles and parchmenty fingers automatically handing her the form might be Christine herself in ten or twenty years—seen now in some diabolical mirror. Her fingers tremble and she has difficulty writing. That's me, that's what I'll be, she thinks, shuddering as she sneaks looks at the dried-out woman waiting patiently behind the counter, head bowed, pencil in her hand—oh, she knows that gesture, the tedium of those minutes of waiting, how you die a little with each one that passes, becoming old, all for nothing, hapless and used up like this mirror-phantom. Christine struggles back to the train, her knees weak. Her forehead is beaded with cold sweat, like a dreamer who sees himself dead in a coffin and wakes with a cry of fear.

When Christine hauls her sore limbs out of the train at St. Pölten, tired from a sleepless night, someone hurries toward her across the track: Fuchsthaler the teacher, who must have been waiting all night. One look and Christine knows it all. He's dressed in black, with a black tie, and as she reaches her hand toward him he gives it a sympathetic shake, his eyes helpless behind his glasses. Christine asks no questions. His discomfiture has said it all. But she's oddly unmoved. She feels no pain, no grief, no surprise. Her mother is dead. Maybe it's good to be dead.

On the local train to Klein-Reifling Fuchsthaler gives a tactful but complete account of her mother's last hours. He looks
bleary, gray in the gray morning, his face stubbly, his clothes
rumpled and dusty. He went to her mother's on her behalf three,
four times every day, kept vigil on her behalf at night. Kind
friend, she thinks silently. If only he'd stop, shut up, leave her
alone, stop talking at her in that sentimental choked-up voice
through those yellow, poorly mended teeth. She's ashamed of
the physical aversion she now feels for a man who seemed so
likable before, but the feeling is so strong it's like bile on her
lips.

Despite herself she's comparing him with the men up there,
those slim, tanned, healthy, sleek gentlemen with manicured
hands and coats with narrow waists. With a kind of malicious
curiosity she notes the laughable details of his mourning getup,
the obviously turned cuffs and collar of his coat, its threadbare
elbows, the off-the-rack black tie over the cheap dirty shirt. This
skinny little man dressed in black strikes her as intolerably lower
middle class, ridiculous beyond words, this village schoolmaster
with his white protruding ears, his scanty, carelessly parted hair,
his red-rimmed pale-blue eyes behind steel-framed spectacles,
his shrewlike parchmenty face above the crushed yellow celluloid collar. And he wanted...he...No, she thinks, never.
There's no way she could let him touch her, submit to the
timid, undignified, tremulous affections of this deacon-like
little man, in those clothes—impossible. The very thought of
it revolts her.

Fuchsthaler breaks off. "What is it?" he asks with concern.
He's seen her shudder.

"Nothing...nothing...I'm just too tired, I guess. I can't
talk now. I can't pay attention to anything."

Christine leans back and closes her eyes. She feels better as
soon as she doesn't have to look at him or listen to the soft
consoling voice, made unbearable by her own humiliation. It's

terrible, she thinks, he's being so kind, he's sacrificed himself. But I can't look at him anymore, can't bear him, I can't. Not these people, not a man like him. Never.

At the open grave the minister runs through the prayer quickly: rain is falling hard, straight down. The gravediggers, shovels in their hands, shift impatiently from one foot to the other in the mud. The downpour becomes heavier and the minister speaks faster. Finally it's over, and the fourteen people who had accompanied the old woman to the churchyard head back wordlessly to the village, almost at a run. Christine is again horrified at herself: she felt nothing during the ceremony, but was preoccupied with tiny annoyances. That she wasn't wearing galoshes; last year she wanted to buy some and mother said it wasn't necessary, Christine could borrow hers. That Fuchsthaler's turned-up coat collar is frayed and worn on the inside. That her brother-in-law Franz has grown fat and wheezes asthmatically whenever he exerts himself. That her sister-in-law's umbrella is tattered, she really should have the fabric replaced. That the grocer lady didn't send a wreath, just a few wilted flowers from her front garden, tied with a piece of wire. That Herdlitschka the baker has had a new signboard made while she was gone. Everything hideous, narrow, disagreeable about this little world she's been pushed back into digs in its barbs until she can't even feel her own pain.

In front of her apartment the mourners say goodbye and, spattered with mud, go sprinting home underneath their umbrellas. Only her sister, her brother-in-law, her brother's widow, and her brother's widow's second husband, a cabinetmaker, climb the creaky stairs to her apartment. There are five of them including Christine, but only four places to sit. The place is uncomfortably cramped and dreary; a damp, musty smell comes from the hanging wet coats and dripping umbrellas. The rain drums on the windows. The dead woman's empty gray bed waits in the shadows.

No one speaks. Out of embarrassment, Christine says, "You'll have some coffee?"

"Yes, Christl," says her brother-in-law, "something hot would be nice. But you'd better be quick because we can't stay long, our train leaves at five." He sighs, a Virginia cigar in his mouth. He's a good-natured, jovial municipal official with a premature paunch (he began putting it on as a baggage-train sergeant during the war and it's been growing more rapidly in peacetime). He only feels at ease when he's at home in his shirt-sleeves; throughout the ceremony he was standing at attention with a conscientiously doleful expression, but now he partly unbuttons the black mourning jacket (it looks like a disguise on him) and leans back comfortably: "It was a good idea not to bring the children. Nelly thought they ought to be at their grandmother's funeral, but I said children shouldn't see sad things like that, they can't understand them yet anyway. And after all the trip here and back is so horribly expensive, a whole lot of money, and in times like these..."

Christine is working hard at the coffee mill. Back five hours and already she's heard it ten times—"too expensive," that accursed refrain. Fuchsthaler thought it would have been too expensive to bring the chief physician from St. Pölten Hospital, said he couldn't have done anything anyway; her sister-in-law said it about the cross for the grave, a stone one would be "too expensive"; her sister said it about the requiem mass; and now her brother-in-law is saying it about the trip. The same phrase on everyone's lips like the rain on the eaves, washing all joy away. It's going to be a constant drip, drip, drip every day: too expensive, too expensive, too expensive! Christine trembles with fury as she works the mill. If she could only get away from here, stop having to see and hear this! The others are sitting quietly around the table as they wait for their coffee, trying to make conversation. The man who married her brother's widow, an unpretentious cabinetmaker from Favoriten, sits with his head down among his half relations; he didn't know the old woman at all. The conversation lurches from question to answer without going anywhere, as though something were blocking the way. Finally the coffee is ready—a distraction. Christine sets down four cups (all she has) and goes back to the window. The embarrassed silence among the four of them is suffocating, an oddly restrained silence clumsily concealing one thought and one only. She knows what's coming, feels it in her bones. Out in the hall she saw that each of them had brought two empty rucksacks. She knows, she knows what's coming now, and is choking with disgust.

Finally her brother-in-law begins, in his pleasant voice. "What a downpour! And that absentminded Nelly didn't even bring an umbrella. The simplest thing would be for you to give her your mother's to take along, Christl! Or do you need it for yourself?" "No," says Christine from the window and shudders. It's coming, any minute now. Just let it be quick.

"Actually," her sister puts in, as though it had been planned beforehand, "wouldn't it be the most sensible thing to go ahead and divide up Mother's things now? Who knows when the five of us will be together again, Franz is at work so much, and you too, I'm sure" (she turns to the cabinetmaker). "And it wouldn't be worth making another special trip here, that would cost more money. I think it's best to divide everything up now, don't you agree, Christl?"

"Of course." Her voice is hoarse. "But please divide everything up among yourselves. You have two children, you can put Mother's things to much better use. I don't need anything, I won't take anything. Just divide it all up among yourselves."

She unlocks the trunk, takes out a few threadbare garments, and puts them on the dead woman's bed (warm just yesterday; there's nowhere else in the cramped attic room). It's not much: a few linens, the old fox fur, the mended coat, a tartan traveling rug, an ivory-handled walking stick, the inlaid brooch from Venice, the wedding ring, the little silver watch and chain, the rosary and enamel medallion from Maria Zell, then the stockings, the shoes, the felt slippers, the underthings, an old fan, a crushed hat, and the dog-eared prayer book. She omits none of the old pawnshop junk, the old woman had so little, then goes quickly back to the window and stares out into the rain. Behind her the two women are speaking in hushed tones, estimating the value of the items before coming to terms. Christine's sister's take goes on the right side of the dead woman's bed and her sister-in-law's on the left, separated by an invisible wall.

Christine is breathing heavily at the window. No matter how low their voices are, she can hear their appraising and haggling; even with her back turned she can see their fingers at work. Her rage is mixed with pity. "How poor they are, so wretchedly poor, and they have no idea. This junk they split up, that junk they hang on to; these shreds of old flannel and worn-out shoes, these horribly ridiculous rags are treasures to them! What do they know about the world? Do they have any inkling? But it might be better not to know you're so poor, so disgustingly poor and wretched."

Her brother-in-law comes up. "Fair's fair, Christl, you can't take nothing at all. You've got to keep something to remember your mother by—the watch, maybe, or at least the chain."

"No," she says firmly, "I don't want anything, I won't take anything. You've got children, that's the point. I don't need anything. I don't need a thing anymore."

When she turns around again, it's all over; her sister-in-law and her sister have wrapped up their shares and put them in the rucksacks. Now the dead woman is really buried. The four of them stand around, embarrassed and somewhat shamefaced. They're glad the awkward business has been taken care of so quickly and agreeably, but they don't feel entirely at ease. Before the train leaves they'll have to find something solemn to say to dispel the memory of the wheeling and dealing, or perhaps just talk among themselves like relatives. At last Christine's brother-in-law has a thought and asks her, "So you haven't told us, what was it like up there in Switzerland?"

"Very nice," she brings out through her teeth, hard as a knife.

"I believe it," her brother-in-law says with a sigh, "we'd all like to go there sometime—go anywhere! But you can't manage it with a wife and two children, it would be too expensive, forget about going to a posh place like that. How much do they charge for a night in your hotel?"

"I don't know," Christine whispers with the last of her strength. She feels her nerves are about to snap. If only they were gone, gone! Thankfully Franz looks at his watch. "Oh oh, all aboard, we have to get to the station. But Christl, don't put yourself out, no need to see us off in weather like this. Stay here now and come to Vienna sometime! Now that Mother's dead, we've got to stick together."

"Yes, yes," Christine says with stony impatience and goes with them as far as the door. They're all loaded down with things on their shoulders or in their hands and the wooden steps creak under their weight. At last they've gone. Christine throws the window open. The smell is suffocating, the smell of stale cigarette smoke, bad food, wet clothes, the smell of the old woman's dread and worry and wheezing, the awful smell of poverty. How terrible it is to have to live here, and why, who's it for? Why breathe this in day after day, knowing that there's another world out there somewhere, the real one, and in herself another person, who is suffocating, being poisoned, in this miasma. Her nerves are jangling. She throws herself down onto the bed fully clothed, biting down hard on the pillow to keep from screaming with helpless hatred. Because suddenly she hates everyone and everything, herself and everyone else, wealth and poverty, everything about this hard, unendurable, incomprehensible life.

PART TWO

"STUCK-UP HUSSY. HOW OBNOXIOUS!" Michael Pointner the grocer banged the door shut behind him. "The audacity of that sharp-tongued creature! I've never heard of such a thing. What a witch."

Herdlitschka the baker was waiting for him in front of the post office. "Now, now, don't get excited. What is it this time," he said soothingly, smiling broadly. "Did somebody bite you?"

"But it's true. Of all the nerve! In all my life I've never seen such unmitigated gall. Every time it's something different. She doesn't like this, she doesn't like that. All she wants is to be a pain and act sniffy. The day before yesterday it was because I used pencil instead of pen on the customs form for the candles. Today she tells me she's in charge here and she doesn't have to accept poor packaging. What if she is in charge? My word, before she started sticking her silly nose in I must have mailed a thousand packages. And the sound of her, so la-di-da, such fancy German, to show us we're clods next to her. Who does she think she's talking to? But I've had it. She's not going to put on that act with me."

Fat Herdlitschka's eyes gleamed with complacent *schadenfreude*. "Well, maybe she just felt like it, you're such a dashing fellow. You never know where you are with those ladies-in-waiting. Maybe she's taken a shine to you and that's why she's being a pain."

"Please, no stupid jokes," the grocer said sullenly. "I'm not the only one she goes after. Only yesterday the administrator of the plant was telling me she snapped at him just because he was kidding her a little. 'I won't have that, I'm in charge here'—as though he were her shoeshine boy. The devil's gotten into her, something's wrong. But I'll drive him out again, you can depend on it. She'll take a different tone with me or she'll be sorry. I'm going to have a word with somebody in the head office if I have to walk to Vienna."

Pointner was right. Something was wrong with Postal Official Christine Hoflehner. The entire village had known it for two weeks. At first no one said anything. My God, the poor girl lost her mother—that's what's bothering her, people thought. The minister had stopped by twice to comfort her; every day Fuchsthaler asked if there was anything he could do; the next-door neighbor offered to sit with her in the evening to keep her company; the woman at the Golden Ox had even asked if she didn't want to board there so she wouldn't have to maintain her own household. But she hadn't even given them a proper answer, and everyone had felt she just wanted to get rid of them. Something was wrong with Postal Official Christine Hoflehner. She hadn't been going to the choral society once a week as she used to; she said she was hoarse. She hadn't been to church for three weeks, hadn't even had a mass said for her mother. She told Fuchsthaler, who wanted to read to her, that she had a headache, and when he offered to walk with her she said she was tired. No one spoke to her now; when she did her shopping she acted as if she was rushing to catch a train and said nothing to anyone, and at work, where she'd been known for her courtesy and helpfulness, she was now invariably aloof, brusque, and overbearing.

Something had happened to her; she knew it herself. It was as though someone had sprinkled some venom into her eyes while she slept, so that now she saw the world in its light: everything was ugly, malignant, and hostile when viewed with malignant and hostile eyes. She began every day in a rage. The first thing she saw when she opened her eyes was the steep smoke-stained beams of her attic room. Everything in it—the old bed, the poor quilt, the wicker chair, the washstand with the cracked jug, the peeling wallpaper, the wooden floorboards—it was all odious. She would have liked to close her eyes and sink back into the dark. But the alarm clock wouldn't permit it, clamoring loudly in her ears. She got up furiously, got dressed furiously: the old underthings, the repulsive black dress. She noticed a tear under one of the sleeves, but let it go. She didn't take up the needle to mend it. Why? Who would it be for? For these hicks, anything's too fancy. Don't bother with that, just get out of this hideous room and go to the office.

But the office had changed too—it was no longer the neutral restful room where the hours rolled slowly and noiselessly by as though on wheels. Whenever she turned the key and entered the terrible silence that seemed to be lying in wait for her, she'd remember a scene from a film she'd seen last year. *Life Sentence*, it had been called. A jailer, full-bearded, hard and aloof, accompanied by two policemen, was leading the prisoner, a frail, frightened youth, into a bare, barred cell. She and everyone else in the audience had shivered to see it, and she shivered now. That was her, jailer and prisoner in one. For the first time she'd noticed that these windows were barred too, and for the first time she'd begun seeing the office with its bare whitewashed walls as a dungeon. Everything in it had a new meaning. A thousand times she looked at the chair she sat on, the ink-stained table where she kept her papers, the wicket that she raised when the workday began. For the first time she saw that the clock never advanced, but ran in circles—from twelve to one, from one to two, and on to twelve, and then the same thing again, always the same progression without any progress, wound up again and again for the day's work without ever getting a break, imprisoned in the same rectangular brown housing. And when at eight in the morning Christine sat down, she was tired—tired not from something achieved and accomplished, but tired in anticipation of everything ahead, the same faces, the same questions, the same chores, the same money. After precisely fifteen minutes, Andreas Hinterfellner the postman, gray-haired but buoyant as ever, brought the mail for sorting. She used to do it mechanically, but now she spent a long time looking at the letters and postcards, especially those addressed to Countess Gütersheim in her castle. The countess had three daughters. One was married to an Italian baron; the other two were single and traveled widely. The most recent cards came from Sorrento. Radiant arcs of blue sea sweeping into the landscape. Hôtel de Rome was the address. Christine tried to imagine the Hôtel de Rome and looked for it on the card. The young countess had made an *X* to show where her room was, among the broad terraces of luminous gardens and surrounded by espaliered orange trees. Christine imagined walking there in the evening, a cool breeze blowing from the blue sea, the rocks still giving off the warmth of the day, walking with...

But there was mail to sort. Onward, onward. Here was a letter from Paris, which she knew right away was from the daughter of ———, the subject of all sorts of nasty rumors. She'd been mixed up with a Jewish oil baron, then she was a taxi dancer somewhere, and to top it off she was supposed to be with someone else now; and in fact the letter came from the Hotel Maurice, on the fanciest stationery. Christine tossed it away furiously. Next the printed matter. She set aside a few items addressed to Countess Gütersheim. *Lady*, *Elegant Life*, and the rest of the illustrated fashion magazines—what difference would it make if the Countess got them in the afternoon delivery? When the office was quiet she removed the magazines from their wrappers and opened them up, staring at the clothes, the pictures of actors and aristocrats, the well-tended country houses of English lords, the cars that belonged to famous artists. She inhaled it all like perfume, remembering. Her fingers shook nervously as she examined the women and their gowns with interest and looked almost passionately at the men, their extraordinary faces burnished by their lives of luxury or illuminated by intelligence. She put the magazines away only to take them out again. Curiosity and hate, desire and envy alternated in her as she gazed at this world that was at once so far away and so familiar.

Then she'd be startled when a peasant clomped with heavy shoes into this world of seductive images, his pipe clamped between his teeth, his eyes bovine and sleepy, to ask for a few stamps, and reflexively she'd find something to dress him down for. "Can't you read? No smoking!" she'd fling into the amiably bewildered face, or some other sharp remark. It would be out before she knew it, as though she were driven to wreak vengeance for the ugliness and wretchedness of her world. Afterward she'd be ashamed. The poor fellows can't help being repulsive, uncouth, filthy from their work, up to their necks in the mud of their village, she thought. I'm no different. I'm just the same. But her despair was hardly separate from her fury, which came out at any opportunity. In accordance with the law of conservation of energy, she had to relieve the strain somehow, and from this one position of power, her pitiful little counter, she discharged it at the expense of innocent people. Up there in that other world she'd been courted and desired— that had been an acknowledgment of her existence; here she didn't exist unless she was angry, unless she was wielding her tiny bit of official authority. It was sad, it was deplorable, it was petty, lording it over these unsuspecting good people, she knew that, but it got rid of some of her pent-up fury for a moment. If there was no one to vent it on, it came out against mute objects. A thread wouldn't go through the eye of the needle— she snapped it. A drawer wouldn't close—she slammed it shut with all her strength. The head office sent her the wrong consignments—she wrote an outraged, belligerent letter instead of a polite one. A telephone call didn't go through right away—she threatened her colleague with an immediate official reprimand. She knew it was pathetic and she was horrified at how she'd changed. But she couldn't help her hatred—she'd choke on it if she didn't find some way to cast it out into the world.

When work was over she fled back to her room. Before, she used to stroll for a bit while her mother was sleeping, or chat with the grocer woman or play with the neighbor's children; now she shut herself in behind her four walls, hiding her resentment away so she wouldn't snarl at people like a vicious dog. She couldn't bear to look at the street with its unchanging houses and faces. The women seemed ridiculous to her in their full gingham skirts, with their greasy hair piled on top of their heads and their plump hands covered with rings, the heavy-breathing, potbellied men unbearable, and, most repellent of all, the boys with their pomaded hair and citified airs. The tavern, reeking of beer and smoke, was unendurable, and the strapping girl who submitted to the lascivious embraces and jokes of the forest ranger's assistant and the policeman struck her as a ruddy-cheeked idiot. She preferred to shut herself up in her room, leaving the lamps unlit so she wouldn't see the hated things in it. She sat in silence, brooding, always about the same thing. Her memories were incredibly vivid and sharp, with innumerable details that she hadn't noticed or felt at the time amid the whirl of activity. She remembered every word, every glance. The flavors of everything she'd eaten were powerfully there; she could taste the wines and liqueurs on her lips. She remembered the sheerness and the silkiness of the dress on her bare shoulders and the softness of the white bed. All sorts of things came back to her, like the funny dogged way the little Englishman followed her down the hallway in the evening and paused in front of her door. The skin prickled on her arm as she remembered the Mannheim girl's affectionate caresses, and it occurred to her that women were supposed to be able to fall in love with each other. Hour after hour she recapitulated every second of every day of that time; how full of wasted opportunities it had been, she realized now. So she sat in silence every evening and dreamed of that time, what it had been like, knowing it was gone—not wanting to know but knowing nonetheless. If someone knocked at the door (Fuchsthaler made repeated attempts to console her), she froze and held her breath until she heard the footsteps creaking back down the staircase. Memories were all she had left, and she wouldn't give them up. Exhausted by them, she'd get into her bed and find herself startled by its coldness and dankness; her skin was spoiled now. She shivered so much that she had to pile her clothes and her coat on top of the covers. Finally, late at night, she'd fall asleep. But her sleep was not a good sleep; it was filled with anxious and fantastic dreams. She'd be climbing in a car, hurtling quickly, horribly quickly up and down the mountains, at once afraid of falling and exhilarated by the speed, and there was always a man next to her, the German or someone else, and he'd be holding her. She'd suddenly realize she was naked, and there would be people laughing. The car would falter, she'd shout at him to crank it up again, quickly, hurry, harder, harder, and at last deep within her she'd feel the thrust of the engine, and a flood of pure joy as it took off over the fields, into the dark wood, and then she wouldn't be naked anymore, but he'd be clasping her to him, more and more tightly, so that she groaned and thought she was dying. Then she'd wake up, sweaty and exhausted and with aching limbs, to see the garret roof, the smoke-stained, worm-eaten slanting beams, and the cobwebbed ceiling, and would lie in bed, tired and vacant, waiting for the implacable command of the alarm clock, and then she'd climb out of the hated old bed and into her hated old clothes to meet the hated day.

Christine kept to herself for four weeks in this morbidly overwrought and foul-tempered state. Then her dreams were spent, she'd recalled every last second of her experiences, the past could no longer sustain her. Tired, depleted, with a constant pain between her temples, she went to her work, doing it half consciously, asleep on her feet. In the evening sleep refused to come. Her nerves jangled in the quiet of the crypt-like garret; her body was hot in the cold bed. It had become unendurable. She suddenly felt an overpowering desire to look through another window at something other than the hideous tavern signboard of the Golden Ox, sleep in another bed, experience something else, be someone else for a few hours. She was roused to action: on Friday she took the two hundred-franc notes left over from her uncle's winnings out of the drawer, put on her best dress and her best shoes; she went straight from work to the station and bought a ticket to Vienna.

She didn't know why she was going there, had no clear idea what she wanted, other than to get away, away from the village, from her work, from herself, from the person she was condemned to be. She just wanted to feel wheels turning beneath her again, see lights, see different people, ones with more intelligence and style, to put up some resistance to the whims of chance, not be trampled underfoot; to move again, feel the world and herself, to be a different person, not the same old one.

It was seven in the evening when she arrived in Vienna. She left her suitcase at a small hotel on Mariahilfer Strasse and quickly found her way to a hairdresser's before the shutters rolled down. She had a mad hope that a pair of skilled hands and a bit of red would do it again, would turn her into the person she'd been. Again the waves of warmth spilled over her; again the clever hands caressed her hair. Lipstick deftly redrew the lips that had once been desired and kissed. Some color brightened her cheeks and a shadow of powder on her pale tired face conjured up her Engadine tan. When she stood up in a cloud of fragrance, she felt the old power in her knees, and she went down the street confidently, her back straight; if her clothes had been right, she might have believed she was Fräulein von Boolen. There was still a late glow in the September sky. It was good to walk in the cool of the evening, and with excitement she registered the brush of an interested glance now and then. I'm still alive, she thought, I'm still here. Occasionally she paused in front of a shopwindow to look at the furs, the dresses, the shoes, her eyes burning through the glass. Perhaps I can do it again after all, she thought; her spirits rose. She walked along Mariahilfer Strasse and onto the Ringstrasse. Her eyes brightened as she looked at the people strolling there, chatting and carefree and a good many of them truly attractive. They're the same, she thought; there's not much between us. There's a way up somewhere, a little step to climb, you've just got to find it. She paused in front of the Opera. The performance was evidently about to begin, cars were driving up, blue, green, black, with glinting windows and shiny paint, to be met at the entrance by a liveried valet. Christine went into the foyer to look at the attendees. Strange, she thought, the papers talk about Viennese culture, the sophisticated public and the opera it's created—I'm twenty-eight years old now, I've lived here all my life and this is the first time I've been here. But I'm still on the outside, only in the foyer. Out of two million people, a mere hundred thousand have seen this building. The others read about it in the papers and hear about it and look at the pictures and they never dare to come in. And who are these people? She looked at the women, and was not just disturbed but indignant. No, they aren't any more beautiful than I was, they don't move more lightly and freely than I did, all they have are the gowns and the invisible advantage of their confidence. Just a short step up, another step inside, and she'd be with them; up the marble staircase and into the loge, into the gilded music box, into the carefree realm of pleasure.

The warning buzzer sounded and the late arrivals hurried to the cloakroom, taking off their coats as they went. The room was empty again and Christine heard the music starting. It was over; the invisible barrier came up again. She walked on. The white moons of streetlamps swayed over the Ring. The avenue was still filled with people. Christine followed the crowd along the Opernring, with no particular destination in mind. She stopped in front of a large hotel, as though drawn to it. A car had just driven up. The liveried bellhops rushed out for the suitcases and handbag of a somewhat Oriental-looking lady and the revolving door swallowed her up. The door was like a whirlpool; Christine was unable to resist a desire to observe the longed-for world for a minute. I'm going to go in, she thought, what could happen to me if I ask the desk clerk whether Frau van Boolen from New York has arrived, it ought to be possible. Just one look, only one, to bring it all back, to really make it come back, to be that other person for a moment. She went in. The desk clerk was talking to the woman who had just arrived. No one stopped Christine from walking through the vestibule, looking at everything. Gentlemen in smart, well-tailored traveling clothes or smoking jackets and handsome little patent leather slippers sat in the armchairs, smoking cigarettes and chatting. In an alcove sat a conclave of three young women loudly haranguing two young men in French, laughing all the while, that careless casual laughter, that music of the carefree that she found so intoxicating. At the rear of the hotel was a broad marble-columned court, the dining room. Waiters in tails kept watch at the entrance. I could go in and eat, Christine thought, automatically checking the leather handbag for the two hundred-franc bills and the seventy schillings that she'd brought. I can eat here, what will it cost? If I could just sit in a big room again, be waited on, looked at, admired, pampered. And the music, here too there was music coming from inside, breezy and low. But the old fear was back. She didn't have the right dress, the talisman that would open the door. She felt uncertain, and the invisible barrier rose again, that impassable magic pentagram of fear. Her shoulders shook and she left the hotel quickly as though fleeing from it. No one had stopped her. No one had even seen her, and that made her feel even weaker than before.

She continued along the streets. Where should I go? Where am I now? The streets were gradually emptying out. A few people hurried past, intent on getting their dinners. I'll go into some café, Christine thought, not a fancy restaurant where everyone will look at me. Some bright place full of people. She found one and went in. Almost all the tables were taken, but she found an empty one and sat down. No one took any notice of her. The waiter brought her something and she chewed it nervously and indifferently. I came for this, she thought, what am I doing here? You can't sit looking at the tablecloth. Ordering and eating only takes so long, you've got to get up sometime and go on. But where? It's only nine. A newspaper vendor came to her table—a welcome interruption. She bought two or three of the evening papers, not to read but to have something in front of her and look like she was busy, or maybe waiting for someone. She glanced through the news without interest. What did any of it matter, problems in forming the government, a murder and robbery in Berlin, stock market quotes, what's the point of this gossip about the singer at the Opera, whether she stays or goes or sings twenty times or seventy times a year, I'll never hear her. When she put the paper down, the bold heading ENTERTAINMENT on the back page leaped out at her. "What's on Tonight?" And underneath, things to do, theaters, dance halls, clubs. She picked up the newspaper nervously and read the ads. "Dance Music: Café Oxford"; "The Freddi Sisters, Carltonbar"; "Hungarian Gypsy Band"; "The Famous Negro Jazz Band, Open Until 3:00, Where Vienna's Best Society Meets!" It would be wonderful to be back among people who were enjoying themselves, to dance, relax, throw off her hated coat of armor. She made a note of a bar, two bars; both were nearby, the waiter told her.

She handed in her coat at the cloakroom, feeling better when the hated carapace was gone and she could hear the fast, aggressive music coming from below. She went down to the cellar. Disappointingly, it was mostly empty. Some white-jacketed lads in the orchestra were giving it all they had, apparently trying to make the few people sitting self-consciously at the tables get up and dance, but there was only a taxi dancer—plainly for hire, with hints of black eyeliner, a bit too soigné and too mincing in his dancing style—guiding one of the barmaids listlessly up and down the middle of the square dance floor. Fourteen or fifteen of the twenty tables were empty. One was occupied by three ladies, doubtless professionals, one with dyed ash-blond hair, another in a mannish outfit with a clinging overgarment cut like a smoking jacket over her black dress, the third a fat, heavy-breasted Jewess sipping whiskey through a straw. All three looked at her, their glances oddly appraising, and then began laughing quietly and whispering, their well-trained eyes having spotted her for a novice or a provincial. There were men sitting alone at a number of tables, apparently business travelers, ill-shaven, tired, and waiting for something to startle them out of their lethargy, slouched over coffee or little glasses of schnapps. Entering this place, Christine felt like someone who descends a flight of stairs only to step into empty space. She would have liked to turn around again, but the waiter swooped down, asking solicitously where the *gnädige Frau* would like to sit, so she took a seat somewhere and waited for something to happen like everyone else in this cold hot spot. One of the gentlemen (actually a dry goods agent from Prague) got up heavily at one point and hauled her around the floor before parking her again. Apparently he wasn't up to it, wasn't interested enough. In some way too he must have felt this strange woman's ambivalence, her odd indecisiveness, her willingness and unwillingness, and it was too much for him to deal with (he had to catch the express train back to Zagreb at 6:30 in the morning). But Christine sat there for an hour. By that time two new gentlemen had sat down with the ladies and were making conversation. She was the only one who was alone. Abruptly she summoned the waiter and paid. She was in a state of hopeless fury as she left, pursued by curious gazes.

Back onto the street. Night had fallen. She had no idea where she was going. Did it matter? Would it matter if someone grabbed her and tossed her into the canal, or if the car now braking on the bridge to avoid hitting this preoccupied pedestrian went ahead and ran her down? She didn't care now. She noticed suddenly that a policeman was giving her a funny look, as if he wanted to come over and ask her something. Maybe he took her for one of those women, she thought, the ones who slunk out of the shadows to accost men. She went on. I ought to go back home now. What am I doing here, what's the point of this? Abruptly she sensed a step behind her. A shadow appeared next to her, followed by its proprietor, who looked her full in the face. "Going home so soon, Fräulein?" She didn't answer. But the man didn't go away and he began to speak, insistently and cheerfully; she couldn't help feeling better. Didn't she want to go somewhere else? "No, I don't." "Come on, it's too early to go home. Just to a café." Finally she relented, just for the company. He was quite a nice fellow, a bank official, as he told her, but certainly married, she thought. In fact he had a ring on his finger. Well, so what, she just wanted a little company. Nothing wrong with absently listening to a few jokes. Now and then she glanced over at him. He was no longer young; he had crow's feet, and he looked overworked, exhausted, somehow rumpled and crushed, like a suit of clothes. But his talk was nice. For the first time she was talking with someone again, or letting him talk, yet she knew that wasn't what she wanted. And somehow his cheerfulness hurt her. A lot of what he said was amusing, but she felt the gall in her throat— gradually she was overcome by something like hatred for this stranger who was so happy and unconcerned while everything in her was mired in fury. When they left the café he took her arm and held it. That other man, in front of the hotel up there, had done the same thing, and the excitement scalding her now had nothing to do with this nattering little fellow next to her, but came from that other man, from a memory. Fear abruptly seized her. She might give herself to this stranger, throw herself at someone she didn't want at all, out of mere fury, out of impatience. Just then a taxi drove by and she raised her arm, tore herself away from the baffled man, and jumped in.

In the strange room she lay awake for a long time, listening to the traffic outside. It was over, she couldn't get around or through the invisible barrier. In sleepless agitation she lay in bed, listening to the coming and going of her breath and wondering why.

Sunday morning was as interminable as the confused and sleepless night. Most of the shops were closed, their allure hidden behind lowered shutters, so she killed time in a café, leafing through the newspapers. What had she been looking forward to? She'd forgotten why she came to Vienna, where no one was waiting for her, where no one wanted her. It occurred to her that she'd have to visit her sister and her brother-in-law sometime. She'd promised to pay them a visit, and of course she should. It would be best to go right after lunch, certainly not before, or they might think she was there for the food. Her sister was so strange now, ever since she'd had her children—she thought only of herself and scrimped on every soup bone. But there were still two hours, three hours until then. Wandering aimlessly, Christine noticed on the Ringstrasse that admission to the Gemäldegalerie was free today. She walked incuriously through the rooms, sat down on a velvet bench, watched the people, and continued on to a park, feeling lonelier every minute. At two o'clock, when she finally arrived at her brother-in-law's house, she was exhausted, as though she'd been wading through snowdrifts. At the front door she encountered the entire family, her brother-in-law, her sister, the two children, all clearly in their Sunday best and honestly glad to see her—that cheered her up a little. "Why, what a surprise! Just last week I was saying to Nelly that we ought to write to find out what's going on, because we never see you. You really should have been here for lunch, but how about coming along with us now? We're going out to Schönbrunn so the kids can see the animals, and it's such a nice day." "I'd like to," said Christine. It was good to have somewhere to go. It was good to be with people. Her brother-in-law hooked his arm in hers and told her all sorts of stories while her sister took charge of the children. As he talked, his broad, good-humored face was never still and he patted her arm in a friendly way. He was doing well, you could tell at two hundred paces, he was content and took a naïve pleasure in his contentment. They weren't at the tramway yet, so he confided in her his great secret that the next day he'd be elected district chairman by the Party, but he had it coming to him, he'd been a representative practically from the minute he came back from the war, and if all went well and the right-wingers were brought to heel he'd be on the next municipal council.

Christine listened amicably as she walked next to him. He'd always been very friendly, this uncomplicated little man who took pleasure in little things, a good person, obliging, credulous, trusting. It was clear why his comrades wanted him for that modest office; he deserved it. Yet as she looked at him out of the corner of her eye, short, pink-cheeked, easygoing, with a double chin and a belly that wobbled as he walked, she was almost appalled to think of her sister: how could she ... I couldn't bear to be touched by this man. But it was good to be with him in broad daylight with a lot of people around. Standing with the children in front of the cages at the zoo, he was practically a child himself. With secret envy Christine thought: If only I could go back to taking pleasure in such little things, instead of yearning for the impossible. At five they decided to return home (the children had to go to bed early). First the children were crammed onto one of the packed Sunday streetcars; there was standing room only, but the rest of them squeezed in. As the tram clattered along Christine thought of the shiny car immaculate in the morning light, the sweet-smelling air streaming over her temples, the cushioned seat, the landscape flitting by. She closed her eyes and lost track of time, hovering in that other realm in the midst of the jostling crowd. Her brother-in-law tapped her on the shoulder: "We have to get off. Why don't you come for coffee before you catch your train. Wait, let me go first and clear a path for you."

He pushed on ahead, and, in spite of being so short and stout, he had no trouble elbowing a narrow path among the bellies, shoulders, and backs doing their best to move out of the way. He was at the door when there was a sudden commotion. "Quit shoving me in the gut, you idiot," shouted a tall thin man in an inverness coat rudely and furiously. "Who are you calling an idiot? You all hear that?" Christine's brother-in-law exploded. "Who are you calling an idiot?" The thin man in the inverness coat, hemmed in, laboriously squeezed through while the rest stared, and a squabble seemed about to break out, but Christine's brother-in-law's angry voice suddenly changed. "Ferdinand! Well, I'll be! Now that really would have been something. I nearly got into a fight with you!" The other man too was astonished and laughed. The two of them gripped each other's hands and looked into each other's faces. The conductor interrupted: "If you gentlemen wish to get off, please do it! We have a schedule to meet." "Come on, you have to get off with us, we live two doors down. Well, I'll be! Come on, let's go." The face of the tall thin man in the inverness coat had brightened. He reached down to put his hand on the shoulder of Christine's brother-in-law. "I'd love to, Franzl." They both got off. The surprise had winded Christine's brother-in-law and he stood at the stop catching his breath, a greasy sheen on his face. "Who'd have thought we'd run into each other again! I've often wondered where you'd ended up and I've always intended to write to the hotel down there and find out. But you know how it is, things get in the way. And now here you are. Well, I'll be! What a pleasure!"

The stranger opposite him was also glad. He was a younger man, more controlled, but a slight trembling of his lips gave his pleasure away. "Forget it, Franzl, I'm sure you did," he said, reaching down to clap the little man on the shoulder, "but now introduce me to the ladies. One of them must be your wife, Nelly, who you always told me about." "Right, right, give me a minute, I'm flabbergasted. Ferdinand, it's such a pleasure to see you!" And then to the others: "You know the Ferdinand Farrner I've always talked about. We were in the same barracks for two years in Siberia. The only one—it's true, Ferdinand, you know it—the only one who was a decent fellow among the Ruthenian and Serbian trash they dumped us in with there, the only one you could talk to and the only one you could depend on. Well, I'll be! But come on up, I'm really curious. Well, I'll be. If someone had told me I was going to be so happy today— why, if I'd taken the next tram we might never have laid eyes on each other again."

Christine had never seen her easygoing, phlegmatic brother-in-law so lively, so animated. He practically ran up the stairs of the building and pushed his friend inside. A faint indulgent smile on his face, the stranger yielded to his war buddy's outpourings of enthusiasm. "So take off your coat, make yourself comfortable. Here, have a seat in the armchair—Nelly, coffee for us, schnapps, cigarettes—now let me look at you. You haven't gotten any younger, you're actually looking damn thin. What you need is a square meal." The stranger obligingly let himself be scrutinized—Franz's childlike joy plainly cheered him. The hard, tense face with the beetling brow and the pronounced cheekbones gradually relaxed. Christine too looked at him and tried to remember—earlier she'd seen a picture in the museum, a portrait of a monk by a Spaniard. The name was gone now but it was the same bony, ascetic, almost fleshless face, the same tension about the nostrils. The stranger good-humoredly smacked Christine's brother-in-law on the arm. "Maybe you're right. We ought to just go on sharing everything the way we used to do with our rations. You could let me have some of your bacon. You'd never miss it and your wife wouldn't have any objection, I hope."

"But tell us now, Ferdinand, I'm dying to know. When the Red Cross got us out back then, I was in the first batch and you were supposed to follow the next day with the other seventy. Then we sat on the Austrian border for another two days. There wasn't enough coal for all the trains. And all that time I was waiting for you to show up. We went to the railway clerk ten times, twenty times to get a wire sent, but everything was such an unholy mess, and after two days we went ahead, seventeen hours from the Czech border to Vienna. What happened to you?"

"Well, you could have sat at the border and waited for another two years. You were just lucky—we got the short end of the stick. The telegrams came in half an hour after your transport left: the railway lines had been bombed by the Czechs, so back we went to Siberia. That was no fun, but we didn't take it hard. We figured eight days, two weeks, a month. Nobody thought it would be two years, and only a dozen out of the seventy of us made it through. Reds, Whites, Wrangel,* war on and on, constantly back and forth and here and there, they shook us around like dice in a cup. It was 1921 before the Red Cross found a way back for us through Finland. Yes, my friend,

* Peter von Wrangel (1878–1928). Commander-in-chief of the White (pro-Tsarist) army in Crimea.

we went through a lot, and you'll understand why we didn't put on much weight."

"What rotten luck, do you hear that, Nelly. All on account of half an hour. And I had no idea. Not a clue that you were stuck in that mess—you of all people! You of all people! What did you do for those two years?"

"My friend, I could talk all day and there'd still be more to tell. I think I did everything a person can do. I helped with the harvest, in the factories, I delivered newspapers, banged away at the typewriter, fought for two weeks alongside the Reds when they were at the gates of our city and begged with the peasants when they entered it. Well, let's not talk about it. When I think back on it today, I'm amazed to be sitting here smoking a cigarette."

Christine's brother-in-law was agog. "Well, I'll be. Well, I'll be. A person doesn't know how lucky he is. To think that you could have been alone here for two years, Nelly, you and the kids, it's unimaginable, and a good fellow like you, you're the one that got clobbered. Well, I'll be. Thank goodness you're in one piece at least. All that bad luck, you're lucky nothing happened to you."

The stranger angrily ground out his cigarette in the ashtray. His face had suddenly darkened. "Yes, well, you could say I was lucky. Nothing happened to me, or almost nothing, just these two broken fingers, on the last day. Yes, you could say I was lucky. I got off easy. It was the last day, we couldn't stand it anymore, the few of us still left, squeezed together in a single barracks, and we even cleared out a grain car at the station just so we could move on, seventy men cheek by jowl instead of the regulation forty per car. It was impossible to turn around, and if somebody had to relieve himself, well, I'm not going to talk about that in front of the ladies. But anyway, we were off, and happy about it. Another twenty got on at a station down the line. They were whacking each other with rifle butts to get to the front and they squeezed in one after another, and then another after that, even though we were already five or six deep, and that's how we traveled for seven hours, in one groaning, shouting, wheezing, sweating, stinking mass. I had my face to the wall and my hands out in front of me so my ribs wouldn't be crushed against the wood siding. I broke two fingers and tore a tendon, and I stood that way for six hours, not a breath of air in my lungs, half asphyxiated. It got better at the next station where we tossed out five corpses—two had been trampled to death and three were smothered—and we went on like that until evening. Yes, you could say I was lucky, just a torn tendon and two broken fingers, it's a little thing."

He held up his hand: the third finger was limp and wouldn't bend. "Yes, a little thing, that's what it is—after a world war and four years of Siberia, a mere finger. But you wouldn't believe what a dead finger does to a living hand. You can't draw with it if you want to become an architect, you can't type in an office, you can't grab hold of things where there's heavy labor to be done. Little devil of a tendon, just a wisp of a thing, and everything you want to do in your life hangs by a thread like that. It's like when you make a mistake of a millimeter on the ground plan of a building, one little thing and it all comes crashing down."

Franz, aghast, helplessly repeated, "Well, I'll be," wishing he could pat Ferdinand's hand. The women too had become serious and watched the stranger with interest. Finally Franz pulled himself together and said, "So go on—what did you do once you got back?"

"Well, what I always told you I'd do. I wanted to go back to technical school—pick up where I left off, as a twenty-five-year-old sitting at the school desk I hadn't seen since I was nineteen. Eventually I even learned to draw with my left hand, but then something else got in the way, another one of those little things."

"What was that?"

"Well, it's just the way things are—school costs a lot of money, and that was one more little thing I'd forgotten about. It's one little thing after another, wouldn't you say?"

"But why? Your family always had money, you had a house down in Merano and fields and the pub and the tobacco shop and the grocery...and...all that stuff you told me about... And then your grandmother who did nothing but save, never gave away a button and slept in a cold room because she was too cheap to shell out for the kindling and the paper. What happened to her?"

"Yes, she still has a fine garden and a fine house, practically a palace. That's where I was coming from on the streetcar —the nursing home outside Lainz where they grudgingly consented to take her on. And she's got money too, a big pile of it, a strongbox full to the brim. Two hundred thousand crowns, in old thousands. She has it in the chest during the day, under her bed at night. All the doctors laugh at her and the attendants get a kick out of it. Two hundred thousand crowns. She was a good Austrian and sold everything down there, the vineyard, the pub, and the tobacco shop, because she didn't want to turn into an Italian, and she put it all into the brand-spanking-new thousand-crown notes that they turned out so brilliantly during the war. So now she has them hidden in her strongbox under the bed and swears they'll be worth something again someday. They started out as twenty or twenty-five hectares and a beautiful stone house and some fine old heirloom furniture and forty or fifty years of work, didn't they, so they couldn't just stay nothing forever. The poor dear is seventy-five and doesn't understand much anymore. She just goes on believing in the good Lord God and His earthly justice."

He stuffed tobacco into a pipe he'd pulled out of his pocket and began puffing away. Christine felt the anger in the gesture— a cold, hard, scornful fury that she recognized, and somehow

she felt he was her ally. Her sister stared off irritably, obviously
conceiving some aversion to this man who was inconsiderately
stinking up the room while treating her husband like a schoolboy. Franz's submissiveness toward this poorly dressed, surly
fellow annoyed her—she could sense the spirit of revolt in him
as he sat there tossing stones into the pond of her gemütlich-
keit. Franz himself seemed stunned, gazing at his buddy with a
mixture of good humor and alarm while foolishly spluttering,
"Well, I'll be." He thought for a moment. "But after that—go
on, what did you do then?"

"All sorts of things here and there. At first I thought if I
made a little extra on the side, that would be enough for me to
go back to school on. But it was never enough—I barely made
enough to feed myself from one day to the next. Yes, my dear
Franzl, banks and offices and businesses just didn't need men
who needlessly took two extra winters of vacation in Siberia
and then came home with half a hand. Everywhere 'sorry, sorry,' everywhere people already parked on their fat asses, people
with healthy fingers, and me always with that one little thing
I'd picked up."

"But—you can go on disability, can't you, since you're unfit
for work or partly unfit? You've got to be getting some financial
assistance—surely you're entitled to it?"

"You think? I agree. I agree that the government has a certain obligation to help someone who's lost a house, vineyards,
a finger, and six solid years. But, my friend, in Austria all roads
are crooked. I thought there'd be no problem too, so I went to
the disability office and showed them I'd served here and served
there and here's my finger. But no, first I had to prove that
I'd come by the injury in the war or that it was somehow due
to the war. That's not so easy if the war ended in 1918 and the
injury occurred in 1921 under circumstances such that no one
made a record of it. Still it would have worked out in the end,
except that the bureaucrats made a great discovery—it'll amaze

you, Franz—which is: I'm not an Austrian citizen at all. According to my baptism certificate I was born and am domiciled in the administrative district of Merano, and in order to have Austrian citizenship I would have had to adopt it by a certain time. So that was that!"

"Yes, but then why...why didn't you adopt it?"

"Good grief, now your questions are just as dumb as theirs. As though they posted the official Austro-German gazette on the walls of Siberian thatched huts and barracks in 1919! My friend, in our Tartar village we didn't know if Vienna was part of Bohemia, or maybe Italy. And we didn't give a damn. All we cared about was stuffing a crust of bread down our throats and getting the lice out of our hair and finding some matches or tobacco sometime in the next five hours. Wonderful—I should have adopted Austrian citizenship there. Well, finally they at least gave me a piece of toilet paper saying that I could expect to be 'an Austrian citizen under the terms of Article 65 as well as Articles 71 and 74 of the Treaty of Saint-Germain effective September 10, 1919.' But I'll sell it to you for a packet of Egyptian, because I never got a red cent out of any of those agencies."

Franz was beginning to perk up now. He had an idea he might be able to help and was suddenly feeling better. "I'll fix that for you, leave it to me. We'll get some results soon enough. I can attest to your war service if anyone can, and the assemblymen know me from the Party, they'll give me an in, and you'll get a reference from the municipality—we'll make things happen, you can count on it."

"I appreciate it, my friend, I really do! But that's it for me. I've had enough, you don't know what kind of documentation I had to lug in—military documentation, civilian documentation, from the mayor's office, from the Italian embassy, proof of indigence, and I don't know what other trash. I've spent more on notaries and postage than I could have begged in a year, and

I pounded the pavement so much that it got me down more than I can say. I was in the Federal Chancellery, the Ministry of the Army, at the police, at the municipality. There's no door I wasn't shown, no stairs I didn't stumble up and down, no spittoon I couldn't have spit in. No, my friend, I'd rather crawl in a hole and die than go from door to door again on that fool's errand."

Franz gazed at him in disbelief. He looked like he'd been caught out—perhaps he was embarrassed by his own comfortable existence. He moved closer: "All right, but what are you going to do?"

"Anything. Whatever comes along. For the time being I'm the technical supervisor on a construction site in Floridsdorf, half architect and half watchdog. The pay's not bad, and it'll keep me going until the building is done or the company goes under. Then I'll find something else, I'm not worrying about that. But what I told you about up there, up there on our wooden pallet, all that about being an architect and building bridges, that's finished. I'll never get back all the time I slept and smoked and frittered away behind barbed wire. The door to the academy's closed and I'll never get it open again—they knocked the key out of my hand with a rifle butt back at the beginning of the war, it's lying in the Siberian mud. But let's drop that. Why don't you give me another cognac. Schnapps and cigarettes are the only thing I learned from the war."

Franz obediently filled his glass. His hands shook. "Well, I'll be. That somebody like you, so hardworking, so smart, such a good fellow, should be slaving away at odd jobs. Such a shame —I'd have bet anything you were going places, and if anybody deserves to, it's you. Well, that's got to change. There must be some solution."

"'Must'? I see! I thought the same for five years after I got back. But 'must' is a hard nut to crack, and it doesn't always fall from the tree no matter how hard you shake it. The world's a tad different from what they taught us back in school: 'Be ever faithful and upright...' We're not lizards whose tails grow back when you cut them off. My friend, once they've cut six years out of your body—the best ones, from eighteen to twenty-four—then you're always a kind of cripple, even if (as you put it) you're lucky enough to make it home safely. When I go looking for work, I've got nothing more to show for myself than some glorified apprentice or teenage layabout, and when I see my face in the mirror, I look forty. No, we came into the world at a bad time. No doctor's going to fix that, those six years of youth ripped out of me, and who's going to reimburse me? The government? That prize no-good, that first-class thief? Name one among your forty ministers, for justice, for public welfare and wheeling and dealing in war and in peace, show me one who's for doing the right thing. They herded us in, played the Radetzky march and 'God Save the Kaiser,' and now they're blowing a different tune. Yes, my friend, from down in the muck the world doesn't look that delightful."

Dismayed as ever, Franz now noticed his wife's evident annoyance; out of embarrassment he began making excuses for his friend. "The way you talk, Ferdl, I'd hardly know you. You should have seen him, the best, most uncomplaining fellow of all of them, the only decent one in the bunch. I'll never forget when they brought him in, a skinny kid, only nineteen. All the others were overjoyed because the storm had blown over for them, he was the only one who was furious because they'd nabbed him during the retreat, pulling him out of the railroad car before he could fight and die for the fatherland. The first night, I can still remember—we'd never seen anything like it— here he is in the middle of the war, straight from his mother and the parish priest, and he gets down on his knees and prays. If somebody made a joke about the Kaiser or the army he'd practically throttle them. That's what he was like, the most decent guy of the whole lot. He still believed everything it said in the papers and the regimental orders—and now look how he's talking!"

Ferdinand looked at him gloomily. "Yes, I bought it all, just like a schoolboy. But you knocked it out of me! Weren't you the one telling me from the first day that it was all a scam, that our generals were idiots, that the supply officers thieved like magpies, that anyone who didn't surrender was a fool? And who was King of the Commies there, me or you? Who was it, buddy, going on about world socialism and world revolution? Who was the first to take the red flag and go over to the officers' camp to yank their rosettes off? Think back a minute! Who stood next to the Soviet commissar at the governor's palace and delivered the great speech saying that captured Austrian soldiers were no longer the Kaiser's mercenaries but soldiers of world revolution and would be marching home to smash the capitalist system and establish a reign of harmony and justice? And now you're back to your beloved boiled beef and your tankard of pils. What's become of the clean sweep? Where's your world revolution, Herr Socialist Supremo, if you don't mind my asking?"

Nelly stood up brusquely and bustled about with the dishes, now openly angry that her husband had let this stranger come into his apartment and tell him off like a boy. Christine felt oddly pleased as she watched all this—felt like laughing out loud at the sight of her brother-in-law, the future district chairman, hunched over in embarrassment and finally apologizing.

"We did everything we could. You know we had a revolution on the very first day—"

"Revolution? Allow me to bum another cigarette so I can blow some smoke too—your milquetoast revolution! You turned the kaiserlich-königlich signboard around and slapped some paint on it, but you obediently and respectfully left every-

thing neat and tidy inside, with the top nicely on the top and
the bottom nicely on the bottom. You pulled your punches to
make sure nothing got shaken up. That was a Nestroy play,*
not a revolution."

He stood and urgently paced up and down, then paused in
front of Franz. "Don't get me wrong, I'm not from the Red
Flag.† I know only too well what a civil war is. I couldn't forget it if they burned my eyes out. Once when the Soviets re-
took a village (it went back and forth between the Reds and the
Whites three times), they brought us all together to bury the
corpses. I buried them with my own hands, charred, mangled
bodies, women and children and horses, all jumbled together,
one horror, one stench. I know what civil war means now, and
I wouldn't have any part of it even if I knew it was the only way
to bring eternal justice down from heaven. I just don't care anymore, I'm not interested, I'm not for or against the Bolsheviks,
I'm not a Communist or a capitalist, none of it matters. All I
care about is me, and the only government I'm going to serve
is my own work. I don't give a damn how the next generation
makes out, whether it's this or that, Communist or Fascist or
Socialist. What's it to me how they're living or how they're going to live? The only thing that matters is that I get the little
pieces of my life back together again at last and accomplish
what I was born for. Once I'm where I want to be, when I can
breathe freely, when my own life's straightened out, maybe then
I'll give some thought to fixing up the world—after I've had my
dinner. But first I've got to know where I stand. You have time
to worry about other things, but I've only got time for my own
problems."

Franz made a movement.

* Johann Nestroy (1801–1862). Viennese comic playwright, celebrated for his wordplay.

† *Die Rote Fahne.* German revolutionary newspaper, founded by Karl Liebknecht and
Rosa Luxemburg in 1918 and published by the Communist Party from 1919 on.

"No, Franz, I wasn't saying anything against you. I know you're a good fellow, I know you through and through. I know you'd rob the National Bank for me if you could and make me minister. I know you're a nice guy, but that's where we're at fault, that's our crime, that we were so good-natured, so trustful—that's why people took advantage of us. No, my friend, I'm past that. I'm not going to buy the line that others are worse off, no one's going to convince me that I was 'lucky' because I've still got all my arms and legs and I don't walk on crutches. No one's going to convince me that breathing and getting fed is all it takes to make everything all right. I don't believe in anything anymore, not gods or governments or the meaning of life, nothing, as long as I feel I haven't got what's rightfully mine, my rightful place in life, and as long as I don't have that I'm going to keep on saying I've been robbed and cheated. I'm not going to let up until I feel I'm living my true life and not getting the dregs, what other people toss out or couldn't stomach. Can you understand that?"

"Yes."

Everyone looked up quickly. A loud "yes," full of feeling, had come from somewhere. Christine flushed when she saw them all looking at her. She'd thought "yes," she knew she'd felt it strongly, but the word had just slipped out. Now, suddenly finding herself the center of attention, she was embarrassed. Silence. At last Nelly had found an opportunity to vent her anger; she leaped to her feet.

"Where do you come in? What do you know about it? As though you ever had anything to do with the war!"

The room was suddenly ablaze with energy. Now Christine could let fly too, and it made her glad. "Not a thing! Not a thing! Just that it ruined us. That we used to have a brother, you were forgetting that too, and how our father died, and everything... everything..."

"But not you, you didn't lack for anything. You've got your good job and you ought to be glad."

"Ah, I ought to be glad. I ought to be thankful to be sitting out there in that hole. You don't seem to find it all that appealing —I didn't see you coming out to see Mother except on holidays. It's all true what Herr Farrner says. They stole years from us and gave us nothing, no peace, no happiness, no time off, no rest."

"So, no time off. Straight from the poshest hotels in Switzerland and here you are complaining."

"I never complained to anyone. You were the only one I heard complaining during the entire war. As for Switzerland... That's just why I know what I'm talking about, because I saw it. Now I know what...what's been taken from us...what they've done to our lives...what I..."

She broke off uncertainly, aware of the stranger's interested and penetrating gaze. Maybe she'd given too much away. She softened her tone. "Of course I don't want to say my situation is the same, of course other people were more involved. But we're all fed up, and we all have our own reasons. I never said anything, I was never a burden on anyone, I never complained. But when you tell me—"

"Quiet, children! No squabbling," Franz broke in. "What's the point of this? The four of us aren't going to fix things here. No politics, that just makes trouble. Let's talk about something else, and above all don't spoil my pleasure. You don't know how much good it does me just to see him again. It makes me happy no matter how much he gripes and growls at me."

Peace returned, like the cooler air after a storm.

For a moment they all savored the silence, enjoying the release of tension. Then Ferdinand rose from his chair. "I ought to go. Call your boys in again—I want to look at them."

The children were brought in. They looked at the stranger with wonder and curiosity.

"This one's Roderich, born before the war. Him I know about. And the second one here, this charmer, the posthumous child so to speak, what's his name?"

"Joachim."

"Joachim! Shouldn't he have been called something else, Franz?" Franz gave a start. "My God, Ferdl. I forgot all about it. Imagine, Nelly, I didn't think of it—we promised we'd be godfather for each other if we got back and one of us had a child. I totally forgot about it. You're not angry with me?"

"My friend, I don't think the two of us could be angry with each other now. If we were going to fall out, we had plenty of time for that. But that's the reason, you see—we've forgotten about that time. But maybe it's better that way" (he ruffled the child's hair, a warm expression flitting across his features) "maybe the name wouldn't have brought him luck."

He fell silent. The boy had awakened something childlike in his face and he said to Nelly, in an offhand but conciliatory tone, "No hard feelings, ma'am...I know I'm not a pleasant guest and I noticed you didn't care all that much for my conversation with Franz. But if two people have spent two years picking the lice out of each other's hair and shaving each other and eating out of the same trough and lying in the same mud, it's a crime for one of them to get on his high horse and talk fancy talk in front of the other. You meet an old buddy, you talk the way you used to talk, and if I chewed him out a little that was just because I was annoyed for a second. But he knows and I know we'll never drift apart. I guess I owe you an apology. I know you'll be happy to see me leave, I assure you I understand that."

What he'd said was just what Nelly was thinking, and she hid her anger. "No, no, you're always welcome here, and it's good for him to have someone around. Why don't you come for lunch some Sunday. We'd all be happy to have you."

But the word "happy" came out flat, it sounded false, and when he took her hand it was cool, a stranger's hand. He took his leave from Christine without a word. She felt his eyes just for a second, curious and warm; then he went to the door, with Franz behind him.

"I'll walk you out."

Nelly flung open the window as soon as they were gone. "The smoke is enough to make you suffocate," she said to Christine by way of excuse. She dumped the full ashtray on the sill outside, the banging sound echoing the harshness in her voice. Christine could see she was trying to get rid of any trace of the man. Her sister was a stranger to her, she thought. How hard she'd become, how skinny and dried-up. She used to be so buoyant and lively. But she was grasping at her husband like someone grasping at money—that was why. She didn't want to give up any of him, not even to a friend. He had to be all hers, under her thumb, go on working and saving like a good fellow so she could be Frau District Chairman. Christine had always looked up to her sister, but for the first time in her life she viewed her with contempt and hatred—because she didn't understand, because she didn't want to understand.

It was a good thing Franz was back now, but then the silence between them grew dangerous again; the room was thick with it. He approached the two women uncertainly, with small gingerly steps, as though the floor were unsafe.

"The two of you sang another long duet downstairs. Well, that's fine with me, I'm sure we'll have the pleasure often now. If someone's down, he likes to climb up where the others are."
"But Nelly," Franz said, shocked, "what are you thinking? You have no idea what kind of a person he is. If he'd wanted something from us, he would have shown up a long time ago. He could easily have found my address in the government directory. Don't you see, the fact that he's in trouble is exactly why he didn't come. He knows I'll give him whatever he needs."

"Yes, you're pretty free and easy when it comes to people like that. You can go see him as far as I'm concerned, I'm not going to say no. But here in the house, never again. Look at the hole he burned with his cigarette, and look at the floor, he didn't even wipe his boots, your friend, leaving us to sweep up after him. Well, if you like that kind of thing I'm not going to stand in your way."

Christine's fists were clenched. She was ashamed for her sister, ashamed for her brother-in-law standing there so submissively, trying to explain something that only fell on deaf ears. The atmosphere was intolerable. She stood up. "I'd better go now too or I'll miss the last train. I'm sorry I stayed so long."

"No, no," her sister said. "Come back soon."

It was like saying goodbye to an acquaintance. One rebellious, the other complacent: each hated what the other had become.

On the stairs Christine had a premonition that this stranger would be waiting for her at the bottom. She tried to push the thought away. The man had given her no more than a fleeting glance of curiosity and he hadn't said a word to her, and she wasn't even sure she wanted to run into him. But the notion wouldn't leave her mind, becoming stronger with every step until it was nearly a certainty.

So she wasn't really surprised when she came out of the building to see that inverness coat wafting toward her from the other side of the street, and then to find the stranger's subdued and troubled face before her.

"Forgive me for waiting for you, Fräulein." He blurted it out in a changed voice, one that seemed practically brand-new— diffident, embarrassed, remotely stricken, nothing like the bleakly hard, forceful, aggressive tone he'd used before. "But I was worried the whole time that you wouldn't ... that your sister was annoyed with you... I mean, because I was so rude with Franzl and because you... because you agreed with me... I'm sorry myself that I went after him so harshly. I know it's bad manners when you're a guest and in the presence of strangers, and I assure you I didn't mean any harm, quite the contrary... He's just such a prince of a guy, such a terrific friend, a totally good person like you hardly ever run across... Really, when I suddenly saw him there in front of me I felt like falling on his neck and smothering him with kisses or somehow showing my happiness the way he did. But, you've got to understand, I was shy... shy in front of you and your sister— nobody wants to see me get sloppy... That's the only reason I got my back up with him, it was stupid, but I was shy... I can't help it, I can't... But it got to me when I saw him sitting there fat and happy with his great potbelly, his cup of coffee, and his gramophone, and I had to rag him a little... You didn't know him out there. He used to be the most rabid one of all, talking of nothing but revolution and destroying and rebuilding from morning till night, and now, when I saw him all soft and dopey, so content with everything, his wife, his kids, his Party, and his council flat with flowers on the balcony, so all's-right-with-the-world and petty bourgeois... well, I just had to needle him, just a little, and your sister naturally thought I was jealous that he has it so good... But, I swear, I was just happy he has it so good, and if I went after him a little... well, it was... it was only because I wanted to clap him on the shoulder so much or seize him by the arm or poke him in the belly, old Franzl, and I was shy in front of you..."

Christine had to smile. She understood it all, even the wish to poke her brother-in-law in his fat belly. "No," she said to put his mind at ease, "I understood it right away. It was sort of embarrassing, even, his being that happy to see you, wanting to treat you like a king the way he seemed to—I know why you felt shy."

"I'm...I'm glad to hear you say that. Your sister, she didn't see it, or maybe she saw him turn into someone else the moment he laid eyes on me...Someone she doesn't know at all, and she doesn't have a clue that he and I go back to when we were locked up together in a cell like criminals, day and night and night and day, and that we know things about each other that a wife never could, and that I can make him do anything I want and vice versa. She felt it, even if she tried to hide it and make out that I was angry with him, or envious...Well, maybe it's true, I am full of anger...But I don't envy anyone, I mean the kind of envy where I'd say I'd like myself to be better off and others worse off...Of course I don't begrudge anyone their happiness...I can't help it, no one can help asking 'why not me' now and then when they see other people living high on the hog...You know what I'm driving at...I don't mean 'why not me instead of him'...Just 'why not me too.'"

Christine was taken aback. The man beside her had said just what she'd been thinking all this time; he'd expressed clearly what she'd dully felt—the wish to be given one's due, not to take anything from anyone, but to have some kind of life, not to be left out in the cold forever while the others were warm inside.

He thought her silence must mean she'd had enough of his company and wanted to be on her way. He stood before her irresolutely and reached up as if to tip his hat. Her eyes followed the gesture, rapidly taking in his cheap, worn-out shoes and threadbare, unpressed pants, and she realized it was his shabbiness and poverty that made this otherwise vigorous man so unsure of himself in her presence. In that second her mind flashed back to the hotel; her hand, the one that had carried the suitcase, trembled as it had done then, and she understood his uncertainty as though they'd switched bodies. This man was herself, and she felt she had to help him.

"I have to catch a train now," she said. His evident dismay

gave her a small surge of pride. "But if you'd like to come to the station with me . . ."

"Oh, if you don't mind, I'd like that." Once again she was gratified by the hint of surprise and pleasure in his voice.

He walked beside her now, but he kept on apologizing. "I was an idiot, and it bothers me, I shouldn't have done it. I shouldn't have been talking and thinking as though your sister weren't there, she's his wife, after all, and I'm just some stranger. What I should have done first was ask about the kids, whether they were doing well in school, what grade they were in—something about the kids. But I got so carried away when I saw him that I forgot all that. I had such a great feeling all of a sudden—after all, he's the only person who knows anything about me and understands me . . . Not that we're really the greatest match . . . He's another sort of person entirely, much better, much more respectable than I am . . . And then he's got completely different things on his mind, and he doesn't understand anything about what I really want . . . But we were thrown together, two years, day after day and night after night, so far outside the world that we might as well have been on an island . . . Probably I wouldn't be able to explain any of what really matters to me, but he'd probably get it deep down, and better than anyone. We don't even have to say anything, all we have to do is be together. I knew everything about him the minute I walked into that room—maybe more than he knows about himself, and he realized that . . . And that's why he was so embarrassed, as though I'd found him out and he was ashamed . . . I don't know about what, maybe his big gut, or that he's become such an upstanding citizen . . . But right then he became his old self, and his wife wasn't there, and you weren't there, and both of us would rather have gotten rid of you two so we could talk, we would have had stories to tell all night long— yes, and of course your sister felt that—and yet still it's better for us now, because he knows I'm there and I know he is.

We both feel there's someone to go to if something's bothering us. Because everyone else—no, you'd never understand, and anyway maybe I can't explain it properly, but ever since I got back from those six years in a different world I've had the feeling I'm back from the moon. There's something foreign about these people I used to live with. When I have lunch with my relatives or my grandmother, I don't know what to say, I don't understand the things they're interested in, and everything they do seems so strange, so pointless. It's as if... it's like being on the street and looking through the glass at people dancing in a café, and you can't hear the music, you can't hear the beat, and you don't have any idea why they're all spinning around with such ecstatic expressions. There's just something about them you can't understand and vice versa, and they think you're envious or angry, and it's really just because you don't understand them and they don't understand you anymore... It's as though you speak different languages, want different things out of life... But forgive me, Fräulein, I've been talking at you so much and it's all nonsense. I don't expect you to understand it."

Again Christine stopped and looked at him. "You're wrong," she said, "I know exactly what you're saying, every word of it. That is... A year ago, even a few months ago, maybe I wouldn't have understood you, but since I got back from..."

She thought better of it.

She'd nearly started telling this stranger everything. She quickly began again in another tone: "By the way, there's something else. I'm not going directly to the station—first I have to get my bag from the hotel where I spent the night. I came yesterday evening, not this morning as they thought... I didn't want to tell my sister, she would have been insulted that I didn't stay with them. But I don't like to be a burden. I just wanted to ask you... If you talk to my brother-in-law, don't mention it to him."

"Of course."

She could tell he was pleased and grateful that she trusted him. They went in together to get her suitcase. He wanted to carry it, but she stopped him: "No, not with your hand, you said yourself..." He was mortified, she saw, and she fell silent. I shouldn't have said it, she thought, shouldn't have shown that I remembered there might be a problem. She let him carry the suitcase. At the station they had three-quarters of an hour before the train was due in, so they sat down in the waiting room to talk. They talked about impersonal things: about her brother-in-law, about the post office, about the political situation in Austria, about trivialities and superficialities. There was no intimacy between them, but they spoke plainly and seemed to see eye to eye; she noted the sharpness and quickness of his intelligence and respected him for it. Finally it was time. "I'd better go," she said, getting to her feet.

He stood up too, looking almost distressed. And she was pleased—and moved—to see that he found it hard to break off their conversation. Tonight he'll be alone, she thought, and she felt a kind of pride: here at last, unexpectedly, after all this time, was someone who wanted to win her over; she, an insignificant postal official who sold stamps, dated telegrams, and made telephone connections, meant something to someone. Seeing his crestfallen face, she was full of sympathy and, suddenly remembering, said, "Or I could take the later train—there's another one at 10:20. We could go for a walk and have dinner somewhere here...If you don't have other plans, that is..."

Again she took pleasure in the joy that radiated outward from his eyes and suffused his face as she spoke, and then his happy exclamation: "Oh, nothing whatever."

They checked the suitcase at the station and walked for a while among lanes and streets, with no destination in mind. A blue mist gradually darkened the September evening; streetlights hovered between the buildings like little white moons. They strolled side by side and chatted about nothing in particular. Somewhere beyond the city center they came across a cheap little restaurant where they could sit outside on a patio with small artificial arbors and ivied trellises between the tables, so that you were alone, yet not alone; you could be seen by other people, yet not overheard. They both felt happy when they found a free corner. Buildings rose all around them. From an open window came an indistinct waltz on a gramophone. Laughter and the quiet peaceful sounds of contented solitary drinkers could be heard nearby. Each table had a lantern standing on it like a glass flower, with small inquisitive black insects buzzing around it. It was pleasantly cool. Franz took off his hat, and Christine saw his face clearly in the light of the steady flame. It was a hard, bony Tyrolean face with chiseled features, little lines and wrinkles at the corners of the eyes and around the mouth, a taut, severe, yet somehow worn face. But behind that face there seemed to be a second face, just as there was a second voice behind his angry one, a second face that appeared when he smiled, when the wrinkles lengthened and the aggression in his eyes softened to a glow. Then something boyishly docile came out, and it was almost a child's face, trustful and sensitive. That was how her brother-in-law had known him, she remembered. That was how he must have been then. The two faces alternated strangely as they talked. Shadows appeared the moment he knitted his eyebrows or pursed his lips bitterly, and it was like a cloud passing over the green of a meadow. Strange, she thought, how is it possible? There seem to be two people in him. Then she recalled her own transformation, and thought of the mirror now being used by other people in a room far away.

They ordered simple dishes and the waiter brought them with two glasses of pale Gumpoldskirchner. Smiling, Ferdinand took his glass for a toast. But as he straightened to raise it there was a small, dry, clattering sound. A loose button had come off his coat. It rolled around on the table mockingly before toppling off. His face darkened. He tried to catch the button, to hide it, but, seeing that the little accident had not escaped her, he became awkward, embarrassed, and grim. Christine tried not to look. There was no mistaking the meaning of this tiny sign. He had no one to care for him, no one to look after him! No woman—she felt sure of it. Her trained eye had already noted his unbrushed hat with its dusty band, the baggy, wrinkled, unpressed pants. From her own experience she understood his distress.

"Pick it up," she said. "I always carry a needle and thread. People like us have to do everything ourselves. I'll sew it back on."

"No," he said in dismay. Nevertheless he did as he was told and bent to pick up the telltale button from the gravel. But then he kept it hidden in his hand, uncertain and reluctant.

"No, no," he pleaded, "I'll get it done at home." And when she insisted, he became vehement. "No, don't! Don't!" he said, roughly doing up the other two buttons of his coat. Christine did not press further, seeing that he was ashamed. Something in their companionability had been disrupted, and in the tightness of his lips she suddenly sensed he was about to say something mean. Out of shame, he was going to become abusive.

And he did. Seeming to take cover within himself, he looked at her defiantly. "Well, I'm not properly dressed, but I didn't know I was going to be inspected. It was plenty good enough for a visit to the nursing home. If I'd known, I would have put on something better. But I'm lying to you. To tell the truth, I don't have the money to dress respectably. I just don't have it, or not enough for everything. I get some new shoes, but by that time the hat's shot. I get a hat, but then the coat is beat up. I get this and I get that but I never catch up. Maybe it's my own fault, but I don't care. So there you are, I'm poorly dressed."

Christine opened her mouth to speak, but he cut in. "Please, don't try to mollify me. I know it all already. You're going to tell me that poverty's nothing to be ashamed of. It's not true, though. If you can't hide it, then it is something to be ashamed of. There's nothing you can do, you're ashamed just the same, the way you're ashamed when you leave a spot on somebody's table. No matter if it's deserved or not, honorable or not, poverty stinks. Yes, stinks, stinks like a ground-floor room off an airshaft, or clothes that need changing. You smell it yourself, as though you were made of sewage. It can't be wiped away. It doesn't help to put on a new hat, any more than rinsing your mouth helps when you're belching your guts out. It's around you and on you and everyone who brushes up against you or looks at you knows it. Your sister sensed it right away, I know the way women look down on you when you're down at heels. I know it's embarrassing for other people, but the hell with that, it's a lot more embarrassing when it's you. You can't get out of it, you can't get past it, the best thing to do is get plastered, and here" (he reached for his glass and drained it in a deliberately uncouth gulp) "here's the great social problem, here's why the 'lower classes' indulge in alcohol so much more—that problem that countesses and matrons in women's groups rack their brains over at tea. For those few minutes, those few hours, you forget you're an affront to others and to yourself. It's no great distinction to be seen in the company of someone dressed like this, I know, but it's no fun for me either. Don't be shy, just go ahead and say what you have to say, but spare me the politeness and the pity!"

He pushed his chair back and made as if to get up from the table. Christine quickly laid a hand on his arm. "Not so loud! Do these people have to know everything? Move closer."

He did as he was told. The defiance was gone, the anxiety was back. Trying to hide how sorry she was for him, Christine said, "Why torment yourself, and why torment me? It's all nonsense. What makes you think I'm some kind of 'lady'? If I were, I wouldn't understand a word you've said. I'd think you were overexcited, unreasonable, and full of hate. But I do understand

and I'm going to tell you why. Move closer. There's no reason everyone has to hear this."

And she told him. She told him everything: the rage, the shame, the exhilaration, the change. It was good to speak for the first time about that delirium of wealth, and good too, even as it tormented her, even as it filled her with bitterness and anger, to describe how the desk clerk took her for a thief just because she was carrying her own suitcase and was shabbily dressed. Franz sat silent and motionless, but his flaring nostrils made her feel he was breathing it all in. He understood her the way she understood him, with the solidarity of anger and invisibility. And once the floodgates were open, there was no closing them. She said more than she really wanted to about herself, her hatred for the village, her anger over the wasted years; it came out powerfully and vividly. She'd never told anyone so much.

He sat in silence, not looking at her, slumping more and more. At last he said, as though from the bottom of a hole, "Forgive me for jumping down your throat like that. It was a stupid thing to do. I could kick myself for always flying off the handle like a fool, so angry, so bullying, as if the first person I ran into was to blame for anything and everything. And as if I was the only one. I know I'm just one out of legions—millions. Every morning when I go to work I see people coming out of their front doors, underslept, cheerless, their faces blank, see them going to work that they haven't chosen and have no love for and that means nothing to them, and then again in the evening I see them on the streetcars on their way back, their expressions leaden, their feet leaden, all of them exhausted for no good reason, or some reason they don't understand. They just don't know it, they don't believe it or they don't feel it strongly, not the way I do, this horrible purposelessness. For them getting ahead means earning ten more schillings a month or getting a new job title, another dog tag, or they go to their meetings in the evening and hear about how capitalism is on the way out, socialism is going to conquer the world, give it another decade, or two decades, and the system will collapse—that whole line. But I'm not as patient as that. I can't wait a decade or two decades. I'm thirty years old, and eleven of those years have been wasted. I'm thirty and I still don't know who I am, and I still don't know what it's all for, I've seen nothing but blood and sweat and filth. I've done nothing but wait, wait, and wait some more. I can't take it any longer, being at the bottom and on the outside, it makes me livid, it's driving me crazy, and I feel time's running out while I'm just doing odd jobs for other people, even though I know I'm just as good as the architect who's telling me what to do, I know as much as the guys at the top, I breathe the same air, the same blood runs in my veins. I just showed up too late, I fell off the train and can't catch up no matter how fast I run. I know I can do it all—I learned some stuff, nobody'd call me stupid, I was first in high school and at the monastery school, I was good at music, studied French with a Father from the Auvergne too. But I don't have a piano or any way to play and I'm forgetting it all, there's no one to speak French with and that's going too. In those two years at technical school I stuck to my books while the rest of them were knocking each other about in the fraternities, and even in the Siberian pigsty I went on working, but I'm just not getting anywhere. I just needed a year, one free year, like a running start before you jump ... One year and I'd be on top of it, where or how I don't know, but I do know I've still got it in me to grit my teeth and use all my muscles, to study for ten hours, fourteen hours—just a few years with my nose to the grindstone and I'd be up there with the others, I'd be tired but happy, I could be at peace with myself, I'd say: Done! Over! But right now I can't, right now I hate them all, those happy people, they get to me so much that sometimes I clench my fists in my pockets just to keep from attacking them and their complacency. Look at those three over there. All the time I've been talking I've been mad at them, I don't know why, maybe out of envy, because they're so stupid and jolly, so respectable and having such a good time. Look at them, here's what they are—that one's probably a sales assistant in some notions shop, all day long he's pulling packages out of drawers and bowing and babbling, 'The latest style, 1.80 per meter, genuine English manufacture, long-lasting, durable,' and then he tosses the package back and gets another one and then another one and then a few ribbons and some trim, and in the evening he goes home and thinks that's a life. And the others—that one's in the tax office, maybe, or the post office savings bank, all day he pounds out numbers, numbers, hundreds of thousands, millions of numbers, interest, compound interest, debits and credits, not knowing who it belongs to, where the money's coming from and for what, who owes what, who owns what, he knows nothing and in the evening he goes home and thinks that's a life. And the third, what does he do? I don't know, he works in a municipal office or somewhere, but I can tell from his shirt that it's a desk job, paper, paper, paper, the same wooden desk, the same hand doing the same work all day. But today, because it's Sunday, their hair's greased up and they're looking happy. They've been at a soccer match or at the races or out with a girl and now they're telling each other about it, and one of them is showing off in front of the others, telling them how smart, how clever, how capable he is—just listen to them laughing, soft, comfortable, self-satisfied, they're machines that got a break on Sunday, working stiffs let out of the morgue for the day, just listen to them, the way they laugh, so excited, the poor sons of bitches, just because somebody let them off the leash for a minute they think they own this place and the world. I'd like to smash their faces in."

He was breathing hard. "But that's nonsense, I know. Always the wrong note, always unfair. They may be poor sons of bitches, but they're far from stupid—they're doing the smart thing: accepting themselves for what they are. They want to be dead and they are, that way you don't feel a thing anymore. What an idiot I am, wanting to smack those happy little men, wanting to shake them up—maybe it's just so I'll have a pack to run in and not be so alone. I know it's stupid, I know I'm just cutting off my nose to spite my face, but I can't help it, these eleven poisonous years have filled me with so much hate that I'm fed up to here, I can barely hold it in. Whenever it starts to come out I run home or to the public library no matter where I am. But I don't enjoy reading anymore. The novels they write these days don't have anything to do with me. The little tales about how Hansel gets Gretel and Gretel gets Hansel or Mary cheats on John and John cheats on Mary, they make me want to throw up. And the books about the war, I don't need those. And I can't get down to studying since I know it won't help and I won't get any further as long as I don't have the academic dog tag, and I don't have the money for that, and since I don't have money I can't make money—you get this rage that grows in your guts, until you have to cage yourself like a vicious animal. Nothing makes you madder than wanting to defend yourself against something you can't even get hold of, something the human race is doing to you, but still there's nobody you can grab by the throat. Franzl knows all about that. All I'd have to do is remind him how sometimes we'd lie on the floor in our barracks at night, howling and scrabbling in the dirt with rage and smashing bottles out of pure moronic spite and plotting to take the pickax and do in poor Nikolai, sweet-tempered, quiet Nikolai the good sentry who was actually our friend, just because he was the only one we could get at out of all the people responsible for keeping us locked up, that was the only reason. And I'm sure you'll understand now too why seeing Franzl made me feel so much better. I'd forgotten there was someone who could understand, but right away I felt that he understood—and then that you did."

She looked up and his gaze flooded her; but immediately he was ashamed again.

"Forgive me," he said in his other voice, the soft, anxious, small voice that contrasted so strangely with the hard, aggressive, angry one, "forgive me, I shouldn't be talking so much about myself, it's bad manners, I know. But I don't think I've said as much in the whole last month as I've just said to you."

Christine stared into the lantern. It was quivering slightly; a cool breeze was making the flame tremble. Its blue, heart-shaped center suddenly shot up narrowly. "Neither have I," she said.

They were silent for a time. The unexpectedly tense and painful conversation had been tiring for both of them. The lights were going out at nearby tables; the windows facing the courtyard were dark now, and the gramophone was silent. The waiter passed with ostentatious urgency and cleared the adjacent tables. Now she remembered the time.

"I think I have to go now," she reminded him. "The last train is at 10:20. What time is it now?"

He scowled, but just for a second. Then he smiled.

"See, I'm improving," he said, almost cheerfully. "If you'd asked me that an hour ago, the vicious cur in me would have attacked you, but now I can tell you the way I'd tell a buddy like Franzl: I pawned my watch. And not even for the money. It's a beautiful watch, gold with diamonds. The Archduke gave it to my father after he'd catered a shooting party, even taking charge of the kitchen—everyone thought he did a great job—and you'll understand (because you understand everything) that if you pull out a gold watch with diamonds on a construction site, it sticks out like a sore thumb. And anyway, where I live it's risky to have a watch like that. But I didn't want to sell it, you could call it my emergency rations. So I just pawned it."

He smiled at her as though he'd accomplished a great feat. "See, I said that quite calmly. I'm making progress."

The air had cleared, as though a storm had passed; the tension had eased and a pleasant exhaustion had set in. They were trustful now, feeling something like calm friendship instead of eyeing each other anxiously. They were enjoying walking together as they approached the street leading to the train station. Darkness had painted over the black inquisitive eyes of the houses; the paving stones were cool. But the threat of parting hung over them, and as they neared their destination their footsteps quickened anxiously.

She bought her ticket, turned, and saw his face. Once again it had changed. Now his eyes were in shadow under his brow; the grateful light that had made her happy before had gone out. Thinking he was unobserved, he pulled the inverness coat tighter, as though he were freezing. Suddenly she felt sorry for him. "I'll be back soon," she said, "probably even next Sunday. And if you have time..."

"I always have time. It's pretty much the only thing I do have, and I have a lot of it, but I wouldn't like...I wouldn't like..." He broke off.

"What wouldn't you like?"

"I wouldn't like...I mean just...don't put yourself out on my account...You've been so kind to me...I know I'm no fun...But maybe on the train or tomorrow you'll say to yourself, why let yourself in for some stranger's bellyaching. That's the way it is with me—somebody tells me something heavy about his life and it touches me, but the minute he's gone I say to myself, the devil take him, why is he burdening me with his troubles, we all have plenty already...So don't go out of your way or think 'I've got to help him,' I'll do just fine by myself..."

Christine turned away. To see him so furious with himself was too agonizing. But he misunderstood, thinking she must be offended, and the angry, obnoxious voice gave way to the small, bashful, boyish one. "I mean of course...it would make me very happy...But I thought only if...I was just trying to say..."

He stammered uncertainly, his childish crestfallen face seeming to be begging for forgiveness. And she understood the stammer, understood that this harsh man so ferociously twisted by shame wanted her to come back but was afraid to ask.

An overwhelming feeling of maternal warmth and sympathy came over her; she needed to console this savagely abject man, to blunt his hard pride with some word or gesture. She wanted to stroke his brow or tell him, "You silly boy," but he was so vulnerable that she was afraid. "I'm sorry," she said awkwardly, "but I think I really do have to go now."

"Are you...are you really sorry?" The question was defiant and he looked at her with the need, the desperation of someone who was being abandoned; already he seemed to be standing alone in the waiting room and gazing despondently after the train that was carrying her away, alone in the city, the world, and she felt the entire weight of his feeling resting on her. She was shaken to feel wanted again—this time more deeply than ever in her life. It was a glorious confirmation of her own existence and sense of purpose. It was wonderful to be loved at last—she had to repay him for it.

She made the decision in a flash, without thinking. It was an impulse, a break. She turned, went up to him, and said thoughtfully (though there was no doubt in her mind), "Actually...I could stay with you and catch the early train tomorrow at 5:30. I'd still be on time for my stupid work."

He stared at her; the sudden light in his eyes took her breath away. His features had come to life, like a dark room lit by the flare of a match. He'd understood, understood it all intuitively. Now he had the courage to take her arm. "Yes," he said, beaming, "yes, stay, stay..."

She did not stop him as he led her away. His arm was warm and strong, shaking with joy, so much that she began to shake too. She didn't ask where they were going. Why bother, it didn't matter, she'd made her decision. She'd surrendered her will, voluntarily, and she was rejoicing. Everything in her—her will, her mind—was limp, as if she'd been switched off. Did she love this man she hardly knew? Did she want him? She didn't think; she was lost in her abandonment of will, in the irresponsibility of pure feeling, in the pleasure of detachment.

Now she didn't care what happened. He felt his arm guiding her and she let herself go, like a twig drifting toward the falls. Several times she closed her eyes, the better to feel him wanting her, guiding her.

Then a tense moment. He fell silent; he seemed deflated. "I would have ... would have liked so much to ask you to come home with me ... but ... it won't work ... I don't live by myself ... I have to go through another room ... We could go somewhere else ... to some hotel ... Not the one you stayed at yesterday ... We could ... "

"Yes," she said, "yes," not knowing why she was saying it. The word "hotel" only added to her happiness. The glittering room, the polished furniture, the thunderous silence of the night, the powerful pulse of the Engadine seemed to float up obscurely before her.

"Yes," she said, lost in a reverie of a blissful, yielding love, "yes."

The streets grew narrower as they walked. Ferdinand seemed unsure of himself, glancing anxiously at the buildings. At last, in a small hidden private way, under an electric sign, he saw it. He steered her gently; she did not resist. The door was like a dark tunnel.

Probably intentionally, the hallway was lit by only a single bulb. A grubby shirtsleeved desk clerk came out from behind the glass partition. The two men whispered furtively. Something, money or keys, exchanged hands. Meanwhile Christine stood alone in the dim hallway, looking at the shabby wall and feeling unspeakably let down by this wretched hole. She couldn't help it—the word "hotel" brought back memories of that other lobby: the glittering glass, the streams of chilly light, the opulence and ease.

"Number nine," the desk clerk bawled and added in the same loud voice, "First floor," as though trying to make himself heard all the way upstairs. Ferdinand came to her and took her arm. She looked at him imploringly: "Can't we..." She didn't know what she wanted to say, but he read the dismay in her eyes and knew she wanted to go somewhere else. "No, they're all like this...I don't know any others...I've never been here either." He took her arm and helped her upstairs. She felt hamstrung, every muscle seemed paralyzed.

A bleary-eyed maid, as grubby as the clerk downstairs, came through an open door: "I'll be right back with clean towels." They went in and quickly closed the door. It was a dreadfully cramped box with one window. Other than a single chair, a coat hook, and a washstand, the only object in the room was a large bed with the covers turned back, a bed that stuck out brutally as the only piece of furniture of interest here. It shamelessly filled the narrow room. There was no way to avoid it, or go around it, or overlook it. The air was musty and acrid with stale cigarette smoke, cheap soap, and something else with a sour, off smell. Involuntarily Christine closed her mouth to keep from inhaling it. She thought she might faint from revulsion and loathing. She rushed to raise the window, breathing in the cool fresh air as though she'd been rescued from a mine filled with gas.

A light knock at the door made her jump, but it was only the chambermaid; she brought in the clean towels and put them on the washstand. When she saw that in this brightly lit room Christine had opened the window, she said, "Please close the curtains first"—there was a note of anxiety in her voice—before slipping out discreetly.

At the window, Christine froze. That "first." That was the reason people came to back-alley places like this, to these stinking holes, the only reason. Perhaps—the idea appalled her—perhaps he thought she too had come for that and nothing else.

Although he couldn't see her face, which remained resolutely fixed on the street, her stooped, tense figure was silhouetted in the window and he could see her shoulders quivering. He went to her but was afraid of wounding her with a word. He touched her shoulders, and her fingers when he found them were cold and trembling. He wanted to soothe her, she knew. "Forgive me," she said without turning, "but I felt dizzy. I'll feel better in a minute. Just a little fresh air . . . It's just because . . . "

She wanted to say: Because it's the first time I've ever been in a place like this, a room like this. But she closed her lips tightly; he didn't have to know that. She turned abruptly, closed the window, and ordered, "Turn out the lights."

He turned the switch and the room was plunged into darkness. The worst was blotted out; the bed, now just a vague white patch in the dimness of the room, no longer waited so brazenly. But the dread was still there. In the silence she heard little noises, cracking, sighing, laughing, creaking, the suggestion of bare feet on the floor, water trickling somewhere. The building was full of the doings of licentious strangers, she felt, it was there for the sole purpose of copulation. Slowly the horror invaded her, as a chill starts subtly on the skin but soon spreads to the stiffening joints; it was in her brain, her heart, because she seemed to be beyond thought or feeling, nothing mattered, it was all senseless and alien, including the breath of this stranger beside her. It was good that he was gentle. He didn't pressure her, but simply took her hand to draw her down next to him on the edge of the bed, where, fully dressed, they sat without speaking. He stroked her sleeve and her hand, waiting patiently to see if the horror would diminish, if the icy dismay would thaw. His humility, his submissiveness, touched her, and when he finally took her in his arms, she did not resist.

But even his passionate embrace couldn't dispel her dread entirely. The chill was too deep; he couldn't reach it. Something in her wouldn't relax, something resisted euphoria. He took off her clothes and she felt his body, naked, strong, warm, radiant, but still the strange clammy sheet was like a sponge. His desire was overpowering, but it didn't stop her from feeling sullied by the poverty and squalor all around. Her nerves were frayed as he pulled her toward him: she wanted to escape, not from him, not from his passion, but from this place where people paid money to couple like brutes—quick, make it fast, who's next?— where embraces were sold like stamps or like newspapers that you toss aside when you're done. The air was choking her, thick, greasy, damp, stuffy air, a vapor rising from the flesh, the warmth, the desire of other people. She was ashamed, not that she was giving herself but that this important event was taking place here, where everything was foul and degrading. Her nerves were stretched ever tighter in resistance, and abruptly she groaned, a cramped wail of misery, of fury, that shook her body. Ferdinand next to her took her sobbing as a reproach. He caressed her shoulders, afraid to speak. Noticing his gloom, she said, "Don't worry about me. I'm just having a silly attack. Don't worry, it'll pass, it's just because..." She paused again. "Forget it, there's nothing you can do about it."

He was silent. He knew what she was feeling, he understood her disappointment, her frantic physical distress, yet was ashamed to say truthfully that he hadn't looked for a better hotel or gotten a better room because all he had was eight schillings and that he'd even considered using his ring to pay for the room if it had turned out to cost more than that. But he didn't want to talk about money—he couldn't—so he sat in cheerless silence, patiently waiting for the agitation to subside.

With her senses strained to the utmost, Christine was aware of a constant stream of noises from next door, from above, from below, and from the hallways, footsteps and laughter, coughing and groaning. Next door someone was with a man who seemed to be tipsy and kept bellowing; then she'd hear the sound of a slap on bare skin and a woman's vulgar titillated laughter. It was unbearable, and the longer her only ally sat beside her without saying anything, the more of it she had to hear. She was suddenly afraid and she cried: "Say something! Talk to me, so I don't have to hear what's coming from next door, oh, it's so awful. It's horrible here, I don't know what it is—I'm terrified. Please, say something, talk to me, just so I don't...so I don't hear that...Oh, it's so awful here!"

"Yes," he said, taking a deep breath, "it's awful, and I'm ashamed of myself. I shouldn't have brought you here...I didn't know either."

His caresses were kind, but they failed to quiet the fear that was still making her shiver. Why was she resisting? She tried to control herself, control her trembling limbs, suppress her shudders of revulsion at the clammy sheets and the coarse chatter from next door, at the whole terrible place, but she couldn't. Shudders wracked her.

He leaned over to her. "Believe me, I understand how awful this must be for you. I went through it once too...and it was the first time I was with a woman...It's not something you forget. When I got to the regiment back then and was immediately taken prisoner, I didn't know anything yet, and the rest of them, your brother-in-law included, always made fun of me...The old maid, they used to call me. I don't know whether they were being mean or were just desperate, but they talked about it all the time...They talked about nothing else day and night, they were constantly talking about women, about this one and that one and what it was like, and each of them told his stories a hundred times so we knew them by heart. And they had pictures, or drew them, awful pictures like something on a jailhouse wall. It disgusted me, hearing that all the time, but of course still, still...I was nineteen, twenty, it gets you excited. You feel sick with desire. Then the revolution came and they moved us on to Siberia, your brother-in-law was gone then—and they herded us here and there like sheep until one evening, when a soldier was sitting around with us...He was supposed to be guarding us, but where could we run?... This guy looked out for us and he liked us...I can still see his open face with the potato nose and the wide, good-natured, smiling mouth...But what was I going to say... Right, so one evening he sat down with me like a brother and asked me how long it had been since I'd had a woman...Naturally I was ashamed to say I never had...Any man would have been" (and any woman, she thought) "so I said two years. '*Bozhe moy...*'—his mouth fell open in horror. I can see it now, the good fellow was thunderstruck...He moved closer and stroked me like a lamb: 'Oh, you poor fellow, you poor fellow...You'll get ill...' He went on stroking me and I noticed that he was thinking hard. Thinking, putting one idea after another, was a real effort for that thick-headed, lumbering Sergei, harder than lifting up a tree trunk. His whole face darkened and he got a faraway look, until finally he said, 'Wait, little brother, I'll do it. I'll find you one. There are a lot of them in the village, soldiers' wives and widows. I'll take you to one at night. I know you won't run away.' I didn't say yes, didn't say no. I felt no desire, no interest...What could it be...A simple brute of a peasant woman. Though to feel warm and connected to someone... not so horribly alone...I don't know if you can understand that..."

"Yes," she whispered, "I understand."

"And in fact one evening he came to the barracks. He whistled softly as we'd arranged. Outside in the dark next to him was a woman, short and stout, her hair as slick as oil under a bright scarf. 'That's him,' Sergei said. 'Do you want him?' The little slit-eyed woman looked at me closely in the dark. 'Yes,' she said. The three of us walked along for a ways—Sergei came too. 'So far from home, poor fellow,' she remarked sympathetically to Sergei. 'And never a woman, always with men, poor fellow...Oh, oh, oh.' It sounded good, heartfelt, it had a nice warm sound. I knew she was taking me in out of sympathy, not love. 'They shot my husband,' she said then. 'He was as big as an ash tree, strong as a young bear. He never got drunk and never beat me, he was the best in the village. Now I live with the children and my mother-in-law. God is being hard with us.' I went with her to her house...It was white, covered with straw, a hut with tiny windows, all closed, and when she led me in, the smoke stung my face. The air was thick and hot, like the air in a polluted mine. She pulled me in. The bed was over the furnace, I had to climb up. Suddenly something moved and I was startled. 'It's the children,' she said reassuringly. I realized now that the room was full of people breathing. There was a cough, and again she reassured me: 'Grandma is sick, her chest is killing her.' All the breathing, the stench in the room, I don't know if there were five or six or more there with me, and it paralyzed me. And it seemed terrible to me to have anything to do with a woman, terrible, unspeakably terrible, with the children lying nearby in the room, and someone's mother, I don't know if it was hers or his. She didn't understand my hesitation and pressed up against me. She took off my clothes, untied my shoes—she seemed almost sad— gently and tenderly she removed my jacket, she caressed me like a child. It was touching how nice she was to me...And then, slowly and insistently, she drew me to her. She had breasts as soft and warm and big as loaves of fresh bread, a tender mouth, and it moved me how humble and submissive she was...She was touching, really, I liked her, I was grateful to her, but still the horror of it was choking me. I couldn't bear it when one of the sleeping kids stirred or the sick grandmother groaned, and before dawn I ran out...I was terrified of being seen by the kids or the sick old lady...I'm sure they would have found it all perfectly natural for a man to be there, but I...I couldn't do it and I ran away. She accompanied me beyond the gate, coming along like a dog or a cat. She let me know that from then on she belonged to me—really touching. She took me into the stable and got me some warm milk fresh from the cow, gave me some bread for the road and a pipe that must have been her husband's, and then she asked me, no, she pleaded...meekly, deferentially: 'You'll come again tonight?'...But I didn't go again, the memory of that hut with the smoke and the kids and the grandmother and the bugs that ran over the floor was horrible to me...And yet I was grateful, and today I think of her with, yes, with a sort of love...The way she gave me the milk from the udder, the bread, her own body...And I know I hurt her feelings when I didn't go again...And the others... they didn't understand...They all envied me, they were all so wretched, so alone, that they envied me. Every day I resolved to go to her, and every time—"

"God," she cried, "what's going on?" Christine had sat up suddenly and was listening.

"Nothing," he wanted to say. But he was frightened too. Something was happening in the hallway outside, loud voices, clamoring, shouting, utter confusion, someone screaming, laughing, giving orders. Something had happened. "Wait," he said and jumped out of bed. He threw on his clothes and stood listening at the door: "I'll go see."

Something had happened. Like a sleeper groaning and crying out as he awakens from a nightmare, the hushed fleabag hotel was suddenly alive with unexplained noises. Ringing and knocking, the sound of people running up and down the stairs, a telephone, footsteps, windows rattling. Shouting, talking, confused questions flying back and forth on every side, and voices, strange voices, knuckles rapping, fists hammering on doors, loud footsteps instead of the slap of bare feet. Something had happened. A woman screamed, men argued loudly and heatedly, something fell over, a chair, a car made a racket outside. The whole building seemed to be in an uproar. Christine heard quick footsteps overhead, the loud, apprehensive voice of the drunk next door, the sounds of chairs scraping and keys rattling from the rooms on either side; the whole building from basement to roof, every cell in the beehive was abuzz.

When Ferdinand returned he was pale and nervous, two sharp lines etched on either side of his mouth. He was shaking.

"What is it?" asked Christine, still huddled in bed. Ferdinand turned on the light. Half-naked, Christine lifted the sheet automatically.

"Nothing," he said through his teeth. "A sweep, they're checking the hotel."

"Who?"

"The police!"

"Are they going to come here too?"

"Maybe. Probably. But don't worry."

"Can they do anything to us? ... Because I'm with you?"

"No, don't worry, I have my identification, and I registered properly downstairs, don't worry, I'll take care of everything. I know this kind of thing from the men's hostel in Favoriten where I used to live, it's just a formality ... But ... " Once again his face became dark and hard. "But we're always the ones who have to go through these formalities. And sometimes they break some poor devil's neck. It's only us they roust out of bed in the middle of the night, they don't chase anybody else around like dogs ... But don't worry, I'll settle everything, but just ... get dressed now ..."

"Turn out the light." Again she felt ashamed and she needed all her strength to get dressed. Her limbs were leaden. They sat back down on the bed. She had no strength left. From the first second in this awful place she'd felt a storm brewing, and now it was here.

The knocking went on downstairs. The sweep could be heard moving from room to room on the ground floor. Each time she heard them rapping on the wooden doors below, it was a blow to her heart. Ferdinand sat by her, stroking her hands. "It's my fault, forgive me. I should have thought, but . . . I just didn't have any other ideas, and I wanted . . . I wanted so much to be with you. Forgive me."

He went on stroking her hands, but they were still cold and trembling. Her whole body shivered.

"Don't worry," he said, trying to soothe her. "There's nothing they can do to you. And if . . . if one of those bastards gets fresh he'll have me to deal with. I'm not that much of a pushover, I didn't go through four years of hell to get leaned on by these uniformed night watchmen, I'll give them something to think about."

"No," she pleaded anxiously as she saw him reach back for what she thought might be a weapon. "Please, stay calm. If you love me a little, stay calm, I'd rather..." She couldn't go on.

The footsteps had moved upstairs and now seemed very close. Their room was the third; they heard the knocking at the first. They held their breaths. They could hear everything through the thin door. The first room took no time at all—on to the second. Three raps—knock, knock, knock—and they heard the door being flung open with a drunken shout: "Don't you have anything better to do than harass decent people at night? Go chase the crooks, why don't you!" A deep, harsh voice responded, "Your papers!," then something else more quietly. "My fiancée, *jawohl*, my fiancée," the drunk bellowed defiantly, "I can prove it. We've been together two years." That seemed to be enough, and the door banged shut.

Now it had to be their turn. There were only four or five steps between doors, and here they came, one, two, three... Christine's blood froze. There was a knock. The police inspector stood discreetly at the threshold; Ferdinand faced him calmly. The inspector's face was actually pleasant—round, broad, with a charming little mustache—though bright red from the tight collar of his uniform. You could see him in mufti or shirtsleeves, sleepily nodding along to some folk song. But now, frowning severely, he demanded, "Do you have your papers?" Ferdinand stepped forward. "Here, and my military papers too if you're interested. A man with those isn't surprised when things turn nasty, he knows all about that." The inspector ignored the sarcasm and checked the identification against the registration slip before glancing toward Christine. Face turned away, she hunched in the chair like a prisoner in the dock. The inspector lowered his voice. "You know the lady personally... I mean... You've known her for a while...?" He was trying to make it easy. "Yes," Ferdinand said. "Thank you," the inspector said. He saluted and made as if to go, but Ferdinand, trembling with rage to see Christine humiliated and redeemed on nothing more than his say-so, took a step toward him.

"I'd just like to know if...if these night sweeps are conducted in the Hotel Bristol and other Ringstrasse hotels too, or just here?" The inspector's face assumed an expression of cold professionalism. He replied dismissively, "I have no information to give you, I'm following orders. But if I were you I'd be glad I'm not investigating too closely. It may be that the information in the register concerning your wife" (he emphasized the word) "would not check out completely." Ferdinand gritted his teeth and choked back his anger. He had to squeeze his hands together behind his back to keep from hitting this representative of the government in the face. But the inspector, seemingly accustomed to such outbursts, calmly closed the door behind him without a second glance. Ferdinand stared at the door, seething with fury. Then he remembered Christine. She'd slipped down on the chair until she was almost lying flat—as though she'd died of fear. Ferdinand stroked her shoulder.

"See, he didn't even ask your name...It was really just a formality...All they want to do is turn your life upside down with these 'formalities' and ruin you. I remember there was something in the paper a week back about how a woman threw herself out of a window because she was afraid she'd be turned in and her mother might find out or...she'd be tested for VD... Better to jump, three stories down...I read about it in the paper, two lines, two lines...It's really just a little thing, we're not used to it, that's all...At least you get your own grave if you do that, not a mass grave as in the old days, that's something we can count on now...Ten thousand deaths every day, what's one person compared to that, if it's somebody like us, somebody with no rights. In the good hotels they salute and they bring in the detectives just so the ladies don't have their jewelry stolen, nobody there goes snooping around the 'citizenry' at night. But why should I be embarrassed?" Christine sank still lower. She remembered something—what was it the little Mannheim girl had said...The doors opened and closed there all night long. She remembered: the wide white beds bright in the early-morning light, the silent doors that seemed to be cushioned, the soft carpets and the vase by the bed. There everything could have been lovely and good and easy—but here...

She shuddered with revulsion. He stood next to her hopelessly, saying, "Calm down, calm down, calm down. It's over now." But her cold body still shrank from his hand. Something in her had torn like an overstretched sail, and her nerves were frayed. She didn't hear him, she was listening only to the knocking that was still moving from one door to the next, one person to the next.

Now it was upstairs. The knocking was suddenly heavy and increasingly violent: "Open up! In the name of the law!" They both strained to listen in the momentary silence. Again the hammering came from upstairs, but now it was the sound of a fist, not just knuckles on wood. The thudding made its way through every door, into every heart. "Open up! Open up!" a voice commanded. Someone was apparently resisting. There was a whistle, then footsteps on the stairs; four, six, eight fists pounded on the door upstairs. "Open up! Now!" Then an impact traveled through the entire building, wood splintered, and a woman screamed, high, piercing, terrified, sharp as a knife. Chairs crashed to the floor, there was a struggle going on, bodies fell like sacks of stones, shrill screams turned to wails.

They listened as if it were them, as if it were Ferdinand upstairs fighting furiously with the policemen, Christine howling and writhing in their trained grips, half-clad and enraged. The scream came with horrible clarity: "I won't go, I won't go!" It was a wailing, screeching, frothing sound. Glass smashed—the harassed woman must have broken a window, or maybe someone else had. And now they'd grabbed her, two or three of them (that was what Ferdinand and Christine imagined), and they were dragging her along. And now they must have thrown her to the floor—the sound of her flailing and struggling came through the brick walls. And now she was being dragged through the hall and downstairs while her terrified high-pitched shrieking became more and more muffled and faint: "I won't go! I won't go! Let me go! Help!" Now they were downstairs. The car started up. They'd bagged her, like an animal.

Now it was quiet again, even quieter than before—gloomy, as though a thick cloud hung over the building. He tried to take her in his arms, lifting her from her chair and kissing her cold brow. But she slumped in his arms like a drunk. He kissed her, but her lips were dry and unresponsive. He tried to sit her down on the bed; slack, dazed, and empty, she collapsed, while he bent over her, stroking her hair. Finally she opened her eyes. "Let's get away from here," she whispered. "Take me away, I can't bear it. Not a second longer." And then she knelt before him. "Take me away, I beg you. Take me away from this terrible place."

He tried to calm her. "But where, darling...It's not even 4:30 and your train doesn't leave until 5:30. Where can we go? Don't you want to rest?"

"No, no, no." Loathing filled her as she looked at the rumpled bed. "Can't we just get away, away from here, let's just get away! And never again...never again...like this...somewhere ...never again!"

He obeyed. In the desk clerk's cubicle a policeman was still poring over the hotel register and jotting down notes. His sharp glance was like a blow. Christine swayed and Ferdinand steadied her. The policeman bent over the register again. Outside in the alley, fresh air and freedom. She breathed deeply as if restored to life.

Morning was still far off, but the streetlamps already seemed to be burning low. Everything looked tired, the empty lanes, the dismal buildings, the shuttered stores, the few people wandering about. Farmers' horses plodded heavily by with bowed heads, pulling long vegetable carts to market and trailing a rank, humid smell. Milk wagons clattered over the cobblestones, the tin milk cans rattling; then the grim, gray quiet returned. There were a few people about, bakers' boys, canal cleaners, other laborers of one kind or another, with drowsy, shadowy faces, looking gray and wan, vaguely unrested and resentful, and Ferdinand and Christine couldn't help sensing the natural animosity between those who slept and those who were stirring in the sleeping city. Without speaking they moved through the darkness to the train station. There anyone could sit down and rest: a home for the homeless.

They sat in a corner of the waiting room. Men and women lay on the benches, sleeping with mouths open and bundles next to them, themselves like battered bundles that destiny had deposited nowhere in particular. From outside came an occasional reluctant wheezing, puffing, and groaning: engines were being shunted about, the stoked-up boilers tested. Otherwise it was quiet.

"Stop thinking about it," he said to her, "there was no harm done. Next time I'll make sure nothing like this happens. You don't mean to, but I think you're holding it against me, and it's not my fault."

"Yes," she said half to herself, "I know that, I know...It's not your fault. But whose fault is it? Why are we always the ones who suffer? We didn't do anything, we didn't do anything to anyone, but every step we take is a trap. I've never asked for much, once I went on vacation, and I wanted to be like the others, free and easy, eight days, two weeks, and then all that with my mother happened...And once I..." She broke off.

He tried to soothe her. "But darling, it turned out all right, be sensible...They were looking for someone, and they just took down the particulars, it was just bad luck."

"I know, I know. Just bad luck. But what happened there... You don't understand—no, Ferdinand, you don't, you have to be a woman to understand. You don't know what it's like as a young girl, a child even, before you understand anything, to already be dreaming about what it would be like to be with a man that you loved...Everyone dreams about it...And you don't know what it's like and what it will be like, you can't imagine it no matter how much your girlfriends talk about it. But every girl, every woman thinks of it as a great event...as something beautiful...the most beautiful thing in her life... in a way, I can't express it very clearly, as what, yes, as what you're actually

living for...as what's going to lift you up above all the meaninglessness...For years, years, you dream about it and imagine
it...No, you don't imagine it, you don't want to and you can't,
you just dream about it, as something beautiful, so very, very
indistinctly, like when...And now it turns out to be so...so
horrible, so appalling, so dreadful...No, you just can't absorb
it when that's been destroyed, because no one will ever be able
to give that back to us once it's been ruined, sullied..."

He stroked her hand, but she stared down at the dirty floorboards without paying any attention.

"And to think that it all turns on nothing but money, filthy,
low-down, vile, despicable money. With a little money, two or
three banknotes, I could have been among the blessed, I could
have left, driven somewhere in a car...somewhere where no
one could come after me, where I was alone and free...Oh,
how wonderful it would have been just to relax, for you too...
It would have made all the difference for you, you wouldn't be
so glum and distracted...But we're like dogs, people like us,
crawling into other people's stables, getting whipped...No, I
never thought it could be so awful." When she looked up and
saw his face, she added quickly, "I know, I know, you can't help
it, and maybe I haven't gotten over it, the horror...You've just
got to understand why it was so awful for me. Give me a little
time, it'll pass..."

"But you'll come...you'll come again?"

His anxious question did her good. It was the first warm
word.

"Yes," she said. "I'll come again, you can count on that. Next
Sunday, only...You know...That's all I ask..."

"Yes," he whispered, "I know what you mean."

She left on the train. He went to the buffet and quickly
drank a few shots of brandy. His throat was parched. The brandy went down like fire and he could move his limbs again. He
went along the street faster and faster, swinging his arms against

an invisible enemy. People looked after him in astonishment, and at the construction site people noticed how furious he was, how unpleasant and dismissive, though before he'd always been so unassuming. Christine sat in the post office as always, depressed, silent, watchful. And when they thought of each other, it wasn't with feelings of passion or love, but with something like pity—not the way you think of a lover, but of a friend in trouble.

After this, Christine went to Vienna every Sunday. It was her only day off, and she'd used up vacation days for the summer. She and Ferdinand got along well. Too tired, too disappointed for passion, for a love affair with any excitement and optimism in it, they considered themselves lucky just to have found someone to confide in. They saved up all week for their Sundays, wanting to spend this one day together without constant pennypinching, to go to a restaurant or coffeehouses, to the pictures, to drop a few schillings without constantly counting and calculating. And they saved up words and feelings too, thought about what they'd tell each other, and they were both glad to have someone who listened intently, with sympathy and understanding, no matter what happened to them. After so many months of privation this was enough, and through Monday, Tuesday, and Wednesday, and with increasing restlessness through Thursday, Friday, and Saturday, they awaited this small joy with impatience. A certain restraint remained. They didn't utter words that are usually on the lips of lovers. They didn't speak of marriage or staying together forever. Everything seemed so vague and far away, and they hadn't made enough of a beginning for any of it to be real. Usually she arrived around nine (she didn't want to spend Saturday night in Vienna; it was too expensive to get a hotel room for herself, and the memory of her ordeal still made her shrink from sharing). He'd pick her up, they'd walk through the streets, sit on benches in the Volksgarten, take the metropolitan railway out of town somewhere, have lunch, stroll through the woods. It was nice, and they were still grateful to see each other's faces when they sat down together, happy to walk through a field with someone else for a change and enjoy those little things that even the poorest people are permitted: a blue autumn sky, the golden September sun, a few flowers, and a free day that was special from beginning to end. It meant a great deal to them, and during the week they looked forward to the next Sunday with the patience of people whose troubles have taught them to keep their expectations low. On the last Sunday in October, autumn had turned mean: winds swept through the streets, clouds sped overhead; it rained from morning until night, and all at once they felt alien and useless. They couldn't wander through the streets all day with no umbrella, just the inverness coat for shelter. Yet it seemed pointless and unpleasant to sit at congested coffeehouse tables, just bumping knees underneath from time to time as a sign of intimacy, not being able to speak because of all the strangers, but not knowing where else to go. Eventually they found that time weighed heavily upon them, even though it was so precious.

They both knew what they needed. It was ridiculously little— a room, a room of their own, a few square feet of privacy, four walls that were theirs for the day. They knew how senseless it was, two young bodies that were attracted to each other dragging about aimlessly all day in damp clothes or sitting on chairs in overcrowded rooms, but they were afraid to risk another night in a hotel. The simplest thing would have been for Ferdinand to get a place so she could visit him there. But he earned only 170 schillings a month. He lived in an old woman's house and to get to his little cell he had to go through her room, but he wasn't about to leave. During his months out of work she'd trusted him to pay the rent and expenses later, and now he owed her two hundred schillings which he was paying off month by month, and there was no hope of being out of debt for another three months. He didn't tell Christine, he didn't explain; despite their intimacy, he was still too ashamed to reveal his poverty or acknowledge his debts. But Christine had an idea it was money that was preventing him from moving out and getting a room, and she would have liked to lend him some, but the woman in her worried that she might wound him by seeming to be paying for the privilege of having him all to herself. She said nothing and they sat hopelessly in smoke-filled cafés, watching the windows, waiting for the rain to stop. The vast power of money, mighty when you have it and even mightier when you don't, with its divine gift of freedom and the demonic fury it unleashes on those forced to do without it—they felt this as never before and were filled with bitter rage when, in the dark of the early morning, they saw the brightly lit windows and knew that those glowing gold curtains gave shelter and freedom to hundreds of thousands of people, men with women they desired, while they themselves were homeless, plodding blindly through the streets, through the rain; it was cruel as only the sea could be cruel—the sea in which a person can die of thirst. Quiet, secluded rooms with light and warmth and soft beds, tens of thousands of them, hundreds of thousands, innumerable unused and unoccupied rooms, and only they had nothing, no place where they might lean close and brush lips for so much as a second, no help for their raging thirst, their fury at the senselessness of it all, except to delude themselves that it couldn't go on like this forever, and so they both began to lie. In the coffeehouse he'd go over the classifieds with her; she saw him write letters of application, and then he said he had splendid prospects for a splendid job. A friend of his, a war buddy, was going to find him an administrative job in a large construction company. He'd make so much money that he'd be able to catch up with his engineering studies and become an architect. She said (this was not a lie) that she'd requested a transfer to Vienna, formally applying to the head office, where her uncle had a lot of pull. In a week or two she was sure to get the good news. What she didn't say was that in fact she'd surprised her uncle one evening. She'd rung the bell at eight thirty after listening at the windows: the family was at home. The bell had rung in the hall and then her uncle himself had appeared, looking somewhat nervous. It was too bad she'd come today, he said, her aunt and her cousins were away (from the coats in the hall she knew this was untrue) and he had two friends there for dinner, otherwise he'd ask her in, but was there anything he could do for her? She'd explained and he'd listened, saying, "Yes, yes, yes of course," and she'd had no doubt that he was afraid she needed money and that he just wanted to send her on her way. None of which she told Ferdinand; why discourage him even more? Nor did she tell him that she'd bought a lottery ticket, and that she, like all poor people, expected a miracle. It was better to lie, to say she'd written her aunt to help her find work or come to America; when she was there she'd bring him over too and get him a job, they needed capable people there. He didn't believe her; she didn't believe him. So they sat around idly, their joy washed away by the rain and their eyes dimmed by the dimness, aware of the hopelessness of their situation. They talked about Independence Day and Christmas when they'd have two days off and go somewhere together, but November and December were far off: there was a long, empty, hopeless stretch of time to fill before then.

They were deceiving each other, but not really. They both knew how senseless it was to be sitting in a noisy room full of people when what they really wanted was to be alone together; to be telling each other transparent lies when body and soul yearned for truth and deeper intimacy.

"Next Sunday it's sure to be nice out," she said. "The rain can't go on forever."

"Yes," he replied, "I'm sure it'll be nice out." But they were too dejected to care; they knew that winter, the enemy of the homeless, was coming, and that nothing would get better for them. From one Sunday to the next they waited for a miracle, but no miracle came. They walked together, ate together, talked, and gradually their companionship became more a misery than a joy. They had a few quarrels, but they were ashamed because they knew they were really angry at the meaninglessness they'd slid into, not at each other. All week long they looked forward to their day together, but by Sunday evening they always felt something was wrong, something made no sense. Poverty was crushing all the feeling they had. It was intolerable to be together this way, and yet they tolerated it.

One gray November day, with dull noonday light filtering through the dirty office windows, Christine was doing figures at her desk. Since she'd started going to Vienna on Sundays, she'd barely been able to get by on her earnings. The train tickets, coffeehouses, streetcars, lunches, and odds and ends—it all added up. She'd torn an umbrella getting on a train, she'd lost a glove, and (being a woman) she'd bought herself a little something now and then before seeing Ferdinand: a new blouse, nicer shoes. Her calculations showed her coming up short. Not by much, twelve schillings in all, what remained of her Swiss francs would cover that easily, but still, how could she keep going into the city every Sunday without an advance or without sinking into debt. Three generations of bourgeois instinct made her dread either alternative. She sat and brooded: Where is this going? The last time, four days ago, it had rained and stormed once again and they'd sat in coffeehouses the whole time or stood under eaves, even taken shelter in a church, and she'd come home with damp, crushed clothes, full of a pervasive exhaustion and misery. Ferdinand had been strangely distracted. There must have been trouble at the site or some-thing—he'd been sharp and unfriendly. Half an hour would pass without his saying a word, and they walked together in silence like a couple of strangers. What could have upset him? Was he angry because she hadn't steeled herself to going to another one of those awful hotels with him (the memory still made her shudder)? Or was it just the weather and the hopeless-ness of their aimless wandering from café to café, the enervating and soul-killing homelessness that took all the meaning and joy out of their time together? Something was beginning to go dead between them, she felt. Not the friendship, the fellow feeling, but both of them were losing heart somehow. They no lon-ger had the strength to go on lying to each other. Once they'd imagined they could help each other, make each other believe there was a way out of this impasse of poverty, but they no lon-ger believed it themselves now, and the dank specter of winter was approaching.

She no longer knew where to look for hope. The left draw-er of her desk contained a typewritten letter; it had arrived yesterday from the post office administration in Vienna. "In response to your application of September 17, 1926, we regret to inform you that the requested transfer to the Vienna postal district is not a possibility at this time, as an increase in the number of positions in the Vienna Post Office within the terms of Ministerial Decree BDZ/1794 is not projected; nor are any posts currently vacant."

She'd expected nothing else. Perhaps the privy councillor had intervened, perhaps he'd forgotten; in any case he was the only one who could have helped. There was no one else. So that meant staying here for a year, five years, the rest of her life perhaps. The world was senseless.

Should she tell Ferdinand, she wondered, her pencil still in her hand. Strangely, he'd never asked what had become of her request. Probably he hadn't believed in it anyway. No, best not to tell him—he'd get the idea even if she never brought it up. Telling him would only add to his torment. It just made no sense. Nothing made sense anymore, nothing.

She heard the door. Instinctively she became alert and began straightening things up around her, something she did mechanically to bring her out of dreamland and back to work whenever someone came. But the sound of the door caught her ear—it was oddly indecisive and cautious. The peasants usually slammed it open like a stable door and then slammed it shut behind them, but now it might have drifted open in the breeze, with only a slight creak of protest from the hinges. Glancing through the window, she was stunned to see the person she'd least expected: Ferdinand.

Christine's mouth opened. The shock was not pleasant. Ferdinand had sometimes offered to come and visit in order to spare her the trip to Vienna. She'd always refused, perhaps because she would have been embarrassed to be seen in the shabby little office wearing the apron she'd sewn herself. It was pride, perhaps, or some unutterable shame. Perhaps too the neighbors might talk. What would they say, the innkeeper's wife or the woman next door, if they saw her out in the woods with a stranger from Vienna? And Fuchsthaler's feelings would be hurt. But now here he was. It couldn't be good.

"Now look how surprised you are, it was the last thing you expected!" He was trying to sound cheerful, but his voice was grating.

"What's the matter? . . . What is it?" she asked with alarm.

"Nothing. What do you mean? I had some time off, so I thought I'd come out. Aren't you glad?"

"Yes, yes," she stammered, "of course I am."

He looked around. "So this is your kingdom? The reception room at Schönbrunn is prettier, grander, but still you're all by yourself and there's no one to lord it over you. That's nothing to sneeze at!"

She was silent. What does he want?

"Isn't it your lunch break? I had the idea that at twelve we might go for a walk and talk."

Christine looked at the clock. It was past 11:45. "Not yet, but soon. Only... only I think... it would be better... it would be better if we don't go out together. You don't know what it's like here when they see you with someone, they ask right away, the grocer, the women, every Tom, Dick, and Harry, they ask who's that, who have I got there with me; and I hate to lie. It's better if you go on ahead, along the parish road to the right. At the bottom of the hill you'll see the Stations of the Cross path— it leads up to St. Michael's Church at the top. And at the edge of the forest there's a big cross, you'll see it as soon as you leave the village, with benches for pilgrims. Wait for me there—no one will be there at noon, they're all having lunch. A stranger won't attract attention. Wait for me there, will you, I'll be along in five minutes and we'll have until two o'clock."

"Fine," he said. "I'll find it. See you then."

He closed the door behind him. The brief bang went straight through her. Something must have happened. He wouldn't have come if he didn't have some reason. What about his work? And the train costs money... six schillings, and then the return trip. There must be a reason.

She lowered the wicket. Her hands shook; she could hardly turn the key to lock up. Her legs were like lead.

"So where are we off to?" asked Frau Huber, a peasant woman just back from the fields, when she saw the post office girl heading toward the woods—an unusual sight at midday.

"I'm going for a walk," Christine said. You had to make excuses for every step you took, they were watching you every second. She hurried on anxiously, almost running up the last steps of the Stations of the Cross path. Ferdinand was sitting on a stone bench under the cross. The man of sorrows hung high in the air, arms twisted by the nails, his head with the crown of thorns slumped sideways in tragic resignation. Ferdinand's profile merged with the tableau as he sat on the stone bench under the outsize crucifix. His head was bowed solemnly; his form was rigid with fanatical concentration. He held a walking stick, which he'd jabbed into the ground. At first he didn't hear her come up. But then he started, pulled the stick toward him, turned, and stared, without curiosity, enthusiasm, or affection.

"There you are," he said simply. "Sit down, we're alone."

Her whole body was quivering with anxiety. She couldn't suppress it any longer.

"What's wrong? What's happened?"

"Nothing," he replied, staring in front of him. "What do you mean?"

"Don't torture me. I can tell, I can see. Something must have happened for you to be free today."

"Free. You're right there. Yes, I'm free."

"But why . . . They haven't fired you, have they?"

He gave an unpleasant laugh. "Fired, no, not at all, you couldn't really say that. The construction is simply done."

"Done? What do you mean? How can it be done?"

"Done, I mean done. Our company is broke, and Herr Contractor has disappeared. A con man, they're saying now, a cheat, and the day before yesterday he was still the *gnädiger Herr*. Saturday I noticed something was up, he was on the phone all day back and forth with people until the workers' wages arrived, and then he only paid us half—an accounting error, it was supposed to be, that was what the company secretary said, they'd withdrawn too little and the rest would be paid on Monday. But on Monday nothing and nothing on Tuesday or Wednesday, and today the jig was up, the boss gone, construction stopped, you see, and that's why people like us can go for a nice walk for once."

She looked at him numbly. What was most frightening was the way he talked about it with such scornful composure.

"Yes, but aren't you legally entitled to severance?"

He laughed. "Yes, yes, I believe the law does say something about that, and we'll see, won't we. For the time being they haven't got a postage stamp, their credit is wiped out—even the typewriters are in hock. We can wait. We've got time, after all."

"And what... what are you going to do now?"

He stared straight ahead without answering. He poked about in the dirt with the stick, digging out little rocks and heaping them up. This was too painful to watch.

"Please... What... what are your plans now... What are you going to do?"

"Do?" He laughed again—that strange bark. "Well, what a person does in these cases. I'll draw on my bank account. I'll live off my 'savings.' Though I don't know how. Then after six weeks I'll probably be permitted to make use of the unemployment compensation provided by our beneficent Republic. I'll try to live on that just like the other three hundred thousand in our blessed nation on the Danube. And if that glorious endeavor comes to nothing, well, I'll just die in the gutter."

"Nonsense." His icy calm enraged her. "Stop talking nonsense. How can anyone take things so hard. Someone like you... You'll find a job, I'm sure you will."

He jumped to his feet and banged the stick on the ground.

"But I don't want another job! I've had it! The word makes me scream. Eleven years now I've had one job after another, always getting by but never getting in, always there but not really anywhere. I was in the war for four years, then after that death factory more factories, one place after another. I've always put my nose to the grindstone for someone else, never for myself, and then they blow the whistle: Out! That's enough! Go somewhere else! Start over, square one over and over. But now I can't go on. I've had enough, I'm through."

Christine was about to say something, but he cut her off.

"I can't go on, Christine, believe me, I've had it, I can't go on, I tell you I can't. I'd rather die in the gutter than go back to the employment agency and stand in line like a beggar and wait for a ticket and then another one. And then go running up and down stairs, write letters that never get answered and fill out applications that the street sweeper picks out of the horseshit in the morning. No, I can't bear it any longer, cringing in the outer office and then finally being let in to see some petty official who blusters and looks at you with that experienced, cool, indifferent smile just to let you know that he has hundreds to choose from and is doing you a favor by even listening to you. And then feeling your heart skip a beat, every single time, when someone carelessly leafs through your file and looks at your references as though he were spitting on them, and then says, 'I'll put you down, you might check in tomorrow.' And then again the next day no dice and the day after that, until finally you find something somewhere, you're on the job, and then you're yanked off it again. No, I can't bear it any longer. I've taken a lot, I've marched for seven hours on Russian country roads with split shoes and torn soles, I've drunk sewer water and carried three machine guns on my back, begged for bread as a prisoner and shoveled bodies and been beaten by a drunken guard. I've cleaned the boots of the entire company and sold dirty pictures so I'd have food for three days, I've done everything, and I put up with it all because I believed that eventually it would be over, eventually I'd get a job, climb the first rung and the second. But I always got knocked back down. I've gotten to the point now that I'd rather kill someone, gun him down, than beg from him. I can't go on now. I can't go on lingering in outer offices and standing around waiting for work. I'm thirty years old today, and I can't go on."

She touched his arm. She didn't want him to guess how terribly sorry she felt for him, but he noticed nothing. She might as well have been shaking a tree.

"So now you know, but don't worry, I didn't come here to whine. I don't want sympathy. Save it for other people—maybe it'll help. It doesn't help me anymore. I came to say goodbye. It doesn't make any sense for us to go on. I don't want to have to depend on you, I've still got my pride. I'd rather starve to death! The best thing is to break up like adults and not burden each other. That's what I wanted to tell you, and thanks for everything—"

"But Ferdinand." She gripped his arm more tightly. She was hanging on to him with all her strength, actually trembling. "Ferdinand, Ferdinand, Ferdinand." She felt such mindless, helpless fear that it was all she could think of to say.

"No, you tell me—honestly, does it make sense? Doesn't it hurt you too to see us looking so shabby in the streets and the coffeehouses and neither of us able to help the other and both of us lying to each other? How long is that going to go on, what is it we're waiting for? I'm thirty now and I've never had a chance to do anything I wanted. Hired, fired, and every month I age another year. I've seen nothing of the world, I've never had a life, I've just gone on believing that at last it's starting, now it's going to begin. But now I know there's nothing else, nothing else ever. I'm worn out, I can't take anymore. And that kind of person should be avoided . . . I know it doesn't do anybody any good, your sister figured that out right away and put herself between Franzl and me so I wouldn't get hold of him and drag him down with me. And you, I'd only be dragging you down too. It makes no sense. Why don't we do the friendly thing and put a decent end to it."

"Yes, but . . . what are you going to do?"

He sat rigidly and said nothing.

She looked up and was shocked. With the stick gripped in his fist he'd dug a little hole in the ground in front of him, and now he was staring at it as though he wanted to dive into it. It seemed to be pulling him down. Christine understood. Everything was clear.

"You mean . . ."

"Yes," he replied calmly. "It's the only thing that makes sense, I've had enough. I don't want to start over, but I've still got what it takes to put an end to it. There were four of our group who did it in Russia. It goes fast. I saw their faces afterward, calm, clear, at peace. It's not hard. It's easier than going on like this!"

She was still clutching him, but now her arms stiffened. Silently she let go.

"Don't you understand how I feel?" he asked, raising his eyes calmly. "You've always been honest with me."

After a moment she said simply, "From time to time it crosses my mind too. Only I never dared to think about it so clearly. You're right—there's no sense in going on this way."

He looked at her uncertainly. He desperately wanted to believe. He said, "You would too?"

"Yes, with you."

She said it calmly and firmly, as though she were talking about going for a walk. "By myself I'm not brave enough, I don't know . . . I haven't given any thought to how it's done, or I might have done it a long time ago."

"You'd . . . " He was stammering with happiness as he seized her hands.

"Yes," she repeated calmly, "whenever you want, but together. I won't lie to you any longer. The transfer to Vienna wasn't approved, and here in the village I'm perishing. Better quickly than slowly. And I never did write to America. I know they won't help me, they'll send ten or twenty dollars—what good's that going to do? I don't want to agonize, I'd rather it was quick, you're right!"

He gazed at her for a long time. He'd never looked at her with such feeling. His hard face relaxed, and a smile began to show behind the challenge in his eyes. He stroked her hands. "I never thought that you... that you'd go so far with me. Now it's twice as easy for me. I was worried about you."

They sat with fingers entwined. A passerby would have taken them for newly engaged lovers who had walked up the little Stations of the Cross path to seal their betrothal. They'd never felt so untroubled, so confident together; for the first time they were sure of each other and sure of the future. They sat for a long time gazing at each other, their expressions calm, clear, and at peace, their hands joined. Then she asked quietly, "How... how do you want to do it?"

He reached into his back pocket and brought out an army revolver. The November sun glinted on the polished barrel. There was nothing frightening about the weapon.

"In the temple," he said. "Don't be afraid, I have a steady hand, I won't shake... And then in my heart. It's an army revolver of the heaviest caliber, you can feel safe. It'll be all over before they hear the two shots in the village. There's no reason to be afraid."

She looked calmly at the gun, with practical curiosity but without agitation. Then, glancing up, she glimpsed the man of sorrows and the cross rising massively above the stone bench on which they sat.

"Not here," she said quickly, "not here and not now. Because..." (she looked at him, her hand tighter than his) "first I'd like to be together again... really together, without fear and without loathing... A whole night... Maybe we've still got something to say to each other... Those last things that people otherwise never get to say... And then... I'd like to be with you once, with just you for one night... Then they'll find us in the morning."

"Yes," he replied. "You're right, one should get the best out of life before throwing it away. Forgive me for not thinking of that."

Again they sat in silence. A breeze caressed them, the sun was warm and pleasant. They felt good—happy and miraculously untroubled. Then the church bells in the village rang, once, twice, three times. She gave a start. "A quarter of two!"

A bright laugh lit up his face. "See, that's what we're like. You're brave and you're not afraid to die, but you're afraid of being late for work. That's how enslaved we are, that's how ingrained it is. It really is time to shake all that nonsense off. Do you really want to go back there?"

"Yes," she said, "it's better that way. I'd like to put everything in order first. It's silly, but I don't know...I'll feel better once I've straightened things up and written a few letters. And then...if I'm there until six this evening, no one will suspect and go looking for me. And tonight we can go to Krems or St. Pölten or to Vienna. I still have enough money for a good room, and we'll have dinner and do what we want to do for once...It has to be nice, completely nice, and when they find us tomorrow morning nothing will matter. Come by at six. It won't make any difference if they see me, let them say and think whatever they want...Then I'll close the door behind me and everything else will be behind me too...Then we'll really be free."

He kept gazing at her. Her unexpected resolve made his heart lift.

"All right," he said, "I'll come at six. Until then I'll go for a walk and have one more look at the world. So—*auf Wiedersehen.*"

She ran down the path, feeling serene and lighthearted. When she looked back, he was watching. He pulled out his handkerchief and waved it. "*Auf Wiedersehen! Auf Wiedersehen!*"

Christine went in. Now everything was easy. The desk, the chair, the counter, the scale, the telephone, the piles of paper, all the objects no longer lay in wait for her like enemies. They did not mock her silently (*thousands, thousands, thousands of times*): she knew now that the door was open. One step and she'd be free.

She felt wonderfully calm, as serene as a meadow falling into shadow in the evening. Work seemed as easy as play. She wrote a few letters—one to her sister, one to the post office, one to Fuchsthaler to say goodbye—and she marveled at the clarity of her handwriting, the evenness of the lines, the precise calligraphic spacing of the words, as effortlessly neat as her homework had been back in school. All the while people were coming in with their mail or requesting telephone connections, piling up parcels on the counter, paying bills. And each time she helped them with special attention and courtesy. Without being aware of it she wanted these insignificant people who meant nothing to her—Thomas, Frau Huber, the forest ranger's assistant, the grocer's apprentice, the butcher's wife—she wanted them to have a pleasant memory of her; it was her last trace of feminine vanity. And when one of them said "*Auf Wiedersehen*" and she responded "*Auf Wiedersehen*" with twice as much feeling, she smiled a special little smile because now she was breathing a different air, the air of deliverance. Then she took up the unfinished backlog, counted and estimated, put everything in order. Her desk had never been so neat. She even wiped off the ink stains and straightened the calendar on the wall—her successor would have nothing to complain about. No one would have anything to complain about, because she was happy now. She was putting her life in order and everything here should be in order too.

She worked so happily, so briskly and diligently, that she lost track of time and was surprised to hear the door.

"Is it really six already? My goodness, I hadn't noticed. Another ten, twenty minutes and I'll be finished with everything, I'd like to leave everything just so, you see. Let me close out the books and lock up the cash and I'll be all yours."

He was going to go wait outside. "No, no, sit down, I'll lower the shutters outside, and it doesn't matter if they see us leave together, tomorrow they'll know it all anyway."

"Tomorrow," he smiled. "I'm glad there won't be a tomorrow. For us anyway. The walk was wonderful, the sky, the colors, the woods. He was quite an architect, old God, a little old-fashioned, but better than I ever could have been."

She took him into the inner sanctum behind the glass, where no other outsider had ever set foot. "I don't have a chair to offer you, our Republic isn't that generous, but sit down on the windowsill and have a smoke. I'll be done in ten minutes" (she breathed a sigh of provisional relief) "done with everything."

She added the columns one after another; it went quickly and easily. Then she took the black money pouch out of the till and balanced the books. She stacked up the banknotes—the fives, tens, hundreds, and thousands—on the desk, moistened her index finger on the sponge, and counted the blue bills with practiced deftness, quickly and mechanically, ten, twenty, thirty, forty, fifty, sixty; she jotted down the total for each denomination, already impatient to check the figure in the books against the cash on hand and draw the bottom line, that final, liberating stroke of the pencil.

She heard a sound behind her and glanced up to find Ferdinand looking over her shoulder. He was breathing hard.

"What is it?" she said in alarm.

"Allow me" (his voice was dry) "allow me to look for a moment. It's been a long time since I've seen a thousand-schilling note and I've never seen so many all at once."

He held one delicately between his fingers as though afraid it would break, and she saw his hand trembling. What was wrong with him? He was looking so oddly at the blue bill. His narrow nostrils quivered and there was a strange light in his eyes.

"So much money . . . Do you always have this much here?"

"Yes, of course, and this isn't even that much, 11,570 schillings. At the end of the quarter, when the winegrowers pay their taxes or the factory sends out wages, it can be as much as forty, fifty, even sixty thousand. Once it was eighty thousand."

He stared at the desk. He kept his hands behind his back, as though he were frightened.

"And it doesn't . . . it doesn't make you nervous to have all that money in your desk? You're not afraid?"

"Afraid? Of what? The building is protected—see those thick iron bars—and Weidenhof and his family live over the grocery next door, they'd certainly hear if someone broke in. And at night it's always put away. No, nothing's going to happen."

"I'd be afraid," he said tensely.

"Nonsense. Of what?"

"Of myself."

Glancing at him, she saw that his mouth was half open. His eyes avoided hers. He began to pace.

"I couldn't stand it, not for an hour. I couldn't breathe with so much money around me. All the time I'd be thinking, that's a thousand schillings, just a rectangular scrap of paper, and if I stuffed it in my pocket I'd be free, for three months, half a year, a whole year, I could do what I wanted and have my own life, and with that much—what did you say?—11,570 schillings, we could live for two years, three years, we could see the world and really be alive for every minute of it, not the way we've been living but the way we want to live, we could live the lives of the people we were born to be, let those people come out of us, become those people, instead of being stuck. All you'd have to do is reach out and take it, like this, one little movement and off you'd go, free. No, I never could have stood it, it would have driven me mad looking at it, having it so close, smelling it, feeling it, knowing it belongs to that idiot puppet, the government, which doesn't breathe and isn't alive and doesn't want or know anything, the stupidest thing people have ever invented, something that crushes people. I would have gone out of my mind... I would have locked myself in at night to stop myself from taking the key and opening the drawer, and you—you were able to live with it! Haven't you ever considered it?"

"No," she said, shocked. "Never."

"Well, the government was just lucky. Scoundrels always are. But finish up now" (he said it almost angrily) "finish up, put the money away. I can't look at it any longer."

She closed the drawer quickly, with shaking fingers. Then they left for the train station. It was already dark. Through the lighted windows people could be seen at their dinner tables, and as they passed the last window a soft, rhythmic murmur rolled out: the evening prayer. He said nothing, she said nothing—it was as if they were not alone. There was an idea traveling with them like a shadow. They felt it in front of them and behind them, inside them, and it was still with them as they took the road out of the village and without thinking quickened their pace.

Beyond the last house, they were in darkness. The sky was brighter than the earth, and the trees along the road stood out against its glassy light; like charred fingers, the black skeletons of the bare branches reached into the still air. Scattered peasants and wagons moved along the road, heard more than seen. Footsteps and the rumbling of the heavy carts told them that they were not alone.

"Isn't there a path across the fields to the station? A path no one uses?"

"Yes," said Christine, "turn here, off to the right." She was glad he'd said something. For a second she could stop thinking about the dangerous, shadowy idea that had been silently dogging them since they left the post office.

Ferdinand walked alongside her in silence, as though he'd forgotten her. His hand never brushed hers. Then abruptly he asked (the words fell heavily, like a stone), "Do you think that at the end of the month there might be as much as thirty thousand?"

She knew what he had in mind, but she controlled her voice to keep from showing it. "Yes, I think so."

"And if you delay the deposits too . . . If you hold on to the taxes or whatever you've got there for a few extra days—they won't be keeping such close track of things if I know anything about Austria—then how much would you be able to scrape together?"

She considered. "Well, at least forty thousand. Maybe even fifty . . . But why?"

He was almost stern. "You know why."

She didn't dare to contradict him—he was right, she did know why. They went on in silence. They passed a pond where frogs were croaking madly. Their snoring, taunting sound was almost painful. Abruptly Ferdinand stopped.

"Christine, let's not kid each other. Things look bad for both of us, really bad, so we've got to be really straight with each other. Let's think clearly and calmly."

He lit a cigarette, and in the light she could see the tension in his face. "Let's think, yes. Today we made up our minds to end it all, we were going to 'take our lives,' to use that cliché. But that's not true. We didn't want to take our lives, you and I. We just wanted out of our ruined lives at last, and there was no other way out. It was poverty we wanted out of—not life but this life, the senseless, abominable, unbearable, inescapable life we have. That's all. And we thought the gun was the only way. But that was wrong. Now we know there's another way after all, one last chance. The only question is whether we have the courage to seize the opportunity, and how to go about it."

She was silent. He dragged on his cigarette.

"It's going to have to be thought through and worked out completely coolly and realistically, like a mathematical problem . . . I won't keep anything from you—frankly, I have to say that this is probably going to take more guts than the other way. The other business is easy. Twitch one finger, a flash, and it's over. This way is harder, because it's longer. You're kept in suspense, not just for a second but for weeks, months, and all the time you've got to be hiding, you've got to be looking out for yourself. Something indefinite is always worse than something definite, a strong fear that doesn't last very long is easier than one that's nebulous but doesn't go away. So what we've got to do first is consider whether we're strong enough, whether we can stand up to the strain, and whether it'll be worthwhile. Whether to end our lives smoothly and quickly, or start again. That's the concern I have."

He started walking again and she followed automatically. Her legs were doing the walking; her mind waited helplessly for what he was going to say next. She was so appalled, so drained of will that she couldn't think.

Now he stopped. "Don't misunderstand me. I don't have a trace of moral scruple, when it comes to the state I feel completely free. It's committed such terrible crimes against us all, against our generation, that we have a right to anything. I'm not worried about doing it damage, we'll just be recovering some damages for our entire battered generation. Who taught me how to steal, who made me do it, if not the state? Commandeering, that's the word they used during the war, or expropriating—Versailles called it reclamation. Who taught us how to cheat if not the state—how else would we know that money saved up by three generations could become worthless in a mere two weeks, that families could be swindled out of pastures, houses, and fields that had been theirs for a hundred years? Even if I kill someone, who trained me to do it? Six months on the drill field and then years at the front! We have an excellent case against the state, by God, we'll win in every court. It can never pay off its terrible debt, never give back what it took from us. Once there might have been a reason to have some qualms, back when the state was a good custodian, thrifty, decent, proper. Now that it's behaved like a hoodlum, we have the right to be hoodlums too. You know what I'm talking about, don't you? There's no reason for us not to even the score—I don't have the tiniest doubt about that, and I don't think you should. Why shouldn't I go ahead and take my disability pension? It's mine by rights, though the hallowed Treasury denies it, along with the money that was stolen from your father and mine and the living birthright that I and everybody like me was robbed of. No, I'm telling you my conscience is clear. Does the state worry about whether we live or die, and die a wretched death too? And if we steal a hundred slips of blue paper or a thousand or ten thousand, nobody in the country's going to be any poorer for it—they'll feel it as little as the meadow misses the grass the cow grazes on. So that doesn't disturb me at all, and I think if I stole ten million I'd sleep as soundly as a bank director or a general who's lost thirty battles. All I'm thinking about is us, you and me. We can't go off half-cocked like some fifteen-year-old sales clerk who steals ten schillings from the till and blows it an hour later without ever knowing why or what for. We're too old for that kind of thing. We've got just two cards left to play and it's one or the other. A decision like this has to be made carefully."

He walked on to collect his thoughts. She could feel his concentration, and his cool logic chilled her. She surrendered as never before to her sense of his superiority.

"We'll take it slow, Christine, step by step. No diving into this. No fantasies or false hopes. Let's think. Pack it in today and we're finished with everything. One little movement and life is over. Actually a wonderful idea—I still remember the way my high-school teacher used to preach that the only respect in which man is superior to animals is that he can die when he wants to, not just when he has to. Maybe it's the one freedom you can always count on—the freedom to throw your life away. But the two of us, we're still young, we don't know what we'd be throwing away. We'd just be throwing away a life we didn't want, a life we rejected, and yet it's conceivable there's another we might welcome. Life is different with money—at least I believe it is, and so do you. And if we believe in something—you do understand me?—then our 'no' to life isn't completely true, and we'd be destroying something we have no right to destroy, the unlived life in us, the chance for something new, maybe something magnificent. That handful of money might allow something still unrealized inside me to flourish, something that can't emerge now, that's wilting like this stalk I've broken off, wilting just because I've broken it off. Something that would grow in me. And you? You might have children, you might... Who can say?... And the very fact that there's no way to know is wonderful... You understand me, I think... The kind of life that's behind us isn't worth living, scraping along miserably from one week to the next, from one day off till the next one. But maybe, maybe it's possible to make something of it, it would just take courage, more courage than the other way. And if it goes wrong after all, a gun isn't hard to find. So what do you think... if the money's pretty much there for the taking, why not just take it?"

"Yes, but... but where would we go with the money?"

"Abroad. I know foreign languages, I speak French, I even speak it very well, I speak excellent Russian, a little English too, and the rest can be learned."

"Yes, but... they'll investigate, don't you think they'd find us?"

"I don't know, no one can know that. Possibly, even probably, but maybe not. I think it depends more on us—whether we can stick it out, whether we're smart enough, careful enough, whether we think things through properly. Of course it'll be a terrible strain on us—probably not a good life, with people hunting us, being eternally on the run. I can't speak for you. Do you have the guts? You've got to be sure."

Christine tried to think. It was all so sudden. She said, "On my own I don't have the courage for anything. I'm a woman—I can't do anything just for myself, I can only do something for someone else, with someone else. But for two people, for you, I can do anything. So if it's what you want..."

He picked up his pace.

"That's just it, I don't know if it's what I want. You say it's easy for you with someone else. For me it would be easier alone. I'd know what I was getting into. A ruined, mangled life—fine, chuck it. But I'd be worried about dragging you along. It wasn't your idea, it was mine. I don't want to drag you into anything, I don't want to seduce you into doing anything, and if you're going to do something, you've got to do it for your own sake, not for mine."

Little lights emerged behind the trees. They were coming to the end of the path across the fields. Soon they'd be at the station.

Christine was still dazed. "But...how are you going to do this," she said anxiously. "I don't understand. Where will we go? I always read in the paper about how they catch all these people. So what are you picturing?"

"I haven't even begun to think about it. You overestimate me. Ideas come in a flash, but only fools act on them without thinking. That's why they always get caught. There are two kinds of crimes (to use the word conventionally): crimes of passion and crimes that are premeditated, thought out beforehand. The crimes of passion may be more beautiful, but most of them go wrong. Those clerks who raid the till in order to go to the races, sure they'll win or somehow the boss won't notice, they all believe in miracles. But I don't believe in miracles, I know that the two of us are completely alone, all alone against a vast organization that's been built up over centuries and commands the expertise and experience of thousands of individual investigators. The individual detective may be an idiot and I may be a hundred times smarter and more cunning, but they have experience and the system is behind them. If we—notice I'm still saying 'if'—if we really decide to do this, it can't be reckless or childish. What's done rashly is done badly. It has to be planned down to the last detail—every contingency has to be worked out. It's a matter of probabilities. Let's think it all through carefully and precisely. Come to Vienna on Sunday and we'll decide then, not now."

He stopped, his voice suddenly brighter. It was his other voice, the child's voice hidden inside him that she loved.

"Isn't it amazing? This afternoon you went back to work and I went for a walk. I looked at the world again—it was the last time, I thought. There it was, so bright and beautiful, so full of warm sunny life, and there I was, still fairly young and quick and spirited. I reckoned everything up and asked myself what I'd actually accomplished in this world, and the answer was painful. Sad to say, I haven't acted or thought for myself at all. At school I studied what the teachers wanted me to study and thought what they wanted me to think. In the war they gave me orders and I went through all their drills and paces. When I was a prisoner I had just one wild dream—someday I'll be out!—but doing nothing wore me down, and when I got home I toiled for other people, mindlessly, aimlessly, just for a scrap of food and a pittance so I could go on breathing. Sunday will be the first time I've had a chance to think for a while about something that concerns me alone, me and you; and I'm looking forward to it. You know, I'd like us to build it like a bridge, a structure where every nail and screw has to be in its place and a millimeter's difference is enough to bring it down. I want to build this thing to last for years. It's a great responsibility, I know, but for the first time it's my responsibility—yours too—not some squalid little responsibility like what they give you in the military or in those companies where you're just a nobody answering to somebodies you don't even know. Whether we do it or not, we'll have to see—but still, just to have an idea, to think it through, work it out, and calculate the alternatives down to the ultimate consequences, that'll be a pleasure I'd never expected to have. It's good I came today."

They were near the station; they could make out the lights distinctly. They stopped.

"Better not come with me. Half an hour ago it wouldn't have mattered whether anyone saw us together. Now I can't be seen with you—that's" (he laughed) "part of our great plan. Nobody can suspect that you have an accomplice, and if someone was able to describe me that wouldn't help us a bit. Christine, we have to start thinking of everything now, I told you it won't be easy, the other way would have been easier. But on the other hand I've never known, we've never known, what it is to be alive. I've never seen the ocean, I've never been abroad. I've never known what life is—always thinking about what everything costs means we've never been free. Maybe we can't know the value of life until we are. Sit tight and stay calm, don't worry, I'm going to work everything out down to the last detail, on paper even, and then we'll review it point by point and weigh the possibilities. And then we'll decide. Do you want to?"

"Yes," she said, loud and clear.

The wait until Sunday was unbearable for Christine. For the first time she was afraid of herself, afraid of people, afraid of things. It became a torment to unlock the till in the morning, handle the banknotes. Were they hers, or were they government property? Were they all still there? She counted and recounted the blue bills and never got to the end of it—either her hand began to tremble or she lost track of the total. Her confidence was gone, and with it any objectivity. She was uncertain, confused: she thought everyone must know her intentions, be in on her fears, be watching her and spying on her. "This is madness," she reasoned with herself. "I've done nothing. We've done nothing. Everything's in order, every banknote's in the safe, the accounts balance, let anyone inspect them." But it did no good: she couldn't bear people's eyes on her, and when the telephone rang, she quailed and needed all her strength to lift the receiver to her ear. And she nearly passed out when, on Friday morning, the policeman came in unexpectedly, his tread heavy and his bayonet clanking. She clutched the table with both hands as though hanging on for dear life, but the policeman, his Virginia cigar in the corner of his mouth, only wanted to send a money order to the young mother of his illegitimate child, his monthly payment, and he joked with good-natured acerbity about how long he'd be paying for his brief pleasure. But she couldn't laugh, and her hand shook as she filled out the money order. Only when the door banged shut behind him was she able to breathe again, pulling out the drawer to convince herself that the money was still there, 32,712 schillings and 40 groschen, precisely as entered in the ledger. At night she couldn't sleep, and when she did she had frightful dreams, since imagination is always more terrible than reality, and what has yet to happen is more dreadful than what already has.

On Sunday morning Ferdinand was waiting at the station. He looked at her closely. "Poor thing! You look terrible, you're a nervous wreck. You've been worrying, haven't you? I was afraid of that. It was probably a mistake to tell you beforehand. But it'll be over soon. Today we'll reach our decision, whether to go forward or not."

She glanced at him. His eyes were bright, his gestures vigorous and free. He noticed her eyeing him.

"Yes, I'm feeling fine. It's been ages since I felt as good as I've been feeling these last few days. At last I know the pleasure of thinking something out for myself, just for me and all on my own...Not just a tiny bit of some project I don't care about, but something I'm building from the ground up, for me and nobody else. A castle in the air for all I know, maybe it'll tumble down in an hour. Maybe you'll blow it away with a word, maybe we'll demolish it together. Even if we do, for once it was my own work and it was fun to do. I had a hell of a good time thinking through every last contingency, working out a campaign against every army, state, police force, newspaper, testing it in theory against every earthly power, and now I'm in the mood for real war. At worst we'll lose, but when did we ever win? Well, you'll soon see!"

They left the station. Fog shrouded the buildings in gray chill. Porters and attendants waited with lifeless faces. Everything was dank; the damp chill turned every word into a puff of condensation. There was no warmth in the world. He took her arm to steer her through the traffic on the street. She gave a nervous start.

"What is it, what's wrong?"

"Nothing," she said. "I'm just so scared. Whenever anyone speaks to me, I think I'm under observation. I have the idea that everyone knows what I'm thinking. I know it's silly, but I feel it's written on my forehead, I'm terrified the people in the village have gotten wind of everything. When the forest ranger's assistant asked me on the train, 'So what are you up to in Vienna?,' I turned so red that he began to laugh, and then I was glad. Better he think that than the other thing. But tell me, Ferdinand" (she pressed close to him) "it won't always be this way, will it, if we...if we actually do it? Because I know I'm not strong enough for that. I couldn't stand always living in fear like that, being afraid of everyone, not being able to sleep, not sleeping because I'm afraid of a knock at the door. It won't always be this way, will it?"

"No," he replied, "I don't think so. That's only here, where you're living your old life. Once you're out there in different clothes, with a different name, in another world, you'll forget the person you were. You told me yourself about how once you were someone completely different. The danger would be to go into this with a bad conscience. If you feel it's wrong to rob that robber baron, the state, then that's definitely not good and I'll call it quits. As for me, I feel totally justified. I know I got shafted, and I'm risking my skin on my own account and not in a war for a dead idea, for the House of Hapsburg or Mitteleuropa or some other political abstraction that has nothing to do with me. But, as I said, nothing's been decided yet, we're just 'playing with ideas,' and playing is supposed to be fun. Buck up, I know you've got what it takes."

She took a deep breath. "I think I can stand a certain amount, you're right, and I also know we have nothing to lose. I've endured plenty, but this part is just so hard, the uncertainty. Once it's done, you can count on me."

They went on. "Where are we going?" she asked.

He smiled. "Strange, the whole thing was so easy, it was downright fun to consider the various alternatives about the escape and where to hide out and how to stay safe, and I really think I've worked out every detail—I can confidently say: it's right, it works. I figured everything out, it was child's play to plan out how we'll get by and be safe once we have money. There was just one thing I wasn't able to do—find a place, four walls, a room where we can discuss the whole thing in peace, and once again it was clear that it's easier to live for ten years with money than for a single day without it. Really, Christine" (he smiled at her almost proudly) "finding a place where we wouldn't be seen or heard was more trouble than our entire scheme. I considered every option. It's too cold to walk out into the country, in a hotel someone might overhear—and I know you'd be anxious and upset—and we need to focus. In an inn the staff would be watching, especially if it's empty. Outside we'd attract attention because we'd be sitting in the cold. Yes, Christine, no one would ever believe how hard it is to be really alone in a city of millions when you don't have money. I came up with the wildest ideas, I even thought about climbing up St. Stephen's. Nobody goes up there in fog like this—but that's too absurd. Finally I approached the watchman at my old work site, the one that's been shut down. He's got a wooden shack there, a hut with a cast-iron stove, a table, and, I think, a single chair. I know the guy, and I gave him a long song and dance about a posh Polish lady I know from the war who lives with her husband in the Hotel Sacher and is too classy and well-known to be seen with me on the street. You can imagine how astonished the dolt was, and of course he considered it a great honor to be of service. We've known each other for a long time, and I've gotten him out of trouble twice. He's leaving the key under the boards along with his identification so we'll be safe even if something goes wrong, and he's promised to light the stove in the morning. We'll be alone there, it won't be comfortable, but since what's at stake is a better life, we can stand crawling into that doghouse for a couple of hours. No one will hear us there, no one will see us. We can make our decision in peace."

In Floridsdorf, far outside the city center, the construction site was boarded up and deserted. The forlorn abandoned building was a shell, with a hundred empty windows like unseeing eyes. Tar barrels, wheelbarrows, piles of cement bags, and bricks lay in wild disorder on the sodden ground—as if some natural disaster had interrupted the bustle of construction. For a workplace the quiet was unnatural. The key was under the boards. The damp fog kept out prying eyes; Ferdinand unlocked the little wooden hut, and the stove was in fact burning, it was warm and comfortable inside, with a nice smell of wood. He closed the door behind them and threw a few pieces of wood into the stove. "If someone comes, I'll toss the papers in. Nothing can happen, don't worry, and besides, nobody can come, nobody can hear, we're alone."

Christine stood in the room, feeling she didn't belong there. Everything seemed unreal; the only real thing was Ferdinand. He pulled some big sheets of paper out of his pocket, unfolded them, and said, "Please sit down, Christine, and pay attention. This is the plan, I've worked it out precisely, written it out three times, four times, five times; I think it's completely clear now. I want you to read it through carefully point by point. Where something seems wrong to you, I'll pencil in your questions or objections on the right, and then we'll discuss them all together when you're done. There's a lot at stake, nothing can be improvised. But first something else that's not in this outline. Something concerning the two of us that has to be discussed. So. We're doing this together, you and I. In so doing we'll be equally culpable, although I fear that the law will regard you as the true perpetrator. You are the official in charge, they're going to search for you and pursue you, you'll be a criminal in your family's eyes, in everyone's eyes; whereas, as long as we're at large, no one's going to know about me as the accomplice and plotter. So you have a bigger role than I do. And you have a job which would provide you with a living and a pension to see you through to the end of your life; I have nothing. So I'm risking a lot less in the eyes of the law and before—how to put it—let's say before God. Our roles are unequal. You're assuming a bigger risk—it's my duty to warn you of that." He saw her look down.

"I had to be tough in telling you that, and I'm going to go on that way, not hiding any of the risks. First and foremost: what you are going to do, what we are going to do, will be irrevocable. There will be no going back. Even if we made millions with the money and repaid it five times over, you'll never be able to come back here again and no one will pardon you. We'll be cast

out once and for all from the ranks of upright, honorable, trust-
worthy citizens, and for as long as we live we'll be in danger.
You've got to be aware of that. And no matter how careful we
are, some accident, something we haven't thought of, haven't
foreseen, might snatch us out of our fine new carefree lives and
throw us into prison and, as they say, disgrace. In a venture like
this there's no such thing as security. We won't be secure when
we're over the border, we're not secure today and won't be secure tomorrow or ever. You have to look at it as a duelist looks
at his opponent's pistol. The shot might miss, it might hit him,
but one way or another he's looking down the barrel."

Pausing again, he tried to meet her gaze. She was looking at
the ground, but her hand on the table was steady.

"So, again, I don't want to raise any false hopes. There are
no assurances I can give you, none at all. Or myself. If we go
into this together, that doesn't mean we're going to be bound
together for life. We're doing this in order to be free, to live
freely. We might want to be free of each other some day. Maybe
even soon. I can't vouch for myself—I don't know who I am,
still less who I'll be once I've tasted freedom. The agitation in
me today might just be something inside that wants to come
out, but maybe it'll stay there, or even grow. We still don't
know each other very well, we've only ever been together for
a few hours. It would be madness to say we'll be able to live
together forever or that we want to. All I can promise is that
I'll be a good friend to you, in the sense that I'll never betray
you or force you to do something you don't want to do. If you
want to leave me, I won't stop you. But I can't promise that
I'll stay with you. I can't promise anything—not that this will
succeed, or that you'll be happy or have no worries afterward,
or even that we'll stay together. No promises. So I'm not trying
to talk you into anything—no, on the contrary, I'm warning
you: because your situation is worse, you'll be the criminal. And
then you're a woman and more dependent. You're taking a big

chance, an awful chance, I don't want you to think anything different. I'm not trying to persuade you. So please—read the plan. Then think about it and make up your mind, but, as I told you: you've got to be aware that the decision is irrevocable."

He put the papers on the table. "Please read it with total attention and total skepticism—pretend this is a bad business deal and you don't trust the contract. Meanwhile I'll go outside and take a walk, check out the building. I'm not going to hang over you. I don't want you to feel any pressure."

He stood up and went out without looking at her. The big folded sheets of paper, covered with neat handwriting, lay in front of her. She had to wait a few minutes for her heart to stop pounding.

The creased manuscript was neatly drawn up like a document from a bygone century. The section headings were underlined in red pencil:

I.   The Crime Itself
II. Avoiding Capture
III. Plans for Life Abroad, Etc.
IV. Plans in the Event of Misadventure or Discovery
V.   Summary

The first section, "The Crime Itself," was again subdivided, as were the others, with each subsection, labeled (a), (b), (c), etc., clearly set off as in a contract.

Christine picked up the document and read it from start to finish.

I. The Crime Itself

(a) Choice of Date: It is evident that the deed must take place either on a Saturday or on the day prior to a public holiday.

This will delay discovery of the theft by at least twenty-four hours and provide the head start absolutely necessary for our escape. The post office closes at six o'clock, early enough to allow for the possibility of reaching Switzerland or France on the night express train; in November early dusk will offer a further advantage. November is the worst month for travel. One can with virtual certainty expect to be alone in the train compartment during the night within Austria, so that there will be few witnesses who could provide personal descriptions once the newspapers have been notified. November 10, the day preceding Independence Day (a public holiday), would be particularly advantageous in that we would arrive abroad on a weekday and be able to make all initial purchases and alterations in appearance that much more unobtrusively. Accordingly, it would be desirable to delay the delivery of all incoming funds until this date (without attracting attention) in order to amass as large a sum as possible.

(b) Departure: We must of course leave separately. We will both buy tickets for short trips only: to Linz, from Linz on to Innsbruck or the border, and from the border on to Zürich. If possible you must buy your ticket to Linz some days in advance, or, better, I will buy your ticket for you so that the clerk, who undoubtedly knows you, will not be able to provide any information about your actual destination. See Section II for other measures related to false leads and covering the trail. I will board the train in Vienna, you at St. Pölten; we will not speak to each other during the entire night as long as we remain within Austria. It is important that no one know or suspect that the crime involved an accomplice; subsequent investigations will then remain focused on your name and description and not on the couple we will appear to be when we are abroad. Until we are well within the borders of another country, any appearance of a connection between us is to be avoided in front of conductors and officials, other than the border guard to whom we will identify ourselves with a joint passport.

(c) Documents: It would clearly be best to obtain false passports in addition to our real ones, but time is short. Once abroad we can attempt to do so. But obviously the name Hoflehner must not be seen at any checkpoint, whereas I may register anywhere under my real name, which will still be entirely unblemished. I will therefore make one small alteration to my passport, the addition of your name and photograph. I can make the rubber stamp myself (I studied wood engraving at one time). I will also (I have made sure of this) be able to alter the *F* in my name with a small stroke so that it can be read as "Karrner," and this name will put the passport into quite a different category even in the eventuality which I believe can be ruled out (see Section II). The passport will then be valid for the two of us as man and wife and will suffice until such time as we obtain proper false passports in some port city. If our money holds out for two or three years, this should offer no difficulty.

(d) Transporting the Money: If at all practicable, precautions must be taken during the final days to collect bills in the largest possible denominations, thousands or ten thousands, so that you will not be loaded down. During the journey, you will distribute the fifty to two hundred banknotes (depending on the denominations) among your suitcase, your handbag, even your hat if necessary. This should certainly be adequate to evade the simple border inspection that is now commonly practiced. In the course of the trip I will exchange some of the banknotes for foreign currency in the Zürich and Basel train stations, so that when we arrive in France we will have what we need to make the important initial purchases without having to exchange a conspicuous amount of Austrian currency in any one place.

(e) Initial Destination: I propose Paris. Paris has the advantage that it can be reached easily, without changing trains; we will arrive there sixteen hours before the theft is discovered and probably twenty-four hours before any arrest warrant is issued and will have time to complete all adjustments in physical appearance (this will affect you only). I speak fluent French, so we will be able to avoid the typical tourist hotels and go to a suburban hotel where we will be less conspicuous. Another advantage of Paris is that the holiday traffic there is enormous, making surveillance of any one person virtually impossible. From what friends have told me, registration of change of residence is also a casual affair in France, unlike Germany, where landlords, even the entire nation, are curious by nature and demand precision. In addition, the German newspapers will presumably provide more details about an Austrian post office robbery than the French ones. And by the time the newspapers publish this initial information, we will probably have left Paris (see Section III).

II. Avoiding Capture

It is essential that the investigations conducted by the authorities be made more difficult and if possible led astray. Any wrong track will delay their progress, and after some days the personal descriptions will have passed entirely out of mind within Austria and certainly abroad. It is thus important from the outset that we envision all the measures that will be taken by the authorities, and take appropriate countermeasures.

The authorities will pursue their investigations via the usual three channels: (1) careful searches of buildings; (2) questioning of all acquaintances; (3) searches for other persons involved in the offense. It will thus not be sufficient to destroy all papers in the building; on the contrary, measures must be taken to confuse the investigators and put them on the wrong track. These will include:

(a) Visa: When any crime is committed, the police inquire at the consulates to determine whether the Person H concerned in the case has recently been issued a visa. As I am obtaining a French visa not for Passport H but for myself (see Section V), and thus, at least for the time being, will not draw notice, it would actually suffice if no visa at all were obtained for Passport H. However, since we wish to divert the trail eastward, I will obtain a Romanian visa for your passport, which will of course produce the consequence that the investigations conducted by the police will concentrate primarily on Romania and the Balkans in general.

(b) To strengthen this assumption, it would be a good thing for you to send a telegram on the day before Independence Day to Branco Riczitsch, Bucharest Station—general delivery. "Arriving tomorrow afternoon with all luggage, meet me at station." It is a safe assumption that the authorities will review all recent dispatches and telephone calls from your post office and immediately hit upon this highly suspicious communication, which will lead them to believe, first, that they know who the accomplice is and, second, that they are sure of the direction of flight.

(c) To reinforce this error, which is important for us, I will write you a long letter in a feigned hand. You will tear it carefully into little pieces and throw them into the wastebasket. The detectives will naturally search the wastebasket, put the pieces together, and find corroboration of the false trail.

(d) On the day before your departure, you will make discreet inquiries about direct trains to Bucharest and the fares. We can be certain that the railway official will present himself as a witness and thus add further to the confusion.

(e) To remove any connection with me, though you will be traveling and will be registered as my spouse, one small thing is required. To my knowledge, no one has seen us together and no one at all except your brother-in-law is aware that we know each other. To mislead him, I will go to his house tonight and say goodbye. I will say I finally got a suitable job in Germany and am going there. I will also pay my landlady what I owe and show her a telegram. Since I will be disappearing eight days ahead of time, any connection between the two of us will be completely ruled out.

III. Plans for Life Abroad, Etc.

A precise evaluation cannot be made until we are there. A few general points only:

(a) Appearance: In dress, conduct, and bearing, we must present the appearance of moderately well-off members of the middle class, because they attract the least attention. Not too elegant, not too humble, and in particular I will pose as a member of a class seldom associated with this sort of undertaking or with money: I will pretend to be a painter. In Paris I will buy a small easel, a folding chair, canvas, and a palette, so that wherever we go my profession will be obvious at a glance and questions superfluous. And in all romantic spots in France, there are thousands of painters roving about year round. It will attract no further attention and from the outset arouse a certain sympathy, like the sympathy one has for eccentric and harmless people.

(b) We must dress accordingly. Velvet or linen, signaling the artist just a little, otherwise total inconspicuousness. You will appear as my assistant, carrying the plate holder and the camera.

No one asks such people what they are doing and where they come from or is surprised that they choose out-of-the-way little lairs for themselves, and even a speaker of a foreign language attracts no special notice.

(c) Language: It is extremely important that, as far as possible, we speak to each other only when no one is around. Under no circumstances may we be observed speaking German together. The old children's language *Be-Sprache* would be best to use when others are present, as it is not only incomprehensible to foreigners but also obscures the very language being spoken. In hotels, we should if possible take corner rooms or those that will allow us to be unheard by neighbors.

(d) Frequent Changes of Residence: It will be necessary to change our place of residence frequently. After a certain time, we may become liable to taxes or otherwise attract official scrutiny, which, though irrelevant to us, may still create awkwardnesses. Ten to fourteen days, four weeks in smaller towns, is the right period of time. This will also prevent our becoming known to hotel staff.

(e) Money: The money must divided up and kept in separate places until we succeed in renting a safe-deposit box somewhere, which will be risky in the initial months at least. Obviously it must be carried not in a billfold or openly, but sewn into the lining of our shoes, in our hats or our garments, so that in case of a random inspection or other unpredictable misadventure the discovery of large amounts of Austrian currency will give no grounds for suspicion. Money must be exchanged slowly and with caution and always in larger places such as Paris, Monte Carlo, or Nice, never in smaller cities.

(f) Insofar as is possible, acquaintances are to be avoided, at least at first, until we have obtained new papers in some way (it should be easy in port cities) and have left France for Germany or another country of our choosing.

(g) It is unnecessary to establish objectives and plans for our future life in advance. Assuming an average, inconspicuous way of life, I calculate that the money should last for four or five years, within which time we must make decisions about what will follow. Instead of carrying the entire sum on us in cash—nothing more risky than that—we must endeavor to deposit it as soon as possible, although this cannot be done until entirely safe and unobtrusive methods are found. The strictest caution, the most rigorous unobtrusiveness, and constant self-monitoring will be required for the initial period. After six months we will be able to move freely and any official profiles will have been forgotten. We must also use this time to improve our languages, systematically alter our handwriting, and overcome the feeling of foreignness and insecurity. If practicable we should also acquire some skill that will make possible another way of life and another profession.

IV. Plans in the Event of Misadventure or Discovery

In an undertaking as founded on uncertainty as ours, the possibility that things will go wrong must be reckoned with from the outset. When dangerous situations may arise or from what quarter they may come cannot be known in advance, and the two of us will have to study them and deal with them jointly as they present themselves. However, certain basic principles can be set down:

(a) If we should become separated through some accident or error on the journey or in the course of our changes of residence, we will immediately return to the place where we last stayed the night together and either wait for each other at the train station or write to each other at the general post office of the city in question.

(b) If, through some misadventure, our trail is picked up and an arrest is made, all measures must be in place so that the ultimate steps can be taken. I will not let my revolver out of my pocket and will always keep it by my bed. Just in case, I will prepare a poison, potassium cyanide, which you can always carry unobtrusively in a compact. The feeling of always being prepared to act on the decision we have made will give us greater confidence at every moment. I for my part am fully resolved never again to set foot behind barbed wire or barred windows.

If, however, one of us is apprehended in the absence of the other, that other will loyally assume the duty of fleeing at once. It would be the grossest error to surrender out of a sentimental wish to share the comrade's fate, for one person alone is always less weighed down and will be able to invent excuses more easily in the event of a simple investigation. In addition, the other, the one who is free, will be at large, able to help cover the trail, send word, or possibly be of assistance in the event of an escape. It would be madness to willingly give up that freedom for whose sake everything was done. There will always be time for suicide.

V. Summary

We are entering into this hazardous undertaking and staking our lives in order to be free, at least for a time. The idea of freedom includes freedom with respect to each other as individuals. Should living together become burdensome or intolerable to either of us for internal or external reasons, he or she will make a clean break from the other. Each of us is undertaking this venture on his or her own initiative without compulsion and without placing the other under duress. Each of us will be responsible for himself or herself only; neither may find fault with the other on that account, whether openly or tacitly. Just as from the first we will share the money that secures our freedom, so we will also share the responsibility and the risk, and each of us will accept the consequences for himself or herself.

In all future planning our individual responsibility will remain unchanged: our conviction will be at all times that we have done no injustice to the state or to each other, but only what was appropriate and natural in our situation. It would be senseless to venture into such danger with a bad conscience. We will embark upon this course only if each of us, independently of the other and after thorough deliberation, has arrived at the conviction that it is the only one and the right one.

She put the sheets down and looked up. He'd come back and was smoking a cigarette. "Read it through again." She did, and when she was finished he asked her, "Is everything clear and concise?"

"Yes."

"Is anything missing?"

"No, I think you've thought of everything."

"Everything? No" (he smiled) "there's something I've forgotten."

"What's that?"

"I wish I knew. There's something missing in every plan. There's some hole in every crime, but you can never know where it is ahead of time. Every criminal, no matter how sophisticated, almost always makes some tiny mistake. He cleans out all his papers, but leaves his passport; he thinks of every obstacle, but overlooks the most glaringly obvious one. Everyone forgets something. Probably I've forgotten the most important thing too."

Her voice was full of surprise. "So you think . . . you think it won't succeed?"

"I don't know. All I know is that it'll be hard. The other way would have been easier. You almost always fail when you go against your own law. I don't mean legal rules and regulations, or the Austrian constitution, or the police. Those one could deal with. But everyone has his internal law. One person rises, another falls; you rise if you're meant to rise, fall if you're meant to fall. So far I've never succeeded at anything. You too. Maybe, even probably, everything's rigged so that we'll go under. If you want my honest opinion, I've got to tell you that I don't think I'm the kind of person who's ever completely happy; maybe it doesn't even suit me. I'll be satisfied with a month, maybe, or one, two years. If we have the guts to go through with it, I won't be thinking of living happily ever after with white hair and a cozy little house in the country, but only of a few weeks, a few months, a few years beyond what we would have had with the revolver."

She looked at him calmly. "Thank you, Ferdinand, for being so candid. If you'd spoken enthusiastically, I would have begun to mistrust you. I don't think we'll succeed for long either. All the time I was away, it kept pulling me back. Probably what we're doing is futile, and it makes no sense. But not doing it and going on like this would be even more senseless. I can't see anything better. So—you can count on me."

He looked at her, brightly, lucidly, but without cheer. "No going back?"

"No."

"Wednesday the tenth, at six?"

She returned his gaze and held out her hand.

"Yes."

⌒

AFTERWORD

AFTERWORD

WILLIAM DERESIEWICZ

Of all the names that ring out from the annals of Viennese cafe society, that storied model for later bohemias, none is more elegiac than Stefan Zweig's. Hitler destroyed that world, but the Great War had already rung the curtain on its golden age. The greatest names and greatest achievements belong to the three decades surrounding the turn of the century: Mahler, Schnitzler, Klimt, Schiele, Freud. After the war, after the Austro-Hungarian Empire, whose tolerance and multinationalism made Vienna's cosmopolitan ferment possible, the mood is all of loss, whether nostalgic or disillusioned, Joseph Roth or Robert Musil. But if Roth and Musil come late, Zweig comes last. He wasn't the youngest or the last to die, but he believed longest in the pan-European culture Vienna represented, and his career embodied the passing of that ideal.

Zweig, the most popular author of his day, knew everyone who mattered in European culture, and he seems to have read every thing that mattered. His outpouring of biographical studies— books and essays not only on Mahler, Schnitzler, Roth and Freud but also on Erasmus and Montaigne, Goethe and Nietsche, Dickens and Dostoyevsky, and many, many others—can be understood as a mission, impelled by a growing sense of doom, to preserve European civilization and the humanistic values for which it stood. But though he escaped the camps, he couldn't escape the sense that everything he cared about was being exterminated. His death in 1942, in a Brazilian backwater, was a suicide.

THE POST OFFICE GIRL

Zweig's fiction is also marked by the two catastrophes he witnessed, especially the first. His best-known tale, "Chess Story," completed, like his memoir "The World of Yesterday", on the eve of his death, registers the Nazi hostility to the life of the mind. But two previous stories—he wrote about twenty in all—allegorize the earlier loss. In "Buchmendel" ("Mendel the Bookman," as it might be rendered), the Great War destroys a living repository of bibliographic knowledge who dared to ignore the political barriers—irrelevant to his universe of culture—the conflict has created. In "The Invisible Collection," a wife and daughter sell off a connoisseur's unparalleled assemblage of engravings to stave off poverty during the postwar hyperinflation. The collector is blind by then, and still lovingly caresses the blank pages his family has slipped into his portfolios to conceal the loss. The image is immeasurably poignant, but it is also double-edged: European culture has been erased by history, yet it is still alive in the minds of those who cherish it.

But nowhere else in his fiction does Zweig confront the legacy of the Great War with as deep a social reach or as detailed a human sympathy as he does in "The Post Office Girl". Zweig completed only one novel, "Beware of Pity"; "The Post Office Girl" was found among his literary remains and published in Germany (as "Rausch der Verwandlung", "The Intoxication of Transformation") only in 1982. Its appearance in English caps a recent spate of republication. Since 2002, Pushkin Press has issued six volumes of fiction, while New York Review Books has published three, all nine of them in attractive editions and many in new translations. Other presses have contributed fresh versions of "The World of Yesterday", "Marie Antoinette", Zweig's most popular biography, and another volume of short stories. We have three recent translations of "Chess Story" and two editions of "Beware of Pity" from which to choose, as well as new versions of some fourteen other tales.

Still, posthumous publication is a dicey business. There's been more and more of it lately, for obvious reasons. Venerated authors represent established "brands" guaranteed to move product, one of the few sure bets in an increasingly anxious business. Artistic integrity and the writer's own wishes don't enter into it. Ernest Hemingway and Elizabeth Bishop, celebrated perfectionists both, are only two of the authors lately subjected to the publication of material they had chosen to suppress. Zweig nibbled at "The Post Office Girl" for years, and the afterword to the German edition describes a manuscript in considerable disarray. Given that he chose his own time of death, and also that he had just finalized two other works and dispatched them to his publishers, it seems clear that he never managed to hammer the novel into a shape that satisfied him.

Nevertheless, we are lucky to have the book, not only for its devastating picture of postwar Austrian life but also because it represents so radical a departure from Zweig's other fiction as to signal the existence of a hitherto unsuspected literary personality. No wonder he struggled with it for so long; he was listening to a new voice, and he may never have fully figured out what it wanted to say. The typical Zweig story is a tale of monomaniacal passion set loose amid the veiled, upholstered civility of the Austrian bourgeoisie, the class into which Zweig was born. A wife in a corseted marriage, an army officer stunted by the regimented routines of duty, an aesthete numbed by his meaningless rounds of pleasure—through a chance encounter or a moment of moral daring, each is precipitated into a state of almost demonic possession by guilt or greed or desire. Zweig, whose obsession seems to have been obsession itself—he speaks in "Buchmendel" of "the enigmatic fact that supreme achievement and outstanding capacity are only rendered possible by mental concentration, by a sublime monomania that verges on lunacy"—was alive to both the life-affirming and the self-destructive potentialities of the situation. Repression, released at last, careens past exhilaration toward derangement. Zweig's newly awakened protagonists finally notice the world and feel its urgency pressing in on them

.

for the first time, but their souls don't know what to do with so much feeling.

There are whiffs of Dostoyevsky here, and of the nineteenth-century Decadents, and even occasionally of Sacher-Masoch, another Viennese—Zweig was largely uninterested in postwar Modernism, and he can feel like a throwback to the fin de siècle—but the major influence, of course, is Freud. Zweig, who delivered an oration at his friend's funeral, saw himself as a kind of Freud of fiction, a fellow spelunker in the caverns of the heart. His prose attends not only to the moment-by-moment fluctuations of his characters' inner turmoil but also to the symptomatology manifested on their bodies: the tremor of a gambler's hands, the shifts of an adulteress's gaze. His characteristic method is also Freudian. Nearly all his tales feature a frame narrator, someone to whom the protagonist confesses her secrets. The encounter typically takes place at a continental resort or hotel, one of those cosmopolitan spaces of luxury and mystery. Storytelling bridges the distance between strangers—culture doing its unifying work—but it also marks the distance between the narrator and the volatile emotional material he handles. The telling of the tale becomes a kind of resocializing device, replacing the containing structures that have broken down within the tale, and the narrator becomes a kind of analyst or, indeed, a connoisseur. In "Moonbeam Alley," the narrator clearly speaks for Zweig when he evokes "the delightful sensation of an experience made deepest and most genuine because one is not personally involved," a sensation, he says, that "is one of the well-springs of my inmost being."

By renouncing the pleasures of vicarious feeling, "The Post Office Girl" achieves an immediacy otherwise unequaled in Zweig's fiction. No frame narrator screens us from the title character, 28-year-old Christine Hoflehner, postal clerk in the sleepy Austrian village of Klein-Reifling. The year is 1926. Christine shares a dank attic with her rheumatic mother. Her youth has been stolen by the war, along with her father, her brother and her laugh. But into the gloom of her days a sudden light breaks—a telegram from her aunt Claire, gone to America years before and now come back a rich lady. Claire invites her niece to join her on holiday in Switzerland. With a limpid and sensuous directness, Zweig renders the intoxication of the transformations that follow: the provincial girl's "first reckless gulp" of "glass-sharp" alpine air as she throws open the window of her train, her newly awakened shame as she creeps into the grand hotel clutching her straw suitcase, the greedy flare of her nostrils as her aunt inducts her into the world of finery. This is Christine in the beauty salon:

> Now fragrance from a shiny bottle streams over her hair, a razor blade tickles her gently and delicately, her head feels suddenly strangely light and the skin of her neck cool and bare.... She's aware of it all and, in her pleasant detached stupor, unaware of it too: drugged by the humid, fragrance-laden air, she hardly knows if all this is happening to her or to some other, brand-new self.

The notation is swift and simple. When Zweig's characters tell their own stories, by contrast, the prose can be overwrought, the effect distractingly self-conscious. Here, for example, is the protagonist of "Fantastic Night" undergoing an analogous awakening:

> No, it was not shame seething in my blood with such warmth, not indignation or self-disgust—it was joy, intoxicated joy blazing up in me, sparkling with bright, darting, exuberant flames, for I felt that in those moments I had been truly alive for the first time in many years, that my feelings had only been numb and were not yet dead, that somewhere under the arid surface of my indifference the hot springs of passion still mysteriously flowed, and now, touched by the magic wand of chance, had leaped high, reaching my heart.

In place of such labored figures, Zweig marks Christine's discovery of the life of pleasure, and the unfolding of her newfound self, with fresh, unfussy imagery: a carnation in a vase is like "a colorful salute from a crystal trumpet"; her first sip of wine goes down "like sweet chilled cream"; the silk dresses her aunt picks out "glisten like dragonflies," their "yielding new fabric" a "warm, delicate froth on her skin." Christine's body is awakening for the first time, and the language transmits the sensuality of that experience.

Zweig was never shy about making use of traditional narrative models. The main archetype here is Cinderella, of course, but Sleeping Beauty enters in, as well. Christine isn't just poor and overworked; she's been in a state of suspended animation ever since the war interrupted her womanhood just as it was getting started. What her fairy-godmother aunt makes possible with a wave of her magic purse is nothing less than Christine's repossession of her femininity. Within the space of a few days, even a few hours, she learns what it feels like to be beautiful, to be fashionable, to be noticed. She falls in love with the image in her mirror and gives herself a new, more elegant name. She runs in the mountains and shakes the dew from her hair. She dances to hot music, makes out in the back seat of a roadster and stays up late gossiping with her girlfriends. She isn't particularly admirable at this point, neglecting her aunt in favor of the fast new set she's fallen in with, forgetting to write to her ailing mother, adjusting all too easily to a life where other people do the work. As usual, Zweig doesn't make our moral allegiances easy. But the story's direction seems clear. Christine is pursued by two men, a handsome young German engineer—he's the fellow with the roadster—and a protective old English general: sexy Herr Wrong and courtly Lord Right, a love triangle in which she seems certain to get caught on the wrong side.

And then, with the suddenness of someone pulling the plug on a carousel, Zweig brings the whole thing to a halt. Christine's friends discover that she's not the young lady she's been pretending to be, and Aunt "Claire (formerly Klara)" fears for the discovery of her own long-buried secrets. After scarcely more than a week, Christine and her straw suitcase are sent packing back to Klein-Reifling. Midnight has struck for Cinderella, but there will be no glass slipper and no prince. If anything, Christine's life is even worse than it was before, because now she knows what she's been missing. Suspended animation is one thing, but this feels like death, the death of the new, true self who had only just begun to stir. The village becomes intolerable:

> The women seemed ridiculous to her in their full gingham skirts, with their greasy hair piled on top of their heads and their plump hands covered with rings, the heavy-breathing, potbellied men unbearable, and, most repellent of all, the boys with their pomaded hair and citified airs.

The sweet little schoolmaster who had courted her shyly before her departure is now "intolerably lower middle class"—a term that would never have occurred to her before. In moving the novel away from the grand hotel toward a more complex counterpointing of social spheres, Zweig opens his fiction for the first time to a world of economic realities that lies below his own experience. The wonder is that he succeeds in imagining those realities with such an intimate specificity.

The expansion of Christine's consciousness, and the novel's, is only just beginning. Visiting her sister Nelly's family on a trip to Vienna, she meets Ferdinand, her brother-in-law Franz's comrade from the war. Whatever reasons Christine has for resentment, Ferdinand has many times over, and whatever awareness has started to break in on her, he has articulated long ago. Ferdinand spent years in a Siberian prison camp, only to return to a country that no longer had any use for him. His dreams of becoming an architect have been dashed by poverty, his chances for even decent employment wrecked by injury. His family wealth evaporated in the hyperinflation. He has beaten on the doors of ministries, climbed the stairs of government agencies, and has nothing to show for his talent and drive but the sense of a wasted life.

When Ferdinand's bitterness comes pouring out in a torrent of savage eloquence, Christine recognizes a kindred spirit. Unlike the priggish Nelly or the paunchy Franz, here is someone who refuses to accept the radically diminished expectations imposed by the war. A potent system of imagery links the two. Christine feels "like a severed finger still warm yet without feeling or strength." A finger is exactly what Ferdinand has injured, but, he says, "you wouldn't believe what a dead finger does to a living hand." But that is not his only disability. "Once they've cut six years out of your body... you're always a kind of cripple." This is what it feels like to be dispossessed, to be marginalized, to be cheated out of the life you could have had and the person you could have been: it feels like you've been cut in half. Zweig is again tracing the commerce of body and soul, and the sensuousness of his earlier, happier descriptions pays off double here, because he renders the life of deprivation with equal immediacy. "The smell is suffocating," Christine thinks of her attic room, "the smell of stale cigarette smoke, bad food, wet clothes, the smell of the old woman's dread and worry and wheezing, the awful smell of poverty." "Poverty stinks," Ferdinand echoes her, "stinks like a ground-floor room off an air-shaft, or clothes that need changing. You smell it yourself, as though you were made of sewage." Poverty isn't just doing without; it is also shame and impotence and self-disgust. War isn't just bullets; it is also what happens afterward.

All of this represents an immeasurable advance over Zweig's other fiction. Instead of a single emotion intensively examined within a narrow social frame—a fair description even, as its title suggests, of "Beware of Pity", though that work is considerably longer than "The Post Office Girl"—Zweig gives us fully rounded lives rooted in a broad historical context. This, he is telling us, is what the war has done to people. This is what history has made of their bodies. This is the fate of a whole generation. The question of historical luck, and thus of the possibility of alternative lives or selves, is everywhere at issue. Franz made it home right after the war; Ferdinand got stuck in Siberia for an extra two years. Klara was sent off to America; her sister Maria, Christine's mother, spent the war working in a damp hospital basement. The postwar generation of girls is bold and shameless, but everywhere Christine looks she sees women like her, who have missed their chance at life.

The affair she begins with Ferdinand, two souls clinging together for friendship more than anything else, is no less immune than they to the withering circumstances of their lives. The couple contemplate suicide, then conceive a plan that will enable them to escape a different way. And that's where the novel breaks off. Did Zweig intend to end it there? He might have. The narrative terminates at the conclusion of a scene, and on a thematically significant word. But it would have taken an even greater departure from his normal practice than any other the novel exhibits for Zweig to have suspended the story on such a radically Modernist note of openness, before even a climax, let alone a resolution. Zweig's own death involved a suicide pact—he was found lying hand-in-hand with his second wife—and perhaps he simply never succeeded in imagining what a different ending could have looked like. On the other hand, by 1942, Christine and Ferdinand's future would have been all too clear. The rage, the feelings of betrayal, the sense of wasted talent: the Great War's toxic human residue, expressed so starkly in Ferdinand's long denunciatory speeches, would fuel the politics of the 1930s. A million Ferdinands, roused by such tirades, would put on shirts of brown or black and dance the death march of Old Europe.

William Deresiewicz is an essayist and critic. His work has appeared in The Nation, The New York Times Book Review, The New Republic, The London Review of Books, and The American Scholar.